ALMOST HOME

Almost Home

All Rights Reserved © 2015 by K John McLaughlin

ISBN-13:978-0692514443 (K John McLaughlin)

ISBN-10:0692514449

To my nephews – thank you for inspiring me every day!

"You are always new, the last of your kisses was ever the sweetest."

John Keats

"Memory is a complicated thing, a relative to truth, but not its twin."

Barbara Kings Olver

PROLOGUE
STEPHEN

The first time I ever laid eyes on the house was Labor Day weekend. The love of my life had just carefully removed a blindfold from my eyes. I hadn't a clue what he was up to. Under the guise of escaping to San Francisco for a weekend, we had left Caden, our nine-year-old son, with a friend and run off up the coast for a romantic getaway. I hadn't wanted to go. My lover Alec was a closeted actor, they all were back then; most still are. He was pretty well known, so the need for discretion was paramount. Even a rumor could ruin his career, and thus our whole happy existence. Amazingly enough, he was best known for playing a gay character on a popular TV drama. An actor could play gay on TV, but couldn't be one in real life, not even in Hollywood. Because it wasn't easy to have a romantic getaway, they rarely happened.

Lately there had been other things on our minds. Romantic getaways, no matter how close to home, seemed frivolous considering what lay before us. It was 1987 and the man I loved had AIDS. He'd been sick several months earlier, which led us to the diagnosis. I hadn't tested positive then, though I did shortly after we moved to San Francisco. Alec had only been sick the one time and honestly we knew very few people who'd had AIDS, and no one who had died because of it, but we knew the stories. We had done our research.

We, especially Alec, tried desperately to stay positive for Caden's sake. I spent nearly every waking moment secretly terrified. Sometimes I felt as if I would drown in it, the fear eventually pulling me under for good. It was my love for Alec and Caden that kept me afloat. I cannot begin to explain how full my heart was when that sweet boy called me "Dad" or my handsome Alec called me "Steph."

My name is Stephen. I'd never been called anything else. The first time he'd done it, the look on my face shocked Alec. I couldn't say whether I liked the nickname or not. Then he started giggling. His laughter could fill a room. It came from somewhere deep within him, at first barely audible, building until it erupted into a roar. I'm ashamed to admit that early on I was embarrassed when he laughed in public. Thankfully, that passed quickly. I loved the man so much; it was difficult to be ruffled by anything he did. Looking back though, at the beginning of our relationship I must have come off as an uptight little bitch.

1

In November of 1992 I watched strangers in white coats carry the lifeless body of the love of my life out of that house. All the warmth, all the light, almost every bit of laughter left with him. I was destroyed, but it was impossible to stay sad all the time with a kid around. Thank God for that boy! Alec was his biological father; I hadn't come into his life until he was nearly three years old.

Once, when Alec was very sick, he morbidly told me how lucky we were that neither he nor Caden had any family besides me. Caden's mother had died in childbirth. Alec's parents had passed away. There were no grandparents, no siblings to come out of the woodwork and demand custody of our son should Alec be the first to die. He'd still insisted we put everything in writing just to be safe. I'd wanted to slap him when he said our lack of family was good, or lucky, but I knew he was right. I'm not certain I would have survived had someone come and taken Caden away from me.

I actually had a family somewhere; a brother and two sisters, a mother. They hadn't disowned me as Alec's parents had him, although I pretended they had.

As part of my heart was being torn out, zipped up in a black, vinyl body bag, and carried out of our lives on a stretcher, just two miles down the hill, hundreds, maybe thousands of gay men and women celebrated. The Castro district of San Francisco was alive with revelry that night. It was certainly not uncommon to hear gaiety coming from the Castro, but that night was special. All evening long, as Caden and I comforted each other, I was reminded of how the day had begun. A quick cab ride down the hill to vote. I hadn't even considered not voting; not that day, not after all we'd been through. Alec had voted by absentee ballot. He, too, wouldn't have missed it.

When the celebration poured out of the bars into the streets, I didn't need a newscast to tell me what had happened. It was November 3, the day Dianne Feinstein and Barbara Boxer had been elected to the United States Senate, the first female senators from California, and the first two women to ever represent any state at the same time. That same night, the wishes of nearly everyone I knew came true as William Jefferson Clinton defeated George Bush and Ross Perot, becoming the forty-second President of the United States. I believed then and I know I was right: had George Bush been re-elected, I would have followed my lover to the grave, as would have countless others. So many had already died and many more were dying; yet nothing had been done to stop it. To some, Bill Clinton symbolized the only hope we had. To others, he was simply the lesser of three evils.

2

Still, I had forgotten a few times throughout the day. By six o'clock that night, it felt like I'd cast my vote days before. Alec had been so ill for weeks, but had rallied. He was weak and frail, but we'd gotten used to him that way. As long as he was joking with Caden and making fun of me, the rest was easy to overlook. I think I was so exhausted, I hadn't a clue what was real or imagined. I'd sent Caden to school that Monday and Tuesday. Monday afternoon, he'd rushed home to reclaim his place at his father's side. I'd found him there later that night, both of them asleep, peaceful. I had thanked God for the opportunity to sneak out back and have a cigarette. Or five.

We all slept in chairs that night. I hadn't the heart, nor the strength to pry Caden away from Alec's side. I don't think I knew it was going to be our last night together or our son's last few precious hours with his father. He went to school on Tuesday less begrudgingly than the day before.

Thankfully, I'd had the foresight to vote early enough in the day that it'd only taken an hour. Our polling place was a mile from home, but straight downhill. On a normal day, I'd have walked down and taken a cab back up. That's how Alec and I usually went into the Castro, an easy enough walk downhill, but perilous to get back home after a few drinks. Instead, I took a taxi both ways to cast my vote. I had never learned to drive a car and thank goodness for that. Where we lived, being a passenger was often times scary enough.

Alec died in his sleep, peacefully and quietly at three o'clock in the afternoon. I knew almost instantly. I could literally hear his breathing stop. I was sitting uncomfortably close, reading only inches from his face. Less than forty minutes earlier he'd said, "See ya later!" It was an inside joke. In the beginning of our relationship and several times near the end, he had caught me staring at him while he slept. My gaze at first questioning, later rapturous, finally loving. In an attempt to poke fun at me, he'd claimed it had never occurred to him to do the same and started saying, "See ya later," instead of goodnight. It was somehow fitting that those were his last words to me. I was so grateful that I responded as I always had: "I love you." Our final words to each other were perfect.

Tears filled my eyes, but I didn't sob. I knew it was coming. Maybe I sent Caden off to school so it would be easier for Alec to let go. Maybe I knew more than I even let on to myself, if that's possible. Mostly I was calm. I sat there and cried for a minute or two and then kissed my baby's forehead. As I stood up, I became aware our son was home. I didn't know if I should try to stop the inevitable. As he entered the house I heard him telling us about the

3

mock election they'd had at school. He had no idea he was speaking only to me. I had no idea what to do.

Surreal didn't begin to describe the next few hours. Eventually I'd gotten Caden to sleep and sat outside on our little patio, smoking. I had quit almost two years before, but started up again about a month earlier. Neither Caden nor Alec knew. Likely they did and just didn't say anything. While Alec was still alive, the only moments I'd allow myself to feel the true magnitude of what was happening to us were when I snuck away to smoke or take a shower. In those instants, I could be distraught. Everywhere else, it was "brave face" for the two people I lived with.

The night air was almost balmy for November. I'd grabbed a sweatshirt and gone out to the deck in the same slippers and the sweatpants I'd worn all day. I sat down, lit a cigarette, and took a tentative sip from my glass of wine, then a second more deliberate swallow. In that moment, I decided I wouldn't choke back the tears, but to my surprise, none came. I was so exhausted. A second drag, exhale; and all hell seemed to break loose in the Castro. Some newscaster had called the election and I'm sure the tears came easily for some of those people celebrating below me. There must have been hundreds of people pouring out onto the street. I thought, *Well, Alec missed it.*

He would have been so relieved, ecstatic. Months earlier, we'd both volunteered for the campaigns, but those activities weren't in the cards for very long. Sitting there, thinking about how we both would have felt about the result if I were able to feel anything but empty, a single tear escaped. It glided down my cheek and when I went to brush it away, the floodgates opened. I shook with the weeping then, unable to stifle my sobs. I sat there in the cool air for an hour or more, listening to the revelry below. I smoked and cried, and smoked and cried, and unable to move; wished that I'd brought the goddamned wine bottle out with me. That night I accepted the fact that some days called for drinking right from the bottle.

The next couple of days were a blur. I had friends who insisted on helping with everything. Though, at times, I just wanted to be left alone. Service arrangements. For once, I agreed with Alec on the convenience of him having no family. There was no one to notify, no one to comfort in their own grief. It surprised me that I phoned my mother and sister Joanna. Neither of them had even met Alec. The only member of my family back in Minnesota who had met him and Caden was my twenty-one-year-old nephew, Kevin. He was a sweetheart, despite his bitch of a mother: my sister Catelyn. He'd visited about a year earlier for no reason other than just to visit. I'm sure Caty had

4

been mortified by her son's visit. I hadn't spoken to her in years, no phone calls, no Christmas cards, not a word since she had run for congress in Minnesota, and won. I thought she might have been pretending I didn't exist.

Alec and I had talked about Kevin visiting sooner, but it was complicated by his mother calling the shots. I could've paid his way, but Kevin wanted to come on his own. God, I love that kid! I'm certain his mother worried that he was gay all through his adolescence. He still hadn't bothered to put her mind at ease.

It was during his visit that he confided in me that a boy from school had given him a hand job his sophomore year. Another time, he almost accepted a blowjob from a college classmate, but had been interrupted before anything happened. In spite of both admissions, he claimed he was, in his words, "About ninety-three percent straight." I wasn't certain how he accounted for the remaining seven percent. Perhaps even momentarily considering an encounter knocked three-and-a-half percent off your score. I had to chuckle at his determination to allow his extremely conservative mother to continue wondering about his sexuality long after he'd stopped. Kevin was of a newish, more accepting, generation. I suppose each generation gets a little more so. Certainly more than their parents.

Thinking of him, I wondered how Joanna's kids had turned out. I'd never met her son, Kelly, now thirteen. It was over thirteen years since I left home. I'd only been back three times. The first was not long after I left. Seven years later, just after Alec and I had moved to San Francisco, I went back again. That was a few years before my dad passed away. There had been a lot of devastation in my family the last couple of years. I had my own battles, those over which my siblings in Minnesota seemed unconcerned. One or two phone calls a year covered necessary communication, with the odd pleasantry thrown in. We were certainly good at appearances. With all the smoke and mirrors, there were surely people in their lives, even family members just outside "immediate" who hadn't realized that I'd only been back to Minnesota three times.

Since my father's death, my mother Moira had become more erratic, according to my sister. She'd been drinking more and was a chain smoker. My brother Patrick or "Paddy," had found her once with a magazine on fire in her lap. He must've gotten there within seconds of it starting. I hated to imagine what would have happened had he not. At any rate, they blamed her drinking. The only people in my immediate family who would see the practicality of drinking straight from the bottle were my mother and I. Moira had drunk less

5

while my dad was around. It's not that he didn't drink. He drank beer every day, including the one on which he died. My mother switched it up, moving from tequila, to vodka, to brandy; always the hard stuff. But I never recalled seeing her noticeably drunk when my dad was alive.

My last trip back to Minnesota was a weeklong visit just recently. It was a fact-finding mission, really. While there, I made a decision that would change our lives. It was on my mind, of course it was. There was no other reason to go back, out of the blue like that. I went on the pretense that I hadn't been able to return when so many things had happened, I owed it to them this time.

I was back a day and a half when I got the idea. The house in San Francisco was on the market and I'd had offers. It was time for Caden and me to make a change. Worst-case scenario, we'd get an apartment. Alec had a life insurance policy I hadn't known about. A few weeks after his death, Caden and I were a quarter of a million dollars wealthier. We'd make close to half a million from the sale of the house, and that was if I took one of the offers pending, all of them below asking price. The sky really was the limit for us. Alec had seen to that. So back in Minnesota, I started to think. Why not move there? The only negative was the weather. Caden had never known a life with aunts and uncles, cousins, a grandmother.

I was in a cab on the way to my mother's for dinner, quite honestly lost, when I saw it: a gorgeous old house, similar to the one I'd grown up in. *For Sale.* It needed some sprucing up, but the asking price was significantly less than what we'd pay to buy a tiny two-bedroom condo anywhere in California. It had a huge kitchen, a separate dining room, three bedrooms and three and-a-half bathrooms, and a basement. I could pay cash for it, and have enough left over that I wouldn't need to work for ten years. I'd still be able to send Caden to any college that would accept him. It was the most spontaneous decision I'd made in, well, fourteen years, and it was a big one.

I returned to San Francisco a brand new homeowner. Oh sure, I owned one there, also, but that one was inherited. For the first time in my life, I'd purchased something that cost more than a few hundred dollars. I was stunned at Caden's reaction. "Okay," he'd said. I had expected more of a fight. I realized, in that moment, how important the change would be for us. This house we'd lived in, even the city, had died for us with Alec. We'd rarely go anywhere that didn't remind us of him. That fourteen-year-old boy was hurting so badly.

6

I had shut out my family and they allowed it. Maybe I was right; it was all easier at the time that I just went away. Not one of them had put up a fight. But they were family. I had family. And some of them even seemed happy with the idea of us moving there. Meghan pretended she couldn't care less, ever the cool sixteen-year-old. I was told, though, that Kelly was ecstatic at the prospect of having a male cousin only a year older than him. Kevin certainly was happy. Joanna had insisted on inquiring about a teaching job for me. I'd taught English at a private high school in San Francisco for three years before Alec got sick. Before that, I taught in a public high school in Los Angeles. Paddy, a contractor, offered to do the renovations on the house while I returned to California; sold our house there, packed up our lives and moved us to Minnesota.

I politely declined my sister's offer. I didn't want to teach anymore. I hadn't a clue what I wanted to do, but at that moment it wasn't *teach*. The great thing was: I didn't have to know. All I really had to do was take care of Caden. We'd both been well provided for by Alec. I was going to take some time to decide what was next for me.

We needed to be moved in by the end of July at the latest, so Caden could become acclimated before starting a new school. Caden would be attending with his two cousins. He would be a sophomore, Kelly a freshman, and Meghan a junior. All of them would attend the school where Joanna was vice-principal.

I quickly discovered that Caden wouldn't require any convincing. I was astonished at how well it was all going. I should've known it couldn't last. I returned to San Francisco the first of May. A couple offered the asking price on our house less than a week later, but they needed to move in by June 1st. That gave us less than a month. I'd told Paddy he'd have six weeks or more. It meant that I would have to get Caden through the final few weeks of junior high school, pack up our belongings, and move both of us across country to an unfinished house in a place he barely knew existed.

So it was, on May 30, 1993, that I stood in an empty house remembering the first time I'd ever seen it. Alec had just removed a blind fold from my eyes. I couldn't have begun to imagine what was going to happen between then and now

7

Chapter 1
STEPHEN

The sunlight stole past the tightly closed blinds into my empty room, and danced just over my head. My eyes were still closed, but I could hear Caden and Kevin awake somewhere in the house. Sound travelled everywhere now that the house was virtually empty. It was the big day. The first day, as they say, of the rest of our lives.

My mattress lay on the floor, the bed frame already packed away by movers and halfway to Minnesota. I lay on the forgotten mattress afraid to open my eyes. What the fuck was I doing? The self-doubt had crept in when I wasn't paying attention. Perhaps I was too busy packing our lives into boxes, sifting through the years, discarding items with memories attached. I had to tell myself the memories were mine to keep long after the stuff we'd accumulated when there were three of us was gone. I woke up some days still expecting to see Alec lying there next to me. It would take a few moments to realize he hadn't been there in months. It was almost exactly six months since he'd died and I was past counting the days. In fact, I'd been so busy I hardly recognized the approaching milestone.

The plan was to stop about halfway to Minnesota and stay overnight. I didn't drive and Caden was only fourteen, so all the driving would fall on poor Kevin. We'd make it to Minneapolis Monday night. The next chapter in our lives awaited our arrival in a house I barely remembered. I'd only seen it twice, and the reality of it hadn't quite set in. Of course, Caden had very few questions about the house itself. A fourteen-year-old boy could care less about the specifics of his surroundings. He knew he'd have his own room—why wouldn't he—and that was all he cared about.

I could tell he was curious about this thing called a family I described to him, but for some reason he was trying to downplay his interest. It was odd to me that Alec and I had never thought to introduce him to my family. They weren't awful people, none of them. Even Catelyn, if I remembered correctly, had some redeeming qualities. We'd never once discussed all visiting Minnesota together. Perhaps Alec didn't want to realize what he had been missing. After he'd died though, I'd become keenly aware of the ache inside.

I opened one eye and looked over at the digital alarm clock. Seven fifty-eight a.m. It was set to go off at eight. We were going to take our time packing up

8

the rest of the truck and head out of San Francisco about ten thirty. There was always traffic, but it wouldn't be horrible the second day of a three-day weekend.

I'd only slept about four-and-a-half hours, but that was only an hour less than what I'd grown accustomed to. On a really good night, I might get six, which was an improvement, certainly, on the one or two hours a night I'd gotten in the beginning. I realized after Alec died that we almost never spent the night apart. He had done a play in Los Angeles after we'd moved to San Francisco and spent five or six nights a week there for more than two months. Alec had done that play and one made-for-TV movie since the series ended. In the four years after the series, it had become increasingly evident that playing a gay character on TV was not a good career move for a gay actor.

That was all the time we'd spent apart since moving to San Francisco, and I hadn't slept well then either. I told myself that it wasn't like he was just away working. I was going to have to figure out something. Maybe a new bed in a new room in a new house in a new city. With both eyes open, I rolled onto my back and moved my forearm to block the intruding sun from my eyes. Summer had arrived for sure. It seemed like just a few days ago it was still dark, or at least dim at that hour. But it had been weeks, the morning light barely vanquished by daylight saving time a month earlier. Time and its passing had become a stranger to me. I hadn't worked but two days since last January. I'd taken two months, suffered through Thanksgiving, Christmas, my birthday, and New Year's without Alec.

I'd planned to return to teaching after a semester's absence, but that didn't work out well. I managed my first day back. First days of just about everything are easy to manage. Just maneuvering through them requires enough effort that you barely have time for thought. On the second day, the bottom fell out. I could not will myself out of bed. After a sub was called, I crawled out to the patio for a cigarette. That cat was out of the bag. I'd not bothered hiding it from Caden and he'd not bothered hiding his disdain over it for a few weeks. He had cut me some slack right after he'd first found out. It was during the gathering after the memorial service when he'd come looking for me and busted my friend Mariana and me sneaking a cigarette, in her little blue Geo Metro of all places. He hadn't said a thing then, nor did he for a couple of weeks after that. Then one night at dinner, he lowered the boom. "So," he said.

"Yes?" I asked.

9

"How long have you been smoking?"

"It's not like I've BEEN smoking. I've had a few cigarettes."

"A few hundred! Jeez! I found a carton in your bathroom cupboard."

"What were you doing in my bathroom cupboard?" I asked, trying to change the subject.

"I was looking for a razor."

"A razor? For what? You're fourteen years old. Were you planning to shave your head?"

"I wanted to be prepared," he answered.

"There's thinking *way* ahead!" He had at least two years.

"Stop trying to change the subject."

"I wasn't. Still, you had no business in there," I said, sticking to my plan of changing the subject.

"Ha! You're so transparent."

"How do you even know what that means?"

"I looked it up in the dictionary and there was a picture of you," Caden said, triumphantly.

The conversations continued. His disapproval had reached epic proportions until finally, I promised him I would make every effort to quit once we were settled somewhere else. This was even before Minnesota had come up.

Caden had gone back to school a little over a week after his dad died. Meanwhile, I was a complete failure. How was it that I was so incapacitated? In those first few weeks, I sat on the patio in my robe and winter coat feeling sorry for *us*. When that grew tiresome, I tried to remind myself that I was the adult, therefore I had to be there for Caden and the self-pity, on either of our behalves, had to go. Eventually it was alright. So many things became encompassed in parenting; grocery shopping, housecleaning, bill paying, feigning purpose. I never went back to teaching. There was vague talk of finding myself, perhaps writing. The people around me, sometimes Caden included, were torn between pity and horror. No one knew what to say to me anymore, no one but Mariana. Obviously, things improved. I mean, I literally sold one house and purchased another. The other stuff had become like a full-time job. I was starting to think I had a future in housewifery, too bad there was no husband to make that earnest pipe dream a reality. I'd almost happily shop and cook and clean and muddle through the days as if I had more purpose than I really did. We were getting by and although there was no such thing as normal anymore for either of us, we'd become somewhat adept at impersonating a family that hadn't been systematically torn apart by grief.

I heard footsteps outside my door and then Caden's voice. "You up? Your alarm's gone off twice. No fair hiding."

"What could I possibly be hiding from?"

"How should I know?" he asked, and was gone back down the hall. I heard him calling after Kevin.

I moved my legs and felt the cat stir. I hadn't realized he was even in bed with me, but there he was. Caden had named Sonic after a video game he played with his father, something about a hedgehog. I was no good at those things. My knowledge of video games began and ended with Ms. Pacman. The kid stuff was what Alec did well; video games, comic books, baseball. They'd just started delving into horror movies, my disapproval noted for the record. I managed some of the nerdy stuff just fine. I knew enough about superheroes to at least contribute. I had taught high school kids for going on ten years, so I could talk the talk and not sound completely grown-up. We all watched *Star Trek: The Next Generation* together. In fact, when it came to naming the cat it was a toss-up between Wesley, after Wesley Crusher in TNG and Sonic. We had a female cat, too, named Meg after a character in my favorite movie, *The Big Chill*. She came with me when I joined the family. She was nearly fourteen and far less likely to make a run for it. I was sure she was hiding, determined to not go anywhere when the time came. Sonic had ended up with me because the house doors were open and they didn't want him escaping, further delaying our departure.

"Time to get up, bud," I told the cat. "Big day."

Sonic meowed his dissent, apparently no more looking forward to this day than I was. Change was something I embraced in theory, but the actual execution usually left me at best disinterested, at worst completely horrified.

11

The self-doubt certainly didn't help. UGH! I'd made this bed, this was my decision, and there really was no turning back now. I decided to blame the cat.

"This was your idea, you know?"

"Are you talking to yourself again?" Caden was back at the door.

"I was talking to your cat." I was on my feet and willing myself to the door.

"How did Sonic get in there?"

"Must've been Kevin," I said, not a question. If Caden or I hadn't let him in, there was only one other option. I opened the door and found Caden standing there, waiting.

"I thought you might've gone back to sleep," he said.

"And miss all of this?"

"Come on. This was your idea."

"Nope. We're blaming it on Sonic. If this turns out to be the biggest mistake of our lives, I'm planning to blame the cat."

"Good plan." He was mocking me now.

"I'm just going to hop in the shower. Ten minutes and I'll show you two how this is done."

"We're pretty much ready to go. Just waiting on you. Kevin didn't want to drive the truck down the hill, so he walked down for coffee."

"How long ago was that?" I asked.

"Just now. I said I'd make sure you were ready to go when he got back."

"Who the hell put you two in charge?"

"Ha! Somebody has to be. I just figured it ought to be the smart one."

"I like where you're going with this, but I have to hold my head under water for ten minutes." *Maybe I could drown*, I thought. "Is the kennel ready in the garage?"

"Ooh, I forgot. You shower. I'll get the cats ready to go."

"Ten minutes." I reached out to muss his hair, but he'd already turned and started to go.

"When have you ever gotten ready in ten minutes?" he said, his back to me. "Come on, Sonic." The cat followed, more like a dog, blindly ready for whatever lay in store. Man, would he be disappointed.

The water felt good. I loved the shower part of the ritual. It was all the crap that came after, shaving, moisturizing, and dressing; so much work was completely unfair immediately after something so halcyon. Sometimes I stood in the shower and thought about what would happen if I refused to ever get out. I'd wrinkle I supposed, which was what all the moisturizing was for. I would eventually grow bored, want for something one couldn't have in the shower; a cigarette, Chinese food, a good book. Still, nothing bad ever happens in the shower. For whatever time you're left alone, it's all warm water and quiet. Heaven. So many showers, though, were rushed. *I'm just going to hop in the shower*. Like you'd be in and out, quick like a bunny. I rarely took a shower anymore when it wasn't a means to something else. Go to work, go shopping, conferences, dinner with friends, goddamned memorial services.

Alec's dying brought people into our lives that somehow we'd managed to avoid. We didn't try to avoid them, just hadn't traveled in the same circles. We didn't travel in any circles. The closest thing we did to socializing outside our group of friends was volunteering for the Democratic Party before things got bad for Alec. Sure, we went to the bars before that, but Alec was always so paranoid about being recognized. We fought once because I struck up a conversation with a guy at the bar while in line to get drinks. The guy assumed Alec was jealous and I couldn't tell him otherwise. We didn't go out again for a while after that. We certainly weren't lonely. There was Mariana, a handful of other friends, mostly straight. All straight. There were acquaintances from school or the other volunteers, but those connections stayed pretty much sedentary. How nice it would be to have something, a way to reach or stay connected with many friends all at once. I'd thought that so many times when dealing with my family.

13

In the last few months, almost a year, we became part of a community, so many lovely people willing to help. I'd never actually gone to a support group until very near the end. I was uncomfortable the entire time. Most of the time, I had no problem crying for other people's pain, but I preferred to do my own crying privately. I guess I'd become accustomed to the necessity of that. Alec would sometimes poke fun when I cried at a movie, but he did too, just not as blatantly. And he was proud when Caden cried watching *My Girl* a couple of years before. That may have been the first time we actually saw our son exhibit empathy. It's not that I didn't cry for myself; I did, more in the last two years than I was comfortable with. Much more. I just hated when those tears were witnessed. Even by Alec, maybe especially by him. There were a lot of tears in that support group. I didn't begrudge them their tears. My own seemed like a luxury I'd rather cash in for something else, the days when Alec and I both smoked and drank, a time we went to an ecstasy bar in LA called The Probe and danced all night, kissing each other and other men at the same time, free love, the closest either of us would ever get to Woodstock. I'd settle for sex, sometimes I imagined it wouldn't make a difference with whom. It had been so long; since a year before Alec died, I realized, so a year and a half. I suppose I'd have marked it in my diary had I known it would be the last time.

There had been a drought after the first time Alec had been sick and when we found out. There were droughts, sometimes weeks or months afterwards, too. My getting it was pretty much a forgone conclusion, but I'm sure there was fear on both our parts. There'd barely been a test back then. I tested positive two years after Alec. You were supposed to be tested every six months in those days, but I had missed one. When I did finally test positive, it had been almost a year since I'd last been tested. We'd already moved to San Francisco. It was the morning of Caden's eleventh birthday party. I knew I was positive already. I just did. I told myself I was being paranoid. I told myself I was being pessimistic. I told myself not to bother getting tested for a year. I actually lied to Alec and told him I had gone. What difference did it really make? I was kidding myself if I thought I wasn't going to get it. At that point, the test itself felt like a formality. What difference would it make to know for sure?

For two years, I'd been full of shit. What it really came down to was this: I was terrified of *feeling* anything about it. How could I go home to someone who was already sick, was terrified of leaving his son, of leaving me, and basically announce that it was all going to be a crapshoot? I could die before him. I was afraid of that, too. We could die together or in close proximity to each other and leave our son completely alone. What if one of us was too sick to care for the other? There were so many variables and absolutely no happy endings.

14

Alec had already been there. When he got sick, we had no idea even what to tell Caden. He was far too young to know something so awful, so we kept it from him. I told myself I was entitled to my own secret; another lie. Everything about then was shrouded in terror, lies upon lies, uncertainty weighed down by our reluctance to hurt each other with something as incomprehensible as communication.

And I was just plain angry! I had been raised Catholic and somewhere inside I still believed in God. Those childhood beliefs fell short of transforming into organized religion anymore. Somehow, though, I believed in a divine purpose. What the fuck kind of purpose was this?

Caden's birthday party was in two hours. I hadn't even told Alec I'd gone to be tested. Riding down in the elevator after having just tested positive, I decided not to tell him yet. I couldn't very well tell him right before the birthday party. I didn't know when I'd tell him, but I knew I'd explode if I didn't tell someone. There was a payphone across the street from the clinic. I nearly teleported through the lobby, onto the street and to the phone. Coins deposited, numbers punched, dialing, ringing... ringing.

"Collect call from Stephen."

"One moment, sir." I think I blacked completely out for the next forty-five seconds or so until I heard my sister's voice.

"Stephen? Stephen, what's wrong?"

"Joanna, what the fuck?" What had I done?

"Why aren't you calling from home? Is something wrong?"

I began to cry.

The memory of that day faded and I was back in the shower. Caden was right. I was not ready in ten minutes. I'd barely even made it into the shower in that time. I loved our shower, big enough for two people. There was no tub, just a glass stall. Alec and I had made love in this shower so many times. I had cried in this shower, hidden from Alec and Caden, while he lay dying in another room. There used to be speakers above the bathroom mirror, piping music from a stereo in the bedroom; and I'd shower listening to Van Morrison or Joni Mitchell or Fleetwood Mac. The stereo and speakers were with the bed

15

frame on their way to Minnesota. There was nothing this morning but the sound of the water. I stood for five minutes just letting the warm water wash over me, enjoying my last shower there. I knew if I didn't get a move on; there'd be another knock on the door. I stepped out of the shower stall, grabbing a fluffy white towel as I went. I used my hand to wipe the moisture from the mirror and looked at my reflection.

I rarely bothered to look at myself in the mirror anymore. Sure, I checked to make sure my hair wasn't sticking up or that there wasn't toothpaste on my chin, but I couldn't remember the last time I just stood and studied the face looking back at me. I brushed my damp hair from my forehead and held it back, moving my face closer to the mirror, squinting. I was blind as a bat, so without my glasses or contact lenses, I wouldn't have been able to properly see without moving closer. My eyebrows were well shaped. Even grief couldn't curb my vanity. I put a small amount of moisturizer in the palm of one hand, rubbed my hands together and began to apply it to my face. I still looked like I was in my early to mid-twenties. Kevin and I could pass as brothers and had when he visited. We both got our looks from my mother, his grandmother's side of the family, Joanna did too. Caty and Paddy looked more like my dad, pale with big Irish noses. I had long eyelashes, brown eyes, and almost shoulder-length light brown hair.

Alec had always been breathtakingly handsome, perhaps even a bit rugged before he'd started losing weight. I was always thin. My five feet ten, one hundred and fifty pound frame betrayed very little body fat. There was some muscle tone, more when I worked at it. My stomach was certainly flat, but I wouldn't say I had defined abs. I did have the faintest hint of a V. As I looked at myself in the mirror still glistening a bit from a hot shower, I thought again, about how long it had been since I'd had sex. I was thirty-three years old and I hadn't even masturbated in weeks. There were so many things I continued doing when Alec was sick, that I'd all but stopped doing after he'd died, jerking off just being one of them. I used to use free weights to add some tone to my arms and sometimes I'd even jog. There were steps going down almost a block into the Upper Castro that I'd run up and down. I was still in decent shape, but I told myself while standing there naked in front of the mirror that things had to change in Minnesota. This was a new start and I had to take advantage of it. At some point, people just grow weary of someone who is sad all the time. I felt I put on a pretty decent front, but sarcasm and half-assed buoyancy could only carry one so far. It was truly time to embrace the course I'd set us on, no more faking it.

16

It was strange, but there in the mirror for a few moments, as I considered myself; I realized that I'd have to do a bit more of that in order to think of my son. I was going to burn myself completely out if I didn't relax into this single parenting thing. It had been six months, but let's face it; really, it had been over a year. I was doing all right really, all things considered, but I could do better. For both of us.

"Okay, so twenty-five is the new ten." I had quickly dressed in loose blue jeans, a light sweatshirt over a tank top, leather flip-flops, and a baseball cap, and was making excuses as I went down the hall into the main room. It took my breath away to see the room completely empty. The hardwood floor gleamed up at me, an empty canvas there for someone else to paint. On the counter that separated the kitchen from the main room was a Styrofoam coffee cup, a duffel bag, a set of keys, and Kevin's wallet. Across the counter was a nearly empty jug of orange juice, a pack of Kool's, and a lighter. Thank God Kevin smoked! It took some of the pressure off me. I didn't think I'd make it through the next two days without smoking.

"Did you say something?" Kevin asked. My nephew was twenty-one years old and absolutely gorgeous. He'd certainly made a splash in the Castro the night he'd arrived. We went to the Midnight Sun and twice I watched men run into things paying attention only to him. He was six feet tall, maybe a hundred seventy-five pounds. His arms were muscular and tan. That morning he wore a tank top and loose fitting denim cut-offs. He was barefoot and his medium-length brown hair hung, absentmindedly, in his face. Sunglasses covered his piercing blue eyes. He stopped in the doorway to the garage and looked at me, smiling.

"To myself mostly," I replied. "Bum one?" I asked, motioning with my eyes to his pack of cigarettes on the counter. I really was trying to quit, but we'd definitely be stopping for a pack of my own on the way out of town. He nodded.

"Ready for this?" he asked.

"I was born ready."

"Coffee's for you." He motioned to the cup on the counter. "Milk and lots of sugar."

He gave me a hug as he moved past me. "I think we're about ready to hit it," he said, already halfway to the guest bathroom.

17

"Hiya, Steph!" Caden was in the garage doorway now. He'd started using the shortened version of my name previously only used by his father. "Ready to hit it?" Caden had come to idolize Kevin in just a couple of days. He was even copying phrases I'd never heard him use before.

"I'm going to have a quick smoke and look down at the city. Wanna join me? I promise you won't die from that little bit of second hand smoke."

"Where's Kev?"

"Bathroom." I had started toward the small patio and Caden followed.

I lit a cigarette, took a long drag, and put the pack and the lighter in the pocket of my sweatshirt. Caden stood close to me, not caring for once about the smoking, and together we looked down upon the city that had been home to both of us for five years. The Castro was just below, and beyond it lay Market Street, then downtown. The first time I'd taken in this view was also after having made my way through an empty house and it felt like a lifetime ago.

"You're going to miss this, aren't you?" Caden asked, moving even closer to me.

"Aren't you?" I replied, meaning to avoid any acknowledgement of regret at what we were about to embark on.

"I suppose. This was always a bigger deal to you and dad."

"I guess," I mused.

"I miss him." He was now so close, I took a quick drag, turning my head to exhale away from him, and moved the cigarette to my left hand.

"Oh kiddo, so do I. So much." Tears began to well up in my eyes, but I managed to push them back. I turned toward him a bit and said, "We can miss him together anywhere, you know?"

"I know. I just wanted you to know that I miss him too." He didn't seem sad at all. I was sure he was trying to cheer me up. Then he looked back down at the city and said, "See ya later." And he walked back into the house, leaving me to my own goodbyes.

18

Chapter 2

<u>CADEN</u>

Grown-ups always wanted to say goodbye to everything like when they were leaving stuff behind. We were all in the truck, *leaving* San Francisco, and I didn't get why. We were still in the city, about to go across the bridge. It wasn't like either of us had anything left there. I was just — I didn't get: why Minnesota? Stephen seemed so broken, like when we used to do puzzles with my dad and we'd get all the way to the end and there'd be pieces missing. I'd get so pissed off that we'd done all that work and then couldn't finish. That was what Stephen reminded me of sometimes; like he was missing the few pieces that would complete him. It scared me. I knew he was trying to smile and I knew that he loved me. It was just that… sometimes I couldn't feel it. Sometimes I couldn't feel anything. Sometimes, though, like when we said goodbye (*see what I mean?*) to the city. *I mean who does that? Grown-ups.* Stephen wanted to say goodbye to San Francisco. He called it symbolism. Did I forget to mention that my dads were gay? Well, my dad was. Stephen was my stepdad. My dad and Stephen were together for eleven years and we were happy. We were fucking off the charts until my dad; my real dad, he died.

Anyway, grownups liked making stuff final. Like they had to tidy everything up so it fit together. Sometimes stuff just didn't go back together, not the way it used to. Sometimes, actually a lot of the time, nothing made sense. Like, I never had grandparents. Stephen said I would when we moved — at least a grandmother — but he also said she was kind of weird. Weird wasn't so bad. Most people got weird when your dad died. And then all you had left was another dad. That, I supposed, *was* really weird. But someone who was at the house after Dad died said, "Not as much so, in San Francisco." Okay, so we went out back to say our big goodbye. He was smoking and it kind of smelled good. I had a cigarette with this guy at school after my dad died and I felt like I was going to puke, but then it wasn't too bad. I wanted to be close to Stephen. Like a puzzle piece. So I moved close and he didn't move away. I really missed my dad, but I realized… I missed Stephen, too. I'd never missed him before. I mean, was that weird, seeing as we weren't apart? He seemed like he was really missing Dad too. I didn't get why adults always thought they had to be so strong. I thought it would be nice to tell him I knew. That was all. So I did. But then I just wanted to get in the truck and go. So I left and I guess he really did say goodbye to the city.

20

I sat in the backseat, careful to sit behind Stephen, next to the kennel. That way Stephen couldn't stare back at me the whole way. At first, he made a big production of navigating. That was what he called it, anyway. I think he felt bad for not knowing how to drive, so he gave himself a job to do.

Kevin was his nephew, the son of the sister he didn't like very much. He flew out to San Francisco to drive us to Minnesota. I guess that was a really big deal. At least that's what Stephen kept saying. We had a new house in Minnesota and it needed some work, another thing I'd heard Stephen say a million times. He tried really hard, kinda too hard most of the time, but I knew he meant well. Adults said that. When my dad died, a lot of people made it a big deal. But they didn't know him that well. Some people wanted to hug me or touch me a lot. Most people don't want to touch me very much at all. I thought gay people, especially, were worried what it'd look like. That was okay, because I didn't always want to be touched. After Dad died, it was annoying getting hugged so much. Stephen kept saying, "They mean well." I think he was kind of over it too. One time I went to look for him and found him in his friend's car smoking. He acted funny, like I didn't know he smoked. I was like, *Dude, I'm not a fucking idiot!*

He thought when he started again, that Dad and I didn't know. My dad said that Steph would feel bad if we let on that we knew and that it could be one of our secrets. Like that we really didn't care about some of the stuff he did, like setting the table. We had this big, long table with a lot of chairs. Sometimes we'd sit in there and eat, but first we'd have to make a big deal of setting the table and everything. Dad said Stephen used to do that with his family when he lived in Minnesota, and he probably missed it. We would've been happy eating in front of the TV, which we hardly ever got to do. Dad said it was the polite thing to do to lie and say we liked eating at the table and to pretend to fight over who got to set it.

My dad died a while ago. He died at home, so it was weird at first. There was a special bed in the living room. We got that after he went away to be sick and I didn't think he'd come home again; but then he and Steph decided it would be nicer for him to be sick at home than in some hospital. That was last October and then he died in November, the same day as the election for President. We did this thing at school, a fake election. Everyone got to vote secretly just like adults did and Bill Clinton won in both of the elections; the fake one and the real one. I went home to tell my dads what happened at school. That was when I sometimes called them both "Dad," but my dad was dead. Steph said "gone." He was *gone*, like what the fuck did *gone* mean?

21

People who were gone came back sometimes, right? My dad wasn't coming back.

Both of us tried really hard not to cry in front of each other after that night. Sometimes we pretended we weren't sad for the sake of each other, kind of like the setting the table thing, I figured. The polite thing. I thought my dad would like that I did that for Steph. We didn't eat at the table for a long time after he died. For a while there were a lot of dead flowers on it, and then just crap; stuff piled up, mostly other people's dishes. I thought Steph didn't like to eat there without my dad. Maybe because he died like ten feet away. We kind of avoided that whole area of the house. It was just a long room with the TV at the other end, though we could never have that on when we ate at the table. I had no idea why!

In the truck, I just listened to music and watched the cats. They were facing me, which I think made them feel better after a while. They were pretty freaked out at first. They couldn't be out of the kennel while we were in the truck, so I liked being able to at least see them; until the second day when they started using the litter box again. Neither of them used it at all the whole first day, but they did when we got to the motel.

Kevin and I shared a room, and the cats got to come out of the kennel once we were in there. Sonic always slept with me at home, but in the motel, he slept with Kevin. Meg slept on the floor in the corner. I guessed she was pissed off at everybody, even Kevin, who none of us knew very well, especially Sonic. We didn't even have him when Kevin visited before. That was a while ago, before I knew Stephen had a family.

Kevin was cool. He didn't act weird around me. He just kind of *was*; like he didn't act one way in front of me and a different way with just me and Steph or just him and Stephen. And he was dope. He had an earring and he talked like an adult, but not all the way. Some things he said sounded cool, like a language in between how kids and adults talked. I liked that he'd be in Minnesota too, and we'd see him a lot.

I had other cousins there, which Kevin said were dope, too. Those kids were Steph's other sister's. Everyone liked her. She'd just gotten a divorce, and Kevin said she's very pretty, not like his mom; who dressed like an old lady and only smiled when someone was taking her picture. That's what Kevin said, and she's his mom. I didn't think I was all that excited to meet Kev's mom. Anyway, I'd have three cousins, three aunts, an uncle, and a grandma. Stephen called it "instant family," which was sort of funny. And weird. But I

22

was okay seeing how they were. Some adults were better than others. Like they could remember what it was like to be a kid, so they didn't act all weird.

My dad didn't have any relatives. Most people did, but not my dad. It was just him and me until I was two years old, but it wasn't like I remembered that. Anyway, it wasn't that Stephen wasn't my real dad. He sorta was. I loved him. I thought about saying that sometimes, but I didn't. I got scared, I guess. Like when I said I thought he loved me, but I didn't feel like it. I wasn't sure I should love him the same way as I did my real dad, but I maybe did. Grown-ups were way more hung up about that stuff. Ownership, like people could belong to other people.

One time when Dad was sick, before he came home again, he and Stephen wanted to talk about something. I knew it was really important because they said so like a million times. I usually saw Dad every day, except the time he was in a play, and when he was in that place. Steph said we were going to take a cab to the hospital to see Dad and talk about what was happening. I knew what was happening. I was thirteen. I knew stuff. My dad was really, really sick and he was going to die. So we took the cab to the place where my Dad was, and all of the adults were extra weird that day.

He wasn't in bed when we got there. He was sitting at the little table by the window in his room. He looked like he was going to stand up, but Steph went right over, hugged him and kissed him on the lips, and then he just stayed sitting. Then I went over and hugged him. He was really skinny and his eyes looked funny. I'd never seen them like that before, but they pretty much stayed like that until he died, like something in a horror movie. He hugged me back, but not as tight as usual. I didn't think he could hug that tight anyway, but he tried, and it seemed like it hurt him. I tried to make it quick when we hugged, so he wouldn't be in pain, but sometimes I forgot and then he'd have this look on his face. I'd feel bad, but he'd smile, and Stephen would smile, so I'd smile and not say anything.

"Do you want a pop?" Stephen had asked. They called it pop in Minnesota and my dad sometimes laughed at him when he called it that. We hardly ever talked about pop, because we didn't usually have it. I looked at Steph and then my dad and it seemed like it would be okay, so I said "Yeah." Stephen went and got us each a pop, but only he and I drank ours. For a while, my dad didn't even open his, but then Stephen did it for him. We talked about school and stupid stuff and then they told me that my dad was dying. Nobody had used that word before, at least not to me. I overheard Stephen and Mariana

23

talking about it one time. That's how I knew. I'd known for a while, but I didn't think I was supposed to know, so I didn't mention it.

My dad had tears in his weird eyes when he said it to me, and then they told me that I'd stay with Steph after he was gone. I never really thought about it before, like it never occurred to me I wouldn't. Where else would I stay? Then I kind of felt weird, and after that I wasn't sure if I was supposed to call Stephen "Dad" anymore. Like maybe, my dad or Stephen would feel bad if I did. I didn't know and I didn't want to ask, so I just went with it. I started calling him Steph because that's what Dad mostly called him. Sometimes he called him "Honey," but I wasn't gonna call him that.

I was still just listening to music in the back seat and watching the cats, who'd relaxed a little. They were sorta getting used to traveling. Sonic even slept a little. Meg mostly sat in the litter box, but didn't use it except for that one time. Sometimes I'd fall asleep a little and wouldn't even notice when the CD ended. I'd wake up and not know how long there hadn't been music. I would quietly change the CD and usually no one would look back at me. I didn't really want to talk, so that was all right. We were in Minnesota, not in Minneapolis yet, but in the state. I only knew that because of the signs. A while back, I saw one that said Minneapolis was 120 miles ahead, but then I closed my eyes again, and I guess I fell asleep. When I woke up, my music had stopped and we weren't moving anymore.

Stephen was looking at me. "We're here," he said. *Here? Where? Oh there!* I sat up and looked out the window and saw all these really big houses.

"This is it," Stephen announced.

"What?" I asked, but I knew what he meant. Sometimes I asked, just to be sure, so I didn't look really dumb if I was wrong.

"I guess we're home," he said. So fucking weird!

"Jesus Christ, it's huge!" It was all I could think of to say. It was! It was fucking huge. Jeez, I was glad I didn't say fucking. No one seemed to mind that I said Jesus Christ, though. They were both looking at the house like they completely agreed with me.

24

Chapter 3
STEPHEN

The Minneapolis house was a two story Tudor in Linden Hills, a few blocks from Lake Calhoun. It was originally built in 1905, and then nearly rebuilt in 1970. The owners had both passed away and their children decided to sell. The carpeting seemed as if it had been laid in 1970 and never seen to since, but there were hardwood floors underneath. With a little TLC they would be beautiful. The plumbing wasn't original, but it might as well have been. Peeling wallpaper, dated paneling, landscaping gone to seed. It was obvious their children hadn't much to do with the parents in their twilight years.

There was bickering over the sale of the house, so the estate still hadn't been settled a year after their mother passed away. The asking price had been $200,000, about on par with the neighborhood at the time, but laughable considering its condition and the repairs that would need to be made. Almost on a lark I offered $125,000 cash, fully prepared to haggle a bit. I knew I'd have to pour at least a hundred grand into it. It took them less than twenty-four hours to accept the offer. The house was a little under three thousand square feet, more than twice what we had in San Francisco. It sat less than five blocks from the spot where I'd first made out with Liam Carpenter. I'd done more than that really, but we'll just leave it there.

Alec's life insurance — the policy I had known nothing about — had netted us; well me specifically, Caden being a separate beneficiary, a quarter of a million dollars. There was a policy we'd taken out together that paid out $100,000, and the sale of the house in San Francisco had brought in another $500,000. Alec had paid about half that when he bought it. I was almost a millionaire.

I had left Paddy pretty much a blank check to rip up the carpeting, redo the floors, build a new staircase, remove the wallpaper and paneling, and replace the roof. Central air had to be installed, as well. My brother would contract that out. We would be in Minneapolis a month ahead of schedule, so I crossed my fingers and hoped for the best.

Pulling up in front of the house at seven p.m. Monday, I was surprised to find someone who wasn't my brother on the roof. Kevin had pulled the U-Haul beside one of those rented Dumpsters people use while renovating. I looked back at Caden; headphones on, Walkman blaring, barely aware we were even in Minnesota. Why didn't I turn around earlier and make him pay attention to

25

the skyline as we drove into the city? My heart was in my throat; I supposed I was feeling enough anxiety enough for both of us.

"This is it!"

"What?" Caden replied.

"I guess we're home!" I joked.

Caden sat up and looked out the window. He really hadn't known where we were. I could swear he stirred a while back, but he was wiping the sleep from his eyes with one hand, removing his headphones with the other. I opened my car door, reminding myself of the drop, and half-leapt out of the truck. Kevin was out of the driver's side, stretching his legs in the street.

"Jesus Christ, it's huge!" Caden exclaimed, joining us in the street. I turned and looked at him, neither shocked, nor disappointed. He was right. The house was so much larger than I remembered. God, what had I done?

"Nice!" Kevin said, walking around the back of the truck.

"You didn't drive by before?" I asked him.

"Nah! Grandma said she had the address, but I never asked. I just knew it was by Lake Calhoun. You bought the whole thing?"

"Yeah Kev, people don't sell houses in parts. I'm feeling a little light-headed. Long drive, I think."

"Don't faint. Jesus!" Caden said.

"Okay. Really! Enough with the language!"

"Chill!" he begged. I wasn't sure about this slang crap he was picking up from Kevin. "Can we see inside?"

"Let me figure out who that is on the roof first," I answered nervously. The guy had disappeared, but as I closed the door to the truck, I could see he had climbed down and was coming around the side toward us.

"You must be Stephen," he said. "Paddy will be back any minute. We've been working twenty-four-seven. I'll bet you have no idea who I am."

"You work for my brother?"

"Yes. I'm Charlie. Charlie Carpenter. We went to Southwest together. Well you went with my brother, Liam. He was a grade behind you."

"God, Liam!" I was sure I was blushing. I'd just been thinking about him.

"I was probably this guy's age the last time you saw me," Charlie said, motioning to Caden, who was clearly anxious to go inside and explore.

"I'm fourteen," Caden told him.

"Okay, I was a little younger."

"How is he?" I asked Charlie.

"Liam died about a year and a half ago."

"Oh God, I'm sorry!"

"Thanks, but you don't want to hear about all that now. You've been on the road for two days. Do you want to see your house?"

That was all the invitation Caden needed. He practically ran up the steps onto the porch, Kevin behind him, the two of them far more anxious than I was to explore the mansion in front of us.

"Go ahead," I called after them. "Be there in a second." I retrieved my cigarettes from the pocket of my sweatshirt.

"Smoke?" I offered Charlie. "I'm just going to sit on the step and have one before I go in."

"I quit. But I'll sit with you?"

"Please." We sat there in silence for a moment or two. It was Charlie who spoke first.

"Liam died of AIDS. I thought you'd want to know. Paddy told me about your lover and —."

"I'm so sorry," I interrupted, not anxious to discuss Alec after less than five minutes in Minneapolis, sitting at the precipice of Caden's and my new life together.

"I'm sorry. I shouldn't have said anything."

"No, it's alright. Tell me what you've been doing with the house," I begged, changing the subject.

"We still have another day on the roof, but the floors are completely finished except the tile in the downstairs bathroom and the carpeting in the master bedroom. The furnace was replaced last week and the AC is working great. There's still some plumbing stuff and I think Paddy ordered the water heater this morning."

"Why don't we go look? I think I can make it without passing out."

"You must be excited."

"Very much so." We both got to our feet and I led the way across the walk and up the steps.

"Most of the wallpaper is gone, but there's a lot of painting to be done. Paddy started tearing down the paneling in the basement this afternoon. He just went home for dinner."

I paused for a moment at the threshold, looked back at Charlie and thanked him. I opened the door and could hear Caden and Kevin somewhere upstairs, their voices reverberating through another empty house. "Oh, the movers came, right?"

"Yes, Saturday. Most of that stuff is in the garage."

"Good. Thank you." I called upstairs to Caden. "For the record, the bigger bedroom is mine."

"I figured. Jeez!"

"Just making sure you hadn't already moved in. Was the phone turned on?"

"I don't actually know," Charlie answered. "I suppose we could check it."

28

"I think we'd need a phone to do that." Caden and Kevin were on the stairs.

"Awesome house," Kevin said.

"Damn Skippy," said Caden. I didn't have a clue what that even meant.

"The upstairs is nice?" I asked.

"Dank," they said, almost in unison. From their tones, I assumed "dank" was a good thing.

"Well, let's see." I started up the stairs. Then asked Caden, "Pick your room?"

"Yep. Right at the top. Is our stuff here? I can start unpacking." It was nice to see him excited. I couldn't recall the last time I had seen him so enthusiastic.

"Your bed should be in the garage."

"There are keys on the counter just inside the back door," Charlie told them, and Caden was off, disappearing in seconds.

"Kev, you must be exhausted, anxious to get home. I bet —."

"I'm good," he interrupted. "I'll help Caden get his stuff upstairs." Then he, too, was gone.

"I'm just going to let you explore," Charlie said. "I'll be on the roof finishing up."

The wood floors were gorgeous. There would eventually be carpeting going up the stairs, down the hall, and at least in the master bedroom, which sat at the end of the hall. At the top of the stairs were two bedrooms of about equal size. Beyond those on the left was a bathroom, and on the right a linen closet. Past the bathroom was the door to the master bedroom. I walked down the hall to my room and stood in the doorway, struck again by how lovely the floors were, rethinking my decision to carpet this room. I crossed to the window, looked down, and watched Caden open the garage door. He must've felt me watching him because he looked up at me and smiled.

There was so much left to be done, but it seemed Charlie and Paddy had done a beautiful job so far. I couldn't help but smile, too. Caden was excitedly rummaging through the garage to find his stuff. I'd thought about staying in a hotel for a couple of days, while we painted, and made decisions about carpeting, but I couldn't do that to Caden now. It hadn't even occurred to me that I was without a bed. The bed frame on which Alec and I used to sleep would go in the guest room with a new mattress and I planned to buy a whole new bed. I guessed I'd be on the couch tonight.

I headed back downstairs, stood in the center of the living room and looked out the huge front window at the U-Haul parked on the street, and suddenly remembered the cats. *God*, I thought, hurrying out the front door and out to the truck. I opened the door to a barrage of angry meows.

"I'm so sorry, guys. Wanna see our new house?" The kennel was heavy and awkward, carrying two cats, two cat beds and a tiny litter box. I wrestled it out of the back seat and set it on the sidewalk. Just then, Caden came around the side of the house.

"Need help?"

"Look who we forgot," I said. "They're pissed."

"Come on, Sonic," Caden said, grabbing one side of the kennel. I grabbed the other and together we carried the kennel up the steps and into the house.

Once securely inside the house, I opened the metal door to the kennel and moved aside. Out came Meg first, tentatively checking her surroundings. She was all white with long hair and beautiful green eyes. She brushed quickly against my leg, apparently excited to be out of that box. Caden got down on his hands and knees and peered inside the kennel. Sonic was sitting in the litter box; frightened, uncertain of what came next. Caden reached his arm in and held his hand out to the cat.

"Come on, boy."

"Maybe just let him come out on his own," I suggested. It had been a long two days. The only time they'd been out of the kennel was in the hotel in Montana. "Did you find your bed?"

"Oh yeah," he said, giving the cat a quick pet and extracting his hand. "Wanna see?"

"I've actually seen it. Did ya find anything out there that wasn't ours before? That I'd like to see."

"Haha. Hey, I had an idea. Since we have three bedrooms and there's just us, maybe Kevin should come and stay here?"

"Oh, kiddo. I'm not sure how his mom would like that, but of course he's welcome. Why don't we get ourselves situated and then we can talk about it?"

"Okay, deal. I should probably go help him move stuff outa the way so we can get the bed frame out," he said, back on his feet. "When's your brother gonna be back? I want to meet him."

"Not sure. Soon I think. Let me lock up the truck and I'll come help you two."

He turned back around and hugged me. I was surprised at first, but relaxed into it. It wasn't one of his quick embraces. He held on for a moment and I raised my hand to muss his hair. "I really like the house." Then he tightened his grip on me for a second before letting go.

"If you do, I do." I assured him, and he was off again.

"Did you find a box in there that might contain a telephone?" I asked after I'd secured the truck.

"Not yet, but I really wasn't looking for one," Caden replied. "There are kitchen boxes over there." He motioned behind him. I looked around and wondered out loud where our couch was.

"It's in the house, just through there." Kevin indicated, pointing to the back half of the living room.

"Oh nice. I haven't even been through there yet. That's where I'll be sleeping tonight. I forgot I no longer own a bed."

Just then, a truck pulled into the driveway, my brother behind the wheel. Patrick definitely looked his age, which was forty, perhaps a bit older. His light brown hair was greying a bit on top. He got out quickly, walked around the truck, and came to hug me. He was about an inch taller than me, around six feet, and maybe twenty-five pounds heavier. Physical labor had left him in good shape. He was muscular; rugged looking even. I couldn't get over how much he looked like our father. After a quick, awkward embrace, he turned to the garage, looked at my son and said, "You must be Caden."

31

"Uncle Patrick?" It was odd, and strangely comforting, hearing Caden call my brother "Uncle."

"Call me Paddy! Hey there, Kev. Just saw your mom on the news."

"What's she done now?" Kevin asked.

"Press conference. Just a lot of talking. You know, the usual," he told Kevin.

"So some things haven't changed," I joked.

Catelyn Bennett-Amble was the two-term Republican congresswoman from the Sixth District. She had run against and defeated the three-term Democratic incumbent in a nasty campaign. My sister was an outspoken advocate of nearly everything the rest of her family opposed. The lone exception to that opposition: her mostly estranged husband, Tom Amble, Kev's father. Kevin actually took the most exception to his parent's politics. My brother and sisters and I had been raised by a liberal-minded Irish Catholic father and a German-Irish mother who couldn't care less about politics. To my knowledge, my parents had always voted Democrat. I remembered arguments between my father and Caty after she'd started dating Tom, who my dad called the "Republican wing nut."

"How was the drive?" Paddy asked the three of us.

"Not bad." It was Caden who answered.

"You did all the driving?" Paddy asked Kevin.

"Who else?" Kevin questioned.

"So no license, yet, baby brother?"

"Not yet. Another year and I'll have Caden to drive me around," I joked. "I figured, why bother?"

"You made decent time?"

"Pretty decent." My brother and nephew were discussing roadways and traffic, so I turned back to the garage and the kitchen boxes Caden had pointed me to.

32

"Did they hook up the phone?" I called to my brother.

"Supposed to have," he answered. "You have a phone? We could check."

"That's what I'm looking for. Might be a while."

"Did you meet Charlie? You and his brother Liam went to school together. I think he dated that foreign exchange student, the girl from Spain." Oh yes, his Spanish beard!

"I should go help him finish up on the roof. By the way, I've enlisted the troops to help painting starting tomorrow night, so we've got to go pick that stuff out tomorrow first thing."

"What troops?"

"Joey, Jannie, and Mom. Shouldn't take long to get the first coat on. We can do second coats Thursday and Friday. Should be able to lay the carpet early next week."

"Speaking of carpet, I may have changed my mind about the upstairs," I told him.

"Oh, you're going to be one of those people?" he laughed.

"Sorry. The floors just look so good. I can't get over how much you've done. Thank you."

"Don't start that again. Besides, you're paying me, so it's not like I did it completely out of the kindness of my heart. It's good to have you home. Mom can't wait to meet Caden."

"How's she doing?"

"You mean after almost setting herself on fire? Jannie says she's in denial. She hasn't even brought it up"

"Wait, what?" Caden asked.

"I'll tell ya later," I answered, hoping he'd forget.

33

"Hey help me with the frame," Kevin interjected, quickly changing the subject. The two of them moved across yard with parts of Caden's bed in hand.

"Jannie gave Mom a pamphlet for Alcoholics Anonymous and she told her to fuck off. You shoulda seen the look on her face." Paddy hadn't been pulled off-topic.

"Do they still fight like cats and dogs?"

"Nah, not really, not since Dad and Colleen died. Jannie takes it easier on her. The burning magazine in her lap kind of freaked us all out, though."

"And you're sure she'd passed out from drinking?"

"What else?"

"Well she's sixty-five years old. It could be any number of things. When was the last time she had a physical?"

"I have no idea, Stephen. That'd be Joey's area."

Patrick, Joanna, and Catelyn had split the responsibilities of caring for our mother three ways. Lawyer Catelyn took care of financial and legal matters. Paddy handled household maintenance, and Joanna took care of groceries and doctor's appointments. I worried they had taken away her independence. She was in her sixties, not eighties. She'd seemed a little off when I saw her the month before, but that could've been due as much to my siblings coddling her as to drinking too much. I'd keep an eye out and see what I could deduce now that I was back. I knew she'd adore Caden. I was sorry that I hadn't introduced them sooner, and sad that my mother had never met Alec. Moira Bennett was a big flirt. She loved men and boys, all but ignoring my sisters if Paddy, Dad, or I were in the room.

In the following hour or so, several boxes labeled "kitchen" had found their way into the living/dining room at the back of the house. While I searched for the cordless phone downstairs, Caden's room began to take shape upstairs. Kevin and Caden had found all of the pieces to his bed, including the mattress. They'd assembled it, carried up two dressers, and a few boxes of his things. Now they had set their sights on emptying the U-Haul. I was going through a box when Patrick came in through the front door.

"Anyone home?" he asked.

"Almost." When I turned around to answer, I noticed that the sun had started to set. Actually, it was nearly finished with that endeavor.

"It's almost nine," Paddy said. "Looks like Kev and Caden have the truck almost empty and the roof is finally done. We were thinking it might be a good time to call it a night. Very busy day tomorrow and my wife will appreciate me actually coming home tonight."

"Oh, God, have you been working round the clock?" I asked.

"Just last night and Friday to get the floors done."

"Once we're settled, I'm making dinner for everyone."

"Nice." Paddy decided.

"Kevin, I'd say you could spend one more night with us, but I'm afraid there isn't a bed or even a mattress for you to sleep on."

"We already have it worked out," Caden announced.

"I'm gonna use the sleeping bag in the spare room across from my goofball cousin. Kinda liking this family unit thing unless you're totally sick of me?"

"God, never!"

Patrick interjected, "So I'm going to head home. I'll be back in the morning about nine. That work?"

"Perfect," I replied.

"I have my car here," added Charlie. "I told the guys I'd stay and help them finish emptying the truck."

"You guys must be starving. I swear there's a phone here somewhere."

"Paddy will call some place called Davanni's when he gets home and have pizza bought here."

"Brought here," I corrected Caden. "Davanni's, oh man! I haven't had Davanni's in years. Great idea."

35

"It was Charlie's," said Caden.

"I'm beginning to find this guy invaluable." I smiled.

"That's my plan," he said, smiling back.

For the first time since we'd arrived, I really took in this new guy in our lives. Charlie Carpenter was about my height. He had me by ten, maybe fifteen pounds, though. His dirty-blond hair hung an inch or two past shoulder length. At the moment, it was unkempt and a little sweaty. He wore dirty blue jeans with work boots and a white t-shirt with the sleeves cut off. It hit me how much he looked like his brother. Liam Carpenter used to take my breath away. He was the first guy I ever kissed, the first guy I had ever fucked. Or had fucked me. We awkwardly fumbled around, trying a little bit of everything that summer before I went back in the closet, never settling on anything. I'm certain I broke his heart, barely even saying goodbye in my haste to retreat back into the closet. By Christmas, I was engaged to a woman and Liam had moved on to someone on the football team. I wondered how much Charlie knew about my past connection to his brother.

Charlie wore John Lennon glasses, a hemp friendship bracelet around his wrist and a small hoop earring in his left ear; in addition, he had a tattoo I'd yet to make out on his right shoulder. He was rather breathtaking. Both he and his brother had deep blue-grey eyes, the blue the shade of sky, wet with rain. I remembered Liam's eyes often appeared as if he'd just been crying.

How weird was it that I was here in Minnesota, standing before my older brother, my nephew, my fourteen-year-old son, and this carbon copy of the boy who'd literally been responsible for my first orgasm; and all at once, I felt as if Alec were in the room? Was his ghost jealously sensing that, for the first time since he'd died, I was appraising another man sexually? Honestly, between Liam Carpenter and Alec Secreti, I could count the number of men I'd been with on both hands. For someone who came out during the gay sexual revolution, I was practically a virgin.

"I think we need beer," I said. "Well some of us, anyway."

"Then you're about to really love Charlie," Paddy said. "Check the fridge. He thought you should have a few essentials and not have to worry about shopping your first day here."

36

I went around the corner into the kitchen and was reminded that it was going to need some work. I'd already decided the cupboards had to go. The refrigerator and stove looked older than Caden, and the countertops were a sort of lemony-yellow Formica. The prior owners seemed to have an affinity for yellow, definitely not a favorite of mine. Wallpaper with yellow flowers, yellow countertops and pale yellow paint, there had even been yellow shag carpet, I remembered, in one of the bedrooms. Thank goodness, that was no longer around to assault my senses. I liked to think of myself as having good taste. I didn't move to California with it, but I'd certainly found it there. Some of my first friends in Southern California had insisted I discard half my wardrobe if they were to be seen with me in public. I learned to bargain and second-hand shop. Apparently, even last season's fashions were better than what I had. By the time I met Alec at a party in LA, I was dressing club kid chic, most traces of the hick from Minnesota gone, or at least relegated to the back of the closet with my cowboy boots. I was looking forward to redecorating the new house. It would give me a hobby, the something to do I had been sorely lacking the last half-year.

I opened the refrigerator and found a gallon of milk, orange juice, some condiments, cold cuts, eggs, a pound of bacon, and some chip dip. I had to laugh. I assumed somewhere was white bread and potato chips. My brother had shopped how he would if his wife had left him to it. Sure enough, in the cupboard right next to the fridge, was a loaf of white bread, peanut butter, and potato chips. Back to the refrigerator, there was a case of Miller Light, some bottled water, regular and diet pop.

"Thank you, guys! This is great!" Caden had followed me into the kitchen and was already making eyes at the potato chips and dip.

"Go ahead, but don't get too used to it." The bag of chips was torn open and disappeared along with the dip, a can of pop and Caden into the other room. "Beer?" I inquired of Charlie and my nephew. "Paddy, can you stay for one?"

"I better not. Told Jannie I'd be home before nine." Did he just hesitate?

"You'd better go then. I'll see you in the morning. Thanks again for everything."

"I'll take that beer." and "Don't mind if I do." Came the responses from Kevin and Charlie.

"I guess we're sitting on the floor for the time being." I observed.

37

"The dining room table is in the back of the garage," Kevin said. "Caden, want to help me?"

"I guess," he replied begrudgingly, not wanting to surrender possession of the chips, but they headed out back.

"So how long have you worked for my brother?" I asked Charlie.

"A year. It started out part-time. I also bartend at a place downtown. You probably know it. The Brass Rail?"

"Oh yes! I know it well, or knew it, anyway."

"I work there a couple of nights a week and on Thursdays, I play saxophone there."

"It's still a piano bar then?" I asked. Charlie nodded.

The saxophone? And he bartends at a gay bar? I started to wonder if homosexuality ran in this man's family. As if he could sense what I was thinking, Charlie said, "I'm not gay, by the way. I could care less though. I knew my brother was even before he said anything. "

"Were you two close, before?"

"Before he died? Not very. He was really distant. He never came out to my folks, even when he knew he was sick. It was sad really. I'm sorry I didn't insist on being there for him more."

"You were young. How could you have known what to do?"

"I knew. I just told myself I was respecting his privacy, but I think I recognized it as an excuse even back then. My parents would've freaked. My mom's still in denial. She refers to "Liam's illness" refusing to call it AIDS. I barely talk to them. Between you and me, I took the job at the Rail to shock them."

"Did it work?"

"Nah, but I like it there. I feel like I get to see what my brother's life was like, or what it would still be like."

38

"I'll have to come and hear you play. I love the saxophone."

"You change the subject a lot," he noticed. "I'm sorry if you're uncomfortable talking about AIDS. We don't have to at all."

"It seems that way, doesn't it? I don't think I'm uncomfortable as much as unused to talking about it. I try not to when Caden's around and I haven't had a lot of adult time since his father died."

"I get it," Charlie said.

"How old are you again?"

"Twenty-six."

"You're not like — well I—I don't know any other twenty-six year old straight guys, but you don't seem at all like I'd imagine they are."

"I'm not. I don't know how I got this way." He laughed. "But I'm glad I did."

"And you're single?" This surprised me.

"Pretty much. There's someone I like, but she pretty much doesn't know I exist. Paddy thinks it's funny." Charlie was blushing now.

"He would."

"No, it's not that. It's just…" He was a little nervous talking about her, not as self-assured as he'd been two minutes earlier. "It's just that the girl is your sister."

I had just taken a swig of beer and nearly choked. "Not Catelyn," I joked, and he laughed. Caden and Kevin were at the back door. Each held two wooden chairs.

"Need some help?" Charlie asked, grateful for the out.

"There are like ten more," Caden answered, exasperated.

I loved our dining room table and chairs. They'd look great in the new dining room. In San Francisco, the long table and chairs had reminded me of family dinners growing up. We'd had dinner every Sunday after church. Paddy had

39

indicated when I was back in April that it had been years since that tradition had ended. I looked forward to having my family over for dinner. My set would be perfect. I went out back to help with the remaining chairs.

"Don't worry about me as far as Joanna is concerned. You'd be good for her, I think. She hasn't—I mean, from what I understand—I don't think she's been very happy. Her ex was an ass."

"That's what Paddy said."

"She is quite a bit older than you, not that I think there's anything wrong with that. I should find myself a younger man."

"A younger man for what?" Caden was right behind me. I'm sure I'd turned bright red. Thank goodness, Charlie rescued me.

"Landscaping," he told Caden.

"Weird." Honestly, most things were weird according to Caden. It was as if no other adjective existed.

"Everything's weird nowadays?" I asked Caden.

"Pretty much," he answered. He grabbed two more chairs and was off, several paces in front of us.

"Thank you," I mouthed to Charlie. We each grabbed two more chairs and headed back into the house, passing Kevin, who'd come to get the table with Caden. I had only met Charlie a few hours ago, but already I felt as if I'd made my first friend in Minneapolis.

Chapter 4
KEVIN

Charlie and I were discussing baseball. It was kind of bullshit. You could tell neither of us cared, but it was what straight guys who barely knew each other did when there was no one else to guide the conversation. Actually, it probably wasn't a straight thing or a guy thing. Maybe all people did that: small talk, I guess they called it. My uncle had been upstairs for a little while and I had started to wonder if he was ever coming back.

"So you don't smoke at all?" I asked Charlie; pretty sure I'd just interrupted whatever he had been talking about.

"Not cigarettes," he laughed.

"You don't have any?" I was trying not to sound obvious.

"Yeah, in the truck. But we can't smoke with your uncle?"

"I'm pretty sure that's not true. You'd be surprised how cool Stephen is for his age."

"Hey, his age is only five or six years older than mine."

"No, that's not what I meant. I just—."

"I wonder where he went anyway," he interrupted. It was all right. I was trying to choose my words carefully and it was slow going.

"I meant that Stephen seems less chill than he is. I think it's on account of Alec dying and him being responsible for Caden now. He worries all the time." I was feeling pretty buzzed. "He's probably up there talking to the kid now."

"He seems pretty awesome."

"He is. Anyway, we should just ask him. I mean if you want to smoke. That'd be cool. He needs to relax."

41

"Here he comes," Charlie warned. I don't think he'd gotten what I was trying to say because then he went back into baseball. We were out back and Charlie was saying something about the Dome when Stephen came outside to join us.

"The Dome? That's another place I need to take Caden," he said.

"Put that on your list," I told him.

"Kev thinks I have too many lists." He was right. Like I said, he needed to relax. He sat on the top step and lit a cigarette. "Were you guys talking about baseball this whole time?"

"Pretty much," Charlie said.

"I've never been to the Metro-Dome. They were building it when I moved to California. Do you like baseball?"

"Caden's pretty quiet up there." I was so done talking about the Minnesota Twins and the fucking Dome.

"He's asleep. Can you believe it? It's astonishing; a fourteen-year-old's ability to make himself at home in a manner of hours. You guys need beers?"

"I'll get them if that's alright?" Charlie stood up. Stephen nodded and slid over to one side of the stoop to allow him to get by. I happened to look up and Charlie made a gesture like I should ask Stephen about smoking pot. At least that's how I read it. Charlie was actually kind of funny.

"So Stephen... we were just talking about smoking," I started. "Would you want to join us?"

"We are smoking, you—" He was quicker than he looked. I could see it register on his face. Then he laughed only a little bit uneasily. "You mean pot?" He whispered when he said "pot," and I laughed.

"I told him you probably wouldn't have a problem with it, but Charlie was nervous, maybe on account of he works for your brother."

"I see. I haven't smoked since we got some to try and get rid of some of Alec's nausea a couple of years ago. It's certainly none of my business what Charlie does on his night off and it's none of Paddy's business either." I knew he'd be

42

cool about it. "I don't know that I should smoke though. Caden's right upstairs."

"But you said he's asleep. Come on." He just smiled at me. I couldn't really tell what he was thinking. Charlie was back at the door with two beers.

"You don't have to worry about me where my brother is concerned," Stephen told Charlie.

"What do you mean?" Maybe I had misread things?

"You two can smoke. I was just telling Kev that it's none of my business. Paddy's either."

"You'll join us?" Charlie asked.

"I don't know — maybe."

"I told you," I said kind of smugly, and also happy we were finally getting somewhere.

"Right on." Charlie set his beer on the cement and started towards his truck. "You're sure?"

"Yeah, of course," Stephen answered.

It was a nice night, not very humid. I was thinking about having smoked pot with a couple of other people in my family. I'd actually smoked with my aunt Colleen a few times. That was when she was sick. My aunt died last year. She had cancer, but that's not what killed her. She'd been better. Her hair was starting to grow back. It wasn't even very long after my grandpa died and then my aunt went to take a nap and never woke up. So much fucking bullshit. Colleen was as awesome as my uncle. Anyway, she died and my grandpa died and Alec died all in the same year, not even year really. See what I mean? Complete bullshit.

I think because my aunt Joanna had her own kids and she used to have a husband, too, and my uncle Patrick has Jannie; I never felt as close to them as I did Colleen and Stephen. Hell, in some ways I felt closer to them than my mom. That was sort of weird, especially with Stephen, because I barely knew him. He'd just come back into my life like a year and a half ago. Colleen bought me a plane ticket to go see my uncle in San Francisco. She said a lot of stuff about how someone from our family should meet my uncle's family and that she couldn't believe she'd never gone to visit him. I barely knew she was sick then, but she knew.

Charlie was back with the pot. He had a cool looking pipe and was sitting cross-legged, next to me, loading it. After a minute, he handed it to Stephen and we both watched to see what he would do.

"Oh, fuck it!" he said, and all three of us laughed. Stephen put the pipe up to his lips, held the lighter to the bowl, and inhaled. See. He knew what he was doing. I always did have a sense about people. It's why I never smoked with Joanna or my mom. I bet I could've smoked with Paddy, except he went and got sober. I wasn't sure if that meant he couldn't smoke pot, either, but I didn't want to offend him by asking. Oh yeah! I said I smoked with two people from my family. No shit. I got stoned with my grandma. It was just a couple weeks ago. I thought I was going to get busted. She came out back when I was smoking, but then she just took the pipe from me and hit it. I almost shit my pants.

"Puff, puff, pass, uncle!" Stephen had taken a hit, held it and the pipe, and was now practically coughing up a lung. "Booya!"

"Oh, sorry. The pleasantries of this have escaped me. I'll find them again, though. Maybe they're in a box somewhere with my telephone." Sometimes my uncle says stuff I think he thinks is funny. I mean right there. He couldn't have been stoned already, not off one hit. Still, he laughed and Charlie laughed, probably to be polite. So I laughed too, not wanting it to seem like I didn't get it.

"I'm glad I stayed behind," Charlie said. "This has been a nice way to spend my night off."

"Your night off? You have hardly stopped working since we pulled up at seven," my uncle told him.

"Yes, but I haven't been on the clock for the last three hours." I had hit the pipe and handed it to Charlie with a nod, like *thank you*.

"I should pay you something. Paddy doesn't pay overtime?"

"Not for moving and assembling furniture." He'd taken a hit and was holding the pipe out to Stephen. He fumbled around with it and finally took a hit.

44

"Tightass!" Stephen exclaimed, not choking as much this time. Then he giggled and I wondered if he maybe was high already. After two hits. So awesome. "Seriously though, I want to pay you something."

"Nu uh! Friends don't pay for help moving," Charlie said. He reloaded the pipe and we went around a couple more times. They talked and I mostly just smiled and nodded. Sometimes I just couldn't think of what to say. People said stupid shit when they couldn't think of what to say, so I tend to not say anything at all. It was self-preservation, man!

It had been a long two days. I'd driven 2000 miles and slept for shit in the hotel with the two cats climbing all over me. It was after eleven and I was pretty wiped. Those guys were talking about having another beer. Not me. "I'm tired you guys. I think I'm going to crash."

"Night, man."

"Goodnight, Kev," Stephen said. "I honestly cannot thank you enough for everything."

"Hey, no worries. It was fun."

On my way upstairs, I went back to thinking about how little I actually knew my uncle. I was eight years old when he moved to California. I remembered when he used to babysit me before that, or maybe before things got weird. I figured out later that it must have been after my uncle had come out. Neither of my parents liked gay people. I was sure they'd been responsible for my uncle not having as much to do with me. I used to think that maybe I'd done something to piss him off. I had come to realize that it hadn't been his decision not to hang out with me anymore. It shouldn't have come as that big a surprise. My mother hadn't spoken to me in a month because I told Stephen that I'd fly to San Francisco and drive him and Caden back to Minnesota. That wasn't the first time we'd fought about me going to San Francisco, though.

We used to be pretty close. Seriously. Then at the beginning of junior high, she just stopped talking to me, and when I talked to her, she was different. Eventually I stopped trying. I missed her sometimes, even though she was pretty much right there. My parents had stopped bothering to fight. When they talked to each other, it was in short sentences and my mom never smiled. I heard them talking one night, about him owing her. The only thing I made out was my mom saying, "If you think you're leaving me now… that's

45

just not going to happen. I'll ruin you. Look at my face and see that I'm telling you the truth." She was always talking like that, like she had a prepared statement. Once when they fought, my dad actually cried. He tried to hide it from me, but I saw tears. I'd stopped caring about him a long time before that.

So my aunt bought me the ticket to go see Stephen and Alec in San Francisco and I was super happy. I was nineteen years old and my mother didn't monitor my savings account anymore. She assumed I had bought my own ticket. At first, she seemed more concerned someone would find out. She was a congresswoman from Minnesota. I told her no one pays attention to what she did, let alone what her family did. She said I shouldn't always be so sure of myself, implying I was stupid because I didn't get good grades. She was always doing that shit. Whenever I said something that sort of made sense to her, she had to put me down, like not let me have the last word.

I couldn't believe that I was getting to go somewhere alone. I'd been places with my parents. We'd been to Washington DC, to New York City, Chicago, even South America and Europe, but we'd never gone west of North Dakota. I'd never seen the Pacific Ocean. It felt good to be doing it on my own. Colleen said it was important for my mother to believe it was completely on my own, and no one needed to know she'd bought the ticket. That was cool with me.

"They recruit people, you know," my mother told me. She assumed Stephen had bought me the ticket.

"You are a stereotype, Mother," I told her. I was shocked she was such a homophobe. I suspected she didn't like Stephen, but for the most part, we avoided the subject. She didn't want confirmation her only child was gay and I didn't want confirmation my mother was a bitch.

"Kevin, I refuse to allow you to go to San Francisco, of all places. We don't even know how he lives, he and that family of his. Do they have a guest room or will you be expected to share a room with all of them?" Sometimes the things she said made me physically sick. Up to that moment I would have sworn that even she wasn't capable of saying such disgusting things about her own brother. There was so much hatred there, but at the same time, it sounded practiced, like she was quoting "A Homophobe's Handbook."

"Hey," Caden said. I think I had just been standing at the top of the stairs. I didn't know for how long.

46

"I thought you were asleep?" I asked him.

"What do you mean?"

"Stephen came downstairs like an hour ago and said you were sound asleep."

"Oh yeah, I sorta pretended to be asleep," Caden said. He was standing in the doorway of his new room.

"Alright." I laughed. I didn't get the kid sometimes.

"Sometimes it's like he wants to say something, but he doesn't, and it's just weird and besides, I didn't want to pretend anymore today."

"What's that supposed to mean?" I almost didn't ask. I knew, or thought I did, where he was going. Caden hadn't wanted to leave San Francisco at all.

"I don't know. Forget I said anything."

"Deal," I told him, and went into the other room.

"Thanks for driving us and for helping with my room."

"No worries. Night."

"Goodnight," Caden told me. He wasn't pissed off or even sad. He kind of half-smiled went into his room and shut the door. I stood there for a minute thinking how fucked up everything was. But then I felt, I don't know, sorta safe, like if anyone could figure it out my uncle would.

Chapter 5
STEPHEN

I was right about a good night's sleep. Even on the couch, I slept like a rock. Our first night in the new house had gone smoothly. Caden had all of his things in his new room, his bed assembled, and had set about making himself at home. I went up to use the bathroom at about eleven p.m., more than an hour after he'd had some pizza and gone upstairs, and found him asleep in his clothes, his light still on. He looked very much at home. I crept in quietly, covered him with a blanket he'd brought from California and turned off the lamp beside his bed. I was tempted to bend down and kiss him on his forehead, but worried that would be weird. So much of this dance we were in was awkward and I hadn't a clue which parts had to do with him just being a teenager and which parts were grief. I was certainly all he had; legally and in every way except biologically his father, but the role felt ill-fitting without my co-parent. Caden felt it, too. I sensed that. He was awkward as well, although not half as much as I sometimes was. In lieu of a kiss, I gently brushed my hand over his dark hair and let it remain there for a second. He stirred a tiny bit, so I snatched my hand back and tiptoed out of the room.

Back downstairs, Charlie and Kevin were chatting casually about baseball. The Twins were having a decent season. I sensed the boys were grateful to have me back though. Neither seemed a huge fan of sports. This was clearly heterosexual small talk.

How I ended up smoking pot with the boys was beyond me. It just happened, and truthfully, I didn't mind that it had. Maybe that's why I'd slept so well. Kev seemed quiet the whole time we were smoking. I was concerned about him. I couldn't put my finger on it, but he seemed lost. I had made up my mind to question someone—I hadn't decided who yet—about my sister's relationship with her son. Something wasn't right and it seemed to go far beyond her apparent homophobia. I'd thought about it a lot over the years and I really believed my oldest sister, or any of my other siblings, didn't have it in them to truly hate. That wasn't how we were raised. It had taken me far too long to realize and accept that. How much time had I wasted believing my ostracism was completely one-sided?

I knew Kevin smoked pot sometimes. He had absolutely no filter when it came to sharing potentially salacious information about himself. I was a bit shocked by the stories he told Alec and me. It seemed Kevin had experimented

48

sexually more than once in high school and college. He'd just blurted that out over a second bottle of wine with Alec and me in San Francisco. Alec had just winked at me then. He'd been instantly enamored with Kev.

It would be an adjustment, for me, accepting the desire gay men, especially my lover, displayed for my nephew. Kevin certainly had "it." Alec was respectful, of course, but I noticed it, having not seen Kev in years. My nephew was striking. He had some of my mother's genes; the resemblance was clear. Anyone could see he and I were related, but Kevin looked nothing like his mother. His eyes were stunning, there was no other way to put it. Look up and your breath is gone. Alec had attempted to put it into words as my nephew disembarked his flight. "Jesus Christ," was what the love of my life had come up with.

During his visit to San Francisco, I became aware of how little attention Kev paid to the aesthetics. He was clueless when it came to the people falling all over themselves in his presence, but it wasn't just that. He didn't pay attention to other people's appearances. My sister's son didn't appear to have a shallow bone in his body.

"He just seems sweet, unencumbered," Alec told me.

"I don't know if you actually get how weird that is," I answered him.

"Why? Why is that so weird? You are one of the sweetest people I know." Poor man.

"I'm a sarcastic, judgmental bitch." I insisted.

"But everything underneath is sweet." I just shook my head. "This kid could have anyone. Fuck their sexual preference! People are going to walk into walls in your nephew's presence."

I'd just sighed. He was right. That poor boy. Kevin was nineteen when he visited us. He'd show up shirtless for breakfast and Alec would gladly sell our house, or me into white slavery, for a fucking smile from the teenager. I fell back in love with my nephew when I realized that Kevin was utterly oblivious to the attention he incited in everyone in his wake.

49

I'd only had two pieces of pizza since lunch somewhere in North Dakota and was on my sixth beer. I did the adult thing in my head where I quickly considered the ramifications of what they were suggesting. My head was a little cloudy and I actually laughed a little. Yeah, the whole thinking thing wasn't going to happen. I was an adult; we all were. Why did I always have to think everything through so thoroughly? When had I become that person? I must have just been standing there for a minute, because when I looked back at them, they were awaiting a ruling on the marijuana thing. My first hit, I nearly choked to death. But I managed to regain my composure as the evening wore on.

Kevin was not even ten when his father put an end to me babysitting him. Catelyn didn't bother disagreeing with him. Joanna's fiancée felt the same way Tom did. I remembered clearly the day she explained to me how glad she was that I could be honest with myself about who I was. Then with her next breath asked me to please not "force the information" on her fiancée. Colleen, the sister closest to me in age had balked, but a part of me understood. She was my confidant, but she was away at college; a sophomore at St. Cloud State. I hadn't wanted to come out in the first place. I didn't care if people knew. I just didn't understand why I had to be the one to tell them. It was 1977 the first time I came out; I hadn't even turned eighteen. Colleen suggested I not tell the rest of the family. We both assumed Patrick would have a problem with it. For a while, I didn't say anything to anyone. At least I had confided in someone. The problem was that the someone wasn't around much. Still, the secret remained between my sister and I for almost six months, until a boy named Liam entered my world.

"I got high with your brother once," I said to Charlie. "Not far from here actually, in his car by the lake."

"Calhoun?" Charlie asked. I just nodded.

"We sat in his car and listened to this mix tape I had made and smoked a joint. I'm pretty sure it was the first time either of us smoked." We had that conversation immediately after Kevin had gone to bed. "Liam and I —," I started.

"You dated?" he interrupted.

"I suppose you could call it that. Two guys didn't really go on dates fifteen years ago. I'm not sure they even do now, but it was something like that. We hung out."

50

"You had sex?"

"Yes." I was a bit astonished at how easily I was discussing it with him. "We were each other's first. I think it hurt him when we broke up. I was always sorry for that."

"How so?" Charlie asked. "I mean, besides the obvious?"

"I was very—I don't know—gung-ho, I guess, about the whole thing and Liam was uncertain. Not about what we were doing, but about people knowing, about coming out. Have you met my mother?"

"I have," he answered.

"She caught us kissing on my bed, and Liam was mortified. We both were, but your brother was truly afraid. I'd never seen him fearful of anything. It was like just the idea of being found out meant we were through. That's what would happen if our parents found out we were gay, at least in his mind. They'd end it."

"What happened?" Charlie asked, quietly.

"Nothing, really. My mother pretended she hadn't seen a thing, but she couldn't have missed it. Liam's shirt was off. It was pretty unmistakable. I had already come out to my sister Colleen, but your brother hadn't told anyone." I had drained my beer can a few moments earlier and was debating one more. Charlie must have picked up on my indecision and got up.

"I think I'll have one more beer if that's alright," he announced.

"Of course. I'll join you. Mosquitoes and humidity, two things I definitely did not miss about Minnesota." I grabbed us each a beer and we moved into the dining room where I continued my story. "Liam didn't talk to me for a few days after that. He avoided me at school. I was sure whatever we had was over, but I couldn't just accept that without talking to him."

"What did you do?"

"I waited by his car after school. He was actually relieved to see me there. It turned out that he thought he'd gotten *me* in trouble. He couldn't understand that my mother didn't think us kissing was a punishable offense. In reality, she

51

may have, but she'd have to talk to me about it to punish me, and that wasn't going to happen." Charlie was looking confused, so I decided I needed to explain my family a little more to him.

"We're a very non-confrontational family. None of us likes, or in the case of some of my siblings, is even capable of discussing anything difficult or painful. We just make a lot of small talk and if a difficult conversation must take place, we pretend later that it didn't happen. I was going to have to be the one to bring it up if I expected my mother to talk about the kiss."

"So Liam didn't want to stop seeing you?"

"No. On the contrary, he told me he'd missed me and was afraid that I was angry with him, which couldn't have been further from the truth. We didn't really talk about it again for a few days. We just went back to doing what we'd been doing: hanging out. A week had gone by, and we were sitting in Liam's car. He brought it up, asked me, 'Did you ever talk to your mom?' I told him that I hadn't and he got quiet. When I asked him what was wrong, he said he was thinking about coming out to your mom."

"No shit?!" Charlie was clearly shocked that his brother had even considered such a thing.

"I think he did come out to her. In fact, I'm sure of it." Charlie was stunned. He'd told me earlier that Liam hadn't come out to their parents. Apparently, their mother was even better at avoidance than my own.

"After everything he went through, I can't believe my mother never said a word. They were so distant towards him. She hadn't disowned him, but she did her best to freeze him out." Charlie was angry. "I really hate that woman!"

"I'm sorry." There was more, but I didn't want him to be angry with me, too. Still, he deserved to know all the truths I held. Alec was the only other person I'd ever discussed Liam with. Very early in our relationship, we discussed our prior boyfriends. I told him there was only one I considered an actual relationship. I'd had sex with a few guys in California before I met Alec, but I had only been in love once before. "I'm afraid I did really hurt Liam. We hung out for a few more months and I eventually talked to my mother. I basically came out to the rest of my family. Their reception was unexpected. Other than my sister Colleen, who already knew, Paddy was by far the coolest about it. I expected my sisters, especially Joanna, to be supportive. It's not that they weren't, to a degree. They just didn't want to talk about it. Catelyn's husband

52

had a huge problem with my sexuality and instead of defending me; my family acted like that was his right. He announced that he no longer wanted me around Kev. Colleen wasn't home for this discussion. Neither of my parents or Catelyn spoke up in my defense. Joey just looked like she hoped the conversation would be over before her boyfriend got there. Jannie stood, saying they should all be ashamed of themselves, then she and Paddy left. I was grateful for their support, but knew it wouldn't change anything."

"Jannie *is* pretty cool." Charlie offered.

"She certainly has her moments," I agreed. Aside from Colleen, Jannie was the only member of my family who'd ever asked if there was anyone special in my life. In fact, other than the superficial crap; those two, and sometimes Patrick, were the only ones who ever inquired about my life in California, period. My sisters and parents knew when I graduated from college; they knew when I started teaching. Of course, they knew that I'd moved from Los Angeles to San Francisco. Those were the things they were interested in. They'd never have known about Alec and Caden had I not insisted on telling them.

Joey came around eventually. As her marriage fell apart, so did her commitment to shielding her asshole husband from the truth. I sensed her guilt over having not done more. She wasn't even a little bit homophobic. She and Colleen were very close. Colleen even dragged Joey to the Gay '90s to see the drag show. I was pissed that I wasn't there, but I expected I'd have another shot at it now that I lived in Minneapolis. I missed Colleen so much, but truthfully, we'd only seen each other a couple of times over the last decade. She could've visited San Francisco. We talked on the phone more than I did with any of my other siblings. Occasionally she would push me to call Joey, but Colleen had her own shit, and so did I. We, none of us, expected her to die when she did and even if we had known in advance, I had Alec to think of.

"Jannie and Paddy have become like family to me. I don't see my parents at all anymore," Charlie admitted. "It was really Jannie who hooked me up working for Paddy."

"Seriously? How did that come about?" I asked.

"Jannie came into the Rail sometimes after work with another social worker, a guy, obviously gay. They used to be close, but the guy transferred counties or something. Anyway, she and I would talk and she mentioned last winter her husband was looking for someone to do snow removal."

53

"I see." If I was going to do this, I'd just have to jump right in. "Anyway, after that night coming out to my whole family, I thought more and more about how, *Yeah I was out, everyone knew, but that didn't change anything*. Things were okay, I guess, but they'd never be the same again. Catelyn and Tom just stopped coming around as much. I'd helped raise Kevin; I taught him to read and write, to play poker. I still got to babysit him some, but that was mostly because Caty told Tom that my mother was babysitting. I'd take care of him and we all kind of acted like what Tom, and even Caty, didn't know wouldn't hurt them."

"I can't believe shit like that happens. People really do suck!" Charlie said.

"Some of them do for sure. Joey had her fiancée, and they would come to the house and kiss. Paddy and Jannie certainly kissed. I mean no one was making out or anything, but even before he was with Jannie, Paddy would bring by girlfriends and Joey boyfriends and they would kiss in front of the rest of us. Colleen, too. And I couldn't help thinking that it would never be the same for me. There was no way I could bring Liam over for dinner and lean over to kiss him in front of everyone. I knew that would never be okay."

"What happened with Liam?" Charlie asked.

"I graduated and he still had a year to go. I was mostly staying with friends in Uptown, wherever I could, doing everything I could to avoid spending time with my family. Sometimes Liam would be there. I certainly had no problem kissing him in front of my friends. He was becoming increasingly comfortable with being gay, in spite of your mom's reaction. He'd come out to a few friends at school and even they were okay with it. While he was getting more comfortable with the idea of being out of the closet, I was getting less comfortable with it—a lot less.

"I had this friend Sara who I hung out with a lot. One night we were alone and very drunk, and we sort of made out. It wasn't awful. I mean I loved her as a friend and sometimes kissing is just kissing. I was definitely turned on by it, but we didn't go any further. I felt guilty, but I didn't say anything to your brother. I wasn't sure what was happening, but I began to think that maybe I could be bi. Maybe I could do all the "normal" things; be in a relationship with a girl, get married, have kids, you know *that*."

"Do you consider yourself bi?" Charlie asked.

54

"GOD NO! Not at all," I insisted. "I was eighteen and I hadn't a clue what I was doing. I loved Liam, but I also loved Sara, both very much—but obviously quite differently, although I didn't realize that then. You guys had gone on your family summer vacation and Sara and I had begun to act almost like a couple whenever Liam wasn't around. I literally started seeing the possibility of a whole different life for myself. I was grasping at straws, I guess, but while you all were away, I asked Sara to marry me."

"You what?" That was the part of the story that shocked Charlie. He evidently hadn't known about or even suspected that I'd gone through a hetero phase. Or that I'd hurt his brother so badly.

"I know," I continued. "We hadn't even had sex at that point. I got turned on by the kissing, so I didn't imagine there'd be a problem. We only ever had intercourse once, but that's another story."

"So you have had sex with a woman, but you're not bi?"

"Well if that's all that's required to be able to call yourself bi, then I guess I am, but I don't consider myself bi. You guys came home from vacation and I had to tell Liam. I had to break up with him. He was so hurt. I mean, really betrayed. I think it was worse that I was breaking up with him because of a woman."

"I bet it was," Charlie replied. "So what did Liam do?"

"He didn't do anything. He started his senior year of high school mostly out of the closet. You were at a different school. I only saw him once or twice after that. Once I realized being with Sara was a mistake, I sought him out, but he was still so angry. I knew he'd been going out to the bars; my friends had seen him. He had no interest in talking to me."

"So eventually you broke up with her, too?" Charlie asked.

"No. She broke up with me. She told me we both knew I was gay and that I was just lying to myself. We'd been engaged for a few months, long enough for me to confuse the hell out of my family. After we broke up and Liam didn't want anything to do with me, I decided to leave. It felt like it might have been easier had no one ever known."

"I get that."

55

"Within a month, I had decided to move to California. Back then, you could go to college tuition-free in California. This guy that Colleen had known in college moved to LA and said I could stay with him temporarily. I had some money saved and my grandpa had died and left each of his grandkids a thousand dollars. It was intended to help with school, but it was mine to do with what I wanted, so I used it to get set up in California."

"And you never looked back?" Charlie inquired.

"Not really. I mean, of course you look back. I was so homesick at first. I called home a lot that first year, but eventually I trained myself not to call about the little things and not to stay on the phone long when I did call. It was like I was trying to wean myself from everyone here. Eventually I succeeded. By that time I had met Alec, and things changed."

Charlie was looking down at the table, clearly trying to choose his words carefully. I expected him to be angry that I had betrayed his brother. When he looked up, his eyes were misty. He had been fighting tears.

"I know you think you're responsible for Liam's choices, but I don't. You did what you had to for yourself. Basically, you were — are a survivor, and my brother was weak. I know I can never understand what it was like to be gay back then or even now. I get that. I do. But Liam let being gay beat him. The stories I've heard, he was a whore and a drunk. You broke up with him, I guess even cheated on him. But doesn't that happen every day to a lot of people?"

"I guess," I replied. I was incredibly moved by this man's compassion.

"I was excited to meet you, because it was clear you were the only man Liam ever really loved. No one who came after you stuck. The one time he and I talked about his being gay, he talked about you."

I had tears in my eyes. It was weird feeling responsible for someone's broken life. It wasn't like I thought about it a lot, but when I did, I felt I was to blame for Liam's anger and for his lifestyle choices. I'd certainly done my fair share of drinking and had had some anonymous sex in LA. That may have continued had I not met Alec. Thank God for that man. I couldn't imagine what my life would have been were it not for him. It was sad that Liam hadn't found someone like Alec, but I finally had someone telling me I wasn't to blame for that. We were gay teenagers in a world that still wasn't accepting. We had both done what we could to survive, and we each ended up HIV positive, just as Alec had. Both Liam and Alec had succumbed to AIDS, and I was likely to, as

56

well. I prayed every single day that God didn't cruelly take me away from that kid sleeping upstairs. I knew life wasn't fair: not at all. There were reasons I moved us back to Minnesota that I hadn't fully worked out in my own mind. To recognize those, I'd probably have to admit to myself how afraid I was that I would go the same way the two men I had loved had already gone.

It was after midnight by then, and neither of us was comfortable, being so emotionally vulnerable with the other. We'd said goodnight shortly after Charlie had told me his brother remembered me fondly, a revelation that meant the world to me. Charlie headed home and I went out to the back step for one last cigarette. That was likely to become my spot, just like that tiny porch overlooking the city in San Francisco. My new spot overlooked a crappy yard, a garage badly in need of a paint job, and an alley. When I was done with the cigarette, I went to the kitchen sink; brushed my teeth, splashed some water on my face and went to curl up on the couch. I was asleep in moments.

Chapter 6
JOANNA

I'd become awfully adept at procrastination lately. In fact, the level of skill I'd developed had started to concern me. I'd already hit the snooze bar on my alarm clock a few too many times. I could hear that the kids were already up and getting ready for school. It was their last day. Funny how a month, or even a week earlier, I'd have been up before them, utilizing any coercive tactic at my disposal to get Kelly, especially, out of bed. But they were both anxious to start the day, and even more so to finish it. At its end was summer vacation; three months of no homework and sleeping in. I, on the other hand, was dreading the day.

My summer vacation wouldn't begin for another week and a half. That was how long I estimated it would take me to get through the mounds of paperwork awaiting me at work.

Then there was my brother and his stepson to deal with later; my whole family, really. I wasn't sure how I felt about Stephen moving back to Minnesota. It wasn't a bad thing, certainly, just unexpected. While I loved my brother very much, I had stopped missing him years ago.

My kids, especially Kelly, were anxious to meet Caden. He fell in line right between my two in age. Their only other cousin on my side of the family was Kevin, and he was much older. My son envisioned Caden as more of a big brother than a cousin. It would only be short bike ride to Stephen's house, a fact Kelly had brought up repeatedly. I had no idea what to anticipate from my brother, or his stepson, who I'd never met. I wasn't certain it was a good idea for Kelly to get his hopes up. I didn't want him to be disappointed if Caden or Stephen didn't meet his expectations.

The alarm clock was beeping again. I peered over at its digital display. I had less than an hour to shower, grab something to eat, and get each of us to our individual destinations. Meghan went to school at Southwest where I was vice-principal. It was the final day of her sophomore year. Kelly was finishing the eighth grade in St Louis Park. In the fall, we'd all be at Southwest, including Caden.

Stephen was an English teacher. I had offered to get him a meeting at Southwest, but he told me he wasn't ready to go back to work. That was the thing: I barely knew the man. He'd moved to California years ago and only been back to visit a few times. So much had happened in the interim, it was hard to choose a place to start. I got married and had Kelly. Our sister Colleen had battled cancer, then died of heart failure at thirty-three. That same year, our dad died, and I divorced Kelly's father. Meanwhile, a world away, Stephen had tested HIV-positive and lost his lover to AIDS. Suddenly, he had a son. We led completely separate lives, and with each new unshared event, the divide grew.

I swung my legs over the side of the bed wondering if that third glass of wine the night before had been a mistake. I rarely drank more than one glass on a school night. But I'd been wound up after another dumb telephone conversation with my mother. She'd asked for my help grocery shopping. My mother was sixty-four years old and had been widowed for more than a year. Far from an invalid, she had just given up. I sat on the edge of my bed trying to shake the fog from my brain, remembering our conversation.

"I need to go shopping," my mother had said. No hello.

"You need me to take you?"

"Yes. Tomorrow. Can you take me tomorrow?"

"Well Mom, I have school tomorrow."

"I know that. I meant tomorrow night." In one conversation she would be excited about Stephen's move home and the next time we spoke, she'd barely remember it was happening. We were all supposed to go to Stephen's new house the next night, I reminded her.

"Stephen? Well of course I remembered that. I thought we could stop quickly on the way." She usually covered pretty well.

"Mom, you're riding to Stephen's with Jannie. I have school until four-thirty. Then I need to run home, change, get the kids and get to Stephen's by five-thirty. Thursday night is the best I can do. Or this weekend." I still hadn't the vaguest idea why she needed help shopping, but that ship had sailed. We had all taken on different roles in Mom's life. There was a long silence on the other end of the line while my mother composed her thoughts.

"I'd forgotten Jannie was driving me. I suppose it won't be too bad. That's, what, a five minute drive? You know she won't let me smoke in her car?"

59

"Well," I began. I knew full well the can of worms my next words would open. "You could always drive yourself. Paddy said they'd be done running their errands by mid-afternoon. You could even surprise them and show up early."

"What? Why would I do that? You know I don't like to drive in Minneapolis," she replied.

"You live in Minneapolis, Mom. Driving in Minneapolis is therefore pretty much unavoidable." It was a battle I'd never win.

"Don't start on that, Joanna. I like knowing I have a car in case of emergencies."

"You're right, Mom," I apologized. I didn't recall the last time I'd seen my mom drive a car. She never did when my dad was alive. "So, shopping? Can we do that on Thursday, or is there something you need right away?"

"I'll figure it out, dear. Don't you worry about me." *Until tomorrow when we have the exact same conversation, likely at Stephen's.* We'd said our goodnights and I opened a bottle of wine. Shortly after, Meghan had come home. I was sitting on the deck well into my second glass of wine, smoking a cigarette, enjoying the evening.

"Just in the nick of time," I told my daughter.

"It's eight fifty-five," she answered. "I'm not late."

"Curfew is at nine. Hence the nick of time comment."

"You're drinking on a school night?"

"At eight fifty-five on a school night."

"You drink more now than you used to," Meghan said. "Did you know that alcohol's a drug?"

"Than I used to when, exactly?"

"When Dad was here," she replied.

60

I wanted to retort that he had done enough drinking for both of us, but there was no point. I was a thirty-eight year old divorcee who my barely sixteen-year-old daughter regularly compared to Nancy Vicious. My thirteen-year-old son missed his father and blamed me for his absence, but at least he didn't believe I had one foot in Hazelden. My mother was losing it; my sister was a bitch. And I hadn't had an orgasm since I took the batteries out of my vibrator to use in the flashlight when the power had gone out. Six weeks ago. That may not seem like such big a deal, but for the fact that I had started getting used to those again since the divorce.

I drained the last quarter glass of wine and stood to get a refill. Meghan followed me inside, watching intently while I picked up the wine bottle. "Crack pipe it is."

She rolled her eyes, a gesture she used to punctuate nearly every conversation she had with her brother or me. As she turned to go, I called after her. "It's still a school night. Your brother should be in his room already. Lights out at ten."

"Got it," she replied, nearly to the stairs.

"I love you." No response. Yeah, that was my life.

It was seven twenty now. In the morning. Last day of school. Meghan had just exited the bathroom.
"Last day of school, guys," I announced. As if they'd forgotten. "Who's excited?"

"I am!" Kelly called from his room upstairs. Meghan's fake smile was her reply. I imagined that meant she was certainly excited about her last day of school and she couldn't wait to leave. In reality, she was more likely plotting an intervention.

I shut the door behind me and turned on the shower. I had less than ten minutes to shower if I was going to do anything at all with my hair. Eight minutes later, I emerged, seconds ahead of schedule. Folded laundry was piled up three feet high on my dresser. Hose up; hadn't shaved my legs in three days. I pulled a navy-blue dress off one of the few hangers in the closet which held garments, stepped into it, adjusted the bra straps and underwire,

61

and pulled the hose snug. Now heels. To accomplish this, I got down on my hands and knees to search. Black three inch, check. Next... under the bed... searching, not there. I turned and sat, my back against the bed, scanning the room. I glimpsed it near the laundry basket, put one shoe on and shimmied across the floor to retrieve its mate. Standing. The shoes felt weird. Oh, well, no time. I took them both off and carried them, running through the house. Downstairs, Kelly was standing at the refrigerator; door open, peering in as if breakfast might jump out at him.

"Morning, love," I said to my son.

"Hey, Mom."

"There should be Pop-Tarts, but have juice or a piece of fruit, too."

"What juice?" Kelly asked. I joined him at the refrigerator, kissed him on the top of his head; an easier feat in heels, which I was still holding, so I had to tippy-toe it. He'd be taller than me soon. He was right, no juice and the milk was almost empty. I hadn't any idea why it was put back the fridge. There was some melon in a container. Mostly leftovers long past their supposed expiration dates, some cheese, pickles, and various condiments. A pizza box, Eureka! Cold pizza it was.

"Pizza?" I asked him.

"I guess," he said. Why didn't my mother do *my* shopping instead of the other way around? No time to even shake my head.

"I'm sorry, baby. I'll try to run out over lunch and grab some stuff."

"It's okay, Mom. We'll eat at Uncle Stephen's tonight, anyway." Oh yeah! Fabulous. I had no idea why I was having trouble getting on board with it. I grabbed the pizza box, kissed my kid again, and shut the refrigerator door.

Meghan had come downstairs. Old concert t-shirt I was pretty sure used to belong to me, a skirt bordering on too short, and Dr. Martens. Her hair was pulled into a high ponytail. She was pushing it with the eyeliner. My daughter was so beautiful without makeup, but I picked my battles, and that one didn't matter in the grand scheme of things. "REO Speedwagon? Didn't that used to belong to me?"

"Still does," she replied. "I borrowed it."

62

"Borrowing implies intent to return the item to its owner. You're walking that fine line between mooching and theft, love. Pizza for breakfast?" I supposed I should check the box and make sure there were at least three pieces. PHEW! Almost a half a pie.

"UGH! I didn't like it the first time." So pleasant in the morning.

"You ate it," I told her.

"I was being polite," she replied.

"You used to love Davanni's."

"I guess," she said. "I'll just have a banana. Is there juice?"

"No juice," Kelly told her. "Just have pizza. You know you liked it."

"Shut up, twerp!" Meghan told her brother.

"HEY!" I reached to touch her and she moved away. "Don't say shut up."

"Are we ready to go?" she asked. I tore off three paper towels, grabbed my cigarettes, tossing them in my purse. Then the shoes, my school bag, a slice of pizza, keys from the dish.

"As ready as we may ever be. Do you have your bag?"

"By the door," Kelly answered.

"Shoes?"

"By my bag."

"Are you ready?" I asked Meghan.

"Yeah, let's go. Can we just stop at SA?"

"There should be time. Okay, everyone in the car. No fighting over the front seat, Kel. Meghan gets it."

63

At the Super America on France, I opened the back door to get my shoes off the seat beside Kelly. I slipped them on, holding myself up on the car door. Halfway into the store, I knew what the problem with the shoes was. FUCK! They were two different heights. One three inch heel, one three and a half. *Why did I buy the same goddamn shoe with two different heel heights? Now what?* There wasn't time to go home. I was going to be lopsided all day. Maybe there was a pair of shoes in the trunk. Cigarettes and coffee, juice and a granola bar for Meghan. Five minutes later, we were at Kelly's school.

"Love you," I told him, as he walked away. No answer. I couldn't possibly be the world's worst mother, but there were days, more and more frequently, when it felt like I was in contention. Meghan was looking at me.

"He misses Dad."

"I know, baby. He'll get to see a lot of him starting next week. Are you still sure you don't want to go?"
"Camping?" She laughed. "Uh-huh, positive. Besides, he's not my dad."

"Of course he is." She changed her mind about that on a dime lately. One minute he was her father, the next she acted as if I were referring to some serial killer.

"I'm staying here." Was all she said. I turned the car into traffic, toward school.

"You remember we're going to your uncle's tonight, right?" She nodded. "I need you to be ready to go by four."

"I'm always ready to go before you and it's the last day. I could be ready to go at noon, if you'd like." We both laughed. "You don't seem very excited about your brother moving back."

"I am," I lied.

"Is it because he's gay?" Meghan asked me.

"How do you even know that?" I was insulted by the mere suggestion.

"GOD Mom, I'm not stupid!'

"I suppose not. Did Grandma say something?"

64

"No. I just figured it out when he was here before."

"It has nothing to do with him being gay, by the way," I explained. "We just haven't been close for a long time, so I'm cautious."

"I know you're angry with him."

"Why would you say that?" I asked her.

"Colleen told me once and you seemed to get even angrier after she died."

"He should've come home when she was sick, or for Grandpa's funeral, but there are things you just don't understand. Your aunt had a knack for seeing things that weren't necessarily there." My sister had needed a reason or explanation for everything. Maybe there was no reason. Maybe our brother had become a stranger. Could someone disappear for fifteen years, then just come home like they'd only been away on vacation? "I'm certain I'm not angry, though."

"It's just that you're really hard on people, Mom, people who leave. Grandma said that sometimes people just have to go where they'll be happier and that doesn't mean we have to follow because maybe we're happy right where we are," Meghan said.

"Grandma said that?"

"About dumbass." Still on the *not my dad* kick. "But I think she meant Stephen, too. She missed him a lot."

"He was always her favorite."

"I thought you said parents don't have favorites?"

"My mother did. Stephen was her baby. When did you two talk about him?"

"After Grandpa died. We did a couple of times, I think. That's how I know she missed him, from how she talked about him."

"You're pretty smart, you know?"

"That's what I keep saying."

65

"I guess we'll just have to see how it goes with Stephen. I'm reserving judgment is all."

"I get it, I guess," she said. We were almost to school. "It's just that when you talk about Uncle Stephen, sometimes it's like when you talk about Dad."

I sighed. She was probably right. God, was I really angry? Why? And how was it that the two women I felt most at odds with in my life had it all figured out before me? It was true that virtually everyone was meeting this move with some level of enthusiasm except for me. Well, and Caty. My brother's return was, for me, alternately a source of ambivalence or suspicion. It was the suspicion I didn't get. I had no reason to suspect him of anything. At any rate, I had no time to think about it that very minute. I parked in the back parking lot and turned to Meghan, changing the subject.

"Have a good last day. I love you."

"I love you, too," she said. Thank goodness I'd already parked the car or I may have driven off the road. I couldn't remember the last time she'd told me that. "I'm sorry if I'm a bitch, Mom. I try not to be bitchy all the time."

"You're perfect," I said. I leaned over to hug my daughter and she allowed it, but just for a second.

"Yeah, not so at all."

"Are too," I countered.

"I gotta go or I'll be late for homeroom."

"Yeah, alright. Get outta here. I'll see you in the office at four." I looked down at my shoes. Let the hobbling begin.

Chapter 7
STEPHEN

We spent the entire day running around. First, there was the U-Haul to be returned, then a run to Menards. There wasn't time to mull over paint colors. With everyone coming later to help, colors had to be chosen, paint and supplies purchased. Then we were off to Target where I had a list a mile long, including a cordless phone, as the one from California continued to elude us. Finally, I needed a bed and some more living room furniture. Slumberland was the place to go for that and we'd need delivery as soon as possible. Caden had opted to join Paddy and me. Maybe he wanted to see more of Minneapolis, but I thought it just as likely that he felt safer with me. There were an awful lot of changes to absorb.

"After this, how do you feel about McDonald's for lunch?" I asked Patrick and Caden. They each murmured their agreement. "Then can we make one more stop after lunch?"

"Where to?" my brother asked.

"The grocery store," I answered. "I should pick up more groceries, bottled water, and pop for everyone. And beer."

"You won't get beer at Rainbow," Paddy countered.

"That's right!" I shook my head. You couldn't buy alcohol, even beer or wine, at a grocery store in Minnesota. "You can't buy on Sundays, either? Right?" I needed to reacquaint myself with the limitations on alcohol purchases in Minnesota.

I bought two couches, a love seat, and two beds at Slumberland. The good news was that for an additional charge, everything could be delivered that afternoon. Even though I had slept fine on the couch the previous night, I was looking forward to making myself at home in my own room, just as Caden had in his.

At McDonald's, Caden ordered as if he were eating for three. It was clear he'd decided to take full advantage of my newly lax nutritional standards. In San Francisco, we only had fast food every couple of weeks. We'd had pizza or fast food at almost every meal for nearly the last week. I sat beside Caden on one side of a booth in the corner.

"How are you doing?" I asked him.

"Good."

"You could've stayed behind with Kev and Charlie."

"It's okay," he said. "I wanted to come with you."

"So, what do you think so far?" I asked him.

"About what?" Sometimes I thought he was just making me work for it.

"The new house, the new neighborhood, the new city. The new uncle?"

"The house is cool." That was all he conceded. I didn't think it meant he disapproved of the new neighborhood, city, or Patrick. Talking to a fourteen-year-old boy required a background in archaeology, considering all the digging that was necessary. I decided to persist.

"Do you like Paddy?" I questioned.

"Oh yeah, he's cool, too." There you have it, two enthusiastic thumbs up from the youth demographic. Paddy was still at the counter waiting for his food.

"You'll get used to everything," I told him. "It's going to be an adjustment for both of us. You know that you can talk to me about anything?"

He just nodded in that absent way kids do so you're not completely certain they heard what you said. I ate a fry and started thinking about "normal."

I'd like to think that things would get back to normal for us, but I'm not certain either of us knew what that meant anymore. What was normal? I could scarcely remember the last time things felt like the pieces all fit. It hadn't been normal when Alec started being sick more often than well. It hadn't been normal when *well* wasn't something we could hope for anymore. And it definitely hadn't been normal since he died. Normal had eluded us for nearly two years. Was it too much to hope that we'd construct a new normal in Minneapolis? It'd only been six months since Alec died, but it'd been years since a pall hadn't hung over our lives.

"What are you thinking about?" Paddy was at the booth with his food. He sat across from us.

"Normal," I answered.

"What's that?" He chuckled.

"That's what I was wondering."

"Patrick, what are Meghan and Kelly like?" Caden asked, changing the subject. He'd hardly said two words to Paddy all day, so it was a good start. My brother seemed a little baffled by the question at first.

"I don't know," he said. "Meghan is kind of quiet. She's very pretty; looks like her mother did in high school. Dresses different and her hair is different, but you can see it in her face."

"What about Kelly?" Caden persisted. I continued to shove fries in my mouth, listening to my brother be put on the spot.

"Kelly is great! Reads a lot. He's quiet, too, but in a different way, I guess."

"He's in the eighth grade?" Caden asked.

"I told you that much," I answered. "He just finished the eighth grade. Meghan will be a junior in the fall. Both you and Kelly have birthdays this summer, so he'll turn fourteen, um... right before or after you turn fifteen. Paddy, when is Kelly's birthday?"

"August sometime, I think," he answered.

"I think you two may be the same age for a few days. Anyway, you'll all be at the same school in September, ninth, tenth, and eleventh grades. Cool, huh?"

"Yeah, kinda cool, I guess." It seemed he was reserving judgment.

"That's cool," Paddy chimed in. "I hadn't realized they were all so close in age. We were all two years apart. We didn't get to go to school together."

"I was in school one year with Joanna. Remember, I skipped a year?" I clarified.

69

"You, Colleen, and Joey were all at Southwest at the same time?" he asked.

"Joanna was a senior when I was a freshman, and Colleen was a sophomore. You and Catelyn went to school together."

"That was back when she was still sorta cool," he laughed.

"Why doesn't anyone like Catelyn?" Caden asked. My brother and I tried not to laugh.

"I'm gonna let you get this one," Paddy said, smiling.

"It's not that we don't like her. I'm sorry we've given you the wrong idea," I tried to explain. "I barely know her anymore. It's just that she's… well, she's very nice, still… but she's… Caty's, uh, well; you know how you say adults are too serious? Catelyn is more serious than most adults. Does that make sense?"

"Kinda, I guess." Caden is very smart. Even after his dad had died, his grades didn't suffer. If anything, they improved. He'd thrown himself into school. I didn't understand why he talked as if he had barely cleared grade school. His vocabulary was a constant cycle of weird, kinda, sorta, and I guess. Occasionally, he'd slip in some actual grammar, but those relapses were typically short.

We finished our lunches and it was on to our last two stops where both Paddy and Caden opted to stay in the truck. I wondered if Caden had more questions for my brother but I didn't have time to worry about it. It was already after one o'clock and I had so much to accomplish before people started showing up.

"The living and dining rooms are taped," Kevin offered, once we were back home.

My nephew was barefoot. He wore loose denim cutoffs and a Garth Brooks concert tee with the sleeves cut off. A red bandana covered his brown hair. He was a couple of inches taller than I was, even barefoot.

"You are wonderful," I told him, leaning in for a hug.

70

"I know, right?!" he replied, and hugged me back tightly. He had a warmth about him that reminded me of his mother a very long time ago.

Catelyn wasn't always cold. In fact, when I was in elementary school and she'd already graduated, my sister doted on me. Picking me up from school, taking me places my parents wouldn't have; the movies or just downtown to goof around. She was twenty-one when she discovered she was pregnant with Kevin. She and Tom had only been dating for a few months. They were married before Caty started to show and Kevin was born six months later. Even then, she continued to dote on me in equal measure to her own son. She and Tom fought constantly after they were married. As I grew older, I began to think my sister felt he was beneath her. I wondered if she'd been given any choice when it came to marrying him. Either way, it seemed, in the beginning that any love she had to give was reserved for me and Kevin, leaving her husband to fight for the scraps. When I was a teenager, Kevin was just a toddler. Eventually I was frozen out too, and Catelyn seemed to care only about her son. I adored Kevin. Everyone did. He was the sole nephew or niece for almost six years. Spoiled wouldn't begin to describe the constant state of adoration that little boy lived in.

"I bought more tape, brushes, the whole nine yards," I told him.

"Sweet," he replied.

"Did you guys break for lunch?"

"Sandwiches and chips."

"What's Charlie been up to?"

"The sink and toilet in the downstairs bathroom," Kevin explained.

"We have the tile for that now, too. Your grandmother will be here soon. Think she'd be good at laying tile?" I joked.

"You're funny," Kevin replied. "Where's that tape?"

"I'm going to have a quick cigarette before I start figuring out where all this stuff goes."

"I'll join you, then." Kevin and I went to smoke out back, me once again on the step. Kevin sat on the sidewalk in front of me, cross-legged.

71

"We haven't talked a lot about your situation," I started.

"What do you mean?"

"You're twenty-one years old. You should be off somewhere at the beach or spending the day sleeping. What gives?"

"I'm not really your typical twenty-one-year-old? Is that what you're saying?"

"I'm just worried," I replied. "Is there some reason you're not anxious to go home after being stuck with us for almost a week? Don't get me wrong, Caden and I love having you around."

"I kind of gave up my apartment at the beginning of May," Kevin admitted, embarrassed.

"Where have you been staying?" I took a long drag on my cigarette. He hadn't lit one. I looked around and noticed he didn't have a pack.

"I stayed on a friend's couch for a few days, then with Grandma, but no one's supposed to know about that," he answered.

"Are you out of cigarettes?"

"Yeah, and money." He looked down at the ground.

"Kevin, why didn't you say anything?"

"It's not your problem."

Kevin had flown across the country to drive Caden and me to Minnesota. He'd seemed embarrassed by any gratitude I showed. He'd been friendly, even loving to Caden, dealt with the cats' almost constant meowing the first twenty-four hours on the road, and even loaned me cigarettes when I was out, all the while refusing to allow me to do much more than feed him along the way. In the past week I had fallen right back into the adoration I'd felt for him as a child; while realizing what a kind-hearted, humble, wonderful man he'd become while I'd been away. His mother must've had something to do with that. I had no idea what went on between them. I knew her marriage was essentially loveless from the start. But she'd been loving toward Kevin in the beginning. Then something had changed in her. At first she was merely

72

distant, unenthusiastic. In the last ten years or so, she'd become extraordinarily cold, unforgiving, even unfeeling. I knew that she and Kevin were essentially estranged, but no one seemed to know why.

"Kev, we're family. I know it's got to feel weird, like we barely know each other, but you need to know that I'd do anything for you. I'm sure Joanna and Patrick feel the same." I felt utterly disgusted with myself for not noticing anything was amiss sooner. He looked up at me and I thought he might actually cry. I couldn't imagine what was going on in his head.

"She stopped paying my rent because I was going out to California to drive you back," he finally admitted. I was dumbstruck. He was angry; I could see that now. There were no visible traces of sadness. He'd grown used to his mother's callousness, so much so that it had ceased hurting him. "I almost gave in. It was clear she had some huge... I don't know: reservations. Then she told me if I went to San Francisco, she'd no longer support me in any way. Then I was like, 'Fuck her'!"

I handed him a cigarette, surprised he hadn't just taken one by now. They were lying on the step in between us. He lit it using his own lighter, which he'd retrieved from his pocket.

"I didn't want to say anything because I couldn't imagine how it would make you feel," he continued. "Grandma thinks she'll come around. I honestly don't care."

"Kev, it barely even registers on my pain meter. I felt hurt fifteen years ago. Your mother and people like her have no power over me anymore. You should have said something," I told him.

"I'm sorry."

"Don't be. I understand, and it was sweet of you. You're an amazing young man and you deserve better. We're going to figure this out. Until then you'll stay in the guest bedroom. Caden will be ecstatic. We'd both love having you around."

So many emotions swam across his face. His expression morphed from anger, to shame, maybe even surprise, and finally... relief. At that moment tears welled up in his eyes. He was more shocked than embarrassed by them. How on earth could Catelyn do that to him? I was angry. How in the hell had my family not noticed? I already knew the answer—they didn't want to. Little had

73

changed. I had finished my first cigarette and lit a second one without noticing.

"God, I'm chain-smoking now," I muttered. "This is actually good. You're such a huge help." He stood up and turned away. I was afraid I'd embarrassed him.

"What are you guys doing out here?" Caden was standing in the doorway. Kevin didn't want Caden to see him upset.

"We're just slacking. Have you put everything away in there?"

"No," he laughed. "You're going to decide where it all goes. I'm not getting involved. I did put all the paint stuff in the dining room and I showed the delivery guys where the new bed went."

"Hey, excellent news: we're going to have a roommate for a while. Kev's going to stay in the guest room."

"SWEET!" He flung open the screen door and nearly threw himself in Kevin's arms. Kevin was as shocked by the gesture as I was. "I told you. I should get to make more decisions around here. I'm good at it."

Kev had composed himself a bit and embraced Caden. For a half-second, I considered a group hug, but oddly, I felt it might be an intrusion. The two of them had bonded, and that was a great thing. Caden had someone to count on in Minnesota. That could never be bad.

"Where's your car and your stuff?" I turned my attention back to Kevin.

"Grandma's." He was still a little choked up. That was the first he'd spoken since starting to cry. I knew that feeling, like you're just maintaining your composure, but having to speak could foil the whole charade. It reminded me of being sent to the principal's office in school or, even worse: the way I felt around my parents the last few months I lived with them. I said as little as possible then.

"You can go back with her tonight when we're finished and get what you can. I'm sure the kid would be happy to help you."

"For sure," Caden volunteered.

74

He was so happy about it, I almost felt jealous. Charlie appeared shirtless at the door. While not as defined as Kevin, he was still a sight to behold, his skin glistening with sweat. He had his brother's pale complexion and freckles. His longer hair was pulled back in a small ponytail. His tiny glasses rested just beyond the bridge of his nose.

"I hope you don't mind us eating your food," he said. "Kevin insisted it'd be alright."

"Of course," I urged. "Starting now, we all have to be a little less polite. Let me just issue a blanket 'help yourself.' That goes for you, too, Kevin."

"If you say so," Charlie replied cheekily.

"You might be sorry," Kevin said, regaining more of his composure.

"Kevin's gonna live here," Caden told Charlie.

"Is that so?" he asked. Caden had pushed past me, still sitting on my step, past Charlie, as well, and into the house. I stood up and turned to watch Caden and Charlie disappear into the house, then back to my nephew. I embraced him for the second time in less than thirty minutes.

"Thank you," he said to me.

"Love you," I countered. Words that had become almost foreign to me in the last six month.

"I love you, too," Kev said, still hugging me.

"Let's get back to work, damn it!" I joked, and the two of us followed Charlie and Caden into the house.

Chapter 8
STEPHEN

Less than a half-hour later there was a knock on the front door. I had become so used to coming and going from the back door, I'd almost forgotten a front one existed. Caden came tearing down the stairs to answer the door. I didn't have a clear view from where I was, on a ladder, taping in the dining room, but I heard my sister-in-law's voice.

"You must be Caden?" Jannie said.

"How'd you guess?" This was the most animated I'd seen him in months.

"I'm Jannie, Patrick's wife, and this Moira." I had climbed down the ladder, smoothed my clothes, and come through the living room, excited to see my mother. It had only been a month. Normally, I would have gone to her house when I got to town, but the circumstances being what they were, it made sense to wait for her to come to me. We'd not even been in Minnesota twenty-four hours anyway.

"Let them in," I called to Caden.

"Welcome home! Did Patrick tell you I love the house?" Jannie rarely called my brother "Paddy."

My mother was in the doorway now and just like a few weeks ago; I was flabbergasted by her appearance. Moira Bennett had always been stunning. I may have been biased, of course. I remembered clearly a time when I looked at my mother and thought she was the most beautiful woman in the world. Growing up, she'd had short, dark hair. All the other moms had long hair. Moira looked like a movie star, always made-up, her hair styled flawlessly, well-dressed. We certainly weren't wealthy, but my mother liked jewelry. She wore a ring on every finger, a bracelet on each wrist. Her nails were always painted.

The woman before me seemed as if she'd shrunk, if not in height, then most definitely in stature. She'd lost weight. Her dark hair had gone completely grey and was longer than I'd seen it. She wore lipstick, but that was all the makeup I could discern. The jewelry was still there. In fact, it may have accounted for a large portion of her weight. She was still beautiful, almost

76

regal-looking, but her aged appearance took my breath away. I stood just outside the doorframe and helped her up the step. Moira was only sixty-four, but I'd heard from Joanna that she acted frailer than she was. I hugged her and she didn't feel quite as thin as she looked. "Hi Mom."

"It's so good to see you," she replied. "Are you going to introduce me to this handsome young man?"

"Caden, this is my mother, Moira." I turned back to see him standing behind me with Jannie.

"Very mice to meet you, ma'am." He reached out to shake my mother's hand.

"Likewise," she remarked and met his reach with her downturned hand. I was surprised she hadn't moved to hug him. "Call me Moira or Grandma, if you like. No need for that ma'am business."

"Yes ma—um, Moira." They weren't as much taking each other in as they were sizing each other up. It seemed oddly cold for my mother, but maybe she was being respectful of a kid who was being thrown into her family headfirst. I moved to hug Jannie.

"Thanks about the house. It's good to see you," I said. "Your husband has done such an incredible job here. He's an artist."

"He's been talking weird like that since he got here." I heard my brother tease from the kitchen where he was washing his hands. "I'll be right in. I started pulling up tile and it's older than we thought."

"He's modest, I guess," his wife said.

"I guess. Do you want to sit down Mom, or would you like a tour?"

"I think maybe my new friend Caden could show me around," Moira declared.

"Mom, why don't you sit down first?" Paddy fussed, coming in from the kitchen.

"I'm just fine." She turned to Caden. "Well, young man. What do you say?"

"Um, okay, I guess so, but I barely know my own way around." He took my mother's hand and led her past the rest of us, back the way Paddy had come.

77

"This is the kitchen. It needs work." He listened to me more than I realized.

"It sure is big," my mother said, their voices trailing off.

"You see?" Patrick whispered.

"We need to start challenging her," Jannie added.

"How do you mean?" I asked.

"Everyone treats her like an invalid and she eats it up."

"How are we supposed to treat her?" Paddy asked. "She refuses to or can't do much of anything for herself."

"Refuses to is more like it," Jannie offered.

"I'm going to reserve judgment a bit." I didn't want to get in between my brother and his wife. I remembered Jannie being free with her opinions, though I did wonder if she was right. It was time to change the subject, anyway. Caden and my mother had come around the other way, touring the dining room now.

"They were talking about one of us," my mother told Caden. She was holding his arm. "You see how quiet they got?"

"It was probably me," Caden told her, not skipping a beat. "I'm new here."

"How does everyone feel about Chinese?" I threw out. It was about time Caden, Kevin and I ate something that wasn't deep-fried or slathered with cheese. "Paddy tells me Rainbow is the place to go?"

"Can we get sweet & sour chicken?" Caden begged. He wasn't going down without a fight on the fried food front.

"Sure," I said. I turned to Jannie. "Your husband tells me you have a host of menus in your car? Any chance there's one for this place?"

"Sure there is," Patrick answered on his wife's behalf.

"Probably," she concurred.

78

"Caden, want to come see Jannie's fancy car?"

"It's a Saab for goodness sake," Jannie exclaimed. Caden followed Paddy outside. My mother had taken a seat on the couch where I'd slept the night before.

"Something to drink?" I asked.

"Do you have vodka?" my mother asked. I wasn't certain whether she was kidding or not.

"Not yet, Mom." I decided to go with not.

"How about a beer, Moira?" Jannie countered. "I know Stephen's got beer. I'll take one, as well." I didn't recall my mother ever drinking beer, but she hadn't declined.

"You're sure you haven't any vodka?" Moira pressed, before taking the can I handed her. "This will be like drinking with your father."

Kevin and Charlie had joined us. "Beers, boys?"

"When did you get here, Grandma?" Kev asked my mother. "Hey, Jannie!"

As I entered the living room, my mother was fumbling with her purse, searching for something. She finally retrieved a pair of eyeglasses. Jannie was still holding my mother's beer as she put her glasses on and turned her attention to Charlie. "You look very familiar."

"That's Charlie," Jannie said, handing her the beer. "He works for Patrick. You've met before, I think."

"No, not from there," she replied. Charlie had crossed the room to offer my mother his hand.

"I'm Charlie Carpenter, Mrs. Bennett." Everyone was being so polite.

"Carpenter?" My mother questioned him.

"It's a pretty common name, Moira," Jannie added.

79

My mother shook his hand, studying him like she was trying to place where she knew him from. Christ! All at once, it came to me. I nearly dropped one of the beers. She was remembering someone different, a boy that looked almost identical to Charlie. Wasn't she? My mother had rarely paid attention to my friends, but I'm certain she recalled the shirtless boy she'd caught making out with her seventeen-year-old son. I remembered thinking it was a shame Charlie had put his shirt back on. If he hadn't, it may have made the memory more vivid for Moira.

"Thank you, Jannie," she said, taking a rather long drink from the can, her eyes still on Charlie. When she spoke again, it was to him, "You remind me of someone else. He was quite pretty, too."

"Moira!" Jannie exclaimed.

"What? He is. Surely, you see that? Or would you like to borrow my glasses?"

I looked at Charlie to see if he was blushing. We had just talked about Liam, and their resemblance, last night. He was smiling at my mother, clearly charmed. I thought he'd told me they'd met. I couldn't tell what he was thinking. Meanwhile, my sister-in-law was shaking her head, opening her own beer. She followed Moira's lead and took a rather large gulp. The evening had the potential to get interesting fast.
Moira was back to rummaging through her purse.

"You can't smoke in here," Jannie told her.

"I know," Moira told her. "Stephen smokes, too. Surely there's some kind of smoking section around here somewhere."

"Outside, Mom. Kev and I will come with you."

There were at least three thoughts currently playing bumper cars in my head. I wondered if Patrick had kidnapped my son. Secondly, I wished that I'd bought lawn furniture earlier. My mother wasn't going to sit on the ground. I grasped for a remnant of the other thought? Oh yes, I was still wondering if my mom had mistaken Charlie for his older brother. Kevin had taken his grandmother's hand and helped her back to her feet.

"Watch my purse, dear," my mother told Charlie, and winked.

"Kev, would you grab one of the dining room chairs for your grandmother?"

80

"Don't worry about me. I'll sit on the step." Once outside, she eased herself down onto the top step and continued. "They treat me like a fucking infant."

"It's okay, Grandma." I nearly choked on my beer.

"I talk like this now. I hope I didn't shock you, Stephen?"

"Just a bit, Mom, but I think I'll live."

"Good for you, son," she continued. "It'll be good that you're here. Poor Paddy's been outnumbered since your dad and Colleen left."

"I'm glad to be here."

"That's wonderful." She took another sip of beer. "And another thing. Don't think I don't know that young man is the brother of that boy you knew from school. He was your boyfriend, wasn't he, his brother?"

"Really?" Kev asked. "The kid you talked about from high school—that was Charlie's brother?"

"I caught them kissing," Moira continued. This time Kevin choked on his beer. My mother looked down at him, then over to me. I knew it. "I'm quiet, dear. Not blind."

I wondered how privy to my mother's newfound frankness Kevin had been, and was even more anxious to discuss her with him now. "Where is Paddy with the menu?" I wondered aloud, changing the subject. I needed some time to process all of this. Considering she hadn't said a word about Liam in fifteen years, even after I'd come out of the closet, I wondered how often my mother had thought about that day. Was her bluntness possible because my dad had died, or could my mother conceivably have made my life easier by broaching the subject when it happened?

So much had changed since 1978. People had certainly changed. Maybe Moira was one of them, though I never thought she was homophobic. My mother, as quiet as she was, was still a bit too free-spirited for that. I couldn't imagine her disliking anyone simply because they were different than her. She put little stock in how the Catholic Church told people they should live their lives. That had been all my dad. Maybe she'd come into her own and my siblings hadn't noticed because they were too busy babying her into submission. I'd

81

grown quiet pondering this and wasn't paying attention to my smoking companions.

"Don't worry, Stephen." I heard my name and snapped out of my musings. "You'll get used to me. I hope you'll persuade your brother and sister to lighten up a bit. It's been a terrible couple of years for all of us, but I hope you don't mind me saying: they died, not us."

I couldn't think of how to respond. Thank goodness I didn't have to. Just then, I heard my brother's voice. He rounded the back of the house first, followed by Caden and another boy. I was so preoccupied with my thoughts it took me a second or two to realize the boy had to be Kelly. My God, he was adorable! Everything about this child screamed nerd, from his glasses to the way he carried himself, to the two books under his arm. He looked like the type of kid for whom one book just wasn't enough. He was a little shorter than Caden, but looked more than a year younger. He was blond, a rare thing in my family, and he had grey eyes. He wore tan shorts, a Polo shirt, and what looked like deck shoes. His outfit was pretty stylish, but the books and his general geek-like demeanor overshadowed the style tenfold. His large eyes were close-set and his glasses, clunky and too big for his face, accentuated them. He reminded me so much of myself when I was his age, I had to fight the urge to hug him immediately.

Meghan was right behind him. I'd met my niece in March. Paddy was right, though. It was uncanny how much she looked like Joanna at that age. I didn't think she dressed all that differently. She'd updated her mother's style. She certainly wore more makeup than Joey had at her age and had longer hair, though it was the exact same shade of dark brown. My sisters, Joanna and Colleen, were as beautiful as our mother. Their popularity in high school was legendary. They were gorgeous, smart, and kind, not a combination found often in teenage girls. Most, especially those well ensconced in the upper-echelon of high school hierarchy, would be embarrassed by an awkward, bookish, geeky little brother. But both of them embraced me and practically demanded the same of their friends. I hoped Joey's daughter would take after her mother in that way. Her little brother would need someone looking out for him. If not his sister, I had faith Caden would do what he could.

Finally, Joanna appeared. My sister's long dark brown hair was pulled back in a ponytail, almost identical to her daughter's. She wore cut-off sweatpants and an oversized t-shirt that had clearly seen its share of paint. She looked like the only one who'd come dressed to work. She wore no makeup that I could

82

see, but she didn't need it. She was barely taller than her kids. In fact, she and Meghan may have been close to the same height.

"Look who we found," Paddy announced, cheerfully.

"Yeah, look who we found," Caden echoed. I almost laughed out loud. Who was this kid?

"You must be Kelly," I said to my nephew. "We keep missing each other." I was about to extend my hand when he moved in for a hug. I watched my sister's reaction as I hugged her thirteen-year-old son for the first time. Her large sunglasses made it hard to read her response.

"It's nice to meet you," Kelly said, politely. I was already hoping he and I would become friends. I moved in to hug my niece.

"Hi," she mumbled, hugging me back less enthusiastically, but not insincerely. She was sixteen. I used to teach sixteen-year-olds. If you found warmth in any of them, you'd uncovered a buried treasure. Both kids went to greet their grandmother. My sister stood a few feet away from me, taking in the scene.

"We've stumbled upon the smoking section," she guessed.

"You've caught us," our mother chimed in.

"Can I bum one?" She moved closer to me. Taking her lead, I moved in her direction, and finally we hugged. The embrace was awkward and forced.

"You want menthol?" I asked.

"Sure. Thanks. It's good to see you." I couldn't measure her sincerity; which was odd, considering it seemed heartfelt. I regretted our weird hug, longing for a do-over. I polished off my fist beer before digging in pocket for my cigarettes. I realized the whole time we'd been outside, my mother had been the only one smoking. I quickly handed out cigarettes; first to Joanna, then to Kevin, and finally myself.

"I'm trying to quit," Joanna continued, lighting the cigarette and taking a long, deliberate drag. "I've just met your son."

83

"Oh, yeah. He's quite a bit more animated than usual today." In that moment, it was like everyone else had faded away. The whole group of them were still within feet of us, but my sister and I were alone in this conversation.

"He looks older than I thought."

"Kelly is wonderful," I babbled, as if he weren't a foot away from me. Surreal. It was so utterly bizarre to be standing here with my sister, smoking cigarettes, discussing having just met each other's teenage children.

"You know we're right here," Caden interjected, and the tunnel vision faded away. Though we were back with everyone else, I felt disoriented. What was it about being there with my family that made me light-headed? Kevin moved to stand next to me. He was close enough that I could lean against him should I need to.

"Of course," Joey answered him. "It's just nice for us all to finally meet."

Fifteen minutes and a hundred dollars later, it was six o'clock and dinner had been ordered. Charlie had offered to go pick up the food and invited Caden and Kelly to go with. Kevin was taking drink orders. It struck me as odd that my brother was the only adult who opted for something other than beer. Paddy had taken a bottle of water and returned to work on the tile in the half bath. That made two days in a row. I could remember at least two keggers growing up, both thrown by him.

I offered Joey a tour and she'd accepted. I had a growing list of things to question her about. Starting with: had Patrick given up drinking? I'd hardly been in the basement since we'd arrived, but I decided to start there. Twenty steps down led to one big room. It was a sort of family room. To the left of that was a small room the prior owners had used for storage, a separate laundry room, and in between a fourth bathroom. I had barely even remembered there was another bathroom down there. I wondered if Kevin might prefer having the room down here since it offered some privacy. He'd be able to come and go without a lot of notice. I was formulating a plan in my head when Joanna spoke.

"How's Kev?" Could she read my mind?

"Funny you asked. I was just thinking about him. It seems he's homeless"

84

"What? What happened to his apartment?" Not wanting to betray his confidence or my mother's, I moved quickly through explaining that our sister had cut him off without giving her the reasons.

"You can't be serious?"

"He was reluctant to say anything," I continued. "I was beginning to wonder why he was still here. I mean, he'd already gone above and beyond. I asked him right before Mom got here."

"So just tonight?"

"Yes, I feel bad. I should've noticed something was weird sooner."

"Well, you had a few other things on your mind."

"I've told him he can stay here, at least until he gets this figured out."

Having seen all there was to see in the basement, we migrated back upstairs. It struck me as odd that Joey didn't seem angry over our sister basically disowning her son. Even her "you can't be serious," was less incredulous than matter of fact. Something had happened with Catelyn, she had turned a corner a long time ago. I don't think anyone ever asked what happened to change her. We all just accepted the fact that she was a bitch now and went about our lives. Even calling her Caty was weird, that name spoke of the girl we'd grown up with. No one called her Catelyn back then, not even our parents. She was Caty, Patrick was Paddy, and Joanna was Joey. It suddenly occurred to me that I'd never had a softer version of my own name until Alec had given it to me. I was always Stephen. At the top of the stairs, I enlisted Kevin's help.

"Kev, why don't you show your aunt and grandmother, if she wants, the upstairs?" I hadn't had a chance to ask about Patrick. I could probably grill Kevin later. At that moment, I had decided to discuss something with Jannie instead.

"Sure," he agreed. My mother went willingly, as did Joanna. Jannie was on a ladder in the dining room with a roll of masking tape. Once the others were upstairs, I went to her.

"Do you guys see much of Catelyn?"

85

"Not really. It's been months. We see her on the news." That seemed to be the stock answer.

"How long has it been that way?"

"Since the campaign I guess. Well, at least that long." She was working it out in her head, thinking back. "I don't know, I think maybe we were relieved. Why do you ask?"

"It just seems odd."

"We see more of Kevin," she offered. "He makes a point to come to birthdays and sometimes he helps your mother out. He's a great kid. Funny, isn't it? That he's Catelyn's?"

"I guess," I acknowledged. "She wasn't always this way."

"No?" I was sure Paddy had defended her to his wife, so there was no point in my doing so.

"She's cut Kevin off," I told her.

"Jesus Christ!" Jannie was angry, but she had never gotten caught up in the negativity that seemed to afflict my entire family. "How the hell does someone do that to their own child?"

"Kev indicated I was the last straw," I admitted.

"What does that mean?"

"I don't know exactly. My being gay?" I guessed. "She told Kev if he flew out to San Francisco to help me, he could forget about her paying his rent."

"I bet she's worried about the campaign," Jannie said.

"I thought so, too, but it's more than that. Colleen told me that my being gay was public knowledge in the first campaign. I'll be local for this election. That's the only difference I can come up with."

"Honestly, who knows with her? It makes me sick though."

86

"I told Kevin he could live here. There's plenty of room, and Caden and I both adore him."

We could hear my mother at the top of the stairs. The tour was winding down. She whispered, "It's good that he has you."

"Your house is lovely, Stephen," my mother said, making her way down the stairs.

"The floors are beautiful!" Joanna called to Paddy in the bathroom.

"Thanks!" he hollered back.

Kevin was the last one down the stairs, and I mouthed "thank you" to him. He smiled in response. He was definitely at ease with the family. Through the big window at the front of the house, I could see the kids coming up the walk, each carrying a large bag of Chinese food. Charlie wasn't far behind. For the next thirty minutes, we all gorged ourselves on Chinese food at the dining room table. It was slightly more casual than the family dinners we grew up with. I was curious if my brother and sister had noticed the similarity. It had been years since we had done anything like this. At one point, I caught Caden's eye. He was sitting at the other end of the table between my mother and Kelly. When our eyes met, he smiled. His enthusiasm on the first day in our new home meant the world to me.

By the end of the night, a first coat of paint had been applied to nearly every wall, except the back bathroom, where Paddy had only just finished laying the tile. Charlie and Joanna had worked upstairs with Caden and Kelly; Jannie, Meghan, and I were downstairs. In the back of my mind, as I said my goodbyes to everyone, I was thinking of making the basement my next priority. I'd assumed the kitchen would be next, but with Kevin moving in, the other should take precedent. I shut the front door behind everyone but Caden and me. I turned to Caden, already starting up the stairs.

"Hey, wait a second, you. Stick around. I want to talk to you." Not as begrudgingly as I expected, he followed me outside so I could have a cigarette.

"What's up?" he asked.

"Just checking in," I said. "Progress report?" He thought for what felt like an eternity. I was never good at waiting for reviews, even Alec's reviews. Most of the time he was less anxious about them than I'd been.

"It's okay," Caden finally said. "I wasn't sure I'd like it, but I guess it's alright. It's cool that Kev is going to live with us."

"I'm relieved, kiddo. I wasn't sure either. I knew we needed a change, but I thought we'd look for an apartment in San Francisco or maybe Berkley."

"I didn't know that. I didn't know we weren't gonna stay at the house until you said we were moving to Minnesota."

"I know I should have at least spoken to you first before buying this house. I promise all major decisions going forward will be made democratically. Deal?"

"I guess," he replied. "It's not like I get a say anyway."

"You do get a say. That's what I'm telling you. I'm glad that you're feeling okay about all of this, but I'm also sorry I didn't consult you before making a decision that affected us both so much. I lucked out."

"I'm still nervous."

"That's understandable. It would be weird if you weren't." I was speaking his language now.

"Anyway, thank you," he said.

"For what?"

"For being there. I mean here. I know you maybe didn't want to be."

I was stunned and hadn't a clue what to say. His comment just sat there. We were looking at each other. I had to figure out something quickly. "I have always wanted to be. I belong wherever you are." I was not going to cry. I studied him for a reaction. His face was actually blank. I desperately wanted to give him more words, but my heart and my head were racing. It was clear he did not know what to say either. We sat there in silence for a full couple of minutes. Finally, I couldn't bear it any longer. "Do you know what I mean, Caden?"

"I think so." He stared back me, still blank. *God, this kid should play poker.* "I'm really tired. Can I go to bed now?"

"Alright." I couldn't force this. He'd already moved past my perch on the step. "Goodnight. Brush your teeth"

BRUSH YOUR TEETH? What in the hell?! I'd never said that before. God, what an idiot! I didn't even know where that came from. It would have been laughable, had I not wanted so desperately to unsay it. It didn't make any difference. He was gone already, the door closed behind him.

Chapter 9
CADEN

I took the stairs two at a time to get to my room and couldn't wait to shut the door behind me. There were so many things in my head knocking into each other. I was breathing like I'd gone up way more than one flight of stairs. After the door was shut, I just sat on my old bed in my new room and cried. It wasn't like a really big cry, not like when my dad died. That night, I felt like I was just completely broken; like I might never do anything but cry ever again. I'd shivered like when you're cold, only with pissed off thrown in. This was stiller and it surprised me. I hated crying, especially in front of anyone, so I wanted to be in that room, the room Stephen kept saying was mine.

My room was in San Francisco and somebody else's parents were probably telling him it was his room. But it wasn't. It couldn't just be that way. That wasn't his room any more than the one I sat in was mine. It wasn't fair for things to be that way, grown-ups making all the decisions about where everyone went and slept and lived. That was pretty much how it was though; and it almost never didn't suck. Then, kind of like they know they're wrong, they cover it up with a bunch of words just like he did. Next time, he said we'd do things democratically and I'd get a say. But it wasn't like we were going to move again soon. Or ever. This was probably it, so what did it matter if I got a say next time? What next time?

Sonic was asleep on my bed when I sat down. It was my bed from San Francisco. We brought it with us. A lot of other stuff was going to be new, not what we had when we were there and my dad was alive. The cat had made himself right at home since we'd moved in—one day—Meg, the other cat, too. She'd slept with Kev the night before. Sonic opened one eye, stretched, and yawned. A minute later, he was brushing against my back as I sat there. I lay back on the bed with my shoes still on because no one could see anyway. Sonic moved around and plopped back down beside me, nestling in close. I pet him and he started purring right away.

My heart had stopped racing and I just lay there on my back and the tears came sideways across my cheeks onto my pillow. After a minute, even those stopped. I could just hear Sonic's purring and the sound of my breathing and I started thinking about *that* night. It was in November. I had slept in the chair the night before and then gone to school because Stephen said it was illegal for me not to on Election Day. It was total bullshit, but grown-ups got really

90

uncomfortable when kids saw shit the grownups thought they shouldn't, especially death. I kinda didn't want to see it anyway, not my dad dying. I'd seen a lot of that already. We all knew it was any day, any minute, but they didn't know I knew. I think some kids know way more than what grownups give us credit for. I usually don't bother saying I know because then we don't have to *discuss* it. I didn't see why everything had to be discussed all the time.

The night before that night, when I slept in the chair and Stephen didn't make me leave and go to my room, my dad was pretty out of it. Sometimes it seemed like he was asleep, but then he would open his eyes and look over at me and smile. At first, it looked like his smile hurt, but then before I fell asleep, I thought he was asleep again. But he opened his eyes and looked right at me, and his smile didn't hurt anymore and he said, really low, "I love you so much, Cay."

"I love you, too, Dad." We looked at each other's eyes for a second and then I looked down and when I looked back up his eyes were closed again. At first, I was scared he was dead already. But then he talked again.

"Don't look down all the time. I know you think when you look down people can't see you're sad or mad or even trying not to laugh. When you look down, it's like you're stealing their chance." His eyes had been closed through all of that, but he finally opened them again. People used to tell me I had my dad's eyes. Not anymore.

"Their chance?" I asked.

"To see your handsome face," he said, so low I almost didn't hear it. I started to look down, but I made myself stay there in his eyes until he closed them again.

I'd stopped petting Sonic and he looked back at me demandingly. "Fine," I told him and started scratching him behind the ears. After another minute, the tears stopped and I used my other hand to wipe my eyes. I didn't know what to feel first. I was pissed that we had just moved, but it wasn't just that. I was scared he wouldn't be able to find us. There were times in San Francisco that I could feel my dad there, like after he died. At first, it kinda freaked me out, like he could see me, you know, doing stuff; even going to the bathroom, but mostly other stuff. After a while, though, it kinda felt safe. Sometimes I would

91

even forget he was there, but then Sonic would look up like someone had just come in our room and I would remember. I even talked to him sometimes. He didn't answer, though. That would've been weird, but it felt good to talk to him out loud. Now who would I talk to? I didn't feel him at all since we had left. My dad was probably still in San Francisco freaking out the new kid. I hoped he scared the shit out of him. It shouldn't be that easy. Fuck easy!

I rolled over and reached for the boom box to turn my music on. Metallica "Nothing Else Matters" had just started on the radio on this station KQ-92 Kev had told me about. I turned the volume up, no headphones.

Never opened myself this way
Life is ours, we live it our way
All these words I don't just say
And nothing else matters

There was something else. I felt like I was pissed off, but not at Stephen. Who then? I didn't really get it, so I went back to my dad and wondered if Stephen ever felt him there in San Francisco. Sometimes I'd look at Stephen and he looked like someone had just sucker-punched him in the gut, like he could just double over any minute from the pain he felt. I knew the feeling. I felt closest to him when I could see he was feeling lousy, like we shared that. If Stephen had felt Dad was there with us in the house, did it freak him out? Is that why he wanted to move? Outside he'd said we had to. I should've asked why.

Sometimes I felt like I wanted to know something, but I didn't want to ask, like in school. The teacher is saying something; and you had a question, but you didn't want to raise your hand because someone might think you're stupid. When that happened, I almost never said anything, but then I'd get pissed off at myself because I didn't know what the fuck the teacher was talking about. Being pissed off at yourself was just weird. It felt way worse than being pissed off at somebody else.

As soon as I thought about that, I recognized the other thing I was feeling. I was mad at myself, but I didn't really get why. I hadn't done anything. Seriously, sometimes life was too fucking hard.

Never opened myself this way
Life is ours, we live it our way
All these words I don't just say
And nothing else matters

I decided to go back over everything like grown-ups say to do when you lose something. *Like your mind.* Retrace your steps. I thought maybe it might work with feelings, too. I was mad at Stephen for just deciding we were going to move. I missed my dad and I sort of knew Stephen did, too. I wondered if Stephen felt stuck with me. I wasn't really his kid. Sometimes I was so pissed off at him, but I knew, deep down, that was just me being an asshole. He didn't have to bring me to Minnesota. I could just be some dumbfuck orphan. Just because Stephen loved my dad didn't mean he had to love me, too. Dad was gone. He wasn't even in San Francisco, not really. That was just a feeling I had sometimes. All that stuff was so hard. I felt the tears come back again, kinda like they weren't really gone in the first place. I buried my face in my pillow. I wanted to scream, but then Stephen would hear me.

I just laid there until I couldn't breathe. The song was over and the DJ talked for a minute, but I wasn't listening. I rolled back over on my back and all at once, I knew. I knew why I was pissed off at myself. I was so scared Stephen wouldn't want me. When we moved, it was a little like maybe he kind of did, you know, want me. He had brought me with. And I didn't hate that he did. And I didn't hate being there either. I liked the new people, and they paid attention to me; kinda like they were trying to figure out if they liked me, too. Sometimes grown-ups didn't really pay attention like that; it didn't matter if they liked you anyway. You're just a kid.

The house was cool, bigger than ours in San Francisco was, way bigger. I told Stephen it was all right, but it was a little bit more than that. I wasn't scared and there were parts I liked kind of a lot. By then, I think I knew. I think I knew, down there, why I was mad. It wasn't at Stephen. I was pissed off at myself. When I said thank you, I remembered I hadn't missed my dad or thought about him since we'd said goodbye to the city. Not even once. I didn't even realize I hadn't felt him since we left until just a minute before. Who was the asshole now? If Minnesota and these people made me forget about my dad, then I hated Minnesota. I hated it so much.

93

Chapter 10
KEVIN

My grandma and my aunt have never gotten along. Jannie talked to her and grandma responded with sarcasm. Or sometimes she'd just swear. Jannie didn't swear hardly at all. I was in the backseat of my aunt's new car on the way to Grandma's to pick up my car and some stuff I'd stored there after I bailed on my old apartment. My grandma was in the front seat.

"You can't smoke in here, Moira," Jannie told her.

"Really? I can't smoke in your brand new car? I'm shocked."

"You're being sarcastic?" Yep.

"I have never once been allowed to smoke in one of your cars. Why on Earth would you think I'd assume I could do so in a brand new one?"

"I just felt I should clarify."

"We're all so glad that you did," Grandma replied snarkily.

"How many beers did you have at Stephen's?"

"Twenty-three."

"Funny." It went on like that for the entire drive. Thankfully, it wasn't far. I was taking my stuff back to Stephen's, where I would be staying. I laid my head back and thought again about how I barely knew him. For some reason, my mother couldn't stand him. That's kind of what started all of the recent shit with her. My mother had gone ballistic when I told her I was going to fly to San Francisco and help him and Caden move back to Minnesota. That was two months ago. My mother didn't like gay people and Stephen is gay. His partner Alec died of AIDS last year. That made things worse, as far as my mother was concerned. She suspected that I was gay, but we didn't talk about it. Except one time, when she forbade me to discuss "my social life," as she called it, with any reporters. My mother was the Republican congresswoman for the Sixth District. She'd be running for re-election next year.

94

The fact that she called my suspected deviancy "my social life" was hilarious to me. I was pretty sure I wasn't gay by then. I'm not sure what about me made my mother assume the worst, but it just made me more determined to keep her from finding out either way. I shouldn't have said "the worst." I don't think there's anything wrong with being gay or even bi. I'd even kind of hoped I'd turn out bisexual, not because of my mother, though that would have been a bonus. I just kind of thought it was cool. Why would you limit yourself? I tried once, well almost twice.

In high school, my best friend gave me a hand job. His name was Marc and he was pretty obviously gay, but he hadn't come out to me yet. He'd been my friend since junior high. It didn't matter to me that he was gay, but my mother had said something like, "Jesus Christ, is everybody gay now?" What the fuck was that supposed to mean? I used to spend the night at Marc's. His parents were always there, but it made both of my parents uncomfortable. My mother was on the school board, so it wouldn't have looked good to limit who I could hang around with. Maybe it was guilt by association that made my mom so certain I was gay. I learned about that in political science at the U, before I dropped out last year. I had considered going to law school. That was what my mother wanted, anyway. After two years of college, she told me I didn't have the grades to get into even a mediocre law school.

A few times, but one time specifically, we told my parents that Marc's would be home, but they were actually staying overnight in St. Cloud. I just didn't want any hassle about hanging out with my friend. Besides, we were both sixteen. That was the night that Marc officially came out to me. I knew already, but I guess it was important for him to say the words. I had kind of hoped he'd hurry up so maybe we could fool around. Then I could figure out if I liked it. If I thought about it, I could see how guys were attractive, just like girls. If I found both attractive, maybe I was bisexual. I figured you could decide to be bi and as long as you liked the way it felt or you know, could get off, then it was cool. I'd really wished my uncle was around then, but he moved to California when I was like eight.

So we got drunk that night and Marc really wanted to fool around. He said that when he was coming out, not meaning necessarily with me. He was just thankful that I didn't get up and leave and end our friendship. He was so relieved; he just started spilling his guts. We drank some more. His mom had sloe gin and we mixed it with orange pop. She usually mixed it with whiskey and orange juice, but both of us had tasted Southern Comfort and didn't like it.

95

After a while, I asked him if he wanted to fool around with me. His eyes about came out of his head. I told him I didn't think I was really gay, but maybe I liked guys *and* girls. The problem was, both of us were virgins. We kissed a little and it wasn't horrible. It kind of made me feel warm and I got a little hard, but he was really hard. He had on these gym shorts and it was like poking me in the leg.

I kissed him again. He was really slobbery and tasted like Hawaiian Punch and Sunkist. I wasn't sure what to do with my tongue. I knew it was supposed to go in his mouth; but was it just supposed to go wherever? I thought that maybe I should've figured that stuff out before, but it was too late for that. So I just stuck my tongue in his mouth. When I did that, he stuck his tongue in my mouth. That was even slobberier, but not totally bad. I couldn't really tell if I liked it. I didn't have anything to compare it to. It felt okay. He was rubbing my dick and I guessed maybe I should touch his, but I wasn't sure I wanted to. It was so fucking hard, I was afraid if I touched it, it might snap right off. That's when he stopped rubbing me and looked at me like he wanted something. I knew where this was going. This other kid we knew had gotten a blowjob from a girl. We'd both heard all about it. I knew from the look in his eyes that's what he wanted to try. I wanted it too, well for him to put me in his mouth, anyway. I still hadn't even touched his dick.

I didn't know what to say, so I just smiled at him and took another long swig from my glass. It was thick, red, and super sweet. He smiled back at me, then tried to reach it with his mouth from where he was sitting. He couldn't bend that way, so I moved around in front of him. He kissed me again and then leaned over my lap. I was really hard. I had started rubbing myself when he stopped. When he was close to my dick, he looked up at me. I smiled at him, and there was no turning back. He opened his mouth wide and looked down at my dick, which was still in my hand. Then it was like he tried to swallow my whole dick, like really fast in one motion. He gagged and I thought he might puke in my lap. He tried it again and I felt the head of my dick hit the back of his mouth. It was fucking awesome! For a second I was harder than I'd ever been. He jammed it down his throat and gagged again. When he looked up at me this time, his eyes were watery. It seemed like a good idea to kiss him again, so I did, and I used my thumb to wipe a tear off his eyelashes. I really wanted him to choke on it again. He pulled away from the kiss.

"I don't think I can do that again," he told me. "I felt like I was gonna puke."

"Maybe you're doing it too fast," I suggested.

96

"We shoulda asked Tim more questions."

We were both so disappointed. I tried to tell him it was okay with my eyes. He wasn't really crying, more like when your eyes get wet if you sneeze hard. He smiled at me kinda sad. I didn't know what to do to make him feel better, so I held his hand for a few seconds and then put it back on my dick. I got my first hand job that night. Marc jacked us both off and he didn't seem at all unhappy about it. I didn't mind either.

I sort of got head from a different guy a couple years later. It was my first year of college and I was still living with Mom. Dad had already moved out. She'd just won her Senate seat and was in a good mood all the time. It didn't matter much because she was never home. I was in a study group, and one night afterward, this guy stayed behind. We hung out for a while. With him, there was no kissing at all. I had gotten up to go to the bathroom. We had five bathrooms, but when I came out, he was standing there, like he was waiting in line. At first, I didn't get it. I couldn't even remember his name. He smiled at me kind of like I had smiled at Marc. Then I got it. He literally just got on his knees in front of me right there in the hallway and undid my belt and my zipper. I was excited to try getting head again. He put his fingers under the elastic on my underwear and my dick just popped up. And out. It had barely gone in the dude's mouth when we heard the garage door opening. My mother had come home early and that was that.

A girl gave me a blowjob my senior year and I wasn't sure it was much better than with Marc. It felt good when my dick was in her mouth. She choked a little bit, too. I had seen porn by then, though, and I knew it wasn't supposed to go in all at once, at least not right away. This girl went right to it, like Marc, but she gagged a little less. The whole time she was down there, I found myself thinking about Marc. I knew that wasn't how it was supposed to go, so for a while I thought I might be gay.

Marc went to college in Chicago and didn't come home for Christmas. At first, we talked a little, but then nothing. I saw him the summer after our first year of college. He was only home for a couple of weeks. We hung out a couple of times, but he had a boyfriend in Chicago who he missed a lot. I thought about talking to him about being gay, but the timing just never seemed right and besides I wasn't even sure I was gay.

"Jannie, you're driving too slowly." I heard my grandmother say.

"I'm driving the speed limit," my aunt barked back.

97

"I'm not certain your speedometer works. Foreign cars. How do you even know?"

"Honestly Moira, when was the last time you drove a car?"

"What's that have to do with it?" Grandma asked. My aunt took the corner on a yellow light, actually going ten miles an hour over the speed limit.

I knew Grandma wasn't perfect. She was funny, but Paddy and Jannie, my aunt Joey, and especially my mom, never laughed. This lady had lost her husband and her daughter in the same year, just last year. She missed Stephen when he lived in California. Mostly she was sad. She told me that some days it just felt easier to let everyone do everything for her, because if she did it, it'd be wrong, anyway. If she let them do everything, she could sleep in. I loved my grandma. There was nothing I'd be surprised to hear her say. She had no filter. When she told Stephen she'd known about him and Liam, that was so *her*.

"Shall we just leap out of the car, dear; or are you planning on coming to a complete stop?"

"Moira, sometimes I think you're just trying to impress the kids," Jannie declared.

"That could be it. It's not like I'd exactly have my work cut out for me."

"Joey's going to come by tomorrow and take you shopping." I didn't think Jannie even listened to her.

"Got it." Jannie pulled up in front of the house, and did come to a complete stop. "Thank you for the ride. Dale Earnhardt has nothing on you, dear."

Jannie had already opened her own car door and stepped out of the car. "Let me help you."

"I've got it," I said. I'd been sitting behind my aunt and was out of the car already. I opened my grandma's door for her and offered her a hand. Instead of taking it, she handed me her purse. I'd been there before. The thing weighed a ton. I wasn't surprised she couldn't lift herself *and* the bag. The car sat low to the ground; still she refused to take my hand.

98

"Thank you, Kevin," she said, and got out on her own. She straightened herself up holding on to the passenger door, turned to me, and reached for her purse.

"Look at that," Jannie exclaimed. My grandmother just rolled her eyes. After they seemed to go all the way back in her head, she winked at me and looked at Jannie on the other side of the car.

"Thank you, again. Kevin can help me in. Slow down on your way home. You don't want to get a speeding ticket, dear."

"Goodnight then, you two," Jannie said. "Do you have your keys?"

"I do." She moved around the front of the car with me right behind her. "Thank goodness I thought to turn on the front light." She was speaking to me this time. At the top of the steps, she turned to wave to her daughter-in-law. As Jannie pulled away, my grandmother raised her middle finger in the direction of my aunt's car.

I was packing some of my stuff in a duffle bag when my grandma appeared in the doorway. She had on pants from a Nike tracksuit and a man's V-neck undershirt. I liked the way she dressed when it was just her at home, like she forgot how old she was. She was barefoot and her toenails were painted dark pink like her fingernails. Her hair was pair pulled back a little and she was holding two beers. She came into the room, sat on the edge of the bed where I had been sleeping before I went to California, and handed me one of the beers.

"Number twenty-four," she joked, opening hers, and we both laughed. "I've never been certain why some of my children are so concerned with what I drink. Or how much. At any rate, I found these in the refrigerator and thought we might carry on."

"Thanks, Grandma." She was really cool. I'd probably have just stayed with her, but I knew it would eventually cause problems for her with my mother.

"Don't be sad, my love," she told me. "Your mother will figure her crap out one day. She's had a stick up her ass for I don't know how long, but I have a feeling it's about to slide right out."

99

"Gross," I said, but then I laughed.

"Not my greatest metaphor, I know." She took a long sip of beer and winked at me. "You know, this stuff is not half bad. I used to have one every once in a while with your grandfather. It's surprising how different something tastes when you're not expected to drink it.

"Stephen's going to be good for all of us," she said after a minute of us just sitting there. "Your mother is going to have to figure out what her problem is. Everyone's angry, but in my experience, anger is usually just covering hurt. It's harder to tell someone they hurt you than it is to be mad at them."

"Who hurt her, though?" I asked.

"I don't know, and honestly it's not really our business unless she wants to say. The important thing is that she figures it out and deals with it. Life is too fucking short to be feeling shitty all the time."

"You don't, do you?"

"I have my moments. Everybody does. No one can be happy all the time. Sometimes I think I should be sadder. I think my children expect that. Your grandfather and your aunt wouldn't have wanted it to cripple me, but that's not my point."

"Who would want you to be sad?" I asked her.

"You'd be surprised. People have an idea of how everyone around them should be, because it makes sense to them. That doesn't mean it makes sense to the people they love. We all made that mistake with Stephen. You know it kills me to admit this, but Jannie was right about that. She said we should be ashamed of ourselves."

"What do you mean?"

"I'm just rambling," she admitted. "You're going to be happy with them. Stephen has a bigger heart than almost anyone I know. When you look at him what do you see?"

"I don't know. That he's sad."

100

"Sure he is," she explained. "Look what he's been through. He's a little lost and, you're right: sad, but he doesn't strike me as angry. My son has so much love in his heart. When he figures out how to love that boy... well he has to figure that out, and he will."

We sat there in silence for a few minutes. I thought I knew what she meant. Stephen didn't seem angry, ever. I didn't know what had happened before he had moved away, but the way my grandma talked, people, probably my mother especially, weren't very nice to him.

"My point is this," she started. "And then I'm going to have you run down those damn stairs and fetch me another beer. No more for you. You've got to drive back across town. My point is that even though you're not gay, you and Stephen have a lot in common."

I couldn't believe she'd just said that. I kind of figured some of them wondered just like my mother.

"I know your mother thinks that you are. We've talked about it. Some of the others probably think so, too. That friend you used to be bring around, but it was more than that. You're sensitive and you've always been drawn to people like yourself—girls, and that boy, and your uncle. I think you living with Stephen and Caden for a little while is going to be good for all of you. You all need each other."

I couldn't come up with a response, so I just smiled, and she smiled back. We sat there, not talking. Then I remembered she'd wanted me to go get her another beer. "They're in the fridge in the garage?"

"That they are. Thank you."

When I got back a couple minutes later, Grandma had folded some clothes and was forcing them in a second duffle bag. I handed her the beer, a little winded from taking the steps two at a time.

"You'd better get going," she said, taking the can from me. "Do you have everything you need?"

"I think so."

"You know I don't go anywhere. You come by anytime to get the rest of this. Bring Caden with you to help."

101

"Thank you, Grandma."

"Now don't." She shushed me. She took some money out of her pocket and pressed it into my hand. "Just between you and me, alright?" I guess I looked like I was going to cry, because she shooed me back.

"You're awesome, Grandma." My voice trembled a little when I spoke.

"You're not so bad yourself, handsome. Now get out of here. Stephen's probably wondering what I've done with you. I'll see you soon."

"Are you coming downstairs?"

"I'll have to so I can lock the door behind you, but I'm going to sit for another minute."

"Okay, but don't forget to come lock the door," I told her.

"Thanks, love, I won't."

Before I left, I figured out that I could bolt the front door and lock the handle on the back door if I left that way. I'd have to walk around the house, but I'd be sure both doors were locked, if not bolted. By the time I got to the backdoor; I heard the floor creak and knew Grandma had gotten up from the bed. *It must be lonely to live all by yourself in such a big house*, I thought. It was lonely sometimes to live alone in a small apartment. I drove almost halfway to my uncle's before I turned the car radio on. Sometimes it's nice to think in the quiet.

Chapter 11
JOANNA

It was such a beautiful night, early enough in summer that the frogs were still mating and their calls could be deafening. Still, there was beauty in it. The humidity had risen twenty-five percent since morning. I'd had a couple of beers at my brother's, and despite my daughter's obvious disapproval, I stopped at the liquor store on our way home to pick up more. It seemed far more palatable than red wine in this heat. We had left ahead of everyone else and I wondered if it looked bad, considering we'd arrived last. While painting, Stephen had mentioned the series finale of Knots Landing and I suddenly remembered the final two episodes, unwatched, in my VCR. In fact, I'd normally enjoy my nightcap on the deck with a couple of cigarettes, but the central air I'd had installed last summer and Abby's return to the cul-de-sac had easily won out over the humidity; even with the amphibian mating call to sweeten to the deal.

First, a long shower sounded lovely. I wouldn't have to compete with my children for hot water or with the lateness of the morning for longevity. Meghan and Kelly had gone in the direction of their rooms. Once in mine, I shut the door, noticing the matching shoe to one I was holding in my hand. The shoe fiasco seemed further away than that morning. I reunited the shoe with its mate, one pair down, one to go. I figured the same thing wouldn't happen again. Then again, who was I kidding? There was still an odd man out. Dress out of my bag and hung up in the closet. I could wear jeans to school tomorrow. No kids! I quickly stripped off the old sweats and t-shirt I'd worn to paint, and removed the underwire torture device I'd worn since eight a.m.

Donning my fluffy robe, I headed across the hall to the bathroom, locking the door securely behind me. I had considered, at one point, installing a dead bolt on the door. Thankfully, adolescence had struck my children; leaving humility in its wake. Before the last year or two, I cannot tell you the number of times one or both of them barged in while I bathed. Even the flimsy lock on the door did not keep my son out when he had to pee.

"But Mom, I have to go!" he exclaimed.

"I'm in the bath, Kel. And the door is locked." I'd lie there and listen to him stomp down the hall and back; stick the Phillips screwdriver into the doorknob and jiggle it, then reach frantically to pull the shower curtain shut as he barged right in.

"What? Get over it, Mom! I said I had to pee."

Thankfully, those days were behind us. When Kelly wouldn't allow me in the changing room last summer when shopping for school clothes, I knew we'd finally turned that corner. Was I wrong, though, to miss helping him change into his pajamas; sitting on the edge of his bed with the Scooby Doo bedspread? Time passed so quickly, taking with it the usually comforting reliance of my kids on me. They never had that with Jim. Of course, Meghan was a girl and wasn't biologically his, but even Kelly deferred to me. He still did in matters of importance, like a missing shoe—little did he know—or a disagreement with his sister over TV privileges or time spent in the bathroom. I could hear him scream "Mom!" from almost anywhere in the house.

The warm water felt amazing washing over me. Not as hot and steamy as the air outside, but warm enough to rinse the day away. The last day of school had gone smoothly enough. A senior boy had tossed a freshman, fully clothed, into the shower. Since neither of them offered an explanation, I could only surmise it had been because it was his last chance to do so.

A sophomore girl had made the painful decision to give her unborn baby up for adoption. She had come to me at first for information on abortion. I had been vice-principal for two years, but before that, I was a guidance counselor. Therefore, I wasn't surprised when this student came to me, bypassing her male counselor. I was obligated by law to encourage her to talk to her parents, while providing her the information. The law didn't require my support or that I give her a shoulder to cry on as she agonized over confiding in her mother. That part I did anyway. The girl was in Meghan's grade, though I didn't think they knew each other well. I did know that fifteen-year-old girls had sex. She wasn't the first girl her age to come to me.

I'd known I would have to have "The talk" with Meghan by the time she was thirteen, and I had. That went about as well as you'd expect. It was as mutually cringe-worthy as a root canal. I'd had insisted she could come to me for birth control when she was ready and made her promise to do so. After a discussion about a friend of hers whose name she refused to give—it has to be tough having a parent as your principal—I was certain my daughter had not had sex. In fact, I was pretty sure she still hadn't. I reminded myself that a refresher might be in order as my daughter had started hanging out with a seventeen-year-old boy. His name was Mickey and he went to private school,

104

so I knew as much about him as a sixteen-year-old girl was apt to confide in her mother. I did know his real name was Michael, that he played football and excelled in parental snow jobs. This kid was so polite the one time I met him; I was immediately suspicious. I hadn't had the talk with Kelly yet. I knew his father wouldn't and it was overdue. I took comfort in the fact that Kelly was far more innocent than his sister.

I had been a single parent long before my divorce. Jim's father was an alcoholic and had drunk himself to death five years ago. Prior to that, there had been years of physical and emotional abuse of his wife and children. Some people would have turned away from drinking after witnessing that, but alcoholism was so engrained in his DNA, Jim was incapable of not going down the same path. My ex had three brothers and a sister; two of his brothers were worse off than he was. One was in prison. His mother and sister were co-dependent and chose to bury their heads in the sand.

Jim had one DUI. Surprisingly, that came late in the dissolution of our marriage. That Kelly had been in the car with him when it happened had pretty much clinched it. I'm sure he felt every bit as horrible about that as I did, but he continued to drink. He now lived with his mother. I had made it clear he'd not see his son again if he drove drunk with Kelly in the car one more time. Not surprisingly, it was Jim's mother who brought Kelly home at least half the weekends he spent with his dad. I would never force Meghan to spend time with her stepfather. That was her choice. Jim seemed less inclined to invite her anymore. In the beginning, I felt safer knowing she was with them. Finally, I'd had a talk with Kelly about how bad a decision it was to get in the car with a driver who'd had more than two drinks. That's likely the reason I said "no" to a third beer at my brother's earlier. I knew three beers would not leave me unable to drive, but I had to practice what I preached. I knew Meghan was disgusted enough by Jim's drinking to confuse casual consumption with alcoholism, hence her disapproval. I imagine she can't see why I would drink at all when I'd had a front row seat for my husband's descent into alcoholism. I also frequently judged my mother for her lack of restraint. I had attempted to broach the topic more than once with Meghan, and I honestly believed she got it. Her jabs were intended to wound me and alcohol was the easiest means to that end.

Standing in the shower, thinking about my children, I suddenly remembered Meghan's doctor appointment this week. It was on my calendar at school, but I'd have to double check. It might have been earlier that day, which meant we'd missed it. Feeling like I was failing as a mother was a luxury I'd decided I could not afford. I knew I was doing the best I could. My children were fed and clothed, and I made absolutely certain they knew they were loved. I grew up in a household where "I love you" wasn't said often. We were taught to assume such things, and it was taken for granted that the lesson was learned. I told Meghan and Kelly almost daily, how proud I was of them and how much I loved each of them. Hugs weren't accepted by them, but I tried them anyway. I set boundaries. I'd seen too many other parents shut down and do nothing; assuming they were failing anyway. Still, I allowed myself five whole minutes of guilt over forgetting my kid's doctor's appointment as I rushed through the last half of my shower. The hot water would be dwindling soon, anyway.

Out of the shower, I barely dried myself off; my wet hair wrapped in a towel as I moved into my bedroom, searching for my school bag. Not there. I found it on a chair in the kitchen. Searching quickly, I located my date book, frantically turning pages until I found the entry: Thursday, June 3 at nine-fifteen a.m. I breathed a sigh of relief knowing we had not missed it. Sometimes just pushing through the day was enough to make you forget half of it.

I towel dried my hair, leaving the towel on the kitchen counter, and went out for one last cigarette. I knew once I went back upstairs, I wouldn't feel like coming down until morning. It occurred to me that the morning would be slightly easier with no kids up. It wasn't likely either of them would wake up before ten or eleven, let alone the scant minutes before seven-thirty I would drag myself out of bed. I found Meghan sitting on the top step to the deck, cordless phone in hand. She hadn't noticed the back door open, so I announced myself. "Sorry love, smoking section is mine."

"It's okay, Mom. Just saying goodnight," she replied. I sat on a bench and ran my fingers through my damp hair. Meghan was still talking, I assumed to Mickey. "It's okay. I'll see you tomorrow. Anyway, I have to go, my mom's here.

"No really, I gotta bounce." A small giggle. Yes, definitely Mickey. "Yeah that. Good night. Okay. Me, too."

"Mickey?" I asked, when she finally hung up the phone. She smiled back at me. I guessed there was my answer.

"Stephen's cool, right?" It was less a question than her attempt to change the subject. I decided to let her have it.

106

"It was alright," I answered. "We don't all need to leap on that bandwagon at once. Is that sufficient enough reason for me not to gush?"

"I guess," Meghan said. "I'm not even sure what that means. Kev said Grandma's missed him, that's all."

"I understand, and I'll get over it. It's just stupid stuff, Stephen and I will figure it out. You'll be sick of the love-fest in no time."

She'd gotten up from the step and I realized she'd worn the same outfit almost all day. She still had the REO Speedwagon t-shirt on, but she'd traded the skirt for a pair of tighter cut-off sweats. Her long brown hair was still up in a ponytail, which started about an inch below the top of her head and ended nearly halfway down her back. Even when it was more practical for her to cut it for cross-country, she refused. Meghan hadn't had more than a trim since she was twelve. Our hair was the same color, and she wore it almost exactly as I had in high school. I secretly wished I could've worn makeup in high school like she did.

"Whatever you say," she told me. "I'm gonna go to bed now before you decide to make this a thing."

"Your doctor's appointment is on Thursday. Don't forget." What a hypocrite. "At nine-fifteen."

"That's so stupid!"

"Maybe, but it's my prerogative to worry about you. Therefore, you're basically screwed in this case."

"Fine," she sighed. "Am I excused?"

"Why does it seem like you always go to bed angry with me?" Oh my God. Except for the slurring, I now sounded just like my ex-husband.

"I'm a teenager, Mother. You have to wait another five years or so until we're really friends again."

"I'll mark it on my calendar. Thank you for helping tonight. I love you."

"Love you, too," she mumbled. I'd learned to take the crumbs. The screen door shut behind her.

107

"Other door, please," I called out. "The air conditioning is on." It was no use. I'd finished my cigarette anyway.

I wondered when my daughter would stop fighting these appointments. She'd have them the rest of her life. It went with the female territory. Had I fought my mother over going to the gynecologist as a teenager? The cordless lay on the counter, less than three feet from the charger, when I went back in the house. *Teenagers!* I turned off the back deck lights, and even though I was a third of the way through my beer; I put the phone on its charger, grabbed another, and headed upstairs.

Chapter 12
STEPHEN

I had sat straight up in bed more than two hours before, confused by my surroundings, and couldn't get back to sleep. After thirty minutes of tossing and turning, I gave in and got up. It served as another example of how frequently I had to remind myself of time and space lately. Six a.m. Thursday. New house. Definitely not in Kansas anymore. Not even in San Francisco anymore. I didn't even have my very own feline version of Toto. Meg had started sleeping with Kevin down the hall. It seemed as if we had gone way past her just being pissed off about the two-day car ride. Now I was afraid she simply preferred my nephew to me. There was too much of that going on for my taste. It'd been a day and a half since Caden had done more than grunted one syllable answers in my general direction, and those were only when questioned directly. He'd spent most of the prior day in his room with the door shut, listening to music. I had no idea what to do, but at some point; I was going to have to formulate a plan.

It was eight o'clock now, and I'd been working in the kitchen for over an hour. It was just too early to start painting again. We'd actually made a lot of progress already. I was pleased with what Kev and I had accomplished in two days. We'd hardly seen Charlie since the night everyone was over painting. I had to remind myself sometimes that Paddy had other customers. His business was mostly landscaping in the summer and snow removal in the winter, with some remodeling thrown in. He was busy, that was for sure. In fact, he'd mentioned that he asked Caden if he wanted to mow some lawns with Charlie until school started. Apparently, Caden had looked at him like he was crazy. Truth be told, Alec had never been big on his son doing any more than the simplest chores around the house, load the dishwasher; take out the garbage, etcetera. We'd barely had any landscaping in the first place. The amount of lawn we'd had could be mown in ten minutes, but we had hired someone to do that. I could never suggest a change, of course, because I wasn't about to do it. My days of mowing lawns had ended when I left Minnesota. Truthfully, I'd have looked at my brother the same way had he invited *me* to mow lawns for money. Still, I thought, it might be good to re-evaluate Caden's responsibilities since we were starting over. First, I assumed it would be a good way to get us back to the point where we were communicating with one another in full sentences.

109

So far that morning, I had washed, dried and put away all of our dishes from San Francisco. I had to do something about the awful appliances, but Paddy had reminded me that meant figuring out the countertops and cupboards first to see what would fit where. All I knew at that point was that everything would be new, but it would have to wait a few weeks, due to Paddy's prior commitments.

I had started on the pots and pans, which didn't need to be washed. As soon as I saw the box marked POTS & PANS & KITCHEN ODDS & ENDS, I knew it. *Aha, you motherfucker*, I thought slicing the tape and opening the top. The very first thing I saw was the elusive cordless phone. We would certainly need more than one, anyway. I didn't have a clue where the phone I'd bought two days ago had ended up. I assumed Kevin had it with him upstairs. There was certainly no one Caden would have called.

I was curious to see what other treasures qualified as KITCHEN ODDS & ENDS, so I removed items one by one, finding only two actual pans. It wasn't long until I was lost in thought again. Leading up to the move, I had figured that I could turn to Joanna for advice on parenting teenagers. She'd seemed distant on Tuesday, and I had meant to ask Paddy if there was anything I should know. The idea got lost amongst paintbrushes and ladders; boxes and shopping lists; and one abnormally silent fourteen-year-old boy.

I had a colander in my hand and was wondering if it would be weird to add, "Ask Paddy about Joanna" to my *To Do* list. I made a couple of quick notations on a pad of paper on the counter. In addition to speaking to my brother, I kept forgetting to find a doctor. I needed to do that ASAP, as I had only one refill remaining on my HIV medications.

It would likely be another hour or more before there was any movement upstairs. Both boys were sound asleep the last time I was up there. Caden, of course, with his door shut. Both cats had been asleep with Kevin when I came downstairs. Once the basement bedroom was finished, I'd either buy Kevin a new bed, or move the one in which he now slept downstairs. I had discovered yesterday that Kev had left his futon behind when he was unable to pay his rent, having had no way to move it. We were both certain his mother's security deposit had paid for its disposal.

"Did you leave anything else behind?" I had asked him.

"A dresser and a desk, but that's about it," he replied. "Nothing I cared about."

110

"I want you to start thinking like we're family."

"We are family, *Uncle* Stephen, but that doesn't really mean much."

"I don't suppose it does," I sighed. "My brother and sisters and I were raised to—have each other's backs. I'm not sure what happened with your mom, but Kev, I really believe that Paddy and Joey would help if you asked. I know they would. Your grandmother, too."

"I know that much," he told me. "She gave me money Tuesday night, and told me not to tell anyone."

"Not so familiar with that concept?" He looked at me, confused. No one got my sense of humor. "How much did she give you?"

"Fifty dollars," he answered.

"That's very generous. See what I mean?"

"I guess," he answered.

"You have to ask for what you need. People who love you will try to pay attention, but they won't always succeed. It's up to you to let us know if you need something."

"It's… I, um… I'm not sure."

"Did you ever have trouble asking your mom for anything?" He looked at me like I'd just asked the dumbest question ever. "Alright, bad example." We'd both laughed.

"Really, though, that's not entirely true. Your mom paid your rent. You went to her house to do laundry. Grandma told me your mother was better stocked than a grocery store, unusual for someone who was never home. You used to go there instead of the store. Right?"

"Yes," he answered, dejected.

"It's not a bad thing. That's what I'm saying. Parents do these things for their kids. That's why your grandmother gave you money, because that was the best she could do."

111

"I get it," he replied. "But with my mom, I didn't have to ask for anything. I just took stuff."

"I get that you're not used to having to ask. That makes sense."

"See? Maybe if I asked my mom for more stuff, hadn't just taken it; I would know how to ask other people for things, for help." He understood more than I thought.

"Yes. That's almost exactly what I mean." Our conversation was going much better than any I had had with Caden recently. "Would you like to stay here; with us, I mean; indefinitely?"

"Seriously?"

"Of course," I replied.

"I would love that," he said.

"Then I have an idea," I confided to him. "I was thinking about making the bedroom and bathroom downstairs a priority, so you could live down there. You'd have more privacy, and could come and go as you pleased."

"That would be awesome," he answered. "What about my mom?"

"I don't think she'd want to move in, but she's welcome, of course." I joked, though I knew what he meant. He smiled. I continued, "Let's take your mom one day at a time, alright?"

"Deal," he said, still smiling.

I had finished the ODDS & ENDS box, and was cutting the tape on the bottom of it when I heard footsteps on the stairs. Expecting Kevin, I turned around and was shocked to see Caden.

"Good morning," I said, a sucker for punishment.

"Good morning," he replied, with no hint of a grunt. He was fully dressed, wearing jeans, an old t-shirt, even his old tennis shoes. I must have looked utterly confused, because before I could speak, he informed me; "I'm going to work." He actually smiled at me, so I smiled back, trying desperately to think of something to say.

"Alright," I managed. "Would you like some breakfast first?"

"I don't really have time," he replied.

"Oh?" I asked, hoping he would elaborate. It took him a few seconds, but he finally did.

"I called Uncle Patrick last night. Remember he told me I could work for him this summer?"

"Yep." We seemed to have switched places, me uttering the monosyllabic responses.

"Charlie's picking me up in five minutes." I checked the clock on the stove. It was eight-forty. "I told Patrick I didn't know how to mow grass, and he told me if he could teach you how; he could teach anyone." Caden laughed at that, and I couldn't help but laugh with him.

"Do you know how long you'll be working today? I should give you some money for breakfast and lunch, or just in case."

"That would be alright," he conceded.

"My wallet's upstairs," I told him, already heading to the stairs. "Don't go anywhere." On my way to my room, I couldn't help but think it was a great development, unexpected, of course, but so great. Back downstairs a minute later, I was careful to check my enormous grin before turning to Caden. I handed the money to him, and said, "Here's twenty. You can offer to buy Charlie breakfast for picking you up."

"Awesome," he smiled. I couldn't believe that he was the same sullen kid who had hidden out in his room the whole previous day. There was a knock on the front door, and Caden shoved the bill in his jeans pocket, turning to go.

"Let me at least say hello to Charlie," I said, following him. He didn't argue, so I guessed he had no objections.

"Hey," Caden greeted Charlie, opening the front door.

"Hey there," Charlie answered.

"Good morning."

"Good morning, Stephen. I guess you don't mind us taking the kid off your hands for a few hours."

"Not at all," I told him. "I think it's great. Any idea when he'll be home?"

"Maybe five hours or so. Paddy won't be long. He's going to meet us at the first house and show Caden the ropes, then head over here."

"Right," I said. "He told me he wouldn't be by until eleven or so."

"Sounds about right," he agreed.

"We better get going," Caden said, pushing past Charlie, heading down the steps. "I don't want to be late on my first day."

"I'll keep an eye on him," Charlie assured me. "He'll be fine."

"I can't tell you how great this is," I whispered to Charlie. Caden was already halfway to the truck.

Charlie and I exchanged smiles. His was sly, a little coy. I bet he made great tips serving drinks to gay men, because Charlie seemed to flirt with his smile, his eyes, even his body language. As he walked away, he brushed his long hair back and held it there, away from his face for a moment, before releasing it again. It fell everywhere; a mess of dark-blond curls. He looked back at me and said, "I'll bring him back later. Have a good morning."

He was at the end of the walk, and turned toward his truck. Before I realized it, I was looking at his ass. It was perfectly round and seemed tight, even in his not-so-tight jeans. I sighed, a little breathless. I was standing in the doorway, my eyes glued to this man's butt, when I heard Kevin's voice behind me.

"What's going on?" he asked.

"Caden's just left for work," I replied. I spun on my heel, shutting the door behind me. My nephew was standing in front of me, his hair a mess, wearing just a pair of shorts.

114

"What the hell!?" Kevin exclaimed. "Caden has a job?"

Chapter 13
JOANNA

Last summer was the first year that I hired Paddy to do our landscaping; mowing the lawn was the extent of what was required. They built a stone wall in front, and a flower bed near the big maple tree in back; things Jim had been saying that he would do for years. I hoped Kelly could take the reins, at least with the mowing; but my bookish and awkward son was about as likely to maneuver a lawnmower around as my sixty-four year old mother was. Anyway, it was nice to give Patrick the business. All told, he probably got a full day's work each week, just from our family. Even Catelyn hired him. They'd had a falling out over business a few years back, but she had hired him to install ground sprinklers and put in lilac trees.

My older brother worked very hard, six days a week. I had hooked him up with a few students to work part-time each summer for the last few years. But it was a relief when Jannie had found Charlie Carpenter, the brother of that boy Stephen was friends with in high school. Charlie worked almost full-time for Paddy. I think the two of them practically killed themselves working on Stephen's house. Some of the work wasn't even in their wheelhouse, but I'm sure the money Stephen paid for the rush job was equal to what Patrick made in an entire winter.

Truth be told, Paddy wasn't the world's greatest businessman. The personal setbacks he and Jannie had endured early in their marriage had taken their toll on him. They'd struggled to have a baby for years. Jannie had two miscarriages within the first three years, but it was the stillbirth of a son, five years ago; that nearly killed them. Jannie was devastated, and something in Paddy just broke. It had taken them two years to come back from that. Paddy drank way too much; there were two DUIs; he nearly lost his driver's license. Had our father not bailed them out, they would have filed bankruptcy as a result of the business being neglected.

He and Jannie separated for almost a year, and my then thirty-five year old brother moved back in with our parents. Twice the man my ex is, Patrick pulled himself out of the debris and despair and got sober. He campaigned to get his wife back, and then worked unceasingly to rebuild his business. To my knowledge, my brother and his wife had given up trying to have a baby. I'm not sure why adoption hadn't been an option for them, or if it had been

116

discussed. At any rate, they seemed good as new the past three years; any discussion of them having children went unheard by the family.

I was shocked when Caden had shown up with Charlie to do the mowing. At first, I didn't even recognize the boy. I had only seen him once a few days earlier, but Kelly certainly knew who he was. I had just gotten home from school, and was upstairs changing my clothes, when Charlie pulled up in the truck. BENNETT HOME & LAWN MAINTENANCE was emblazoned on either side. There wasn't that much to do for us, so Charlie usually came alone, but there was someone, not my brother, in the front seat with him.

I turned away from my window when I heard the door to Kelly's room open. He raced through the hall, down the stairs, and out the front door. My son did not race. There weren't more than one or two things in life that excited him enough to walk fast. I couldn't imagine anything short of a house fire had sent him outside in such a hurry. I pulled on a tank top and turned back to the window. There was no sign of Kelly, though he'd definitely gone out the front door. I strained to see who was with Charlie, and as soon as I placed Caden; I knew. I imagined my thirteen-year-old son had seen the boy right away, and after racing down the stairs; maybe stopped briefly at the door to appear casual; then stepped outside, acting surprised to see anyone there. He had talked nonstop about his new cousin for two days, until Meghan finally told him to shut up about him.

I left my room barefoot, shutting the door on my unmade bed. My bedroom door stayed shut most of the time these days, my lack of motivation hidden behind it. There was never enough time in a day and I'd stopped caring about stupid things like putting away laundry and making beds. It was awful on one hand, because try getting your son to make his bed when you didn't make yours. Single parenting was about picking your battles, and I chose ones I knew I had at least a fighting chance of winning. I was at the front door barely a minute after Kelly. Sure enough, my son was standing awkwardly on the step, gawking at the two boys unloading a lawnmower. He should have brought a prop, I thought, a book perhaps; like he had been planning to sit on the step and read. Barefoot as well, his hands empty, he appeared to have just randomly exited the house for no reason whatsoever. Standing beside him, I mussed his hair and asked, "Playing it cool, huh?"

"What, Mom?" He feigned ignorance.

"I thought at first that your father must have shown up. Up until earlier this week, no one else's arrival has ever inspired such enthusiasm."

117

"What does that even mean, Mother?" I was called "Mother" instead of "Mom," more frequently lately. When spoken by Kelly, the title sounded as if he were addressing someone other than me.

"Never mind, sweetheart. Your secret is safe with me," I told him. Charlie and Caden had wrestled the lawnmower and weed whacker onto the sidewalk, and were now headed towards us. "Be cool," I told Kelly.

"Good afternoon," Charlie said.

"Good afternoon," I echoed.

"Hey," Caden added.

"New employee?"

"It's his second day on the job and he's already running things," Charlie answered, to which Kelly laughed too loud, sounding uneasy. *So much for playing it cool,* I thought.

"Hey," Caden said, like throwing a bone to a dog. "What's up?"

"Oh, nothing," Kelly replied.

"You guys want something to drink?" I asked, rescuing my son. "Maybe Kelly can bring you pops or something. I have iced tea?"

"I'll take a soda please," Caden answered.

"That's right. You don't call them pops in California. Charlie, anything for you?"

"I'm just dropping Caden off," he answered. "I have an errand to run for Paddy, I'll be back in an hour. He'll be fine. But may I use your bathroom quick, before I head out?"

"Sure thing." Then to Caden I said, "Kelly will bring you a *soda.*"

A few minutes later, Kelly had brought his new best friend a pop, and I was in the kitchen considering ordering pizza again for dinner, when Charlie appeared.

118

"Thanks again," he said.

"No problem." I turned to face him. "It's nice that Caden can help out. You guys must be way behind with all the extra work at Stephen's. How's it coming?"

"Great," Charlie answered. "We're putting new walls in downstairs, and Paddy's putting in a new bathroom down there tomorrow."

My little brother had bought a house that easily had mine beat by 1500 square feet. He had four bedrooms and three-and-a-half bathrooms. Before he was finished, the whole interior, including the appliances, would all be brand new. My freezer desperately needed defrosting, and we didn't use the dishwasher anymore because it leaked. The hot water heater was older than my daughter, and we shared one bathroom. I shouldn't have been, but I guess I was jealous. Stephen, when he worked, was a schoolteacher. The increases in pay that I had received in the two years since I switched from guidance counselor to administration were paltry. I knew where Stephen's money came from, and I felt ashamed of myself for coveting what he and Caden had. But still, *three-and-a-half bathrooms*. For two guys. An entire minute must have passed; I suddenly realized Charlie was still standing there.

"I'm sorry," I told him. "I'm a little distracted today, well this week, okay; this year."

"No worries," he chuckled. There was something awkward about him standing there, grinning at me. He sensed it, too, because he said, "I suppose I should check on Caden and get going."

"Probably not a bad idea." I followed him as he walked to the front door. "If Kelly is in the way, I'd suggest threatening to put him to work. He'll clear out quickly."

"I'll give it a try. Thanks again."

I had reached the door just a few steps behind him. Standing there, I couldn't help but notice his butt as he walked away. His jeans weren't exactly tight, but they clung exquisitely around what appeared to be a perfectly proportioned, very round ass. I'd never given the boy much thought before. His long, dark-blonde hair fell in waves across his neck, and I recalled him forever playing with it. It was an enticing habit. I stood there watching him say goodbye to

119

Caden, lost in the moment far longer than was appropriate, before my son suddenly appeared behind me.

"What are you looking at?" Kelly asked.

"The lawn," I lied, changing the subject. "Where've you been?"

"I got a book to read on the deck," he answered. Aha, props. He was catching on. He turned and made his way through the house. I turned back the other way to take one last look at Charlie Carpenter's ass.

An hour or so later, I found Kelly reading right where he said he would be. Caden was mowing the back lawn. Charlie was right. The kid was a natural. As I stepped outside to have a cigarette, a car pulled up in the alley, and Meghan got out of the passenger seat. I had considered objecting to her riding around town with her newly licensed seventeen-year-old boyfriend, but I knew that in the grand scheme of things, riding in a car was small potatoes. Even if the car was driven by a teenage soccer player with blue eyes and manners I didn't quite trust. My career had taught me that two-thirds of all teenage boys were not polite. Of the third that were, half had ulterior motives. I suspected this boy did not give a crap whether I'd had a good day, though he'd ask when calling my daughter on the telephone. He also called me Mrs. McCullough, even after I had asked him to call me Joanna. Mrs. McCullough was my mother-in-law. I'd had to get used to being called "Mrs." at school, an occupational hazard. Outside of school, however, Meghan's friends, even those who went to Southwest, called me Joanna.

I couldn't help but sigh every single time I thought of my daughter dating. Ten years had gone by in the blink of an eye. In my mind, Meghan was in Girl Scouts, with pigtails and a pink backpack just last week. Our biggest dilemmas then were what bedtime stories to read, and what to be for Halloween. I stood on the deck and lit a cigarette, taking in the scene before me. Kelly's head was buried in his book; Caden also had his head down, focusing on the job at hand. Neither of them had noticed the car pull up. They hadn't noticed the door of the car slam behind Meghan over the noise of the mower. I exhaled, thinking it was odd Mr. Polite had not opened my daughter's door for her. I had witnessed him do so before, probably for my benefit.

Meghan wore a man's dress shirt with the sleeves cut off. It was so old, and had been washed so many times it was nearly opaque. The shirt itself wasn't

120

the problem; it was the fact that it was unbuttoned. Any attempt it made to conceal my sixteen-year-old's chest was negated by the navy blue bikini top she wore. I knew Meghan had breasts; I bought her bras. Still, the sight of them made me a little queasy. Her dark hair was pulled back in the standard ponytail. She wore denim cutoffs, not too tight. Perhaps because the bikini top was tight enough for the whole outfit. She was barefoot, carrying a tan denim backpack; a peace sign drawn in black Sharpie. It used to belong to my sister, Colleen. I hoped it held her shoes and a towel. I assumed her wardrobe choice was for swimming, not some slutty fashion statement. Either way, it would have caused a huge fight with her stepfather, had he still been around.

In spite of my ex, I thought I had taught my kids self-respect and the difference between right and wrong. I was, as a result, far less concerned with what they wore and how they treated others. My worries centered on their education, their grades, how I'd afford college. Whether Kelly would be an alcoholic like his father, or Meghan would be as unyielding through life as she was in adolescence. She had almost nothing to do anymore with the man who, for all of his faults, had loved and helped raise her like his own.

I had dated *her* father my junior and senior years in high school, and a year into college. My sophomore year, I stayed at the University of Minnesota and he transferred to the University of Illinois. We succeeded at the long distance thing for about a semester, but he ended it over Christmas break. After summer school, but before junior year, he was home for a couple of weeks. He was already engaged to a girl from Chicago. One night we got drunk and literally fell into bed together. I am surprised either of us could perform well enough for conception, but five weeks later; I was late. A drug store test confirmed the pregnancy. I had a ten-minute phone conversation with Meghan's father and informed him of the pregnancy. Our call was cut short when the fiancée returned home. I never heard back from him. He didn't come home for Christmas or at all the following summer, not that it would have made any difference. I finished the first semester of my junior year, and dropped out to have a baby. I met Jim before Meghan's first birthday and we were married before her second. He was the only father she ever knew, yet she wanted nothing to do with him. She never asked about her own father. The one time Kelly brought it up, her reply was, "Why would I ever want to have anything to do with him?"

Meghan crossed the un-mowed portion of lawn as Mickey sped off down the alley. Caden had his back to her, pushing the mower. When he turned the mower around to go in her direction, he looked up for a second and noticed her. He ran the mower into one of the huge flowerpots at the edge of the

121

deck, and it stalled. Once recovered, the mower started right back up and there was no damage to the flowerpot, just the boy's pride. I think I was the only one who noticed. Meghan didn't even realize who was pushing the mower.

I laughed to myself. It was cute, right? They weren't related, and *I* could barely contain my shock when presented with my daughter's breasts. How could I expect a teenage boy to not take notice? I knew as soon as Meghan reached the deck that something was wrong.

"Sweetheart," I said. Kelly looked up, oblivious, thinking I was talking to him.

"What?" Meghan asked, angrily.

"Are you alright?"

"Slammin'," she replied; and disappeared into the house.

"Nice chatting," I called, more to myself than her. Kelly had already returned to his book, apparently far less fascinated by Caden than he'd been a couple of hours ago. I sat across from him at the table.

"Are you okay?"

"You're asking me now?" He looked up again. I took a drag on my cigarette and nodded. "I'm fine. Caden said he had to work, or he wouldn't be done with the lawn when Charlie came back."

"He's a nice kid, huh?"

"He's okay, I guess."

I wondered what had happened, with both of my kids now. Kelly would come and talk to me later. He always did. I was more concerned about Meghan just then, so I finished my cigarette and leaned across the table to muss my son's hair. He anticipated the gesture, ducking to avoid my touch.

"Ha, missed me!" he exclaimed.

"There's always later." I turned to go back inside, then thought of something. "Hey, are you wearing sunscreen?"

122

"No," he replied. "You'll never guess."

"We're out?" I asked, not surprised. "Okay, I have an idea."

"Does your idea involve me going to the store with you?"

"And out to dinner, before. After all, it's a big mistake to go grocery shopping on an empty stomach." I was shamelessly bribing him, knowing he would request one of two places.

"Can we go to Perkins?" Not the one I was hoping for, but at least it was close to the store. I was debating calling my mother to see if she wanted to go tonight, but that would mean dinner, too, and I'd get far less of my own shopping done helping her.

"I suppose. Let me go see if your sister has plans or if she wants to tag along." From behind her bedroom door, I could hear Garth Brooks' *Ropin' the Wind* cassette playing. The last I knew, my cassette was in my car; I guess not anymore. "Rodeo," the second track, was playing as I knocked.

"May I come in?" I said to the door.

"Suit yourself," Meghan called back. I tried the handle, but it was locked. "Oops, sorry." I heard the floor creek as her bare feet hit it. A second later, the lock turned and she opened the door. "Help you?"

"Do you have dinner plans? You seemed upset a minute ago, everything okay?"

"Not anymore." Was all the explanation she offered.

"No plans? Your brother has chosen Perkins, as if that's a surprise, and then we're grocery shopping. Care to join us?"

"Not really," she said, flopping back down on her bed. "I'd rather be alone. I'm kind of pissed off right now."

"You and Mickey have a fight?" "Rodeo" had ended and "What She's Doing Now" had begun to play. Most people preferred "Shameless," but this melancholy tune was my favorite on the tape. "Is that my cassette?"

"It's my tape," she replied. "And I'm pretty sure we just broke up."

123

"Oh sweetheart, what makes you say that?" I sat at the foot of her bed and reached to touch Meghan's foot.

"He's a 'bama and only interested in one thing!" she exclaimed.

"I don't know what that means," I told her. The slang changed faster than some of the kids changed clothes. I could not keep up, even exposed to it every day. Kelly didn't use any, but Meghan lapsed into an entirely different language more and more these days.

"It means he's a red-neck dickhead." *Oh, that.*

"Did he do something?"

"Not really," she said. "It was really more what I didn't do; I mean wouldn't."

"Are you," I started to ask if she was all right, then realized what she'd said. "Wait, are you saying — ?"

"He wanted us to have sex and I wouldn't." She knew what I was going to ask. In that moment, I knew that I was an awful person and an even worse mother. I knew it because I was thrilled. My daughter had just broken up with her first boyfriend and underneath the angry facade, was probably really upset. How could I be happy about that? Maybe happy wasn't the right word. Relief, was it relief? My face was blank, thank God. I couldn't think of what to say, so I just caressed my baby's dirty foot until she pulled her leg away.

"I get that you don't want to talk, and that you'd rather be alone, but I think maybe Kell and I will skip Perkins and shopping. Stick close to home, you know; in case you change your mind."

"Thanks, Mom," Meghan said. "But I'm really, I don't know; I'm okay. He doesn't get to decide this for me."

"What did you tell him?" I asked.

"You probably don't want to know."

"Try me."

"I told him to fuck off."

124

"Good for you!" I told her, and I meant it. Under most circumstances, I'd have been against the language, but I was proud in that instance. I was right; I had taught my daughter self-respect. I was proud; I hoped I was not beaming with it.

"Seriously?" she asked, confused, though she wore a half-smile.

"Why not?" I liked to keep them guessing.

"Don't look now, Mom; but you're kind of sounding like Grandma." The smile was bigger, self-satisfied.

"That's not the worst thing you've ever said to me."

"I'm okay, Mom. I swear. Go grocery shopping. You wouldn't believe how much stuff we need."

"Fine. If you're so all right, why don't you come with us? How can you pass up Perkins?" Now she was trying not to smile.

"Okay, fine! Can I take a shower first, and can we not talk about it anymore?"

"You may. And deal. No more talking. Not a word for the rest of the day. We will just let Kelly steer the conversation. I hope you're prepared to talk about *Star Trek* all night."

"And Caden," she added. "Don't forget about him."

"Did you even notice that was him mowing our lawn down there?" I asked.

"Nice. Maybe Kelly will decide he wants to do stuff around here."

"He does do stuff."

"I mean boy stuff," she added.

"He takes the garbage out," I told her.

"He can barely lift the can, Mother." She was right and, since he wasn't around, we both laughed about it.

125

"He is about due for a growth spurt," I said, still laughing. I was certain that my daughter was fine. Her fortitude astonished me and, in this situation, her stubbornness would serve her well. Maybe that was not such a bad thing, after all. "Okay, shower and meet us downstairs in forty-five minutes. Is that enough time?"

She nodded. I got up from the bed and she rolled off the other side, onto her feet. She walked around the bed, past me, to her dresser. I hadn't noticed, but my daughter was far more organized than I. No reason to keep her door shut, though she did, and perhaps that was why I never realized it. Her bed was made and all of her clothes were put away. The most clutter were shoes in a pile next to the closet. We had that in common.

"I'm going to hug you now. Deal with it." I moved two steps toward her, and she actually met me halfway. She smelled like coconut. I would have been all right holding onto her for far longer than the thirty seconds she allowed.

"Thanks, Mom," she said, grabbing things for her shower. "Can you get the door?"

"Forty-five minutes," I said, as I shut her bedroom door behind me. I hesitated in the hallway. If there was a way to stop time, just for a year or two, I wanted to know it. Time was going way too fast. Meghan would be gone before I knew it and after her, Kelly. Maybe I should get a dog?

There was something else nagging at me that I couldn't quite get a handle on. Sure, I was leery of my brother's return and what it would mean for all of us. I was shocked no one else was. I was angry, maybe just hurt; but that wasn't it, either. In fact, I was pretty sure I was holding onto that so that I didn't have to look at my other emotions. My little brother was going to get sick, and it would be awful. I didn't know what to do with that. I hadn't allowed the thought to cross my mind, not completely, not until just then. I allowed it for a second before going back downstairs to make a shopping list. I did not want to be standing awkwardly just outside Meghan's door when she came out. At the bottom of the stairs, I lingered for a moment and wondered if Stephen was afraid, too. He had to be.

126

Chapter 14
STEPHEN

Two weeks had gone by since Caden started working for my brother, and we'd been busy. The walls were up in the basement, and the painting was done everywhere but there and the kitchen. Kevin and I were ready to paint his new bedroom and bathroom so he could move down there, but first; a couple of days off were in order. It was Friday, June 18, 1993, and we were all a little bit fried. I personally didn't care if I ever saw another roll of masking tape or paintbrush again. With plans finally drawn up for the kitchen; new cupboards, countertops and appliances purchased; work there was going to start the following Monday.

I had grown up going to the antiquated zoo at Como Park, where lions and tigers paced sadly back and forth in tiny cages. According to Paddy, the modernized Como Zoo was an entirely different place, with hundreds of thousands of dollars in renovations having been made. There was a lot of that going around. There was a second zoo, in Apple Valley, which had opened the year I left Minnesota, so I'd never been. And there was Valley Fair, a Six Flags type amusement park. All were considerations as we planned our weekend activities.

I desperately wanted to get Caden excited about Minnesota, so I had solicited Kevin's help, and we planned a surprise attack on the fourteen-year-old. He was not working until Monday, and was; in fact, still dead to the world at 9:00 a.m. That was his norm before he'd started working.

Our conversations had become increasingly less monosyllabic over the last two weeks, but we were still just making small talk. Maybe that was normal, too. I didn't see the harm in just letting him be, as long as he didn't seem overly sullen or upset. The move was a huge change for both of us. I would probably be more concerned if no adjustment period had been necessary. Still, I wondered constantly if I was messing the kid up.

There was no handbook for how to parent when the other, *realer* parent, had died. I'd expected to be able to confide in Joanna, seek advice on raising teenagers from someone who had hands-on experience; but that situation was weird. I'd been out of her life for most of the last fifteen years; I didn't expect we'd be having sleepovers and braiding each other's hair any time soon, but she was distant. The temperature coming from her wasn't exactly

127

cold, but it was at least sweater weather. I'd asked Paddy what was up there, and he said he hadn't noticed her behaving any differently. Maybe she'd just changed. I'd had little interaction with my sister since we'd become adults.

She was twenty-three when I left, with a two- year-old daughter. Joanna had just married Jim and they had announced she was pregnant around the same time that I revealed I was moving to California. I had never met my nephew, but I saw Kelly once, when he was about a year old. The two times that I'd returned since, he and his father hadn't been around. I couldn't be sure if that was planned or if I was just being paranoid. I'd thought about inviting Kelly to go with us to the zoo or the amusement park, but it felt awkward. The only person in our little group he knew was Kevin. Maybe I would ask him to invite the boy. I was beginning to think that my younger sister had become more like the older one in the years I'd been gone; but surely she wouldn't object to her son hanging out with his two cousins.

That brought Catelyn to mind. I'd been back three weeks and I hadn't seen my big sister, except on the evening news. I didn't think Kevin had seen her, either. Was that odd? I wasn't sure what to think. One thing was certain; my family had changed and I had no idea what had happened. Maybe it was the passing of time, but the whole dynamic was skewed. I'd seen my mother a couple of times since our painting night, and I was going to see her again for lunch.

I planned to run a few errands in Uptown, and then pick up Chinese takeout for us both. It was to be my first solo trip more than a few blocks from home. One thing I didn't factor into the equation was how far away, on foot, certain things were. There was a lake smack dab in between Uptown and us; so short of swimming for it, I had to walk several blocks out of the way to get anywhere.

I thought more and more about learning to drive. I was thirty-three years old, for Christ's sake, and a parent! Wasn't it time? Since I had no idea how to operate a vehicle, never mind that I didn't own one, walking was my preferred mode of transport. I grabbed my Walkman, the Bon Jovi *Keep the Faith* CD, a notebook, and my canvas backpack and hit the road. I turned right from the front of the house and headed north toward Lake Calhoun. I had grown up here, so I knew right where to go. I had often been told that I had an excellent sense of direction, as well. At the corner, I dug out my headphones. Before I made it across the street, Jon was singing "I Believe" in my ears. By the time I had made it to the cemetery, my favorite track had begun.

Sitting here wasted and wounded at this old piano
Trying hard to capture the moment this morning I don't know

For a weekday morning, there were quite a few shirtless, sweaty joggers. Occasionally, I was tempted to turn back and see them from behind after they passed me. One unbelievably hot guy ran so close that I could smell his sweat and a faint whiff of his cologne. It had been ages since I'd taken in such an intoxicating mix of pheromones and virility. I didn't feel awkward or guilty breathing it in, it just felt good. I wondered if I'd ever have sex again. It was silly to think I wouldn't, but what would that even look like? I had been with Alec for more than ten years. Yes, I was still young, but two things loomed as heavily as the humidity. I didn't remember how to go about getting laid. And I was HIV positive.

As I crossed the street, I saw a bus. I was surprised public transportation hadn't occurred to me sooner. I had taken those same city busses in the eighties; and I was certainly adept at them then. I boarded the bus and took a seat near the front, so I could see where we were headed. I needed stamps, cigarettes, a pharmacy, and a bank. I wanted to reacquaint myself with Uptown and where things were, so I knew what I could accomplish on my own and what I'd need a ride for. I was tired of relying on Kevin or Paddy for rides. I planned to just wander around a bit and figure it out. It felt liberating to be on my own. Nothing desperately needed to be done; no decisions had to be made. I hadn't even set a specific time for lunch with my mother, so I wasn't in a big hurry. Within a couple of minutes of boarding, I was stepping off the bus to run into the drugstore to drop off my prescriptions.

An hour later, I had taken my notebook out and made notes a half-dozen times. I'd been to the bank and opened a checking account; taken note of the location of the library, a used bookstore, a high-end market, restaurants, and even a smoke shop where I bought a carton of cigarettes each for Kev and me. So much for quitting smoking for the time being. I was on my way back to the pharmacy to pick up my prescriptions.

I was made to wait ten minutes, while the head pharmacist checked the validity of my prescriptions. I wasn't sure why that hadn't been done while I'd been gone. After a bit, a grey-haired man with possibly the thickest glasses I'd ever seen appeared at the counter and called out my full name. It wasn't necessary; I was the only person within twenty feet of the counter. The pharmacist rudely insisted on seeing identification. Then, after a thorough examination, sniggered at the San Francisco address. It didn't take me long to figure out what his problem was, nor to decide then and there that I wouldn't be doing any further business with that particular pharmacy. The prescriptions, of course, were for HIV medications, which were stocked. Apparently, they were forgotten on a dusty shelf at the back of the store, because that asshole acted as if he'd never filled a single prescription for them before.

There was an issue with the insurance, snider questions and short, rude demands, and finally, nearly two hours after I'd dropped the prescriptions off, the pharmacist returned to the counter wearing gloves. He kept them on while passing back my insurance card and ID, taking my credit card, and *finally* placing five pill bottles into a white paper bag, pushing them at me from across the counter.

Nothing like that had ever happened in San Francisco and I wasn't prepared for the inevitability of it happening in Minneapolis. I was seething by the time I made my way out onto the street. Surely, there was some kind of directory or gay rag that advertised gay-friendly establishments in Minneapolis. I had no wish to repeat the encounter. I sat for a moment on a bus bench at the corner, feeling like the wind had been knocked out of me. I was digging through my bag for my notebook when my eyes welled up. *Fuck,* I thought. *Really, here on the street? Just fuck.*

Giving up on the notebook, I stuck the prescriptions in my backpack and lit a cigarette. I took several deep breaths, willing the tears away. I sat until I had finished my cigarette, missing San Francisco, Alec, our life, and wondering if I'd made a mistake moving back. I finally decided that the whole thing was ridiculous. It was 1993 and I was in Minneapolis, not some backwoods country town. I was going to write a letter to the drugstore chain's corporate office and complain. I had lived rather blissfully behind rose-colored glasses on the west coast for so long; I had forgotten there was a big, awful world out there full of stupid people. I had blindly run right out into it.

I stood up, determined not to let one asshole ruin my plans to explore. At the crosswalk, I took a deep breath and willed myself across the street. Once across, I met the eyes of a guy about Kev's age. He had short, dark hair, piercing green eyes and a tan, and as we passed each other he smiled at me. He had the most beautiful smile, I couldn't help but turn and look back; and when I did, our eyes met again. He was looking back at me, as well. Another smile and I turned to continue on my way.

I had gone two blocks; passed a salon, a couple of consignment shops, a hardware store, and some other shops when I saw a video store on the

130

corner. I hadn't thought to look for one of those, but decided to go in and check it out.

I pulled the door open and a bell jingled as I stepped inside. Past a cardboard display for *A League of Their Own* was a small counter, beyond which were four long rows of videos; arranged side by side, according to genre. A stereo somewhere played "What a Wonderful World" by Louis Armstrong. I wandered in, not looking for anything in particular. At the back of the store was a sign for New Releases, so I started in that direction. As the door closed behind me, the bell chimed again. I discovered there was no stereo after all; there was a television mounted to the wall and on it, the movie *Good Morning Vietnam* played.

I couldn't help but stop and stare at the screen, smiling. Alec and I had gone to the Kabuki Theater in San Francisco to see that the week it came out. It was certainly a happier time for us. Movies had been a huge part of our lives. It was easy to sneak in and out; sometimes to even hold hands in the darkened theater. It wasn't unusual for one or all of us to see one or two movies a week in the theater, and in addition, we rented more. I felt at home in a video store. The only other stores that inspired in me such childlike abandon were music or bookshops. I could spend hours in a video store searching for a hidden gem. After the green-eyed guy on the street with the generous smile and happening upon a video store, my entire outlook had quickly improved. I decided to find some movies to watch with the boys, in addition to our other weekend adventures. Turning back toward the New Release section, I heard a woman's voice.

"Can I help you?" someone said, behind me. I turned to see a heavyset woman of about fifty-five had appeared behind the counter. I realized then that there was another room behind her, probably an office or storeroom. "I'm so sorry. I was in back and I don't hear well."

"No problem," I assured her. "I'm really just looking."

"Well, you just let me know if I can look up anything for you, alright sweetheart," she said, climbing into a stool with some effort. She seemed arthritic, or perhaps older than I had first thought. Instead of forcing her from her perch, I went up to the counter to ask if she had *Dead Poet's Society*. In my hands already were *The Fisher King* and *Good Morning Vietnam*. In my estimation, Caden was certainly old enough to watch it.

131

The woman introduced herself as Betty. It took her several minutes to look up the movie, during which time she talked constantly. A few times she stopped searching to tell me about herself, her cats (she had three, all named after characters in her soap opera), even a granddaughter who lived with her. She didn't watch videos all that much, she preferred TV to movies, and magazines to books. When she finally did announce that *Dead Poet's Society* could be found in the comedy aisle, I had to ask what in the world she was doing owning a video store.

"Oh, I don't even know," she said. "My son and his friend owned it."

"Owned?" I asked. Her face hardened a bit at the question, and it seemed like she might not answer, but she plowed right on.

"I had two kids. My granddaughter is my daughter's. She was never really mother material, if you know what I mean. One day she dropped my granddaughter off for me to baby-sit. That was ten years ago and we haven't seen her since."

"Oh, I'm sorry!" I hadn't a clue what else to say.

"My son was gay, like you, sweetheart. He died in February." She waved her hand across the store, as if she were presenting me with a prize. "This, this place was his thing. He and his friend loved movies. I have no idea what I'm doing. My granddaughter is better at the computer, but she's only here some afternoons, after summer school. She'll be a senior at Southwest this fall, if she passes summer school. I used to help my son out here one or two nights a week. Now I run the place."

"I'm sorry to hear about your son," I told her. She certainly volunteered a lot of information, but she did so in a way that kind of drew you in. There was something about her, a warmth, or feeling of familiarity. Normally, I'd have been uncomfortable with the intimacy of the conversation, but not with Betty. "You said he owned the store with a friend?"

"His partner," she sighed. "He died last year. AIDS."

"I'm very sorry." I actually reached out my hand and patted hers.

"You're a doll," she said. "I knew I liked you the second you came up to the counter. A lot of guys like you come in here, but I don't remember you from before."

132

"I just moved back to town from San Francisco. My partner died last year, too." I really was shocked at how personal this conversation had become.

"Oh, shit," she said. "So many of you, such a tragedy. Thank God we're through with those dumb asses in the White House!" I smiled at her and moved to find the movie. The comedies were literally just behind us.

"Have you thought of selling the store?"

"Every day, but honestly I wouldn't know how that works. I have no head for this. I do know I don't want to wake up five years year from now and find I'm still hauling my hind end down the block, working sixty hours a week. I'm sixty-five years old. I retired two years ago." She snorted.

"You don't look it," I said, bending down to reach the bottom row. Aha, right where she said, but *Dead Poet's Society* was not a comedy. Tape in hand; I turned back to Betty.

"Bullshit, I don't!" she exclaimed, and laughed. "God, my mouth!"

"I like it," I said, without a hint of sarcasm. She reminded me of my mother.

"I'm not built for customer service. I was a maid at the Hotel Remington for twenty-five years, if you can believe it. Cleaning up after people is far more solitary than this. I almost never saw guests, and I worked alone, mostly. Oh, look at you, you found the movie!"

We talked for ten minutes while Betty typed my information into the computer one key at a time, stopping once or twice to swear. Thankfully, she could just scan the videos in and out, so at least that wasn't an ordeal. I told her a little bit about myself, how Caden and I had moved from San Francisco after his dad died. I rented four videos, some kind of Friday-to-Monday special, and when my transaction was complete, I was rewarded with a hug from my new friend. As I left, two guys were coming in. They greeted Betty warmly and I could hear her laughter until the door shut completely behind me. I had spent too long in the video store, so I decided exploring would have to wait until another day.

Minneapolis was not like San Francisco by any means, but I decided to try hailing a cab instead of walking to the Chinese restaurant and then to my mom's. During the cab ride, I couldn't stop thinking about the video store and that poor woman stuck there because, in her words; she just didn't know where to begin to sell it. The food was ready in about fifteen minutes. It was just five blocks to the home I had grown up in until I went to California. A short twenty minutes after I left Betty, I was on my way up Nicolet Avenue.

I wondered about my mother. I hadn't spent very much time alone with her since I'd been back, but she didn't seem as feeble or helpless as I'd been lead to believe. My sister-in-law considered anyone who drank daily to be an alcoholic, but I didn't think my mother had a drinking problem. Moira Bennett had raised five kids in the sixties and seventies. Growing up, I hardly remembered seeing my mother without a cigarette in one hand. Both of my parents drank daily, but rarely to excess. My father would have a beer when he got home from work, and two or three more after dinner. My mother would have a cocktail before dinner, and depending how quickly she fell asleep in front of the television, one or two after dinner. They drank more on the weekends, depending on what was going on. For years, my father gave up beer and cigars for Lent. In solidarity, my mother would have her before dinner cocktail before my dad got home from work, then wait until he'd gone off to bed before fixing herself another. Her idea of a Lenten sacrifice was to limit herself to two a night; doing everything she could to... not hide it from Dad exactly, as much as shield him from the temptation.

My father was a church-going Catholic. My mother converted when they married, but rarely went to church and wasn't about to sacrifice her drinking or smoking out of some silly observance. That said, I had friends whose parents I saw drunk from time to time; and mine were rarely, if ever, that way. It was a different time. If my mother was drinking more now, I believed she'd earned it. She had lost a husband and a daughter in less than a year. She lived alone, and as far as I could see, was treated like a burden by her daughters. As far as the helplessness, Moira didn't like to drive. She never had. My father had always done all of the driving. Her need for rides to grocery shop, to the doctor, or to get her hair done seemed to be the reason she'd been suddenly deemed feeble. I certainly couldn't criticize, and even if I could; I wouldn't. I tried to reserve judgment until I got to interact with her more, one on one.

I raised my fist to knock on the door of the place I once called home, but my mother opened it before I got the chance. Moira Bennett had a lit cigarette in her left hand. Her grey hair was pulled back in a clip, but loose pieces fell about her weathered face. She wore tracksuit pants and a lightweight sweatshirt that didn't match. Her feet were bare, her toenails painted red.

134

"Come in! Come in!" she demanded, like if I didn't get off the street immediately, I'd be shot. As soon as I was inside, she shut the door, bolted it, and put the chain on. Perhaps we were under siege. "It smells wonderful," she said, walking away from me, into the house. I breathed in and realized she was right. It smelled divine. I followed my mother, just then hoping she'd offer me alcohol soon.

"I thought vodka lemonade," she called, too loudly. I was now right behind her, crossing into the kitchen. "I have raspberry lemonade if you prefer."

I loved my mother. It really went far beyond our mutual affinity for alcohol. It was funny how I had trained myself to forget my love for her in San Francisco. Moira was, at times, volatile. I had come to believe that she was perhaps bipolar, but that was long after I'd left home. She was also fun, an amazing hostess, organized, creative. I put the Chinese food on the kitchen counter, threw my backpack next to it, and I gave my mother a hug. It was stiff for just a beat and then she relaxed into it. My mom could hug. That close to her, I smelled lilacs, tobacco, and aerosol hairspray. The embrace lasted longer than either of us expected. I'm not sure either of us wanted to be the first to let go. After half a minute or so, I finally did. "Raspberry lemonade sounds great, Mom."

"Without the vodka?" she asked, incredulously.

"Of course not," I answered. She had a look of relief on her face, as if she had expected me to hassle her like everyone else did.

"That's my boy," she said, almost proudly.

"Not too strong, mom," I told her. "I'm not a big vodka drinker."

She fixed our drinks and brought out plates, we dished up Kung Pao Chicken over white rice and Chicken and Onions in Black Bean Sauce over crispy fried noodles. We retired to the dining room, where we sat at the far end of a table that used to seat all of us.

No matter what we were doing growing up, regardless of any sports or extracurricular activities my siblings and I were involved in; we had dinner together as a family on Sundays. We'd have dinner nightly, of course, but often times not everyone was there. It got so that, in the last year I lived at home, my parents and I would eat dinner on TV trays in the family room. Not on Sundays, though. On Sundays, the whole family would eat dinner, well lunch, due to the earlier hour; every one of us around the table. It made me happy, because it made my mom happy; and I truly loved my family.

That was before I realized that the people you count on the most for unconditional support can let you down. It was before I realized that love, even within a family, isn't always given freely. In my family, it was seldom given without reservation. I left Minnesota because I couldn't bear knowing all their misgivings; I took off at almost the first sign of them. I tried to be someone else, and when that failed, and I saw the reactions of those I loved the most, I decided to go away. I hoped someone would object. I would still go to California, but it hurt when it seemed as if my entire family agreed that we'd all be better off for it.

It wasn't uncomfortable sitting there; just my mother and me, eating where we had eaten hundreds, even thousands of meals. It was familiar, almost easy. Suddenly, I was thinking of all the meals I hadn't had there, everything I missed when I was away.

"You think too much." My mother was saying. She was probably right, I had no idea how long I'd been in my head, a fork in my hand, not eating.

"What do you mean?" I asked, taking a bite, pretending I'd been present all along.

"When you get to be in my position, alone almost all the time, you start to appreciate not thinking. It's a luxury, not being stuck with only your thoughts to keep you company," she said.

"You don't have to be alone all the time," I told her.

"Oh, now; I'm not complaining. It is what it is. I just meant that it's nice not to think, but you think all the time. Surrounded by people and you're somewhere else."

"It's that obvious?"

"I don't know if it's obvious all the time or to that many people."

"My brain won't shut up," I explained.

136

"I get that. I sometimes tell mine, 'Thanks for sharing, but it's time for you to shut the fuck up.' I know I shock all of you. I get it. I wasn't Catholic when I married your father. He was an altar boy, well you know that from when you were one, but your father was an altar boy literally and figuratively. He never swore. I think it feels good to swear, but for forty years I didn't because it made him uncomfortable. It felt so good to say 'Fuck' after he died. There are a lot of things you do in a marriage, pieces of yourself you trade away, and you don't always realize that's what you're doing."

"I see that," I said. "I may not have been legally married, but—."

"I didn't mean to imply you couldn't relate. I'm just talking. What I was getting at, is that your sisters see how I am now and they compare it to how I was before your father died. That's an unfair comparison. I'm not a married woman anymore; I can be who I want to be; just me, no one else's feelings to consider."

I took a sip of my drink. It was still almost full and my mother had made it about half as strong as hers. Meanwhile, she was nearly ready for a refill. She continued as if my attention to my drink had reminded her of something.

"It's true. I drink more now than I did when your father was alive. It doesn't mean I drink too much. I happen to think I drink just the right amount. Between you and me, I think Jannie is just pissed off that she can't drink as much because Paddy's sober. Caty is embarrassed by everything, especially her family. Joey is the only one of the three I cut any slack."

"Joanna's different, Mom."

"We're all different, Stephen." She had finished her drink.

"She seems distant, kind of cold."

"I think she's just tentative. Your sister has lost so much in the last two years," Mom explained.

"So have you."

"I lost a husband and a daughter," she continued. "Joanna lost a husband, then a father, and then; in Colleen, she lost her sister and her best friend. And she has two kids to raise. You know what that's like. You get no time off to grieve. The sun just keeps fucking coming up."

137

"I never thought of it like that." I was getting used to the F-word peppering every other sentence.

"I didn't imagine you had. When your sister died, it's like she took some of Joey with her. She'd been so strong up until then. After your dad died, the thing we all held onto was that Colleen had beat cancer." My mother stood up with little effort, but once on her feet, she moved slowly, like she had to will herself forward. "I'm going to have another drink. Would you like me to add some more lemonade to yours, dear?"

"I don't drink when I'm eating," I explained. "Don't worry, Mother, I'll catch up."

"Did you and Alec drink much?" she called from the kitchen. I realized, quite suddenly, that my mother had never asked about Alec before. She was the first person since I'd been back; except for Caden, to bring him up. It meant something to me I couldn't explain.

"Once upon a time, we did. I carried the torch after he got sick."

"You have a funny way of putting things. You always have. I remember, at one time, you talked about writing. Whatever came of that?" I could hear her tossing ice cubes into her glass. She hadn't finished her lunch. Really, she hadn't eaten half of it.

"I did some in college. I haven't written in years, though."

"Mightn't you get back into that with all your free time? You're not going to teach this year, and Caden will be in school. What are you going to do with yourself?" She appeared around the corner with another drink in her hand.

"I hadn't thought much about it, really, until today," I answered. I was thinking about Betty and the video store. I hadn't completely formed the thought in my head, yet. I supposed I could construct it aloud, with my mother to help.

"What happened today?"

I told her the story of how I'd happened upon the video store, met Betty, her situation, all of it. Then I just sort of blurted out, "I'm thinking about buying it. I'm thinking about buying a video store in Uptown."

138

"Nobody saw that coming," she laughed.

"Not even me," I said. "I can make her a decent offer, and it's a good business. People are always going to rent movies."

"I guess. I know the store you mean. We, I mean I, have a membership there. Can't think of the last time I rented a video."

"I love movies," I continued. "I felt instantly at home in the store. I could talk to people for hours about movies. I think Caden would like it, too."

"A family business?"

"Yeah, kind of." I laughed.

"It sounds like you have it all thought out." She was just moving her food back and forth with her fork.

"You used to hate it when we did that." I motioned to her plate.

"I think that was more your father. I eat less and less. I had to force myself to eat after your father died. There wasn't anyone to cook for and I wasn't hungry. I guess my appetite never really came back."

"You have to eat, Mom."

"Oh, I eat, not as healthy as I should, but I do eat. I just don't need that much to sustain me. I'll finish this later." She pushed the plate a couple of inches away. I wanted more food. That whole lost appetite thing barely visited me after Alec had died. I didn't eat much for a couple of days. As soon as people started bringing food, though, it was all over.

"I can put it away," I said, getting up.

"No, I'll do it in a few minutes. Finish your lunch and your drink. So, a video store?"

"I haven't thought that much about it. I was just there an hour ago. I have no idea what would be a fair offer for a business like that. I don't know if she owns the space, or rents it. I guess I'll need to do some research."

139

"Then do it," she said. "It doesn't sound like the store is going anywhere."

I couldn't have imagined the turn my day would take when I woke up that morning, but I was excited, just thinking about it. I took the last bite of food from my plate. The fork had barely left my mouth when my mother lit a cigarette.

"I'm sorry. Were you waiting for me to finish?"

"It is the polite thing to do." I took a sip of my drink. It was strong, even watered down a bit. I stood up, taking my plate and hers, and my glass into the kitchen. "I think I will add just a little bit more lemonade."

"Nothing to be embarrassed about," my mother said, smiling coyly.

"I'm not embarrassed," I lied. It was clear, at least when it came to hard alcohol, that my sixty-four year old mother could drink me under the table. I called to her from the kitchen. "I'm going to leave the food here, so I'll just put what you didn't eat back in the container, alright?"

"Thank you," she said. "I've been meaning to say something to you since you got back"

"What's that?" I poked my head around the corner.

"I think you should know that I am so proud of how you're handling your life, and I know your father would be, as well. I didn't even need to be involved in it to know you would do the right thing where that boy was concerned."

I was shocked. I really hadn't expected those words to come out of anyone's mouth, but that they came out of my mother's was like a punch to the gut; a good punch. Is there such a thing? The wind went out of me, and all I could do was duck back around the corner and half-whimper, "Thank you, Mom."

"Don't worry about your sister, well the one of them anyway." She just kept talking. "I know that Joanna is happy you're back. She just hasn't realized it yet. You'll fill in nicely for Colleen, too. Joanna needs a friend right now."

A friend to my sister who'd barely spoken to me in the three weeks I'd been back? A video store? My parents' pride? I stood at the kitchen counter, tears in my eyes, knowing full well nothing about the day was going according to plan.

140

Chapter 15
KEVIN

Stephen was about to completely freak out. I wasn't sure what to do, so I just made sure he was looking at me and listening, and I told him, "It's not that big a deal."

The day had started out all right. Stephen, Caden, and I picked up Kelly at his house, and then the four of us piled into my car and drove to Valley Fair. It was my uncle's idea and it was cool to see Caden excited. As excited as Caden was, you wouldn't believe Kelly. It was like Christmas at Disney World for that kid. We went on every ride, all of us, no kidding. My mom wouldn't get on a rollercoaster if it meant a thousand votes. I couldn't picture Aunt Joanna or Uncle Patrick on one either; maybe Grandma. Anyway, Stephen didn't hesitate. He was different from most grown-ups. First of all, he didn't have a job. He used to teach high school, and I bet he was a good teacher. Sometimes, he corrected Caden's and my grammar. It was more than the job thing, though. He wasn't a hundred percent hung up on adult stuff, like what we ate. Last night, we watched videos, and he said we were starting a Friday night tradition, "Movie and junk food night." Caden kind of looked at him like he was trying too hard, but I liked it. So did Caden, because he didn't go up to his room once, all night.

After Caden finally did go to his room, Stephen and I went out back for a cigarette. He'd bought nice patio furniture; a table and umbrella, and cushy chairs; but he still sat on the steps with his legs up to his chest and his drink on the step below him, between his feet. He didn't light a cigarette right away. He was thinking about something. Not wanting to butt in, I just sat and watched him. After a few, he realized we'd just been sitting there, and smiled.

"Your grandma told me today that I think too much. Guess she was right."

"I probably don't think enough," I joked. He laughed and told me that the video store in Uptown might be for sale. He'd stopped there kind of accidentally, and then decided, after talking to my grandma, to look into buying it. That was another way he wasn't like a lot of people. He could just be spontaneous, like, more than anyone I'd ever known. When he got an idea, his face lit up and it was nice, because he seemed so sad and serious most of the time. Seeing him that happy was really cool. He smiled a lot talking about it, and described it to me, even though I told him that I'd been there. We had

141

been drinking root beer with Caden all night. After he finished his cigarette and had pretty much finished telling me every detail about the video store, he got that smile on his face, like he had another idea, and asked if I wanted a "Beer-beer." He got us each a beer and sat back down on the step, lighting another cigarette.

"Now *you're* thinking," he said.

"I guess I was just thinking about how different you are."

"Different how?"

"Just now, when you decided to have a beer; it was like the idea just came to you, and it made you happy," I explained. "Other people just get a beer. It's not a big deal, you know?"

"Your grandma is quite a bit different now, than when your mom and I were kids. Everything was ordered; not like demanded, but organized. I guess my mom was pretty controlling. The dishes had to be done immediately after we ate, like it was a matter of life or death. Sometimes, maybe you'd want to do them in an hour. Was someone really going to die if they waited an hour? What about leaving them overnight?" He took a drag off his cigarette and opened his beer. "When I moved to California and had my own place, sometimes I'd leave the dishes until the next morning just because I could. I'd think about your grandma and it... I don't know; it made me happy to defy her."

"I totally get that." I smiled.

"I wasn't even really defying her," he said. "She didn't know or probably care anymore. I don't know why, but I just got such a kick out of being able to decide things for myself."

"That's kind of what I mean," I told him. "You do get a kick out of things most people just take for granted. It's cool."

"Being an adult sucks so much of the time, why not wring all the enjoyment you can out of it?"

He smiled. If only Caden appreciated what he had in my uncle. It's not like he didn't, exactly; he got it, and he said please and thank you. I knew his dad died. I couldn't understand what it must've been like for him, but it sometimes seemed like he was ashamed to have fun. He was so serious since we got to Minnesota. Anyway, I really liked living with my uncle. I guess that was all I meant.

We had a total blast at Valley Fair. The boys loved the Wild Thing, the newest roller coaster there. They loved it so much; they wanted to go on it again. I'd have gone again, too, but it was kind of cool Caden and Kelly had suggested going on their own. We agreed to let them go off by themselves for an hour, and arranged to meet at the gift shop at five o'clock. Stephen and I sat at the saloon next to the gift shop; had a beer, and talked more about the video store. He hadn't said anything about it, yet, to Caden, but he had gone that morning to talk to the lady who owned it. She loved the idea, Stephen said, and they were going to talk more about it on Monday.

We went to meet Caden and Kelly. That's when things changed. At first, we didn't see them anywhere. Then this girl who was working in the store saw that we were looking for someone and came over to talk to us. She told us that two boys had been caught shoplifting and were in back with the other girl who worked there. Sure enough, it was Caden and Kelly. When she took us in the back and Caden saw Stephen, he just looked down at his feet. Kelly looked like he might cry. Really, so did Stephen. He looked embarrassed and disappointed; he said he was sorry about a hundred times to the girl who caught them.

No one was going to do anything. I really meant it when I told Stephen it wasn't that big a deal. They probably caught shoplifters every day. The girl who had taken us in the back was cool, and finally just told the other one they should let us all go. They went off and talked for a minute and then the cool one came back alone and told us we could go. Then she smiled at me and kind of blushed. I wasn't completely oblivious to the fact that girls liked me. Still, it was completely weird sometimes. As we left, the other one called after us to not come back in the store. *Like really*? I was pretty sure we were all over it enough to not even come back to the park. Everyone was quiet until we got to the car. Stephen was pretty obviously pissed, but so was Caden. Kelly looked like he might pee in his pants any minute.

"So what happened?" Stephen asked once we were in the car. No one answered. We were quiet again, until we got on the highway, then Stephen tried another approach.

143

"Don't you have your own money?" he asked Caden. "I don't understand why you would try to steal something. What was it, by the way?"

"A bracelet," Caden answered. I realized no one had said what they'd tried to steal.

"For whom?" Stephen sounded unconvinced.

"No one."

"Great! Our day ruined for 'no one'!"

"It wasn't—."

"I'm really sorry, Uncle Stephen," Kelly interrupted. Stephen sighed and turned around to face them.

"We're going to talk more about this at home," he said to Caden. "Kelly, was your mom planning to be home all day? I think we'll drop you off a little early."

"We're not going to the restaurant anymore?" Caden asked. Stephen looked at me.

"You're the boss." That was all I had to offer. He shook his head and sighed again. In the rear-view mirror, I could see Kelly look at Caden; embarrassed, guilty. Caden just looked back at him and shook his head. I wasn't about to say anything like, "Everyone shoplifts." I thought, for once, Stephen had forgotten they were two *kids* in the backseat.

"I think it's a good idea to skip the restaurant and eat at home," he finally said.

"Fucking great!" Caden said. For a smart kid, he really wasn't getting it.

"Excuse me?" Stephen twisted back around. Dirty looks were flying everywhere.

"Never mind."

"Good call." We all thought so. Thank God Caden chose not to pursue his objection. We were quiet all the way to Joanna's. "I think I'm going to leave it

144

up to you what you tell your mom. I don't want to get into this with her. Maybe we just chalk this up to—I don't know—a bad first day. We'll do this again. You two had a great time, right?" Kelly nodded. He had relaxed a little, and Caden almost looked like he could fall asleep.

"It's over and done with, I guess," Stephen concluded. I knew it was hardly over.

"Thank you," Kelly told him. He couldn't wait to get out of the car. "I did have a really good time."

"I'm glad." Stephen had barely spoken and Kelly was gone. I guessed he was afraid Stephen would change his mind and follow him in to talk to his mom. I was thinking the same thing, so I pulled away from curb quickly. It was just the three of us again. And silence. As soon as I pulled up in front of the house, Caden was out of the car. He was up the steps and halfway up the walk before Stephen sighed again.

"It's not that big a deal." That's when I said it.

"It is, though," my uncle said.

"I mean, I know, as a parent, you have to make it a big deal, but I shoplifted my first pack of cigarettes. It's obvious they both know it's wrong. It was just some sort of game to them. Or maybe a dare?" That's when I realized there were tears in his eyes. I hadn't expected that.

"I'm sorry. I don't know what to do. I think I've lost him, and I don't know what to do." I was thinking *Don't look at me*, when he apologized again and got out of the car. I didn't know what to do. I rolled my window down, lit a cigarette, and just sat there. I figured I knew where my uncle was coming from. Even though it wasn't a capital crime, he worried—I guess parents had to—that it was a sign of worse stuff to come.

I sat there, kind of wishing we'd already finished the basement, so I could just hide down there the rest of the night. Eventually I went in the house. I didn't immediately see either of them. I took my shoes off and started up the stairs. I guess Stephen had the same thought as me, because he met me halfway up the stairs, on his way down; dressed to paint.

145

"I'm fine," he lied. "I thought we might just order a pizza and get started on your bedroom. The sooner we finish it, the sooner you won't have to deal with us every minute."

"Sounds like a plan." I regretted saying that right away. Did that make it sound like I felt it was a bad thing, *having to deal with them every minute*? I continued up the stairs to change. Then I called down to him. "The pizza sounds great. Thanks for today."

I heard Stephen head out back, probably to have a cigarette before we started painting. Caden's door was, of course, closed. I thought about knocking, but I knew I should stay out of it. I also knew he didn't really have anyone to talk to. Maybe Charlie when they were working, I wasn't sure about that. I knew he wasn't talking to Stephen. I was standing at the top of stairs, outside both of our rooms when Caden came out of his. He looked gloomy, not uncommon for him, but it was obvious he'd also been crying.

"Hey! We're going to get pizza and paint the basement. Fun, right?" I joked. "It's not like we haven't painted anything for two whole days."

"I'm not hungry," he told me. "I just came out to use the bathroom. Besides I'm in trouble, remember?"

"He's just worried about you. I don't even think he's mad anymore."

"If I tell you something, will you promise not tell him?"

"I guess." I wasn't sure I liked where this was going.

"Kelly took the stupid bracelet. I wasn't even there. I mean I was looking at the key chains. They never spell Stephen the right way. And they never have Caden."

"Why didn't you tell someone?" I knew the answer.

"I told Kelly to put it back. I could've even bought it for him. I had money. We were fighting about it when the lady came over and busted us. Then I didn't want to get him in any more trouble. Plus it's kind of a dick move to play it like that." He stood waiting for me to agree with him.

"I see your point."

146

"The thing is Stephen should've known I wouldn't steal a bracelet. I mean, he said it; I had my own money."

"I think you should still tell him. If he was going to get Kelly in trouble, he'd have already done it." I wasn't sure how much I should push, but now I was kinda mad, and that made too many of us angry over something so stupid. "I think it's kind of a dick move to test him like that."

"What do you mean?" Caden shifted his weight from one leg to the other. It was clear he was nervous.

"How should he know you wouldn't steal a bracelet? It doesn't have anything to do with having money or not. Kelly was just showing off for you, I bet."

"That's what I figured."

"You used to be kind of a cool kid. You still are, I guess, but how would anyone know that? If Stephen's supposed to give you the benefit of the doubt, you have to give it back, you know?"

"I don't—."

"This is hard on both of you, but you've spent almost every minute that you're home in your room and seriously, man, you are a complete dick to him." I was on a roll.

"I—," he tried to explain.

"No, dude, really? You're going to say 'He moved me to Minnesota'. Did you ever think he might not have wanted to move either?"

"Then why did we move?" he demanded.

"For you!" There, I'd said it. Somebody should've days ago. My uncle was afraid to, and maybe it would've been a dick move from him, but still. "Look man, how long have we been in Minnesota?"

"I don't know. A couple of weeks."

"Almost three. Before that, it had been almost two months since I talked to my mom, and I haven't talked to her since we got back. Stephen's here, right downstairs, and he's dying to talk to you." I could tell he was going to be

147

stubborn about this, and when I got that way, it was best to let me think about it. At least somebody had finally said something, and it felt good to finally have it out there.

"I gotta pee, man."

"Go!" I told him. "Think about what I said, douche."

"You're a douche," he answered.

"Takes one to know one," I laughed. He closed the bathroom door behind him. I went in the guest room, shut the door, and sat on the edge of the bed. I knew two things right then. I had to keep trying to get Caden to talk to Stephen. And I had to talk to my mother.

I eventually changed into an old pair of jogging shorts and a tank top and went downstairs, barefoot. Stephen had just come in from having a cigarette. The paint and stuff was already in the basement, so I headed down while he called and ordered the pizza. He asked if I'd talked to Caden and I said we'd run into each other in the hallway, but didn't elaborate beyond saying that the kid was starving.

"A life of crime will do that." He laughed as I was walking away. It was Saturday night at seven-thirty, so I wasn't surprised when Stephen came downstairs five minutes later, and told me Pizza Hut said it would take ninety minutes. We were both surprised when the doorbell rang thirty minutes later.

"That was fast. The money is on the table right inside the door." Stephen was willing me to go answer the door.

I ran up the stairs wondering how I was going to get Stephen to tell Caden to come down for dinner. I knew if I asked, he'd just blow me off. If Stephen asked, it would be more work for Caden to avoid eating and he'd probably just do it, whether he was hungry or not. I remembered acting the same way. As I reached the top of the stairs, I realized I'd probably get a second chance at getting Stephen to talk to Caden. It wasn't Pizza Hut at the door, but my aunt Joanna.

148

Chapter 16
JOANNA

I woke to sunlight and a hangover, but no alarm clock. That was something. Sundays were my guaranteed no alarm clock days, so as unexceptional as it was for a Sunday, my summer break had started, and it was the third day in a row I had not woken to the infernal beeping. I loved my job, but I'd been feeling restless, even unfulfilled; so this vacation was happily received. The hangover not so much. About that, the night before was not my best moment. The fight with my brother was huge and regrettable, the drinking afterwards completely necessary. I rolled over in bed and covered my face with a pillow. The original idea was to shield my eyes from the sun pouring in through the crappy blinds, but self-suffocation was not out of the question.

It started innocently enough when Kev called to invite Kelly to go to Valley Fair with him, Stephen and Caden. Kelly would have refused to speak to me for the rest of the month had I said no. Really, I welcomed the break. My intention had been to put a serious dent in a mile long To Do list. Entertaining a thirteen-year-old was not on the list. I should've said no, seeing as how things turned out. Add my son to the growing list of family members who were not speaking to me. I lay in bed for a few minutes, until the pounding in my head was audible and I could no longer breathe through the pillow over my face.

I sat up too quickly and wondered if I'd left my head, torn off my neck, lying on the pillow. It had been years since I'd felt so horrendous as a result of drinking. I sat on the side of my bed waiting for the room to stop spinning, then stumbled onto my feet, steadied myself on the bed frame, and finally staggered to the door. *Why didn't I drink water before bed?* I crossed the hallway into the bathroom and searched the medicine cabinet for pain reliever, nothing. *Jesus Fucking Christ.* Meghan was working, or I'd have considered crawling to her room and sending her downstairs on a mission. It wouldn't have helped my case, though. My daughter already thought I was an alcoholic, only a step or two up from Kitty Dukakis. *You can do this. Better yet, you can do this without puking on the carpet.* I steadied myself on the wall and crept down the hallway past Kelly's door. The sign stating "GO AWAY, MOM!" was still on it from the night before. Message received. Anyone who thought teenage girls were difficult should spend a month with a thirteen-year-old boy. Kelly blamed me for banishing his father, and pretty much everything else after that; including homework, pollution, and war. I sat down

149

at the top step to recuperate a bit, praying my kid did not pick that moment to come out of his room. My head had stopped pounding quite so loudly and the fog had cleared a bit from my brain, allowing some room to go back over the events of the previous day.

I had woken up about nine-thirty and thrown a load of laundry in the washer. I was searching the bathroom medicine cabinet for something that was more suitable for cramps, at that hour, than red wine. Then the phone rang.

"MOM," Meghan yelled, from the bottom of the stairs.

"Who is it?" I asked, still in the bathroom, but not yelling.

"WHAT?" she screamed.

"WHO IS IT?" *If you can't beat 'em, join 'em* was sometimes the only way to go with teenagers. Regardless, I gave up on the medicine cabinet and hurried to the top of the stairs before my daughter yelled again.

"KEVIN!" Too late and even louder than before.

"Okay, enough! Who?"

"Your nephew, my cousin." She held the cordless out, standing firmly at the bottom of the stairs.

"Alright, smartass." Three steps from the landing, I took the phone from my daughter. "You couldn't bring it to me?" And then, "Hello."

"My nails are wet, Mother. You don't want blue nail polish on the carpet, do you?"

"Sorry, hello." I ignored Meghan.

"Um, hi," Kevin muttered on the other end. "Good morning."

"How are you?" I could not remember the last time my nephew had called me.

"I'm good. How are you?"

"I'm— just fine. What's up?"

150

"Stephen, Caden, and I are going to Valley Fair and we were wondering if Kelly wanted to come with us?"

"Really? That's very nice of all of you. When are you going?"

"Well today," he said. "I know it's late notice. If you're busy—."

"No, God, we're never busy," I lied. Well Kelly was never busy, unless you counted reading, playing video games, watching TV, or daydreaming as prior engagements. I went over it quickly in my head and I couldn't come up with any reasonable objection. *Why not?* I knew my nephew pretty well. Therefore, I gathered the whole outing had been Stephen's idea, which was kind of sweet really. "I guess we should leave it up to Kel. I'll let you ask him yourself."

"Okay, sure." Kevin played along. Kelly materialized at the bottom of the stairs at just that moment.

"Like magic," I said to no one, holding the phone out to Kelly. "It's your cousin. He'd like to ask you something."

Their conversation went something like this. "Yeah… What… Seriously… For sure… What time… Okay, I'll be ready." He hung up the phone and took the stairs two at a time, pushing past me. At the top, he looked back at me and thanked me. His bedroom door slammed shut in his wake, for once not angrily.

An hour later, I had scavenged two Midol from the pill bottle in my purse that also contained four aspirin and an assortment of unidentified mystery meds. Kelly was dressed and ready to go five minutes after he'd hung up the phone. I'd given him a ten and a twenty from my purse, and the two of us had waited impatiently for more than forty-five minutes; him to get on with it, me so that I could rush to the store for more Midol. I was thinking, *More wine, too. Fuck cramps.* The car barely come to a complete stop, when my son was beside it, ready to go. I walked, barefoot, to the top of the steps and thanked Stephen for inviting Kelly.

"We'll have him back, I don't know, about eight thirty. Is that okay? We'll stop for burgers on the way back?" Stephen asked.

"Sounds awesome," Kelly exclaimed, climbing in the back seat of Kevin's car.

151

"That works. Thank you." I waved as Stephen got back in the car and Kevin pulled away from the curb.

I'd been sitting at the top of the stairs for at least five minutes when the pounding started again. I was considering sliding down them on my ass, but the noise I heard on the other side of Kelly's door prompted me to my feet. I pondered how odd it was to be afraid of being busted for being hungover by either of my teenage children, until I got to the bottom of the stairs. As a parent, I had gone from feeling like an adult, my own person; back to almost feeling like a teenager, not leery of my parents, but of my children. I reached the bottom of the stairs when I heard Kelly's bedroom door open, and I hurriedly tiptoed around the corner, out of sight. I was an achy, uncoordinated, possibly still-drunk-from-the-night-before shell of the girl who had bold-faced lied to my mother about drinking not that long ago. It was insane the kind of stupid courage some Visine and a mouthful of Scope could give a teenager. As adults, we knew a teenager would not be stupid enough to buy that act. How did we not know the reverse as teenagers?

My throat ached from the pack of cigarettes I had chain-smoked the night before, so I grabbed a glass of water from the refrigerator, a fistful of aspirin, and sat at the kitchen table. I had sat on the deck for hours last night, thinking. I'd eventually given up and brought the bottle of wine outside with me. *I mean really, what was the point of going in and out every thirty minutes?*

Earlier in the day, I'd sat in the exact same spot, having not accomplished much. Two loads of laundry, I unloaded the dishwasher, and took a bath. That was pretty much it. I considered it an accomplishment having not opened a bottle of wine until after four thirty. I was just finishing my bath and first glass of wine when I heard the front door slam. Across the hall, my alarm clock said it was five forty-five. Neither of my kids was due home for hours. I left the wine glass on my dresser and went into the hall in time to see Kelly's bedroom door slam shut behind him. I could only guess at the cause of the emotion with which both doors had been slammed.

"Really I just want to be alone," Kelly called from the other side of the door when I knocked.

152

"I respect that, sweetheart. But I'm your mother, and I want to see that you're alright. Then you can be alone."

"Ugh! Fine!" There wasn't even a lock on his door. That had been removed when he kept locking himself in at four years old and never been put back on.

"Okay then, I'm coming in." I turned the door handle and opened the door slowly. He'd backed away from the door, was standing in the middle of the room, his arms crossed in front of his chest. "You're home early."

"Yeah, we got bored." That was a bold-faced lie. I had not seen Kelly so freaked out since his father let him watch *Nightmare on Elm Street*.

"You did, huh? Did you have dinner then?"

"Nope. No one was hungry."

"You're not going to tell me what happened, I gather."

"What makes you think anything happened?" he countered uncomfortably.

"Because you're home three hours early and you haven't eaten. You've just come from Valley Fair, but you're acting like you had a root canal instead."

"What's that?"

"It's not good. Trust me."

"It was fine. Really. We had an awesome time." He seemed to be relaxing into the lie.

"Alright. I guess I'll just have to call your uncle and find out what happened."

"Please don't," he begged.

"Then start talking."

"Ugh!" That was new. I wasn't certain what it meant, but it didn't sound good.

"Caden and I, um, we—at Valley Fair we, we got caught—." He didn't even have to go on. I may have feared it the second it became apparent something had gone wrong.

153

"Did you steal something?" I sighed

It had happened a few times more than a year before, but almost six months of counseling, after the separation; led me to believe we were past it. Kelly had stolen nail polish, of all things, from the grocery store while I shopped. He presented it to me as a gift, but couldn't explain how he'd paid for it. I'd been separated from my husband for less than a month at the time. All I could think to do was make him go back to the store, return the polish, and confess; but I wasn't about to do that. That was something my father had made Stephen do, and it was humiliating. He'd shoplifted an address book when he was eight or nine. I remember thinking it had been an extremely odd thing for someone his age to steal. To my knowledge, my brother had never stolen anything else, so it had worked. I didn't believe in humiliation as a form of punishment. Plus, it was nail polish. I agreed to a week's grounding, which included canceling plans with his father, a serious punishment to Kelly. Then a month later, he had stolen a bracelet from a female classmate. I wondered if there was something else going on besides the separation, so in spite of my ex's objections, I found a counselor and we started going weekly. I went in with him at first, but after a couple of weeks, the therapist felt it would be better to talk to Kelly alone. I would be called into the office for the last few minutes of the session.

The therapist asked to see me on my own about a month in. He explained that my son had decided he needed to replace his father. This was manifesting in a number of ways, one of which was giving me things. The thefts seemed to coincide with times he perceived me to be lonely or upset. I could not imagine why he would pick the behavior up again. I was fine as far as anyone knew. I certainly was far better than I had been. I'd become more adept at hiding the major crap, at least from Kelly.

"I'm really sorry, Mom."

"I know you are, sweetheart. But love, that doesn't make it okay. Once, even twice, but not anymore. Why today?" As soon as I asked, I knew. "What did you take?"

"A bracelet." He looked up at me.

"For Meghan?" He nodded. I was stunned sometimes how sweet my child was, in spite of his father. Jim was alright. He could be thoughtful, even kind, especially in the beginning. He was a good father, too, even to Meghan, but

154

that man didn't have a sweet bone in his body. Honestly, I wasn't terribly sweet, either, and neither; for sure, was his sister. "Not okay, though. You know your sister is fine, right?"

"Then why does she cry sometimes?"

I'd no idea she had been. In that moment, I wondered how many ways I had failed as a parent. Meghan had insisted she was fine, and I finally took her at her word. At her request, we moved on. Well, I guess I did. "Crying isn't always a bad thing, kiddo. Sometimes it's good. After you cry, you actually feel better; you know like when you have a stomach ache and you throw up?" *What a horrible example!* I scanned my brain for a better one. I was lost.

"There's something else." Kelly turned to look out the window. "I didn't say anything."

"What do you mean?"

"I think Uncle Stephen thinks that Caden did it."

"Oh, kiddo." That was *so* not good.

"I know, but you can't say anything, Mom." He turned to face me.

"You know what? Let's get you something to eat, and then I need to go see your uncle."

"No! You can't. God, Mother!" His mood changed from reticence to anger on a dime.

"Kelly, we cannot let Stephen think that Caden stole something when he didn't." It pretty much devolved from there. After five minutes, we had reached an impasse. I left my son's room, making it clear I was going to at least call Stephen. Kelly made it clear he wouldn't be speaking to me *ever again* if I did.

I waited thirty minutes to see if Kelly would come around. Before I left, I went back upstairs to try to talk him into coming with me. That is when I found the sign on his bedroom door. GO AWAY, MOM! Subtle. He was doing a better job filling in for his father than he knew. I waited for Meghan to get home a few minutes later. I explained things to her, and then left for my brother's. I wondered if any parents ever got used to apologizing for their kids. I'd never

155

gotten used to it. It wasn't often a problem. All things considered, I had great kids. I would eventually make Kelly understand why it appeared I'd sided with someone else's son over him. That was how he colored it in his mind. I didn't think that was what I was doing, but in all reality; I had made mistakes before, many of them parenting. Who could be certain I wasn't just making one more of those?

I had only been to Stephen's once before; well, inside. I'd driven by before Stephen and Caden had arrived from California. Then I'd driven by about a week ago, by accident, I told myself. Charlie was in front, no shirt on, and I slowed down as I passed. The work on the house was mostly done, from what I understood. It felt weird to drop by for no reason. I told myself I had to wait for another invitation, or at least a specific purpose. This was not what I had in mind. I parked my car behind Kevin's and rang the bell a minute later. I could hear music playing inside; someone had to be home. I rang the bell a second time and was considering going around back, when Kev came to the door.

"Hey, we thought you were the pizza."

"Sorry to disappoint." I realized my hands were in my pockets, and it seemed weird to me; so I took them out. "I was wondering if I could talk to Stephen for a minute."

"Sure, come on in." Kev stepped aside, holding open the door.

"IT'S JOANNA. NOT THE PIZZA," he yelled, in the direction of the basement.

"I'll be right up," Stephen called.

"Want something to drink?" Kevin asked.

"No. I'm good, thanks."

"Well, I'm going to get back to the painting. If we finish the first coat tonight, I can actually move downstairs by Monday."

"Of course, don't let me keep you."

He was no sooner gone from sight, then my brother appeared. Stephen was a little bit shy of six feet tall. He had a runner's build. He had always been thin growing up. I'd never forgotten when Paddy told our dad that Stephen needed help with the mower. They had argued about it for days. Stephen was

156

so small; he was barely able to push the thing. Dad really had no idea Stephen was different. I think he saw each of us exactly the same. When it was time to mow, Paddy would sneak back to help, even after he had moved to a dorm at the U. Our dad never knew. I had never thought how similar my brother and my son were until just now. Stephen had hit a growth spurt late and grew at least two inches in his last year of high school. He had filled out more in California, developed a sense of himself that he didn't have before leaving. He had always been shy in high school; I was shocked to learn he was teaching just a few years later. Besides my own reflection in the mirror, looking at my little brother was what betrayed the passing of time to me. It was so much more potent than looking at my mother. That was because he had not been around much, I had looked away and he'd become a man. Actually, I hadn't looked away at all. He moved away and came back a man.

"What's up?" he asked.

"Kelly told me what happened."

"Do you want something to drink?"

"Do you have wine?" I half-sighed.

"I have White Zinfandel. I never learned anything about reds or whites, so I don't know what to buy. Alec was the wine connoisseur. I'd have drunk the pink stuff out of a box if he hadn't made so much fun of me."

He was nervous. As a kid, if he were nervous, he'd give away way too much information. He'd gotten Colleen and me in trouble a few times. Our mother had known to question him first. He was still talking, and I realized that he'd gone into the kitchen and I hadn't followed.

"The house looks amazing, Stephen." It did. My brother had remarkable taste. That was something else he'd developed in California.

"Thanks" He seemed surprised by the compliment. I could have been reading too much into it. "I need a ruling on the wine. Or I have beer? I really haven't stocked a liquor cabinet. I suppose that will be necessary before I have Mom over?"

"The wine will be great. Thanks." I had not had White Zinfandel since my bridal shower. I watched as he uncorked the bottle and filled a gorgeous, hand-painted wine glass half-full.

157

"Listen, about today, I don't know what came over Caden. He's never done a thing like this before—."

"He didn't today either," I interrupted.

"What do you mean?"

"Kelly took the bracelet. From what he told me, it sounded like you'd assumed it was Caden, and neither of them bothered to correct you."

"Why would they do that?" He just wasn't getting it.

"My guess is that Kelly was scared and Caden didn't want to be a narc." I took a sip of the wine. It wasn't bad.

"Seriously?"

"That's my guess. Kelly was afraid to say anything and is so embarrassed."

"I'm surprised he didn't come with you to say so himself," my brother asserted.

"Well, it's like I said, he's embarrassed." I was growing defensive.

"Aren't you supposed to make them, then?" I could not tell if it was a question or an accusation. "I mean, I'm asking. I'm the novice here."

"I'm not sure what you mean." I had no idea why I felt so defensive.

"If that situation had been different, and my kid had let your kid get in trouble for something he'd done; should I have insisted he apologize?" Going back over it the next day, I could not recall a trace of defensiveness in his tone. I was defensive enough for both of us.

"I think it would depend on the situation." I took a long sip of wine and set my glass on the counter.

"I guess." It seemed as if he was reluctant to disagree.

"You have to admit, it's odd." I really should have stopped myself.

158

"What is?"

"You've just sort of insinuated yourself, and especially Caden, into our lives." I regretted it the second I said it. *Jesus Fucking Christ.*

 "Excuse me?" There was the defensiveness; actually, he seemed to have leapt right over defensive, landing on angry. "I can't get over you."

"What is that supposed to mean?"

"Where the hell did that chip come from?" he demanded.

"What chip?"

"The great-big-fucking one on your shoulder." Definitely angry.

"Look, I shouldn't have said that. I'm sorry."

"No really, let's have it; say your piece. Clearly you've something to say."

"I don't," I lied. "It's been a very long day."

"It's been a very long fucking year." I typically only swore in my head. I didn't used to be that way. Did I train myself not to swear around the kids? My ex swore, so what difference was I really making? Clearly, my little brother was quite comfortable swearing. "You've been a bitch ever since I've been back. No. Correction—you were a bitch when I was back a few months ago, too."

"I've been myself." I could not recall when I'd been more uncomfortable.

"Then you've changed."

"Fifteen years does that, Stephen! You don't think you've changed?"

"I'm sure I have. For the better."

"This was clearly a bad idea." I picked up the wine glass, finished it, and then turned to go.

"Sure, go ahead, bail!"

159

"Me bail? That's hilarious. Where the fuck have you been for fifteen years?!" *I said fuck. Out loud.*

"I've been being gay, remember? Somewhere else."

"Is that what you told yourself? Did that make it easier to disappear?"

"Was there ever a time you didn't know where to find me? You never tried once." He was incredulous.

"That's not fair, is it?"

"How's it unfair, Joanna? Tell me. By my count, I visited you three times. Let's count how many times you came to California." He was so goddamned smug, just then. The bottle of wine was still sitting beside him on the counter. Neither of us had even sat down. We were standing there, on opposite sides of the counter, preparing for battle. He spotted me looking at the bottle of wine.

"More wine?" he asked, and pushed the bottle toward me. For a second, I wasn't sure if my pride would stop me from reaching for the bottle. Apparently not. I poured half of what was left into my glass. Those beautiful glasses. My brother had so much. I couldn't believe I was feeling jealous again. I wanted to cry, but I didn't do that anymore. Not for myself. My tears were reserved for my children. I hadn't cried for myself in well over a year. What was the point?

I couldn't get over him pretending not to remember. It was three hundred fucking dollars! Looking at him, I couldn't tell if he was faking the memory loss. I drank half of what I had just poured into my glass. Courage. "You took money from me and just left. No thank you. No goodbye."

"What the hell are you talking about?" Maybe he wasn't pretending. How did you forget something like that?

"I can't believe you." I shook my head, still not a hundred percent convinced. Stephen finished his wine, reached for the bottle in front of me, and emptied the rest into his glass.

"Well?" he demanded.

160

"You'd asked Colleen first. But she didn't have any money. Catelyn alluded to the fact that you'd asked her, as well. So I wasn't even your second choice."

His face was still blank. I could not get over it. "Three hundred fucking dollars, Stephen!"

Suddenly it registered. He hadn't been pretending. I took one last big gulp of wine. There was no turning back now, even though I could see how hurt he was. The look on his face seemed to plead with me to not say the words. Less than twenty-four hours later, I wished I hadn't. I swear I wished I hadn't. "For your fucking abortion! Was it even yours?" *Jesus Fucking Christ!* I swore far more proficiently in my head. I supposed, in that moment, if I could have been a horrible mother, I could have been just as awful a sister. Too much water under a bridge I did not even recognize anymore.

"Was what mine?" my little brother asked, resigned. "The abortion, or the baby?"

Chapter 17
STEPHEN

I hadn't thought about the abortion in years. A few minutes before, when my sister left, I was certain that made me a horrible person. Sitting on the back steps alone, holding an unlit cigarette, my eyes filled with tears. I'd cried, sure. I was a goddamned crybaby. Had I gone an entire day in the last fucking two years without crying at least once? I was so tired of my own crying, I could scream. I hadn't cried for the baby; though, not in years.

That was 1979 and I was nineteen years old, gay, and leaving for California in less than a month. I had sex with a woman exactly once in my entire life. I got her pregnant. Seriously, what were the odds? Sarah had come to me a month after she called off our engagement. She said she didn't want to have a baby. She didn't mind being pregnant, just didn't want to raise a kid. She made me an offer; if I wanted the baby, our baby, she'd have it and walk away.

I wanted a child more than anything, certainly more than I wanted to move to California, but I knew I wasn't ready. I was in a situation where I didn't have my family's support; the additional dilemma wasn't going to make the first one any more palatable. It was amazing to look back, after everything that had happened, and realize that in Ohio, another kid my age had been presented with an almost identical predicament at almost the same time. It was Alec who taught me how wrong my thinking was, even if I hadn't been ready. He had lived it, and of course, he'd felt the same way in the beginning. We'd been together for a year, had been living together a couple of weeks. I told him about Sarah, and the baby we aborted. At the time I was afraid he would judge me for having taken the easy way out; especially given his own choice when faced with a similar situation. Not at all.

"Oh baby," Alec had said. "It terrifies me how close we were to not having Caden." I knew that Caden's mother had been Alec's high school girlfriend, his best friend. They had dated, on and off, all through high school, had only slept together a handful of times. Alec and I had each only had sex with one woman. "We'd gotten the money together for an abortion and had an appointment. But in the end, she couldn't go through with it. I had no idea how relieved I would be. I hadn't felt like I had much say in the decision."

"You weren't terrified?"

162

"Fuck yes! I didn't think either of us were ready, but we were committed to doing it together. The thing is Stephen, looking back; we weren't ready, not at all. But we got ready, well, I did. What choice did I have?" Caden's mother had died in childbirth.

"So you don't think I'm an awful person?" We were sitting in bed, on a Sunday afternoon, both of us wearing boxers.

I'd loved Sundays like that. We had many, barely getting out of bed, the Sunday paper strewn among whatever books either of us was reading at the time. Depending upon the time of day, there would be the dishes from breakfast and champagne glasses half-full of Mimosas on the bedside tables, or half-empty takeout Chinese cartons. In the beginning, Alec had tried to teach me to use chopsticks, but I was hopeless. Caden would play on the floor on Alec's side of the bed; sometimes even nap, right there at our feet. We would talk endlessly, still getting to know each other after a year. It was, on Sundays especially; that each of us would show the other movies we loved. We had almost a desperate need to share with each other every single good thing we'd ever taken in. So many movies were tossed back and forth. Often times, I would start talking about a movie I adored and Alec would finish my sentence, having seen and loved it, too.

The entire time I spent with Alec was happy. Even amidst the sadness, we were happy. But those first two years we lived together, in that tiny *one-bedroom-plus* apartment in Los Angeles, were my favorite. Caden slept in a single bed in the *plus* room. After he had gone to bed, we would make love with such complete abandon; we shared breath. We explored each other's bodies by candlelight, feeling our way in the dark. I had never experienced such pleasure in my entire life. I had no idea that sex was supposed to feel that way. Alec taught me the difference between sex and making love.

I loved looking at him. I couldn't get over how lucky I was. I'd never met anyone as comfortable with themselves; as secure, as Alec. I wore a t-shirt on those days, just hanging out, but not Alec. He was always shirtless. He'd have been naked if it weren't for Caden. I wouldn't have complained. Alec was prettier than the handful of men I had been with before him, Liam included, but not always in the best shape. If he had a shirtless scene coming up on the show or when he would be naked on stage for most of a scene, I'd be expected to join in the diet or increased workout routine. I was blessed with an amazing metabolism, so I didn't gain weight in the times when neither of us paid attention to what we were eating or how much exercise we got. I

163

never had visible abdominal muscles, but with some effort; through exercise and diet, Alec could achieve them.

"I could never think you were awful," Alec told me. "I just told you, we almost did the same thing."

"But you didn't."

"That had nothing to do with me. Look, it sounds like you had—I don't know— more say in your relationship; Caden's mom had more say in ours. Had it been left completely up to me, I'd have assumed she wanted an abortion, and Caden probably wouldn't be here." He kissed me and we both looked at Caden sleeping at the foot of the bed.

"I always felt absolutely horrible that I didn't go in for the procedure with her. I don't know why I didn't. I didn't think of it. When it was over, a nurse wheeled her out into the waiting room. I was determined not to cry in front of her."

"I can't even imagine." He reached down, brushed the hair out of his son's face. "The two greatest things to ever happen to me are you, and my son, *our* son. I can't imagine my life without either of you."

I still struggled with saying "I love you." Of course, we had told each other more than once. The words still stuck in my throat sometimes. Alec barely noticed. "I mean it, Steph. I'd be fucking lost."

I looked at him, and there was so much love in his face. It radiated across his features, danced in his eyes. When I saw myself in his sea-green eyes, I was perfect. I supposed that was what love did. He certainly was perfect in my eyes. I wouldn't say we didn't find flaws in each other, but the awareness of their existence arrived through different senses. I didn't know how to explain it, except it was like gazing out at the ocean. When we looked at the endless waves, flirting with the sand and the beach, we didn't see pollution, or a force powerful enough to drown us; we just saw the majesty of the ocean. When I looked at Alec, I didn't see the man who snored when he drank, or the man who laughed too loudly in public, or left his bath towel bunched up on the rod or, worse yet, on the floor. I just saw someone who loved me. From the very beginning, I never doubted his love. I saw someone who met my gaze with equal rapture. Held in my glance, his flaws melted away. I wasn't as adept at vocalizing my love on the spot. Given ten or fifteen minutes to put words on

164

paper, I could have blown him out of the water with pure sentiment. Finally, I managed the words, "I love you."

After that, we did not talk about the abortion, and I didn't think about it often. I didn't need to. I felt the ache. I didn't need to talk about it or think of it; it just was. Was that how it felt when you lost a child? I guessed that my brother and his wife felt something very different when they lost their baby. That child had a gender and a name. That child was tangible.

I didn't speak to Sarah after that day. Not until we ran into each other, almost accidentally, when I was home a year and a half later. We talked for an hour, and both had exactly the same excuses. The *I thought about you all the time, I thought about calling, but didn't know what to say, the longer we went without talking, the more strange a call, out of the blue, seemed*. We were both fine. She was always far stronger than me. She barely seemed phased, except the ache in her eyes that I recognized a mile away. We shared that. I would never know if our aches were equal. I can't believe they were. She sacrificed a part of herself. I just lost an idea, an inkling of something I'd never have; never grasp the reality of.

When I decided I wasn't ready to be a father, I knew it was my responsibility to come up with the money for the abortion. I had a thousand dollar inheritance, but I needed that to make a start in California. I had also saved a couple hundred dollars from working since I had graduated. That was meant to cover airfare to Los Angeles. I decided I could take a bus, one-way for thirty dollars instead. Looking back, even though Sarah had put the decision in my hands, I still felt powerless. My making it about the money helped me feel in control of a situation which was totally out of my control.

I needed to come up with about a hundred fifty dollars more. I went to Colleen first, of course, but she didn't have it. Then I asked Caty, she had been like a mother to me for years. I spent almost as much time at her house after she got married as I did at home.

When Kevin was about four, my sister stopped wanting me around. I still babysat Kevin, just not as often, and always at my parent's house. Catelyn withdrew from me, shut down. It was as if she had changed overnight. There was no longer a place for me in her life. I saw my brother-in-law less frequently, until he existed only in memories. At family dinners, on the rare occasions when Caty came, her husband was conspicuously absent. Still, I had no doubt that she would have helped, if she could have. I never dreamt that she would refuse me out of some moral obligation to her new church. Catelyn

165

converted from Catholicism to Christianity when she married Tom. I had always thought they were the same, but apparently, they weren't. At any rate, she left me with an, "I'll pray for you," instead of cash for the abortion, so I finally turned to Joanna.

She didn't hesitate. She gave me three hundred dollars the very next day and told me to keep the money I'd saved as something to fall back on in California. Joey told me that I had made a good decision to take the bus. The more money I had once I got to Los Angeles, the better, so she paid for the entire abortion. She even offered to drive us to the clinic, but Sarah insisted on taking the bus there and a cab home. I think she was embarrassed I had discussed it with my sister. She had no idea that Joanna was the third family member I'd told, or that Joanna had given me all the money we needed.

In hindsight, I could see that when things are remembered from a distance, omissions occur, even embellishments. Maybe it was self-preservation. I left Minnesota disappointed by almost everyone in my family. I had been told my homosexuality was inconvenient to them, and that they would rather not discuss it further. No one disowned me or cast me away. They just didn't want to walk in the very next gay pride parade, not most of them, anyway. In the 1970s, that would have been expecting an awful lot. It was expecting quite a bit in the 1990s. I left Minnesota hurt and angry; some might say for no reason. I was glad things turned out the way they did. Had I not gone, had Sarah not had an abortion, I would have never met Alec or Caden. I needed to take my share of the responsibility for the bad of it, as much as for the good.

Joanna and I had been arguing and I had worked up quite a thirst. The day, which I would have to say felt more like a week, had gone from pretty good, to amazing, to kind of perfect, to bad, to worse, to completely FUBAR. We had already finished a bottle of wine. That was gone in twenty minutes with just the two of us drinking. My sister had just asked if I was sure the baby she'd paid to abort was mine. Classy. Someone had been watching too many soap operas.

"Was it even yours?" She had asked.

"Was what mine? The abortion or the baby?" I was fighting fire with fire, although I wasn't quite sure what that meant, the thing I said. Was the abortion mine? I am not sure I was paying attention to the conversation anymore. I was wondering if I should open another bottle of wine. Two thoughts stood out. If I opened another bottle, was that an invitation for

166

Joanna to stay? Also, was my sister going to think I had one foot in Alcoholics Anonymous with our mother? Maybe we could book adjoining rooms at Hazelden, get a family discount.

"I assume you had sex with her?" It was definitely meant as a question. Did my sister think I was a fucking idiot? Despite being gay, I had a decent idea where babies came from.

"Yes." That was all I could manage in reply. It was completely possible I was losing my mind. I couldn't land on a single thought for more than a few seconds; and well, I needed to sit down. A cigarette. Could I invite my sister outside to have a cigarette with me while we were fighting? Would she go for that? Maybe if I carried a bottle of wine with me, she would follow, like a dog with a bone.

The mention of the abortion had knocked the wind out of me, but I wasn't down for the count. I had at least another couple of rounds left in me. I took another bottle of wine out of the refrigerator. God, I'd be glad when that eyesore was out of my life for good. Lemon-yellow appliances. Yuck! I opened the bottle, grabbed it and my wine glass, and turned to Joanna. "I'm going to have a cigarette. You're welcome to belittle me out back, if you have more to say." At that moment, I really hoped she would exit through the door she came in, but in case she was following me, I kept going when I got to the steps.

I usually sat on the steps to smoke, but I had bought nice patio furniture. It was expensive and I was hoping maybe I'd left the price tag on it. I sat down at the table, and something from above caught my eye. Caden ducked back inside his bedroom window just as I looked up. We were giving the boys quite a show, now the neighborhood would get act two. Great! My sister had indeed followed me outside, but she had not brought her wine glass.

"We'll have to be a little bit quieter out here," I told her. "I'd rather not have my neighbors know everything there is to know about me in the first month."

"I don't have much else to say," Joanna countered.

"No more wine?"

"I have to drive home, and I'm not staying much longer."

167

"Well then, first of all; I did say thank you, a hundred years ago when you gave me the money. And it goes both ways. Like I already said, I called and I visited. Where were you?"

"I was here, Stephen. Here raising two kids. Here taking care of our parents. Here the entire time our sister fought cancer." Joanna was practically seething. How long had she held all of that in? "I was here when Dad died and—."

"I cannot get over how fucking self-righteous you've become," I interrupted. "Do you think you're the only one with a life? Jesus Christ!" I had forgotten, for a minute, why we had come outside until Joanna lit a cigarette. I took one of my own from the pack on the table, lit it, and took a long drag. Then I filled my wine glass almost to the rim. She hadn't said a word, so I decided to forge ahead. "You and Caty made it abundantly clear that you didn't want either of your husbands to find out about me."

"You're so full of shit, Stephen! That's not even close to how it went, and if that was the case, why would I give you money?"

"I don't know. Hush money?" I knew that wasn't the reason, but seated, with a cigarette and a full glass of wine, I was feeling angrier. All of this was water under the bridge. How had she not let it go? If she wanted her three hundred dollars back, she could have it. With interest. I took another drag off my cigarette and a long sip of wine. She hadn't sat down. I looked up at her, suddenly feeling a little exposed with her standing over me. "Look, I know you feel I should have come home more—."

"Or at all," she interrupted. "You didn't come home once while Colleen was sick. You didn't—."

"Colleen went through two rounds of chemo, and was in remission." It was my turn to interrupt. "You do know I actually talked to her? While she was sick I talked to her at least once a week."

"Good for you," she said, insincerely. "How about when Dad died?"

Alec had pneumonia when my father passed away. He was weeks, maybe days away from hospice care. I had a thirteen-year-old boy and a thirty-year-old man who looked seventy years old and sometimes could not feed himself. I couldn't get over how selfish my sister was being.

"I was a little busy."

"And Mom? You may not have cared about Dad, but what about Mom?" Yeah, she really had no idea.

"Fuck you, Joanna! Dad wasn't sick at all, and Colleen was sick for less than a year and then better. Alec was sick for two-and-a-half years, and yes, I was busy. I had my own kid to raise. Maybe you forgot about him. He's the one who took the blame for your kid's shoplifting." I was done with this fight.

"If you were doing such a great job raising Caden, how did you not just know he hadn't stolen anything?"

"I think you should just leave." She was right about Caden, but that did not stop me from being pissed. Moving back here, I was counting on Joanna the most. Her crap made me sick to my stomach. How had we even gotten to this place? I took one last drag off the cigarette and stamped it out in the ashtray in front of me. Then I stood up, gathered the wine and went inside, leaving my sister still standing in the backyard.

I waited a few minutes and then went to the front window. Out of view from the street, I stood there and watched for my sister to come around the house, get in her car and leave. I remained there and watched her car drive slowly out of sight and then I stood there some more, just looking out the window, unable to move. Finally, I remembered the pizza. Had it come? I turned around and surveyed the room for answers. Seeing none and hearing absolutely no movement in the house, I turned back around, looking back at the street. Sure enough, Kev's car was gone. *Jesus Fucking Christ.*

Walking into the kitchen, I remembered something my sisters and I; well Colleen, Joanna and I, used to say. "God Bless America!" It was more like, "God," then a pause, and then, "Bless America!" The "Bless America" part replaced "Damn-it." Our father didn't approve of swearing and he certainly didn't approve of taking the Lord's name in vain. My mother and I had just discussed this the day before. I cannot believe I didn't think of this then. If any of us had started to say, "Goddamnit," and saw my father, we would change the expletive. I'm certain my father knew exactly what was going on, but after a while, it just became a thing with my sisters and me. I exclaimed, "God Bless America!" all over Southern California, for a couple of years after moving. I grew tired of explaining what I thought was a funny story, but came out more like a *you had to be there* kind of thing. I hadn't thought about it in years.

169

In the kitchen, I found a note from Kevin, telling me that he and Caden had gone out for a bit and would be back before ten. The note was placed on top of two still warm pizza boxes. *Good*, I thought, leaving the note there with the pizza. I didn't even take the wine back outside with me.

I missed my sister, Colleen. I missed Alec. I missed our life in San Francisco. I missed when Caden was happy. I missed when I was happy, when we all were. I missed so much so badly; I had forgotten there was anything left. It was a mistake coming back. I was sure of that now. I was failing so miserably as a parent. God, how could I have possibly done this on my own, fourteen years ago? So many times, I had wondered how things would have been. I could see clearly: not well. I sat there on the step, not smoking for the longest time, just holding a cigarette; lost, going over everything that was wrong. I eventually smoked the cigarette, and when I was done; I got up, went back in the house, put a wine stopper in the bottle of wine, put it and the pizza in the ugly lemon-yellow refrigerator. The wine that was left in my glass, I dumped down the sink. I washed the wine glasses and left them to dry on a towel beside the sink. The clock on the stove told me it was eight thirty when I left the kitchen and went upstairs to my room, but I paid very little attention. I looked at the time again on the alarm clock beside my bed, but again; I paid no attention. I was in a daze... not thinking anymore... so tired.

I went into my bathroom and looked at myself in the mirror. I had on an old Mondale for President t-shirt. Just above the "I" in president was a blotch of dark plum paint the size of a dime. That was new. The accent wall in the living room downstairs was that color. Below the "D" in Mondale were two specks of grey paint. Those were old, all the way from San Francisco. That was the color of Alec's and my bathroom. There were specks of blue and brown from this house, and red from the house in San Francisco. An array of colors that represented the last decade of my life. I had worn this shirt to paint Caden's new bedroom in the house in San Francisco, before he'd set foot in that house for the first time. I had worn it to paint his new bedroom in this house, just a few weeks ago. In the time between those paint jobs, Caden had grown four feet. Why didn't we have a growth chart on some out-of-the-way wall in the old house? It wouldn't matter now anyway. We would never see it again, if we had. Caden would be fifteen in a few weeks. A couple of weeks after that, he'd start high school. Still standing in the bathroom mirror, now leaning in close, studying the lines on my forehead, I heard that boy's laughter.

He was four years old and playing on the floor beside our bed in that apartment in Los Angeles. The apartment had been Alec and Caden's first. I had a few months left on my leased studio apartment in West Hollywood

170

when Alec asked me to move in with him. We'd found the apartment and they moved in. I lived between places while we waited for my lease to run out. It was a different Sunday than the one I'd remembered earlier. From the boom box on the dresser, we listened to *Hungry Like the Wolf* by Duran-Duran. I had given the cassette to Alec for his birthday. I was about halfway through A Cry to Heaven by Anne Rice, lying on my stomach with my right leg in the air. Alec sat up, beside me, pouring over listings in *Variety*. Suddenly, from over the side of the bed, a dinosaur appeared a few inches from my book, and behind it, more laughter.

"Hello Donald!" I smiled. The dinosaur's name was Donald, after a boy in pre-school who had moved to Orange County. *Donald the Dinosaur*, I wondered whatever happened to him. I searched the toys from Caden's childhood that had remained and had made the trip from San Francisco to Minnesota. There was a teddy bear named, aptly, "Bear" that Caden had slept with for years. Bear sat on a bookshelf now, down the hall, watching over the teenager who was too old to sleep with stuffed animals. There were others, too, but no Donald. Donald was red and did not look like any specific type of vertebrate. Forget the fact that there weren't red dinosaurs to begin with, not that shade anyway. For several months, Donald the Red Dinosaur was a favorite playmate of Caden's. Bear typically remained in bed, relegated to sleep time, but Donald went nearly everywhere Caden did that summer.

"Hello Stephen," the dinosaur seemed to say, followed by the giggles of a soon to be five-year-old boy. Donald flopped onto his side then, and it was Caden I was talking to.

"Donald wants to know what to call you," he told me. Alec looked up.

"Well... He could call me Stephen, like he just did. That's my name."

"He calls Dad, 'Dad', but Dad's name is 'Alec'."

"I see." I still hadn't made out where the conversation was heading. I rolled over onto one side, marking my page in the book, my back to Alec now. He leaned in and rested his body on my side, then nestled in and kissed my neck.

"You're kind of our dad, too," Caden wondered out loud.

"Not kind of, kiddo. Stephen is your dad, just like I am," Alec corrected him. We had never discussed this before. It was news to me. Prior to that moment,

171

I had existed label-free in Caden's life. We'd known each other over a year and he'd only ever called me Stephen.

"Then me and Donald are going to call Stephen, 'Dad,' if that's okay," the boy declared. He spoke for both himself and the dinosaur, apparently.

"I don't know. What do you think, Steph?" Alec asked. I twisted my neck a bit to look up into my lover's eyes, saw them dampen. He leaned in then, to kiss me on the lips. I felt more in love with those two, in that moment, than I had from anyone my entire life.

"I would love that!" I turned back to Caden. "Donald is, after all, my very favorite dinosaur in the entire world."

"What about me?" Caden peered up at me, seriously.

"Well, you are certainly not a dinosaur."

"If I was a dinosaur, would you love me as much as Donald?"

"More," I told him. "But I think you make a much better boy."

"I guess."

"Hey kiddo, it's almost nap time," Alec interrupted.

"DAD!" Caden was not a fan of naptime. What four-year-old was?

"Ten minutes, bud."

"You are my most favorite boy anywhere," I told Caden.

"You don't make me take naps, so you are my most favorite dad anywhere!" I looked back at Alec and his damp eyes were full of love.

"The nap was actually Stephen's idea. He whispered it to me just a minute before Donald showed up," Alec lied, smiling.

"Seriously?" Caden asked. I swung my legs over the side of the bed, sitting up next to him. I lifted my hand to brush the brown hair out of his eyes.

"You need a haircut," I said.

172

"You're full of terrible ideas," Caden answered, seriously.

"How about if I tuck you in?"

"Okay. Can I have two stories?"

"Two stories?! For a nap? I don't know."

"Yes. You can read one and Dad can read one. One for each dad!"

"You drive a hard bargain, but how about if I read both? Dad's looking for jobs."

"I suppose," Caden agreed. I stood up and turned back to Alec, now lying on his side, stretched across the bed.

"You okay?"

"Never better," he said, smiling up at me.

I turned away from the bathroom mirror, the memory fading. Back in the bedroom, I walked over to the dresser and picked up a frame. Caden did not get two stories that afternoon. He barely got one. The picture in my hand was one Alec had taken that day almost ten years ago, of Caden and me, asleep with a red dinosaur, in Caden's single bed in that tiny room in our first home together.

After a moment, I put the picture down and picked up another one. It was one of Alec and me at the surprise thirtieth birthday party Caden and I had thrown for his dad. It seemed like a lifetime ago, in spite of only having been a few years. Caden had taken the picture with a 35 mm camera we had given him the Christmas before. I remembered Alec was not certain Caden was old enough for such an expensive gift, but it turned out the worry was unnecessary. He rarely set the damn thing down. He loved it and must have taken a million pictures. We hadn't the time or money sometimes to develop them all. The one in my hand now was my absolute favorite.

It was pretty benign really, but it was snapped before things had gotten bad, before Alec had really started to look sick. Alec had just blown out the candles on his birthday cake, with little effort. I was behind him with my arms around his shoulders and we were both laughing. He had been sick twice already

173

when the picture was taken. We'd both started HIV medications. I was constantly exhausted from them, but Alec's energy never diminished. In the beginning, we took exactly the same medications; it was odd how the side effects differed so dramatically between us. In the last year and a half or so, every Christmas, every birthday was somehow approached as if it were our last together. The apprehension went mostly unspoken. The photo was representative of a time before all of that, before the vomiting and diarrhea took over our lives, before Alec had started to wither away before our eyes. Our expressions in the picture looked almost as if we had no idea what was coming. I suppose, to a huge extent, we didn't have any idea how bad it would be. People had begun to live longer. Alec had lived five years. I was going on four since my diagnosis.

The unknown was a constant. Fear was a part of my daily life. I didn't like to admit it to myself; I couldn't even bear to think it. However, the truth was; I'd come home to Minnesota so that when I died, there'd be someone to take Caden. Standing in front of the mirror, I just laughed. *What a fucking joke!* My sisters were certainly out, one being dead and all. The other two having turned out to be selfish bitches. That left Paddy and Jannie or Kevin. It wasn't ideal, but Caden had already formed bonds with my brother and my nephew. When it came to that, Kevin would get the house. I would leave it to him. His mother would love that. Actually Joanna, too. *Bonus!* More laughter. I was beginning to really lose my mind, cycling between crazed laughter and hopeless tears. I contemplated going back downstairs for the wine; but instead, I took one last look at the picture in my hand, feeling farther and farther away from the people in it by the day. Then I crossed over to the bed and crawled under the brand new down comforter, still fully dressed. I lay there, no longer thinking, until I fell asleep.

174

Chapter 18
CADEN

Stephen had not come downstairs all day. We didn't see him when Kev and I got home last night, either. He and Joanna had been fighting before we left. I was in my room, and Kevin knocked on the door and said we should get out of the house and give them some privacy. We went through the drive thru at McDonald's and just drove around Minneapolis.

"This is cool," I told Kevin. "I really haven't seen much since we got here. Just people's lawns."

"You'd actually have to leave your room to see anything but that, Cay." Kev had been calling me "Cay." I guess I didn't mind. I called him Kev, but so did everyone else.

"I guess you're right. You know, I really don't want to be a dick to Stephen."

"Then don't be." He'd stopped me in the hall, about an hour before that and told me I was being a dick.

"You make it sound like the easiest thing?" It was more a question than a statement.

"Not easy, but it's pretty simple."

I didn't understand that. Weren't easy and simple the same thing? Kevin turned up the radio, the same classic rock station I now listened to. He didn't have air conditioning in his car, so we had the windows rolled down all the way. It wasn't super-hot, so it was okay. I had flip-flops on, so after a while, I just kicked the right one off and tucked my foot under my left leg. My left leg was always bouncing. It used to drive my dad crazy, because Stephen did it, too. My dad said we shook the whole house in San Francisco. He said he'd never know when there was an actual earthquake because he was so used to the house shaking all the time. There was a song on the radio that I didn't know, but Kev was singing along, kind of low. "It's cool you know all these songs."

"Everyone knows Kansas. You've never heard this? It's "Carry On, Wayward Son."

175

"I don't think so. This is definitely not the kind of music my dads listened to. I mean my dad. Stephen maybe—."

"Why'd you do that?"

"What?"

"You said 'My dads,' then changed it," Kevin said.

Did I? I didn't notice. I used to call Stephen "Dad." I stopped after my dad died. I think I thought Stephen stopped being my dad then. He never said he still was. No one did. No one talked about it, so I just kind of assumed.

"You've done it a few times. You're careful not to slip up around Stephen; you're pretty guarded when you talk to him. You must have used to call him Dad?"

"Who? Stephen?" I asked. Kev just nodded, so I did, too.

"Why'd you stop?"

"It was weird after my dad died. I don't know. I guess I just stopped."

We drove for a ways and just listened to music. Kev was still shoving French fries in his mouth and drinking a pop, and paying attention to the road. I was remembering a few days after my dad died. There wasn't a funeral. He and Stephen didn't want one. I guess that was okay, because I didn't have to wear a suit then. I'd only been to one other funeral, a friend of my dad's, someone he had worked with who hung out with us sometimes and was always nice to me. His name was Marty. He was an agent or something. Anyway, I went to his funeral and I had to wear a suit; other people there were wearing weird things on their heads, and almost all the women were crying really loudly. My dad didn't have many friends. Marty was kind of it. And Stephen. Stephen had a couple of friends, but I guessed maybe there wasn't anyone who would've come to a funeral, anyway. Some people came over to the house and a few of those people were determined to hug us. I didn't mind that much, except that sometimes, when I was being hugged, I felt like I might cry. The people also brought food. I was told they "meant well." Sometimes we'd just throw the food away after they had left. We usually tasted it first, but there was one time when we didn't even do that. Stephen said, "God no! That woman can't even order take out and have it taste good." I thought it was funny. Who

176

doesn't know how to order takeout? So I remembered it. After my dad died, we just kind of stayed at home; and people came to us. That stopped after a few days, too, and it was just the cats and us.

It was a Sunday afternoon and I hadn't been to school since the Tuesday before, the day my dad had died, the day of the election. I was in my room with the door open. Stephen just sort of appeared in the doorway. He'd do that sometimes, like the shape shifters on *The Next Generation*, stealthy, but not as cool. We told each other, "Hey."

"I'm kind of sick of lasagna, and although that tater tot thing Mrs. Thompson came up with was tasty; I'm over that, too."

"Pizza," I suggested.

"I was thinking we could head down the hill and get some Chinese, maybe go to the movie theater. We haven't left the house in three days. Are you up for it?" He talked like grown-ups do when they're trying to talk you into something, but they're pretending not to be.

"Sure." I played along. I liked Chinese food, probably not as much as my dad and Stephen, but it was cool to go to the restaurant on Market, by the theater. My dads called it date night, which I didn't really get. Then I thought about the whole "My dads" thing and I wondered what was going to happen. First of all, I didn't have two anymore, but did I even have one? I wondered if asking about it would've made it real, so I decided not to say anything. It was real enough anyway, wasn't it?

We walked down the hill about an hour later. It looked like it might rain, so we brought umbrellas, but it wasn't that cold. Stephen said we could catch the bus or hail a cab when we got into the Castro, depending on the weather. It ended up being a bus. We had to sit next to each other, pretty close. Stephen put his arm behind me, I guess because there was nowhere else it would fit. I leaned in a little and he didn't move away. It felt good being so close to him.

I felt so confused and unsure about what was going to happen. I'd been waiting for days for Stephen to tell me where I'd be going, what was going to happen next. Thinking back on it, I wondered that for weeks, until it just seemed like nothing was really going to change. Other than my dad being gone and Stephen being weird and me being weird. I went back to school and we lived in the same house and we did the same stuff and ate the same food.

177

I had the same chores. We just didn't talk about it. But then, we hadn't talked about what we were going to do when Dad died. And we knew he was going to, before everything happened. Why did I want to talk about it right then? Why did I need to talk about it right then?

Stephen hadn't been teaching, even before my dad died. I didn't even think about him going back to school. It would have been my school, and eventually I'd have ended up with him as my teacher. I guessed it was good he wasn't teaching anymore, not that it would have been bad, just weird. What would I call him then? There was enough of that confusion when we were at home.

At the restaurant, we sat across from each other in a booth and Stephen opened his menu. I always got Chow Mein with Fried Rice. Stephen always got Kung Pao. It seemed dumb that he even bothered with the menu, but he always did. It was like he wanted to order something else, but nothing ever jumped out at him like the Kung Pao did. The waiter asked if we wanted anything to drink. I got root beer and Stephen got some kind of wine, I think. As soon as the waiter left to get the drinks, Stephen put his menu down, and looked across the table at me. That was it. All of a sudden, I knew he was going to tell me I was going to an orphanage or something like that. We'd come out to where people were, so I didn't cry or something. I held my breath and waited for him to say it for what seemed like a really long time.

"Do you feel like you can go back to school on Tuesday?" That was it? That's what he took so long to say? I almost didn't notice that I hadn't taken a breath until I went to answer.

"I guess." I was so relieved. I took a deep breath, like I was about to go underwater or something.

"That gives us one more day to get our bearings, but if you're not ready yet, you have to tell me. You know that you can talk to me, right? You know that?" I nodded, but I didn't really know that, did I? I didn't really know many things. I wanted so bad to ask him what happened next, but the waiter was back with my root beer and to take our order.

"We're just going to do this one day at a time for now," he said, after the waiter had left again. I didn't say anything, so he kept talking, but his voice shook at the next part. "Maybe it'll be a while before either of us is ready to do anything more than one day at a time."

178

He said it like it was a question and then he looked down at the table and rubbed his eyes. For a while, we just sat there in silence. At least I had a drink in front of me. The root beer tasted funny, not good, like it used to. That was weird, right? I mean things shouldn't taste different, but they did anyway. We hadn't really had anything normal to eat in days, nothing we usually ate, anyway. I wondered if the Chow Mein would taste different when the waiter brought it out. When we'd gone there, before, we couldn't fit in a tiny booth. The owner, this little Chinese man would seat us at one of the larger booths on the other side of the restaurant, by the window. He wasn't there to seat us when we got there, but I saw him come out of the kitchen as the waiter was getting my root beer from the bar. I looked up just then, and saw him bringing a glass of wine on a little brown tray to our table.

"You haven't been in for a while. Is Mister Alec sick?" I thought my heart would come crashing out of my chest. I stood up quickly and hit the glass of root beer, knocking it over.

"Shit!" Stephen took his napkin and tried to clean it up right away. "I'm sorry. I had to; I mean I have to go to the bathroom."

"It's alright," Stephen was saying, but it wasn't like it was totally out loud, it sounded like it did when people talked to you and you had headphones on, like after you turned the music down, but it was still ringing in your ears. I couldn't make out what he'd said right away. The other sound had to drain away. "Go on to the bathroom."

I just turned and hurried away, not sure what I might do if I had to stand there for another second. I felt like I might scream, or worse, cry. I heard Stephen apologize to the man as I was leaving. I wondered what he would tell him after I was gone. I wondered if he felt like he might scream, too.

In the bathroom, I didn't cry. Or scream. I just stood there and tried to catch my breath. I didn't want to be there anymore. I didn't want to be anywhere really. Not yet. I definitely didn't want to go to a movie anymore. The bathroom was only big enough for one person, and the sink was on the outside in the hall. I was in there for a few minutes, I think, and then somebody knocked on the door. I called out that I'd be right out. There wasn't even a mirror in there, just a toilet. The room was smaller than my closet and had just a light bulb that hung down. I thought I should flush the toilet at least, so it didn't seem like I'd been hiding in there. I took another couple of deep breaths and turned the lock on the door. There was a woman in the hall, waiting to get in. She was older, like someone's grandma, I thought, and she

179

smiled at me, like she knew I was in there being sad. I just looked down at the floor and let her squeeze past me and the sink into the tiny closet. I washed my hands at the sink, even though I hadn't done anything in the other room except stand there.

We never went to the movie that day. I guess Stephen felt like me, like it was too soon to be anywhere but home, because when I got back to the table, he'd drunk almost the whole glass of wine, and our waiter had just brought our food in a brown paper bag, instead of on plates. The owner had disappeared, probably embarrassed. I felt sort of bad for him.

"I decided we could stop quick and rent a video, instead of going to the theater. I'm sorry, kiddo. Maybe we should have stayed home, period."

"It's okay." I didn't want him to feel like it was his fault, but I was really glad he decided we could go home.

"I had Mister Chan switch our order to go as soon as you left. One minute and I'll be ready. We can walk up a couple of blocks and pick out a video, and then hail a cab. That alright?" He picked up his wine glass and gulped it down, then he stood, careful; unlike me, not to spill anything on his way up.

It took us a little while to pick out a video. We settled on *White Fang*. I wanted *Silence of the Lambs*, but Stephen said no. He had gone to see it in the theater like a year earlier, and I stayed with my dad. My dad didn't like movies like that, and besides, he was too sick that day and kept telling Stephen to go. I remembered him promising he'd just stay in bed and read or sleep. Stephen finally agreed to go. When he got home, he complained how long the movie was and told us that he almost couldn't pay attention through the second half, until the end, because the movie was so long. My dad told him he'd only been gone three-and-a-half hours, so it couldn't have been that long, with time getting down the hill and catching a cab and everything. I was disappointed then that I couldn't go, but Dad told me after Stephen left; there was no way I was seeing a movie like that at my age.

It was a year and a half later, and I guessed I was still not old enough to see it. I remember deciding that I'd have to figure out a way to get my hands on the video and watch it by myself. I mean how the hell old did I have to be for God's sake?

"Have you seen *Silence of the Lambs*?" I asked Kevin.

180

"Yeah why? What made you think of that?" He'd finally finished the French fries because he crumpled up the white paper bag and handed it to me. "Garbage." I guessed that meant I was supposed to put it in the box he kept behind his seat. Kev was sort of neat for a guy, I mean a guy who wasn't gay, anyway.

"Stephen wouldn't let me watch it last year. I have to be old enough now. Don't you think?"

"Not up to me."

"Why are adults so hung up on movies? I'm not a kid."

"Look, I could care less what you watch, but I guess that's why I'm not the parent."

I wasn't going to get anywhere with him, so I went back to my memory. By the time we got a cab and got up the hill that night, it had started to rain. It had been kind of grey all day, so I barely noticed the sky going almost completely black. I could feel the rain, but I couldn't see it. I had my own keys, but Stephen unlocked the front door. He stayed outside to smoke a cigarette, and I went in with the food. By the time he came inside, I had gotten us all set to eat. I was dishing out my Chow Mein when I heard him come in the front door. I listened to him turn the lock on the front door and hang up his coat. I could hear the closet door open and shut. Then I heard it open and shut again. He must have picked up my coat and hung that up, too.

"You just threw your coat on the floor."

"I didn't exactly throw it. I took it off and set it on the floor. I had the food." I was right.

"Sure. That's it." He was in the kitchen watching me now. "How about we eat in front of the TV?"

"Which one?" I was done dishing my plate up.

"In our—I mean my room." I pretended not to notice what he'd just done. "Why don't you take your food into my room? I'll meet you in there in two minutes. Can you carry all your stuff?"

181

"I'll bring a tray." I had turned to go, but he kind of grabbed my arm and pulled me close. I didn't expect it. We hadn't hugged since that night, unless you counted the bus, earlier. For the last day and a half, about, it seemed like we were kind of avoiding each other. Once, I actually got up and started to go out of my room, to find him and tell him something. Then I remembered nothing was the same, and just shut my bedroom door and went back to lay in my bed. He held onto me and I could smell cigarettes and wine and his cologne and, for a minute I felt protected. I felt like he was my dad again. I hugged him back, tighter than usual, and wondered what he was feeling.

Lunchtime the day after Stephen and Joanna fought had come and gone, and so had dinner. Kev and I ate the pizza from the night before at the counter. He said we should leave Stephen alone, but I was worried. I didn't know what to do. It was weird. He didn't even come down, that I knew of, to have a cigarette since the night before. Finally, Kevin agreed I could put some pizza on a plate and take it up to him. That was a good excuse to knock on the bedroom door, he told me. I actually didn't know if Stephen was still angry with me. He thought I'd stolen a bracelet at that place yesterday. Kelly had done that.

I was surprised Stephen even assumed it was me who had stolen something, but since that's the way it was, I just went along with it. I didn't want Kelly to get in trouble either. It was such a mess, and for the first time in a long while, I didn't want to just accept it. With Stephen not right there, I couldn't stand the mess. I had thought a lot about what Kevin told me. I even thought about what Stephen had said right after we got to Minnesota, the night I had gotten so mad. He said he belonged wherever I was. I had heard him. It was just everything that came before that sucked. That part wasn't enough to make up for us moving, but Kev said we moved for me. I didn't exactly get it, but if it was true, maybe Stephen should be mad at me and not the other way around.

I really didn't think he was, not about that anyway, but even so, I never thought of it that way. I hadn't thought of much really; except myself, in weeks. Maybe not since we said goodbye to the city, still back in San Francisco. I actually wanted to tell Stephen I was sorry. I wasn't sure how I'd say it, but I just knew I had to. I could see that I had worried for so long that he would leave me alone that I never paid attention to the fact that he was still right there. Kevin got me to see that. Grown-ups really did know stuff that at least had to be explained to kids. If they took the time to explain it, then we could work out the rest. I was glad Kevin told me stuff. He was kind of the first grown-up that had done that in a while. He was rinsing his plate in the sink

182

with his back to me. I thanked him, but I think I was too quiet. I said it again, louder, "Thank you."

"For what?" Kevin set the plate on the counter next to the sink and turned around to face me.

"You're cool to tell me stuff."

"Why wouldn't I?" He smiled.

"You'd be surprised," I told him.

"I think it's harder for some adults to remember what it's like to be a kid. It wasn't that long ago for me, and besides, I don't always feel like that much of an adult."

"You're pretty old, though," I said, only kind-of joking.

"Douche!" he called me.

"You're a douche!"

"You're welcome." I had gotten up and walked around the counter. Kevin took another plate out of the cupboard and handed it to me, taking the dirty plate in trade. "Go bring Stephen some pizza, and don't be a dick."

"I'll try my best." He had turned back to the sink and I moved next to him. It felt like I should say one more thing, but it was weird. I stood there for a second until Kevin stopped what he was doing again and looked over at me. He was taller than Stephen. I had to look up to make eye contact with Kevin.

"I love you," I said fast, and turned back around. I don't think I actually knew those were the words that would come out of my mouth. I wasn't sure; again, whether he'd even heard me. I stopped breathing for a second.

"I love you, too, man," Kevin said, our backs to each other. I could breathe.

A few minutes later I stood outside Stephen's bedroom door with some microwaved pizza. I still hadn't worked out what I was going to say. I guessed I would just fake it. It worked for my oral report, the last week of school, a

183

month ago. I had thought I was screwed then, but I actually got a B-plus. It was the lowest grade I'd gotten all year, but definitely not a D or an F. I knocked on the door, hoping for a similar grade today. No answer. I knocked again. I wanted to just give up then. I'd tried. It occurred to me that I could just go back down the hall to my room and eat the pizza myself. I couldn't hear a thing on the other side of the door. Maybe Stephen wasn't even in there. How did we really know? Shit! Okay, one more time. I knocked again and tried the doorknob. The door wasn't locked. Should I just go in? It had been almost twenty-four hours since I'd seen Stephen. I was really scared, not like Freddy Kruger scared; but all of a sudden, I realized how much uncertainty there was. The whole situation blew. I had just taken for granted that Stephen would be there, all the while worrying that he wouldn't be. How fucked up was that? I wanted him to be okay, for us to be okay, more than anything. I did that thing you do when you kind of hold your breath as the teacher hands you your test, the one you didn't really study for, and you just kind of pray before looking down at the grade. I did that and I turned the knob to the right until it wouldn't go any further. Then I pushed the door open a crack and said his name.

There wasn't an answer, so I pushed the door open halfway and stepped inside the room. I could see that he was in his bed. I could only see the top of his head and one hand. The rest of him was covered.

"Stephen," I called again. He moved and I almost lost it. My heart wasn't where it belonged. It was all the way up in my neck. "Are you okay?"

"What?" His voice was hoarse.

"Kevin and I were worried," I told him. He turned a little.

"Why?" He cleared his throat and rolled to the side, pulling the blanket away from his face. The shades weren't drawn, so the room was full of light. The sun was right there, setting.

"You haven't been downstairs all day. And you didn't answer when I knocked on the door or called your name."

"It seemed like I was dreaming," he said. "Like I wasn't really hearing your voice. I didn't hear you knock at all." He rolled completely over onto his back and moved to sit up a bit.

"I brought you some pizza." I tried to sound cheerful.

184

"Oh, thank you." He made no effort to take it from me though.

"Are you alright? You were fighting with Joanna, so we left. Maybe we should have stayed."

"Oh, kiddo, don't worry about that." He gave me a look, not really smiling, but like a parent gives; safe, like everything was really okay. "That was just us being silly."

"So you're okay?"

"Getting there." He was now sitting up, and he moved a pillow behind himself.

"I'm sorry about yesterday." It just came out. There was a lot of that inside. I felt like I might just explode like a piñata.

"You have nothing to be sorry about. Joanna told me it was Kelly who stole the bracelet. Honestly, I shouldn't have thought it was you in the first place."

"I have been kind of a dick lately," I offered. Now he was looking at me. At first I thought disapprovingly, but it wasn't that. It was like how you get when you finally work out an answer.

"Kiddo, you're fourteen years old. Being a dick is kind of in your job description." Now he smiled. "I'm sorry I worried you."

"It's okay. It was just different is all."

"How do you mean?" Stephen asked. He reached out for the plate of pizza, even though I was still too far away. I figured that meant I should come in. I was still a little weirded out, but I moved towards the bed. I handed him the plate and he thanked me and put it on top of some books on the little dresser next to the bed. He motioned for me to sit next to him in the bed. I couldn't remember the last time we sat like that. I'd barely even been inside his bedroom in the new house. I looked around the room quickly, not sure what I was actually looking for.

"I know. It's been a while. I kind of miss our movie days."

"Me, too." I meant it.

185

We used to spend hours watching movies in my dad's bed. I thought maybe the last time was just Stephen and me, right after my dad died, after that whole thing in the Chinese restaurant. That night, for a couple hours, it was like nothing had changed. Stephen had come down the hall with a big tray. There were takeout containers, some silverware, and an empty plate, a bottle of wine and an empty wine glass, and one of those cups little kids use to drink out of so they don't spill. At first, I was confused when he handed it to me.

"Root beer. Try not to spill." Then he laughed and I laughed. It was really funny after me spilling at the restaurant. We sat there and ate our food and I was careful not to spill anything. After the movie was over, Stephen piled all of our dishes on the tray and took them and the leftover food back to the kitchen, and I went to my room. We were broken again, like when you'd tried to glue something and it looked fixed, but then fell apart again as soon as you stopped holding it together. I didn't know why things happened the way they did sometimes. I missed hanging out with Stephen. I missed him being my dad and not some not-really-friend you were just polite to. I never thought he might miss it, too. How did life get so stupid?

"I have a lot to be sorry for," Stephen said. He looked like he might cry. I didn't know what to say, so I finally sat next to him. There was a lot of blanket bunched up in between us. Stephen was now sitting cross-legged. "Maybe I shouldn't have moved us here. I certainly should have discussed it with you first."

"It's okay. I like it here. It's different. I like Kevin a lot, and Charlie and Paddy. And Kelly. I don't know how sometimes. I mean, I don't know how to be."

"What do you mean?"

"All the family I ever had was you and my dad. I forget these people aren't just people or, like, friends." I turned more towards him and moved my legs under me. We were facing each other now.

"That's pretty profound. It's exactly how friendships are, you know."

"I don't get it."

"First of all, you can just know someone and feel like you're going to get along, but then, all of a sudden, you realize you don't just know them. You realize that they're important to you now, just like family. I know you don't

186

have any point of reference for that. I barely do, but friends can become family and family can become friends."

"I guess that makes sense," I told him.

"You were too young to really remember this, but a long time ago, the three of us were hanging out in bed in our first apartment in LA. Do you even remember that apartment?"

"Kind of. I mean I do, I guess."

"You were four. You had this red dinosaur that you just loved."

"Donald," I said. I loved that dumb dinosaur. I didn't remember what had ever happened to him.

"Yes! Donald. You were playing by yourself on the floor and your dad and I were reading. All of a sudden, you were right next to my head, and you pretended to be Donald, well you pretended Donald was talking to me."

"I did?" I really didn't remember that.

"You did," he kept going. "Donald asked me if it would be okay if the both of you called me Dad. Up until that point, we just kind of knew each other. I loved your dad so much. We had just all moved in together, but I didn't quite know where you and I stood. You were a smart little kid, even then. You figured it out before me. That's what I mean. You must have just decided that we were going to be more than acquaintances that shared your dad."

"Really?" I kinda liked the story.

"Really! Do you see what I mean now?"

"I think I just had that with Kev." I told him.

"That's pretty awesome, right?"

"I miss it," I conceded.

"We; you and I, are going to figure this out." He sounded pretty certain.

187

"I don't know how." I was glad we were talking, but everything was still so fucked up.

"I'm not sure either, but it's time we start to figure it out. We're here now. Mistake or not, we're just going to have to make the best of it."

"That night when you first told me that you were sorry you didn't ask me first," I started, and he nodded. "I just figured out something. In San Francisco, I could still feel Dad. I got mad at you because I couldn't feel him anymore. Not here. Then I got mad at myself because I didn't see it right away."

"See what?"

"I didn't see that he was really gone." My voice shook as I said it. "I should've noticed. I didn't even say goodbye." Shit! My eyes were wet. Oh, fuck it!

"Caden, I am so sorry! I should have talked to you about this. I don't know why I didn't. I think I was just scared it would only make it worse."

"I was too." I was crying now, full-on. I looked at him and his eyes were dry. I felt stupid suddenly and swiped at the tears. He reached out and held my hands in his.

"Never be embarrassed to cry. Your Dad was so proud he raised you to be as sensitive as you are. He used to try and get my attention when he noticed you cry at movies."

"He was proud of me?" My heart felt tired.

"Your dad was so very proud of you. Everything about you filled him with joy. I never saw another person so filled with love for someone else until I met your dad. He taught me how. I had loved people before. Of course I had, but it was like I hadn't loved them completely, not even myself, until I saw myself in your dad's eyes. Love was everything to him, and he had so few people to give his love to."

"How do you mean?"

"Most people have parents; some have brothers and sisters, and friends, so many people they can share their love with. I did, but I shut it out. That's why Joanna is angry, but that's a whole different story. Your dad just had you and

188

me. Maybe that's how his love got so big. He didn't have anywhere else to put it all."

"I really miss him."

"I do, too." Stephen leaned forward. Our faces were almost touching. He moved the rest of his body to line up with his head and the blanket scrunched up between us and then he hugged me. It was tight and I shook a little and just let him steady me. "You know what though? He is here. I feel him all the time."

"How come I don't?" My head was resting on his shoulder.

"I don't know. I think, Caden, that you got so mad at yourself, you won't let it happen. Your dad wouldn't have ever wanted you to be so sad."

I didn't say anything. I didn't know what to say, but it felt okay. Even confused, I felt safe now. I let myself cry some more and Stephen just held on. My face was turned away from his, but he sniffled like he was crying, too. I wasn't by myself.

"I really missed this. I'm so sorry we stopped. I thought it was best to give you space after your dad died."

"It always felt like we had broken." I'd never said that stuff aloud before. "I thought maybe you would fix it—us." He looked so hurt just then, his lower lip quivered. I felt like I had been a dick again. I couldn't think, right away, what to say to make it better.

"I should have fixed it," he said, letting me off the hook. "I'm going to do better now. I have to do better. That day that you asked me if you could call me Dad—." He stopped, thinking. I brushed at my eyes, not embarrassed, though. "That day was the best day of my life. I thought the best day would always be when I met your dad, but you made it better somehow. There was an empty piece I didn't know was empty, and you, Caden; you showed it to me."

"I'm sorry." I was confused again.

"No. It was a good thing. I don't know if I'll ever be able to explain to you how much."

189

"I actually get that part. I think. Kevin told me I was being a dick to you." I needed to tell him I was sorry. It felt like that would fix things, like that might be all we needed to be normal again, but I didn't know exactly what to be sorry for. I was glad he wasn't still talking though. "I missed my dad so much at first. I mean I still do, but I missed him so much, that night when we went to the restaurant, that was the first time I ever thought about it."

"Thought about what?"

"What was going to happen? I know you guys didn't think I knew that he was really going to die, but I did. I knew it for a while. No matter what either of you ever did or said, you just looked sad." He sat there and looked at me, and tears just kept falling out of his eyes. I knew we were the same then. I knew he needed me as much as I needed him.

"It was our job to protect you," he sighed.

"You did that. Maybe just too much. Does that make sense?" He nodded. We sat for a minute, neither of us saying anything. Then I just thought of it. I knew what I had to say. "I'm sorry I stopped calling you Dad. I don't know why I did that."

There. I said it. It kind of just sat there. I looked down just then, but Stephen lowered his head and turned to look up at me. He was still crying a little, but he was smiling, too. "When you do that, you make it really hard for people to see how handsome you are." He actually looked like he didn't really get what he had just said, but I did. My dad said that same thing. I wondered if they had talked about it. "You can start calling me it again whenever you want. And you don't ever have to be sorry for being sad or confused. Okay?" He was still smiling. He moved his head back up and took his hand and pushed mine up, too, so we were looking at each other normal.

"Okay, Dad." It was easier to just say than I thought it would be. Dad. Dad! We were still both sitting cross-legged on the bed and I was feeling like I was smaller, no… lighter. He reached his hand up and moved my hair away from my forehead. He used to do that all the time. I sniffled, not really crying anymore.

"We need to get you a haircut." Suddenly I was barely listening. I had turned my head for a second. The sun was right there, blinding me. I moved my eyes back quickly and there he was smiling, right next to us in the bed. My dad. He didn't even look sick anymore.

Chapter 19
STEPHEN

"Dad!"

I opened my eyes partway, and then closed them again. For a moment, I wasn't certain why I'd ever wanted the title back. I also wasn't sure who thought it was a good idea to go to the bar the night before the first day of school. I was asleep, lying on my side, facing the clock; all I needed to do was open one eye and check the time. The effort it required to accomplish the task seemed insurmountable. What the hell had I drunk the night before? I tried going back over the night. Nope. Too early. Not enough caffeine. Not any caffeine.

"Dad!" The voice was closer this time, just outside my bedroom door.

"If you yell that name one more time I'm going to sell you into white slavery," I replied, hopefully not loud enough for anyone but myself to hear. *Okay, you can do this.* Eye open. It took a few seconds to focus my vision in the direction of the digital display two feet from my head. Seven sixteen. I assumed that was a.m. What day was this? Yes, okay. Okay. The first day of school. THE FIRST DAY OF SCHOOL! FUCK!

I shot up so quickly, I thought my head would explode. I was going to kill Charlie. The general consensus had been that I needed a night out. I had opened the video store almost six weeks ago. We had closed it for less than a week when I bought it, during which Caden, Kevin, Charlie, and even Betty; had worked tirelessly to overhaul the store. We had just finished the house when I took on that project. It turned out that Betty's son had owned the building, so I was now landlord to a florist, a smoke shop, and two apartment units upstairs. I had bought all of it for a song and it had needed far less work than the house. Charlie had done a lot of the work on the store and building. One of the units upstairs was vacant, so work was done there, too. Things were really going swimmingly, but I was exhausted. I'm sure we all were.

Things at home were good, also. My relationship with Caden was great, possibly better than it had been since before Alec had gotten sick. It seemed the end of my relationship with Joanna had been the catalyst for Caden and me to finally talk, figure out where we stood with each other. I might have been a bit over dramatic where my sister was concerned, but we hadn't

191

spoken since that night. I hadn't intended it to go on so long. Paddy stayed out of it. I'm not certain our mother knew the full extent of what had happened, and of course, we hadn't seen or heard from Catelyn. I tried not to pry where Kevin was concerned, and he offered very little information without being coerced. I had no idea if he'd spoken to his mother.

Caden had turned fifteen a couple of weeks before. We went to the New Zoo in Apple Valley, all of us. Joanna had even allowed Kelly to join us. I told Caden he could invite my sister, that was the last she had been discussed. I didn't know if he'd opted not to invite her out of consideration for me, or if he had invited her and she chose not to come. My life was far too busy to worry about it. We shared several relatives, and as of today, she was my kid's principal. Our paths were bound to cross eventually.

Between myself, Betty and Kevin, we had the video store hours covered. My intention was to hire someone else once we got underway, but things were working well for the time being. I knew there would be complications once school started, but we hadn't had to address that. Truth be told, I was enjoying as much status quo as I could get. It was new to us, but Caden and I were beginning to get used to it.

Caden had less than a three-block walk to the city bus that would be his ride to school. We had practiced, although he had insisted such ceremony was unnecessary. He had been taking a bus to school on his own, in a much larger city, since he was thirteen. That had become necessary when Alec got sick. So many things had become necessary when Alec got sick, and all things considered, Caden had handled them miraculously well. It still amused me that he worked for my brother. He continued to do so of his own accord. I wondered what Alec would think of any of the changes we'd made. A year before, I couldn't have dreamt a single thing about our lives the way they'd become. I didn't imagine Alec would have conjured up anything close, either. We hadn't even discussed a move to Minnesota. It was funny how things just came together, random decisions, bizarre coincidences and unexpected inspirations; like puzzle pieces in a life you never imagined for yourself; yet they fit.

Charlie had been asking me to come down to the bar for weeks. We had become friends over the three months since we moved. In fact, the four of us—Caden, Kevin, Charlie and I—had become almost inseparable. We had gone to the Minnesota State Fair on Saturday night and saw Def Lepard and Ugly Kid Joe, all of us thrilled. Caden had never seen a spectacle like the Minnesota State Fair. There was nothing like it in San Francisco; anything even similar would have included drag queens and rainbow flags. We ate and ate, and Caden won me a gigantic teddy bear.

That bear was, in fact, the first thing I saw when I woke in the morning. It was so large, and cast such a shadow in the light from the tiny nightlight in my bathroom, that it scared the crap out of me the night before. I looked over at it and sighed.

"We're going to find a new home for you today, bear." I needed to get up and see to it that Caden had everything he needed. I didn't think he'd allow me to walk him to the bus stop, but I thought I might suggest it just to be funny.

"Stephen!" He'd decided to take a different tact.

"WHAT!? What? For heaven's sake." I stood up and all the blood rushed to my head. Surprisingly enough, I may have over-sold the hangover. I really didn't feel that poorly. A couple of Tylenol and I would be good as new.

"Can I come in?" Caden asked. I wasn't sure why my bedroom door was closed all the way.

"You may. What's the crisis?"

"It's locked." He was trying the handle. I checked quickly, to make sure I was wearing shorts.

"I can't find my backpack," Caden explained, once I'd opened the door.

"I thought you were going to set it by the back door, so it was there when you were ready to leave this morning."

"Oh, yeah," he said. "Did you have fun last night? Why was your door locked?"

"I'm not—," I started to say that I wasn't sure, but it came back to me mid-sentence. Shit! I had kissed somebody last night! I scanned my memory. Yeah, I had certainly enjoyed myself, so much so that I'd not have been able to sleep had I not masturbated. Nothing had really happened. I was sitting at the bar talking to Charlie, who was bartending. It had been months since I'd set foot inside a gay bar and years since I'd done so as a single gay man. I wasn't accustomed to being paid attention to, not like that night.

193

There had always been a fairly common standard in gay bars across the country. It had been a very long time since I had experienced it firsthand. Charlie had reminded me that I was "new meat" to the bar's patrons. I rolled my eyes at the suggestion, but after I'd been bought a drink, a shot, and been cruised more than once, I had to concede he was right.

Then I'd seen a familiar face. It took me several minutes to work out from where. He had the most beautiful sea-green eyes. They shone, even in the dark bar. He was the guy I'd seen on the street the day I first set foot in what was now my video store. He was completely gorgeous, but looked very young. Still, I couldn't help but look. After an hour of shared stolen glances, an older guy that had been sitting on the barstool next to me left, and green eyes moved his cocktail, his cigarettes, and his self, down two stools to sit next to me.

"Hi there!" he said, smiling.

"Hello." My heart was suddenly in my throat. His leg brushed mine and I felt myself begin to harden. Jesus Christ! Was I sixteen fucking years old?!

"I saw you on the street in Uptown, what, a couple of months ago?" It was less a question than a declaration.

"How do you even remember that?"

"You have an amazing smile," he answered. "When I saw you crossing the street, you looked so sad, but then I smiled at you and you smiled back, and your whole face lit up."

"Really?" I wondered if the entire bar could see how red I was turning. Certainly, this guy could. "My name is Stephen," I managed, extending my hand.

"God... sorry... Matthias, my name's Matthias." His grip was firm as he shook my hand. "Nice to meet you."

"It's very nice to meet you. You've made my whole night!"

"May I buy you another one of those?" I couldn't stop myself from laughing. "What did I say?"

"It's nothing really. It'll sound arrogant."

194

"New meat?" he asked, chuckling. See? Everyone knew. "I haven't seen you in here before."

"What a line!"

"Haha, you know what I mean."

"Can I get you another, Matt?" Charlie was suddenly standing in front of us. He set a beer down in front of me.

"Please. Can I buy that one, too?" He motioned to the bottle Charlie had just set in front of me.

"Nope, that one's on me," Charlie answered.

"Hey, get in line," Matthias demanded. Charlie just laughed. I wondered if he kept his heterosexuality close to the vest here. He was working in a gay bar, after all. I studied him, pouring vodka into a tall glass. He wore almost skin-tight blue jeans and a tank top that, at the right angle, revealed his nipples. His long hair was pulled back into a ponytail, and he had in contact lenses. He was working it. It had been weeks since I had checked out his ass, but God, in these jeans it was phenomenal. His arms weren't terribly defined, but there were hints of muscle, particularly when he shook a drink. I had noticed that much already. We'd been spending so much time together; I'd stopped thinking of him as anyone but a friend. I didn't even see his brother anymore when I looked at him. In truth, they were very different. I had to look purposefully to see similarities to Liam anymore.

"I take it you two have introduced yourselves?" Charlie asked.

"We're old friends."

"We really are old friends," Charlie told Matthias. "Stephen dated my brother in high school."

"Seriously?" the kid asked.

"Guilty! It was a long time ago."

"Want a shot, you two?" Charlie inquired.

195

"Sure. You call it." I wasn't certain if Matthias was talking to me or to Charlie.

"Okay, but seriously, this has to be it. First day of school tomorrow."

"You go to school?" Matthias asked, slightly surprised.

"Oh, no! My son does."

"Really?" Charlie had walked away to take someone else's order.

"He's fifteen and starting high school," I answered, taking a sip of my beer.

"Shit! You don't look that old!"

"I'm not. He's my stepson." I realized the entire situation demanded more of an explanation, so I gave Matthias a brief rundown, leaving out any reference to AIDS or HIV. I'd only met him three minutes ago.

"Jesus Christ," he said, when I'd finished. "No wonder you were sad that day."

"I'm still kind of surprised you could tell that from a look."

"I'm pretty perceptive. Hey, I've got to hit the men's room. Can you watch my stuff?"

"Sure, no problem." I wondered if I had scared him away. *Away from what,* I thought? This wouldn't go anywhere. It was fun to flirt and it felt incredible to be on the receiving end, but my life was so full of complications, I couldn't quickly make sense out of them all. First and foremost, I was HIV positive and that wasn't something I'd even thought about having to tell some random guy in a bar. I didn't rule out ever having to figure out how I would share that fact. Then there was the fact that my lover had died nine months ago. It hadn't even been a year. It was way, way too soon. Still, it felt blissful and I was really hoping Matthias would return. I told myself that he'd left a full drink, a pack of cigarettes, and a lighter. Of course he was coming back.

"He's cute, right?" Charlie was back.

"You crack me up."

"How so?"

196

"'He's cute, right?' Really? How do you know?" I'd meant it rhetorically.

"You don't think I know when a guy is cute? Plus, oh my God, his eyes! So what kind of shot are we doing?"

"Fuck, I don't know! I don't do shots. You're the bartender," I told him. "Not whiskey! Or anything with milk!"

"Got it," he said and turned away, searching the bottles on the wall in front of him. He grabbed a bottle of blue liquid. Or was the bottle blue? I was seriously buzzed. "Windshield washer fluid."

"What the hell is that?" I asked, suddenly frightened.

"You'll like it." He started pouring from the bottle into a shaker.

"Windshield Washer Fluid?" Matthias asked, back from the bathroom. *He had come back!*

"Apparently," I answered.

"They're really good!"

"See?! Oh ye of little faith," Charlie chimed in. Someone yelled out "bartender" and he was gone again. He'd told me earlier that the paying customers came first.

"So how do you two know each other again?" Matthias asked. I studied his face for a sign that he was joking. Seeing none, I began to wonder.

"I dated his brother," I repeated.

"Oh shit! Yeah, that's right! I'm a little drunk."

"I'm sorry! Do you even want a shot?"

"Oh, hell yeah," he exclaimed, reclaiming his bar stool. Charlie was at the cash register.

I was suddenly so nervous. I was warm all over and my dick had been semi-hard for twenty minutes. Thankfully, my jeans were not as painted on as Charlie's. I decided to excuse myself and go to the bathroom, if only to catch

197

my breath and attempt to do something about my dick. The place was long and narrow, with two bars. The bathrooms were all the way at the back. I was at the front bar, so had to maneuver myself through about fifty people to get there.

In the bathroom, I decided to pee. I stood at the urinal waiting to be able to do so for almost a minute. There were two urinals next to each other and a single stall with no door, pretty standard for a gay bar this size. Behind the urinals, against the opposite wall were two sinks. I finished at the urinal finally, happy to be back to somewhat normal and turned around to wash my hands. Behind both sinks was a large, plain mirror. I stood there letting warm water wash over my clammy hands, checking my face and hair in the mirror. I typically felt much older than I actually looked.

I was just a couple of months away from my thirty-fourth birthday and I was sure I could pass for mid-twenties. I dried my hands with a paper towel and turned back to the mirror. I ran my hand gently through my hair to give it a little body. It was shoulder length, thick and wavy on its own. I had never thought my brown hair and brown eyes were anything exceptional. I hadn't had so much as a trim since we'd moved, and I needed a haircut. How had I not considered that until just that moment?

I smiled at myself in the mirror, mostly to check for anything in my teeth. But since I hadn't eaten anything since I got to the bar, maybe it was mostly because I was drunk. One more adjustment to my hair and I turned, almost running right into a guy who looked about seventeen. How did guys progressively look younger, the older I got?

"Excuse me." He just stood there, sizing me up for a few seconds. "You're hot!"

At least words alone didn't get a rise out of me. I had started to sweat, and my head was spinning a little. All I could manage to say was, "Thanks. You too," before moving past him to steady myself in the doorway. I could do it. I stood there for just a second, considered turning back around to check out the first guy who had called me hot in a decade, but I was on a path. It was best to just keep moving forward. Somehow, a minute or two passed and I was back at the bar. I breathed a sigh of relief as I climbed back on the barstool. I noticed Matthias had disappeared again, leaving behind his belongings.

"Making a call," Charlie said, noticing I had returned. "If you two are planning on hooking up, you're going to actually have to remain at the bar together. You know; like at the same time."

"Excuse me?" I practically choked on the mouthful of beer I had just taken.

"Who would blame you? I—."

"You're not going to start on how hot he is again?" I interrupted.

"No, but since you said something," he started, leaning closer. "He said you have a great ass."

I had to wonder if it was all some kind of practical joke. How surreal was it for Charlie, Mister Perfect Ass, a straight guy with a crush on my sister, to be relaying another guy's assessment of my ass? To me! Also, the attention I was getting was bizarre. I was alright, but I was absolutely nothing special, not compared to Matthias or Charlie. Even the teenager from the bathroom, not to mention at least a dozen other guys I'd passed going to and from the men's room. I had hardly considered how I looked in two years. I took care of myself; I'd even started jogging again. I picked out my clothes carefully and even checked myself in the mirror more frequently. I had completely forgotten what it was like, judging myself according to how others saw me. I could not recall the last time I'd considered what Alec would think of my appearance. Was there a point in a relationship where you stopped wondering, at least stopped caring about that sort of thing? Or had our circumstances dictated it? How shallow would it have been to spend minutes at the mirror when the man you love is dying down the hall? Either way, it was all new to me.

"I just don't get it," I told Charlie.

"Ass?" He chuckled. "Look, I get this must be weird."

"You have no idea. And now you've gone and gotten me drunk, so I'm not sure I have an accurate sense of what's going on."

"Anyone who's able to say 'accurate sense of what's going on' is definitely not too drunk to get a little."

"You're incorrigible. Besides, I wouldn't know what to do with 'a little' if I did get it."

"You better figure it out," he said, looking across the bar. "Matthias is on his way back."

"Goody!" I turned and watched him approach. He was tall, at least six feet, though it was hard to tell because we hadn't actually stood next to each other. He wore a tight t-shirt, black or navy blue, and shorts. God, how had I not noticed he was wearing shorts? No wonder I had the reaction I did when his leg brushed mine. His hair was short and dark with a little curl to it. He was muscular, but not ridiculously so. As he sat next to me, I noticed he had a tattoo on his left arm. He was sitting to my left, so I barely caught a glimpse when he sat down.

"What's your tattoo?" Was that a line? I simply had no idea what I was doing.

"On my arm?" he asked, turning. He rolled up his sleeve and showed me what looked like the branches of a tree. "It actually just starts there."

He turned back around, facing the bar again, and lifted his entire shirt. I almost fell off my barstool. First torso, then abs, then chest, and finally a perfect nipple. I hardly noticed the tattoo right away. I had passed two guys in the back who had no shirts on. I saw Kevin and Charlie somewhat regularly without shirts, but Matthias was showing me himself. He was tan even in this light. The tattoo looked to be three separate pictures. All at once, I saw it. Under the last picture were six words tattooed in cursive: "and she loved a little boy." It was The Giving Tree. They seemed to be exact replications of artwork from the Shel Silverstein book.

"You liked The Giving Tree?" I squeaked, focusing on his abs again. I felt a bead of sweat drip from the nape of my neck down my back. It was hot in that bar.

"I did. It's a long story really, a childhood thing. My dad taught English in a Catholic middle school."

"I taught English, but high school level." An even tone had returned to my voice.

"That's cool." He put his shirt back down, and I finally looked straight ahead.

"What's with the show?" Charlie said, back in front of us. "A guy at the end of the bar almost choked on his drink."

"I was showing him my tattoo. Hey, how about those shots?"

"If you'd both sit still, we could do them," Charlie picked up the shaker and turned it almost sideways in his right hand, shaking. The gesture looked oddly like something else entirely. I decided it was as good a time as any to light another cigarette, seeing as how I wasn't holding my breath anymore. Charlie lined up three shot glasses and turned the shaker the other way, carefully emptying what looked like windshield washer fluid into the glasses. He handed a glass to each of us and took one himself, raising it across the bar to make a toast. "To getting laid."

I was getting used to the sexual innuendo, the casualness with which Charlie approached his job and this situation. The extraordinarily hot guy next to me not opposed to exposing himself at the slightest suggestion. I clinked glasses with the other two and downed the shot in one gulp. It was sweet tasting, blue raspberry, like a slushy. Matthias carefully slammed his glass on the bar in front of him. Charlie had turned around. I set my glass down and turned to look at Matthias.

As our eyes met, he leaned forward and kissed me on the lips. My lower lip touched his upper lip and I could taste the blue raspberry shot. His breath was a mix of it, mint, and tobacco. I was startled at first, but Matthias pressed closer and there was his tongue. Before I knew what was happening our tongues were mingled, his in my mouth, mine in his, our lips pressed together. I thought I might slide off my bar stool, so I moved my leg in. An attempt to brace myself against the slide that only pushed me closer into Matthias. He pushed back. His tongue felt amazing in my mouth, like it belonged there with mine. I felt my dick get almost completely hard. His breath filled my mouth, wherever his tongue wasn't. I had forgotten what this was like. After a minute, he pulled away, not far. He was still close enough to whisper to me and be heard. "I'm horny as hell. Do you want to get out of here?"

I giggled then, like a twelve-year-old girl. Trying to reclaim some of my dignity, I picked up my cigarette and took a long drag. "I can't. I'm sorry."

"Hey, no worries. Just thought I'd ask." I turned back to look at him, his green eyes, and that smile, and let out a small sigh. He picked up his glass, downed the last quarter of his drink, and leaned forward enough to look me in one eye. "It's really alright. But I'm gonna take off. I can still make two-for-ones down the street. I'll see you around." He picked up his cigarettes, slid around off his bar stool, and kissed me again, this time on the cheek.

201

"Have fun," I managed, and Matthias turned and walked out of the bar. I took a long drag off my cigarette, and for a split second considered running after him.

"You must be a lousy kisser," Charlie said.

"As a matter of fact—," I started.

"Dad?"

"Yes, Caden?"

"Why was your door shut?" he asked again.

"I thought I'd walk you to the bus stop, or is that against the rules?" It was worth a shot.

"Seriously, are you crazy?" Caden asked.

"Certifiable." It had worked. "Is that what you're wearing?"

"What's wrong with what I'm wearing?" He turned around and looked in the mirror above my dresser.

"Hadn't you picked out the t-shirt from the concert?"

"I don't want to make that much of a commitment right away," he replied.

"What does that mean?" He was still looking at his reflection, so I went to stand next to him. "So handsome!"

"Please!" he said incredulously. He was looking at my reflection in the mirror, not actually at me. "What if the kids in school don't like Ugly Kid Joe? Or the teachers? I don't want to make that bold a statement on the first day of school."

"Way to stay true to yourself." I went to touch his head, but he pulled away. It was six of one, half a dozen of another, whether I could get away with touching or hugging. He was nervous this morning, so I let it be.

202

"Hey, I've never seen this." He was looking at the picture of him and me sleeping with the dinosaur from when he was four years old.

"Of course you have! It's been on my dresser for years, not just here, but in California."

"It's Donald!" He picked up the frame and studied it more closely. "How come you didn't tell me about this, this summer when we were talking about it?"

"I thought you'd seen it. Come on. Let's get this show on the road." He put the frame down carefully, back where it came from, then turned to face me.

"If you wanted to walk me to the bus stop, I guess that would be okay." He was smiling. We were almost eye-to-eye. He'd grown another inch in the last two days, I would've sworn to it.

"If you're sure."

"How about if you agree to stop and go back, no questions asked, if we get close and there are other kids waiting?" he suggested seriously.

"How about if we compromise and you give me a hug at the door, at our door?"

"Deal!" He turned and left and I picked up the frame to look at the picture again. More than ten years had gone by. When that picture had been taken, I'd carried him to bed. Ten years later, he was nearly as big as me. I did not have time for a walk down memory lane, so I put the picture back quickly, and followed Caden down the hall. As I passed his room, he was shirtless. The shirt he'd had on was thrown on the floor and he had the concert tee in his hand.

"What the hell?"

"Did you eat anything?"

"One of Kev's Pop-Tarts," he answered, sitting on the edge of his bed to slip on his tennis shoes.

"Great. I'm making a mental note to add nutrition to the board."

"Perfect," he said, snarkily.

"Key?" I asked.

"In my backpack." I had been standing in the doorway and he tried to move past me.

"Lights," I demanded.

"I was getting there." He flipped the light switch and we both started down the stairs.

At the bottom of the stairs, Caden grabbed a navy blue sweatshirt that used to be his dad's. We both wore it. I guessed it would be his armor that first day of high school. We walked down the hall, through the kitchen. Going by the counter, he grabbed a half-eaten Pop-Tart, not on a plate, and shoved it in his mouth. It was almost eight o'clock by the clock on the stove. His bus came at about ten after.

"Come on, kiddo. You're going to be late."

"Not late. Just not as early." Sure enough, his backpack was on the floor just inside the door. He grabbed it, slung it on his shoulder, removed the Pop-Tart from his mouth, and turned to hug me. "You wouldn't have even been ready to walk me."

"I know. But I'm getting what I really want anyway."

"You're good," he told me. I had begun to love his hugs. I always had, but somewhere along the line, I'd forgotten, or maybe I couldn't allow myself to remember. I played games constantly to get him to hug me. He played right along, because I knew, secretly, it wasn't nearly that big a deal to him. He had started to gain some muscle working for my brother. We hugged for nearly twenty seconds, almost a record for any regular hug. He shoved the last piece of Pop-Tart in his mouth and turned to go.

"It's going to be fine. High school is easy!" God, I was so full of shit!

"I got this," he told me, and was gone.

As soon as the door shut, I turned and ran through the kitchen, down the hall, to the coat stand. I grabbed a sweatshirt of Kev's, put it on, and retraced my steps; stopping quickly at the back door, to make sure I couldn't see him. I opened the door and ran across the grass, then across the driveway to the

204

alley. From there, I could see him. He was almost to the end of the block. I stood there and watched him until he rounded the corner and was out of sight. I waited there for another couple of minutes in case he got scared and turned back around. *What is he, eight years old?*

When he didn't come back, I got an idea. I wanted to have a cup of coffee and a cigarette. Maybe even see if Kev had any Pop-Tarts left, but first I had to do something upstairs. Back in my room, I crossed to my dresser and picked the picture of Caden, me, and Donald back up. I looked at for longer than I would willingly admit before I could put it back down. Then I went back downstairs for my coffee and cigarette.

Chapter 20

JOANNA

I had gone from teaching to guidance counselor to vice-principal in a little over ten years. It was all part of the plan and, even though I had serious doubts turning that last corner so soon, the rest of the plan had gone to shit when my husband decided he preferred alcohol to his wife and children. I felt so powerless. I lost so much in such a short period, my husband wasn't even the first loss.

My sister Colleen was my best friend. I'd never forget the look of terror on her face when she told me she had found a lump in her right breast. She was young, though, barely thirty, and the cancer was found early. Two rounds of chemo later and she got to keep her breast. We celebrated with a sister's only weekend on the North Shore. Catelyn, of course, was too busy, but that was just fine as far as we were concerned. She was a bitch and that weekend was about celebrating life, pampering ourselves, and getting drunk; not necessarily in that order. Caty would have come with a completely different agenda. She always did and there was always a fight. I would come to cherish the memory of those two days. We did get drunk and pamper ourselves. But most of all, we celebrated life.

Three days later, our dad died. It was sudden, so none of us was prepared. He'd had a massive heart attack and hadn't made it to the hospital. Our mother was lost. She and Colleen were inconsolable. Catelyn was steely. Patrick was strong. Stephen was, well, absent. I, oddly enough, found solace in Colleen's good health. I had been so terrified I would lose her. For six months, there had been a knot in my stomach. My husband had lost his father a year and a half earlier, and then surrendered, once and for all, to the alcoholism that ran rampant in his family. My family drank, but I believed Paddy was the only alcoholic.

I was literally watching my marriage dissolve right before my eyes. Perhaps it was a bit Pollyanna of me to latch onto something positive so fiercely that I allowed it to disguise almost everything bad around it. When I looked back on those few months, I'd been stunned at how oblivious I was. Oblivious might've been too strong a word. I certainly wasn't unaware. Clearly, I knew my husband's drinking was out of control, our marriage crumbling. There was no way to miss my dad's death. The fact that I was still happy somehow, was tenacious self-preservation. If I had allowed myself to feel the effects of all

206

those events when they occurred, I may have started screaming and never stopped.

Not five months after our dad's death, we were at our mother's house, finally going through some of dad's things. It was the house where Colleen, Stephen, and I had grown up.

Colleen had a headache.

Kelly and I had spent the morning going through my dad's closet, while Meghan and Colleen had sorted dusty boxes in the attic. My sister attributed her headache to a dust allergy. She'd taken a couple of Tylenol after lunch, and gone back upstairs to lie down in our childhood bedroom. I went to check on her a couple of hours later; we thought it was odd she hadn't come back downstairs. Kelly, who was eleven at the time, had followed me up to use the bathroom. He stopped in the hall with me when I knocked on the bedroom door. Even as I knocked, I knew something wasn't right. I told Kelly to go back downstairs and ask his grandmother to come upstairs, begging him not to argue with me. "Please go downstairs and get Grandma. Now! Then you and Meghan stay in the kitchen. Kelly—Go!"

Colleen had an aneurism. She died very quickly; possibly even in her sleep, the EMT speculated. She looked peaceful, lying in her old twin bed, covered with a quilt our mother had made.

With her death, my entire façade crumbled. The world I had constructed, however imperfect, no longer made one bit of sense, so I completely fell apart. Catatonia, it turned out, was even lovelier than the steady diet of lies and bullshit I had been feeding myself for a year. I laid in bed for days, not caring about the laundry, the groceries, or the bills. I certainly didn't care about my husband, though that particular lack of concern wasn't novel. For a day or two, embarrassingly, I barely considered my children. For a while though, I wondered about my little brother.

It had been three years since the phone call. It was a Saturday afternoon in August, way before anything had changed. Before Colleen had gotten sick, before Jim's dad died and he'd lost control of his drinking. It was a normal Saturday afternoon. I mightn't have been home, being that it was a summer weekend. After I got the call, I remembered thinking how glad I was that I had been home. It was a collect call from a payphone in San Francisco. I hadn't thought about the call in years.

207

It was before we'd gotten a cordless phone and I was outside watering the garden before the summer sun got too hot. I'd probably gone in for something to drink. At that time, the back deck was just a few months old. Jim had built it earlier that year, so we spent a lot of time on it. I practically lived on the deck when it wasn't too humid. The kitchen phone was ringing when I opened the back door to go inside. I only had to reach out to pick up the handset.

"Hello," I said.

"COLLECT CALL FROM," came a recorded voice, and there was a pause. Then I heard my brother's voice say his first name. His voice trembled a bit when he spoke.

"Stephen? Stephen, what's wrong?"

"Joey, what the fuck?" My brother said sounding, I didn't know... confused.

"Why aren't you calling from home? What's wrong?" As soon as I said it, he began to cry. I could hear it in his voice. He wasn't sobbing. It was quieter than that. Maybe I didn't really hear it as much as sense it. I couldn't describe it. It wasn't as if I was accustomed to hearing his voice on the phone to begin with. The sounds of a big city were in the background; traffic, honking horns, and people.

"Stephen, what is it?" I asked, again.

"I'm, um... I'm supposed to be home by now." His voice was weak, almost desperate. "It's Caden's birthday party today. Alec's son," he explained. I grabbed a cigarette from the counter and lit it. We were still smoking inside back then.

"Is Alec alright?" The question seemed foreign. I had never met my brother's... what? Friend, partner? But I knew from Colleen that he had been sick. Back then, we talked in generalities. *He'd been sick* was code for AIDS. There weren't many questions and even fewer answers. Mostly we were just afraid to know. Colleen had assured me that Stephen *had not been sick*. I wondered, for a moment, why on earth he was calling me and not Colleen.

"Alec is alright. Thanks. Colleen's told you then?"

"Yes, of course. She talks about you nonstop."

208

"That must get old," he joked, his voice lightening for a moment.

"Not at all," I lied. We both laughed awkwardly. "If it's not Alec—."

"It's me," he interrupted, the tremble back. "I'm positive."

"Positive of what?" I asked, sincerely.

"HIV positive," he almost whispered. I hadn't known how to respond. I wasn't completely certain what that even meant then, though I could venture a pretty good guess.

"How do you know?" I asked, blindly.

"There's a test. I hadn't gone in for one in a while. Alec doesn't know."

"You just got the results?"

"Yeah. I had the test a couple of weeks ago. It takes that long for the results to come back. I'd almost forgotten they'd be in." His voice, just then, told me he was trying to convince me this whole process had been as casual as he was implying.

"Oh, Stephen, I'm sorry." He didn't answer right away and I didn't know the appropriate thing to say. The whole conversation was surreal. I took another drag from my cigarette and exhaled. The smoke stung my eyes, which had begun to fill with tears. "It has to be weird to discuss on a payphone? Where are you?"

"Outside the clinic."

"Did you try Colleen first?" I was determined to keep my voice still.

"I needed to tell someone I wouldn't be seeing later at home. Colleen's always one paycheck away from being disconnected. I was sort of in a trance when I worked this out. I just thought I'd save her the collect call, I guess," he explained.

"Do you want me to tell her?"

209

"No, don't. I will call her later tonight or tomorrow, after I've told Alec. There will already be people at the house for the birthday party. I won't be able to say anything until much later."

"You okay?" I asked him. The three of us had said that thousands of times to each other. "You okay?" was our question. I sighed. What had the launching point for all of it been? I had been watering the tomato plants and gone in for a cold beer. Where did this sudden carnage originate? For a split-second, I imagined it all started when Stephen fled to the west coast. That was the uncommon denominator. There couldn't have been another explanation.

"I don't know," he said. "There should be a shorthand for this. I'll have to go on explaining it until I'm, until I'm just done."

The strangest thing of all was that we should have both been sobbing over this. It was sad, right? It felt a little like the adults were way out of their depth. Meanwhile, I had forgotten what it was like to consider so many people. How did normal people do this? Perhaps the bigger the quandary was, the larger the capacity for denial. We exchanged a few more words and I told my little brother that I loved him. He hung up the phone without saying it back. The slight was easy to overlook. In fact, I was certain it was unintended. I placed the handset back on the cradle and stamped my cigarette out. It wasn't completely smoked. The call hadn't been long enough for me to finish an entire cigarette. I felt I would choke if I took another drag. I had been facing the counter. I turned my back to the counter and felt myself crumble to the floor, sobbing.

Before that day, I had been obsessively jealous of how protective Colleen was towards Stephen. Their relationship was odd. They were a little over two years apart and did not share many interests. Had Stephen not skipped a grade in school, they'd have not even been just a grade apart. They didn't share a gender like Colleen and I did. She and I were almost two years apart, yet when they were together growing up, or when they talked; their bond was impenetrable. All three of us were close, since there wasn't five years between us. All of us, even Paddy and Caty, doted on that little brat, and when he left the rest of us, our relationships with each other fell apart somehow, except for Colleen and me. In Stephen's absence, our bond grew stronger. There were times when Colleen shoved that ungrateful little bastard down my throat. He had left. She missed him. I missed him. But there was a stupid and selfish part of me that liked having no competition for Colleen's affection.

Colleen had talked about moving to San Francisco. I never really got it. That was when we were still teenagers. I doubt Stephen knew a place called San Francisco even existed then. I loved Minnesota and never thought of leaving, but Colleen was a free spirit. To my knowledge, she was the first person I was related to who got a tattoo. She had a yin and yang, ironically placed just above her right breast. She wore flowing skirts that dragged on the ground behind her, billowing in the wake of her tiny bare feet, which were adorned with toe rings and hemp anklets. Her long, wavy hair was often wild. Colleen wore lipstick and occasionally, mascara; that's where the makeup ended. She didn't need even that. It was like she glowed. She worked part-time in a bookstore, and as a massage therapist for years; barely able to make ends meet. We had the same degree, a Master's in Education, each of us with a different focus. Hers was journalism; mine was psychology. After getting her master's degree, two years before I did, she went to Europe for six months. When she came home, she started massage school. Colleen never thought outside the box, because she would never have considered that the box was there.

I was flabbergasted she never followed Stephen to San Francisco. I lived in constant fear from the moment we knew he'd moved there that Colleen would follow and I'd lose my best friend. She never even visited him, though. In bed, those days after she died, I wondered if that had been because of me. I found it astonishing the things we kept from those we loved the most. Not secrets, but ideas, plans, and even dreams. Fear of losing the one we loved prevented us from belittling, or squashing, their hopes and dreams. We'd just, selfishly, not go out of our way to encourage. Certainly we didn't remind our loved one of that dream they once shared with us, even though it was glaring, like a bright-red neon motel light.

When I finally got out of bed, I'd found the resolve to end my marriage, once and for all. I'd also decided I had to focus on the things on my list I could bring to fruition. My heart ached and I didn't think I could go on as a guidance counselor. The administration position therefore got fast-tracked. It had only been a few more years down on the list. In those months, as I filed for divorce, mourned the deaths of my father and sister, and changed course in my career, I held onto my children and my control, no matter how fleeting most of that was.

211

It was later in the afternoon of the first day of the 1993-94 school year. Two students who had moved from schools in other states had issues with their credits being transferred. One student had too few credits for her grade, while the other had too many for his. I was now waiting on the boy. I had been absolutely dreading meeting with him all afternoon, and talking to students was normally the best part of my day. I missed teaching, missed the interaction with the actual people that had been my motivation for going into education. Still, the next meeting had my stomach in knots. I was sitting at my desk, arranging papers and files in front of me, carefully aligning the three stacks, when there was a knock on my office door.

"Come in," I called.

"Um, hi," the boy said. "I'm not sure what to call you."

"How about Joanna. We're somewhat informal here, Caden."

"Alright," he agreed.

"Have a seat." I motioned to the two chairs on the other side of my desk.

"Did I do something wrong?"

"Of course not. Why would you think that?"

"I got a note in class that the principal wanted to see me," he said. "That usually means—."

"Occupational hazard," I interrupted.

He was still standing up. I thought it might put him at ease if I joined him on the other side of the desk, so I stood up and moved around beside him. He had an Ugly Kid Joe concert t-shirt on. I wondered if Meghan had seen it yet. She loved them and I was the worst mother ever because I would not allow her to go to the State Fair, alone to see the concert. Fantastic! My brother just continued accumulating the cool parent points. He owned a goddamned video store. I was a high school principal. *Get it together, Joanna!*

"Come on, sit down. This will be awkward at first, but I hope not too bad. I wanted to talk to you about your credits from your school in San Francisco. You were in the ninth grade last year, right?"

"Yes, ma'am," he answered, still a little uneasily.

"The thing is you are only six credits shy of being in eleventh grade. When that happens, we tend to round up. It's better for you to make up a few credits and catch up to the class ahead of you, than to hold you back when you're, let's just say, that much further ahead."

"I don't understand." Having finally sat down, he shifted uncomfortably in his chair.

"First of all, I know that Stephen and I aren't necessarily seeing eye to eye right now, but that doesn't mean that you and I can't. We would like for you to start the eleventh grade, instead of tenth. You are taking an advanced science class, which is basically subject matter you've already covered. I'd like to move you into a computer science class, which is new this year. That class is senior level, but looking at your grades, I think you're up to it."

"Computers? Cool!"

"You're really missing the bigger picture. You would graduate a year early."

"No, I get it. I guess it would be a lot harder if I had already been going to school with the kids in my class."

At some point, I was going to have to get over being jealous of my little brother. I was jealous and I was afraid. I usually vacillated between the two. Occasionally, I felt sorry for him. Sitting next to his fifteen-year-old stepson whose transcripts could already get him a decent scholarship to a pretty good school, I knew very well that my brother could easily send him to an Ivy League; no money concerns whatsoever. But the kid next to me had lost his father to AIDS and had no family at all, except for my brother, and us, by default. He'd lost his father last year, and still managed to bring home a 4.10 GPA. Caden was the kind of student teachers dreamt of. He was perceptive, smart, and somehow unassuming. And he was polite, but genuinely so. Over the couple of months since I met him, I'd seen him weekly. Charlie would just drop him off to mow the lawn most of the time. My little brother had been in Caden's life for more than ten years. He and Alec had done something right. I had to give them that. My sister, Catelyn would argue that homosexuals should not be parents. In fact, she seemed to believe they shouldn't be allowed to interact with children in any capacity. From where I sat, the family Stephen had made for himself in California, certainly gave evidence to the contrary.

"That's very perceptive," I told Caden.

"So, I'll be a junior? I'll be in Meghan's grade?"

"If you and your dad, I mean—."

"You can call him my dad," he interrupted. "I do."

"I certainly don't want to force this on either of you. I just want you to be challenged while you're here." I was dreading the next part of this, but it was my job. I was an adult and my brother was as well. Caden meant the world to him. The thing that set him off more than anything else I said when we fought was my implication that he wasn't as good a parent as he claimed to be. I had thrown his ex-fiancée's abortion at him, called him ungrateful and selfish, a horrible brother and son. But he didn't tell me to leave until I suggested he might not know his son as well as he claimed to. "I need to talk to your dad now, Caden."

"Oh!" He looked frightened, suddenly.

"What is it?"

"It's just that everything has been so good."

"What do you mean?" I really did not get it.

"He seems happy now," Caden explained. "He told me that I could invite you to the zoo, you know, when we went for my birthday, but I didn't obviously. He was sad for so long after my dad died. I know a lot of that was my fault."

"No, I can't imagine—," I started.

"No really, we hardly talked. I was afraid Stephen wouldn't want me anymore and if I needed him, that meant I didn't love my dad. So I just hung out in my room a lot and didn't say much."

"That's a pretty scary place to be," I told him.

"It wasn't until we got here and things were weird with you, that I saw how disappointed he was, and then I just felt stuck. I didn't know what to do," he explained.

214

I understood it then. God, it must have hurt my brother when I suggested he didn't have a great relationship with his son. I couldn't imagine. I felt sorrier than I had that night and most of the time since. They clearly had something very special.

There had been so much water under the bridge between us, between all of us. I knew that he was right when he said the street went both ways, but it had been easier to just blame him. If I accepted any responsibility, that meant I hadn't been there for him. In fact it meant I'd asked him to be someone else to make life easier for me, and then just allowed him to walk away when he couldn't do that; making my life that much simpler. That part had been so long ago, it was easy to cover it up with a new coat of paint and call it bygones. Colleen had alluded to it before; even our mother had said once that we had failed Stephen. Perhaps I'd just done the self-preservation thing again. But on the day of the Valley Fair fight, I truly was oblivious.

"The thing is Caden; you're not responsible for him. He's responsible for you. Also, there are plenty of grown-ups who are culpable."

"What?" he asked.

"The parts of this that can't be attributed to your dad's death." I wanted to choose my words very carefully. "Those things should be blamed on us, here. I'm not sure it can be fixed anymore, but you have to leave that up to me, okay? I will try to make it better." He nodded, though I wasn't certain he understood what I was telling him. "At any rate, I don't think me talking to him about what grade you're in will make it any worse."

He sighed a little bit and I thought, *My sentiments exactly.* "You have study hall now, right? Then gym? It wouldn't hurt for you to go to either of those. Are you finding everything alright?"

"Yes, ma'am."

"Good, and it's Joanna. Why don't you go to study hall and I'm going to give your dad a call. If I reach him before the end of the day, I'll come find you."

He left and I returned to the other side of my desk and sat down. Relationships are so delicate, sometimes even tricky. They need constant attention. We had allowed a decade to go by and paid such little attention to our relationship; Stephen's and mine, all of ours really. It was relatively easy,

215

after a while: out of sight, out of mind. Could it be fixed? If so, we were going to have to begin with small steps. Stephen had seemed willing and ready to let bygones be bygones when they arrived in town. I hadn't felt nearly as able and not at all willing. I took a deep breath, picked up the phone, and dialed. I'd had his number jotted down on a legal pad in front of me the entire time. The phone rang several times. In fact, I was about to hang up when my brother finally answered.

"Stephen, it's Joanna," I announced.

"What's wrong? Is Caden alright?" There was a trace of panic in his voice.

"No, no, everything's alright," I assured him. "I just need to talk to you about his credits from San Francisco. It won't take long. Can you come to the school, today, maybe Kev can—."

"I can be there in an hour," he interrupted. "That okay?"

"Of course. I'm in the administration office."

"I'll see you in an hour." Though he'd been short, his voice was matter of fact, but not cold. Or unforgiving. I put the receiver down and breathed a sigh of relief. I decided to head to the teacher's lounge to have a cigarette.

An hour later, I was trying to take my mind off of the meeting that was about to happen. I had started wishing I'd escaped to the lounge for one more cigarette when I saw my brother. My office door was open and Stephen had stopped at the secretary's desk. I got up and went to the door to wave him back.

"It turns out, it's no less nerve-wracking to be called to the principal's office as an adult," he joked.

"You found it alright?" Small talk seemed as good a place as any to start.

"Yes, I remembered the way."

"If I remember correctly, you didn't spend much time here. Now, Colleen...."
He laughed a little uneasily.
"Have a seat. I wanted to talk to you about Caden's credits."

"Didn't the school send his records?"

216

"Please, sit." He pulled the chair away from my desk, finally sitting. He was dressed casually, blue jeans and a Polo shirt, with canvas shoes. When he crossed his legs, I could see he was wearing no socks. His brown hair was still damp, brushed back. He must have showered quickly before coming over. His cologne hung in the air, beautifully. I studied his face for a sign of how he was feeling. His smile was uneasy, but it betrayed very little. I got a lot of uneasy smiles in my line of work. I decided to put his mind at ease and plow ahead. I explained everything to him, just as I had to Caden. "We'd like Caden to be a junior this year. He'd be a classmate of Meghan's."

"Really? Wow! He's only fifteen."

"He's done very well in school. His grades are phenomenal. He was particularly excited about the computer class," I told my brother.

"He would be. Anything computers. It's practically science fiction to me."

"Oh, me, too," I agreed.

"He'd graduate at seventeen." He was processing. "I'm sorry. I honestly had no idea. I mean, I knew he was a great student, always on the honor roll. His dad talked it up and, I guess I thought he was just being a dad."

"You had other things on your mind," I said, in as understanding a tone as I could. He looked at me, confused, perhaps not expecting the compassion.

"But I was a fucking teacher," he said, and then got a shocked look on his face. "I'm sorry. I forgot where I was for a second. I was a teacher. I certainly know about GPAs, credits, and all of that. I guess I was out of practice, and he barely mentioned it."

"He told me that you two hadn't been talking that much, but are now." I wasn't sure how, exactly to have a conversation with my brother. Had Caden said that in confidence? I wasn't a guidance counselor anymore, and I was related to the parent sitting across from me.

"He told you that?"

"He was worried about us talking. I think after the last time—."

"About that," he interrupted. "I shouldn't have asked you to leave."

217

"I shouldn't have been such a bitch," I whispered. "See? I swear, too. We did have the same mother, after all."

"She was telling me that she never swore around Dad," he said, chuckling. "I don't think she was paying very close attention."

"To be fair, she didn't swear as much when we were kids as she does now."

"Back to Caden...." He changed the subject. I couldn't tell if he was uncomfortable again, or had just realized we'd strayed from topic. "What was his reaction to all of this, besides being excited about the computer class? I mean, I guess it won't matter all that much what I think."

"I don't think he minded the idea. He said it would be easier because he was just starting here and didn't know the kids in either grade."

"He's right. I guess it's the perfect time for this to happen. God, this means college stuff already!"

"I do think it should be up to him, but obviously you're there to guide him. And he's well set for college so far." I told him.

"I certainly didn't expect this today."

"Neither did Caden. He's in gym now. I could send for him and we could discuss it now?"

"All we have to do is say yes and it's done? He's a junior?" Stephen asked.

"Pretty much."

"Why don't you let us discuss it at home tonight? May I call you after we have?"

"Of course!" I was thinking that the conversation was going far better than I'd expected it would, but then my brother abruptly stood up.

"Thank you, then," he said, turning to go. I guessed the improvement was going to come in baby steps, if at all. We hadn't yelled at each other. That was something. It was good we were in the school environment, too. The situation, or location, had rather made up our minds as to what sort of

218

goodbye to offer each other. I tentatively extended my hand to my brother, and he shook it. There was an odd look on his face and I wondered if I had misread something. He turned to go. That was that.

"Thank you for coming in. Just call me at home later." He turned back around and nodded. I crossed to the door of my office to see him go. My secretary looked over at me and mouthed the words, "He's cute." I was certain she knew he was my brother, but as I closed the door to my office, I wondered if I knew what having Stephen for a brother meant anymore.

Chapter 21
CADEN

It was the second day of school, the beginning of my junior year. So unreal. The first day of school, I was a sophomore; it had to be the shortest school year in history, just one day. Stephen told me to meet Joanna at her office. That's what he was told to tell me after they talked last night. When I got there, the secretary told me to wait in the outer office. The door to Joanna's office was closed. I sat in a chair against the wall and waited. After a minute, my mind started to go back to another time I had to wait in the principal's office.

This was in San Francisco. Stephen was a teacher there, but we had to act like we didn't really know each other outside of school. It had always been that way. As we got closer to school from home, we had to pretend that we hadn't actually gotten on the train and ridden halfway together. Stephen was out. The closeted stuff was because of my dad. He was an actor and wanted to continue to work, and especially because he had just played a gay character on TV, it was important that people didn't know who Dad was in his personal life. I never had Stephen as a teacher. I would have last year, but he stopped teaching when my dad got really sick and never went back. I guessed that was good. It would've been weird for my dads to pretend they didn't know each other at teacher conferences and stuff. Also Stephen had to be careful not to react like a parent would if anything happened at school, like the time I was thinking about while I waited for Joanna.

I punched a kid for saying the F-word, not fuck, the other one. I was in the eighth grade, so that was two years ago. My dad was sick then, but not so sick that he couldn't participate in the lie. He had to. I was sitting in a different chair in a different outer office when I saw my dad come in. He had on a big sweatshirt and baseball cap and sunglasses. Stephen told me once, that people probably assumed he was trying not to be recognized. That was good, because we didn't want anyone to think that he was trying to hide anything else. He had already lost a lot of weight and no one wanted anyone to wonder any more than they already did. They both explained to me over and over how important it was, not that we hide; because, they said, "There was nothing at all to be ashamed of," but that we keep our personal lives to ourselves for the sake of my dad's career.

It felt weird to me, because it didn't matter for Stephen's job. I guess it mattered more if an actor was gay, than if a teacher was—at least in San Francisco. Stephen told me when we were talking about moving to Minnesota, that things would be different there, that people wouldn't be as accepting of, for instance, a gay teacher. I didn't know. Sometimes, it was hard to remember where or when we were in the closet or not. I thought it was pretty fucking dumb. Why did people even care what my dads did? It really pissed me off when people said shit like that kid said that day.

"It's gross that they think they can just kiss wherever they want," he said, not to me, but as I walked by. The kid's name was Steven. Funny, right? He was in my advanced math class, so it wasn't as if he was dumb. Stupid people, I guessed, got more of a pass than smart ones. Steven was talking to a girl I didn't know.

"What do you mean?" she asked. I didn't even think I'd ever seen her around.

"Two guys on the BART this morning, like I said, kissing. I mean, what the fuck?!"

"They're all over," the girl agreed with him. I almost laughed. I mean, we lived in San Francisco. What did they expect?

"What's your fucking problem, Johnson?" I stopped and asked.

"Dude, who's even talking to you?"

"It's not like you were whispering."

"And anyway, it doesn't bother you?" the other Steven asked me.

"Why should it matter what people do in private?"

"Well, that's the point, right? They're not doing it in private. It's like they insist on rubbing our faces in it."

"As soon as I'm out of school, I'm outta here," the girl chimed in, nearly spitting her gum out. "It's gay central."

"Fucking San Francisco!" Steven agreed.

221

"Exactly," she nodded, still trying to keep her gum in her mouth. I was about to give up and walk away. I mean there wasn't any point in arguing with those dumbasses. Plus, it was lunchtime and they were serving pizza. But then Steven really pissed me off.

"They act entitled, like that fucking English teacher," he said.

"Which one?" the girl asked.

"Bennett," he spat. "He's a fucking faggot!"

I knew there were obnoxious people, and people who my dads said were "full of hate," but that was the first time I had experienced it firsthand. It was worse because it was directed at one of my dads. I thought about walking away; I really did, but I kind of just snapped. I had sort of turned away already, so I stopped and turned back around. I was only a few feet away from Steven. I took a couple of steps towards him. The girl looked up, but didn't say anything right away.

"Hey, Johnson." When he turned around, I punched him. It was right on the left side of his face. I meant to center it more, maybe catch his eye, but I totally missed. Then Steven Johnson punched me back. Apparently he had more experience with that sort of thing, because he didn't miss, not one bit. Then we kind of rolled around on the floor, fighting for a minute, until a teacher came out of his classroom and told us to break it up. The girl didn't say a word, none of us did. I turned on my butt and pushed myself away, against a locker. My hand hurt and there was something warm and wet on my upper lip. I swiped at it and realized that my nose was bleeding.

Then I saw Stephen (my dad) standing there. He looked; I couldn't even tell, was he pissed off or scared? He actually looked like he might cry. I knew the feeling, but then he took a breath, and asked if we were through. *Through what?* It had only been a few seconds, but now my eye hurt, too. The other teacher called out that the fight was over to anyone who had stopped to stare, then told Johnson and me to get up and follow him to the principal's office. Stephen just continued to stand there, like he was glued to that spot. I was all of a sudden kind of pissed off at him, especially if he was pissed at me. Maybe it was because I thought I might start crying if I continued to face him and that would not help the situation. The other teacher said something about the three of us "Taking a little walk." Then to Stephen, he said, "I've got this." I'd gotten up and was holding my nose. I turned my back to Stephen and

222

followed the other teacher. I knew, somehow, that Stephen wouldn't follow. He couldn't.

I was worried about my dad probably having to come into school. Some actor named Rock Hudson, who was a big movie star, had died of AIDS, like five years earlier, and Stephen said my dad had been paranoid ever since. That's why we moved to San Francisco in the first place. I was worried they'd both be mad at me. I didn't want them to know what Johnson said, because I was pretty sure they'd both already heard stuff like that, and it must have hurt their feelings, like in the worst way possible. I was confused because I kind of wanted Stephen to come with me to the principal's office. I knew he couldn't, I knew he couldn't even react, or people would know. I wouldn't actually care who knew. Fuck them. I could punch more people, if I had to. I was sure I'd get better at it with some practice.

The walk to the office felt like it took an hour. Then, instead of waiting in the outer office, I had to go to the nurse's office first. My nose was bleeding, and the secretary was freaked out. The whole time the nurse screwed around with my face, I was determined not to cry, so I kind of checked out. When she handed me something, I realized that I already had something in my right hand, actually two things. She was holding a t-shirt, like a gym shirt. Then she looked at my hand and said, "I told you, one for your eye and one for your hand. And change your shirt. It's covered in blood."

I looked down, and she was right. I had blood on the front of my shirt and my right hand was sore and had started to swell. I didn't even want to look in the mirror. "You're going to have a black eye," the nurse said, handing me an empty plastic bag. "For your shirt."

I changed shirts quickly, rolled mine up in a ball, and put it in the bag. Then the nurse told me to go wait in the outer office. I got down off the table and thanked her. That's when she smiled at me. "Steven Johnson is a little asshole. They should give you some sort of prize for this."

I started to smile, but that hurt my eye, so I just turned and went out into the other room. I looked at the clock on the wall and it had already been forty-five minutes since we fought. Johnson was sitting at one end of the chairs, so I took a seat at the other. *Little asshole* was right; he hardly had a mark on him. I was as far away from him as I could get and tried to just look straight ahead. Another forty-five minutes went by before Steven's mom got there.

After she and her son had gone into the principal's office, the secretary told me that my dad was on his way. *Great! Fine! Fuck!* From where I sat, I could see most of the office. Stephen came in once, and went right into the nurse's office, then left about five minutes later. When my dad finally got there, I could tell he was uneasy. I couldn't make out if he was angry—I mean he had to be pissed off that I was in trouble—or afraid to be seen. I wondered if he'd seen Stephen. They could have almost run into each other in the hallway. My dad came and sat down next to me against the wall.

"You okay?"

"Great," I said, my voice cracking.

"Yeah, this principal's office stuff still makes me nervous, too." I figured he was joking. We were more touchy-feely; Stephen called it, in private. My dad put his hand on my shoulder, and when I didn't look up, he whispered, "Hey, I'm not worried."

I was sent home early that day. It was a Thursday and I was told to not come back to school the next day either, because I wouldn't tell anyone why I punched Steven. I don't really know what happened after that, but I got to go back to school on Monday and I didn't see Steven in class or around school for another week. The stupid girl turned out to be in the tenth grade, and by the end of that school year she was pregnant. I don't think it was Steven Johnson who was the dad. Someone said it was a senior. I guessed she probably wasn't going to get far away from "Gay central" after that.

"Caden?" someone was saying. I looked up and Meghan was standing in front of me. "What's up?"

"Oh, hey, how's it going?" I asked.

"You were kind of out of it for a sec," she told me.

"Yeah. Too early."

"I know, right," she laughed. Meghan was pretty tall, like almost an inch taller than I was. Her hair smelled like summer, when I was close enough to smell it. She was the prettiest girl I had ever seen. Weird, right? I mean, we were almost cousins. I felt nervous whenever she was around. When she talked to me or looked at me, it got hard to breathe. I had to try really hard not to show it though. That would've been so uncool.

224

"My mother will see you now," she said, kind of joking. "I have to get to homeroom."

"Yeah, alright." I tried to sound nonchalant.

"I think we'll have a couple of classes together. That won't be weird." I was pretty sure she was kidding again, but just about the weird part. Then she just turned and left.

"Caden," someone else said. Joanna was there now.

"Morning—um—Ma—um—Joanna." My face felt hot.

"Come on in," she said, and went into her office. I stood up and looked around. I guess it was to see if anyone was looking. Then I just followed her in.

"Are you nervous?" Joanna asked me.

"A little, I guess."

"Have a seat." So I did. She had gone around to the other side of her desk and was thumbing through some papers there. She took one out of a stack and handed it to me from across the desk. I had to stand up to take it from her. "Your new schedule."

I scanned the sheet for the computer class she had talked about yesterday. It was fourth period, right after lunch. "Intro to Computer Science—Sen Level." Was printed on the sheet. There was a whole room with computers in it, two doors down from the office. It was seriously cool.

"If I take a senior level class now, what do I take next year?" I asked Joanna.

"Well, that's the thing; it's all new to us. This is the first computer class we've had. I imagine there will be others. In five years, people will have them in their houses."

"That's so cool," I blurted out, probably not sounding cool at all. I started to wonder if I could talk Stephen into getting one ahead of that schedule.

"Time has a way of getting away from me," she said. I didn't get it.

225

"Should I just go to class? It's like the second day. Do I need a note or something?"

"All of your teachers are expecting you."

"Meghan said we have a couple of classes together." I sort of regretted saying it right away. So not cool.

"I think just one. Social Studies. Second period. But now I've made you late. Let me show you where English is."

"Okay, cool." We both stood up and she smiled at me. I was glad she didn't think it was weird I asked about Meghan. Was it weird? Sometimes life was just completely confusing. And it was kind of scary that it had, like, jumped ahead a whole year overnight.

I coasted through first, second and third periods, even for it being my second first day. Meghan was not in my second period social studies class like Joanna said she would be, but there were empty desks. It was time for lunch already after third period. The cafeteria was bigger than my last school, but Kelly found me right away. We'd made up, kind of, since he stole the stupid bracelet and I got blamed for it. I guessed that all happened for a reason, actually. That's what adults said when things turned out way better than you thought they ever would, especially when they started out sucking. Stephen and I were totally cool now. He and Joanna actually talked on the phone for a half an hour the night before. And he didn't yell once. Kev and I sort of held our breath the whole time, but it was all good. I had invited Kelly to go to the zoo when we had my birthday there. We saw each other when I mowed their grass. At first, it was really intense, because nobody knew where anyone stood. Joanna and Stephen had fought big time and me and Kelly really hadn't talked since he bolted from Kev's car that day after Valley Fair. And I felt sort of queasy whenever I was even around Meghan, except a couple of times, she walked close to me, and I smelled coconut, like an Almond Joy or something. Summer.

"Hey," I said to Kelly. He really was kind of cool. He was the same age as I was when I had that fight with Steven Johnson, actually older, but he didn't seem as old. My Stephen said that people in Minnesota ripen slower because of the cold. Funny, right? Although I wasn't actually sure I got it?

226

"Oh, hi." Kelly looked over at me like he just noticed I was next to him in line.

"What's up?"

"Nothing. Well, this school is really big. I got lost, like five times, yesterday."

"I know. It's way bigger than my last school." The line moved, so I moved with it. The kid next to me smelled like an ashtray. Some kids went to their cars or hung out behind the school and smoked cigarettes. I think a couple of kids smoked something else, which smelled way worse than cigarettes. The joker next to me probably didn't know he wasn't fooling anyone.

"I'm just glad I didn't have to ask my mom for help." Kelly talked a little like he was out of breath a lot of the time. Maybe it was like he was really excited to say almost everything.

There were two options for a main course, macaroni and cheese that didn't look cheesy at all, and some kind of brown thing with gravy on it. I had reached the point where a decision had to be made, so I motioned to the macaroni. "That would kinda suck, but it's not really bad to ask for help. You could ask Meghan, or even me."

"I can't ever remember where her locker is. I found it once, but that was an accident."

"We're sort of the same," I told him.

"What do you mean?"

"I mean we're both new here."

"Oh, right! So how are you going to help me find stuff?"

"I guess you're right." I laughed. The kid had a point.

"What's up?" somebody said and we both turned to look. Meghan was right there. I almost dropped my tray. Standing up, next to her, I may have misjudged our height difference. We were almost exactly the same height. She was more than a year older. She took a step closer and I felt my face get warmer. "Mac and cheese, huh? Good call. No one knows what that brown stuff is. It's a mystery."

227

"You're not having either one?" I asked. Kelly just kind of stood there gawking.

"I just have yogurt and a salad," Meghan answered.

"This definitely doesn't look like the macaroni and cheese mom makes," Kelly added.

"My boy and I decided to live dangerously." I motioned to Kelly. Meghan smiled at me and I felt a drop of sweat roll off my neck, down my back.

"Anyway, I saw you two in line, and thought I'd come and invite you to sit with us," she said. My tray suddenly felt like it weighed eighty-three pounds. I looked around to see where she meant. There were two girls and one boy, looking over at us from straight back. Where we were standing was just thirty feet or so from the furthest table in that line. One of the girls kind of waved.

"Don't mind her. That's Amy. She thinks you're cute, but I'm not supposed to tell you that." She smiled at me and I felt dizzy.

"Me?" Kelly asked.

"Um, yeah, not likely, goofball," she told him.

"Hey, keep the line moving!" I heard, and realized that along with the room getting warmer, everything around me had stopped for I didn't know how long.

"Okay, I'm heading back to our table," Meghan said. "You guys come over when you're done in line."

"Sure, okay," I managed.

We had to maneuver around like a hundred kids to get back to that table after we'd gone through the line. Also, I thought Kelly might trip any minute. It was like he didn't know how to walk in the forward direction, using both feet. I noticed he'd grown at least an inch since we met. Maybe that was it. Maybe he was always going to be awkward. I steadied him once with my left hand; my tray was in my right hand. If I didn't think it would look weird, I'd have just carried his tray for him. Finally, we reached the table, and the girl Amy looked up, and choked a little on her food. Meghan turned around. Her back was to the rest of the cafeteria.

228

"It's about time! Lunch is practically over."

"They have like a half an hour," Amy disagreed.

"Okay, you guys know my little brother, well except Keaton. Keaton, this is Kelly, my brother and this is Caden, um, my mom's brother's kid."

"Your cousin?" Keaton asked.

"Um, no," Meghan answered.

"I'm her mom's brother's stepson." Keaton was so gay he made some of the queens on the Castro look like football players.

"Sit down," he motioned to me.

"Okay, what does it matter? Caden, that's Keaton. Keaton, Caden."

"And Kelly," Kelly added, and we sat down. Kelly sat next to Amy, which was cool, because she stared, and it wasn't cute through her glasses. They were so thick, her eyes looked three times the normal size through the lenses. Keaton moved down, freeing up the seat next to Meghan. As I moved my right leg over the bench and started to sit, I smelled it again. I had never really thought about summer smelling any certain way, not until I met Meghan Bennett.

"So your uncle married Caden's mom?" Amy asked. I had just figured they all knew my story. Kelly choked a little on whatever he had just put in his mouth. Meghan looked at me and I looked back, wondering if my eyes could actually open any further. I searched her face for some signal for what to say. She just smiled at me. That didn't actually help. All it did was make me sweat more. My silence was creating a panic on Kelly's face, and everyone else at the table had looked up from their food. All eyes were on me, so I decided to just go for it. I knew that Stephen had said we had to be careful, but I had to hope Meghan wouldn't be friends with a bunch of assholes.

"Actually, um, her uncle was with my dad. He died last year, so we moved here." There. I said it. I looked down at my tray and forced myself to take a bite of the dry-looking macaroni. It wasn't awful. There was a faint taste of something cheese-like. I chewed, swallowed, and looked back up. Yep! All eyes were still on me.

229

"Nobody here cares," Meghan finally said. "Right?" I couldn't tell if she believed it. She seemed pretty sure of herself most of the time, but just then, I couldn't make out what she was thinking. Girls could do that. It was like some kind of superpower.

"Oh, yeah, completely," Keaton agreed. He was kind of like that kid in *Pretty in Pink*, only gay. I supposed I was making a big assumption, which probably wasn't cool. I should try to remember to ask Stephen how you knew if someone was gay, just for like knowing in the future. But anyway, I assumed, at least for the time being, that Keaton, at least, didn't care. I already knew that Meghan and Kelly didn't give a shit, so that just left four-eyes, across from me. I started to think it would be better where Kelly sat. At least he wasn't under the magnifying glass. Directly across from Amy, I felt like I was being studied, like a bug in science class. Still, I had to look her in the huge eyes and figure out what she was thinking. She didn't really have the super power.

"You're not gay, right?" she asked, the second our eyes met.

"Amy!" Meghan cried.

"What?! I can't ask that?" No kidding, her eyes got bigger when she was determined.

"It's fine. No, definitely not gay," I explained to her.

"His dad, I mean his step-dad, is pretty cool," Kelly contributed. I looked across the table and noticed his tray was almost empty.

"Came up for air, finally?" Meghan asked him and we all started to laugh, even Kelly.

"Stephen is pretty awesome," I agreed. I meant it, too. It sucked that I forgot that for as long as I did. Sometimes you forgot about something for so long that you didn't really miss it anymore, like a shirt. One day you noticed it in the drawer and it's the only shirt you'd wear for, like, days? You didn't miss it when you didn't remember it existed, but then; there it is again and you kind of miss it, in retrospect, like Monday morning quarterbacking.

"He used to teach high school," Meghan added, after a beat of silence. That was followed by more silence. I figured, since we were in the lunchroom and everything, that maybe I should eat. The faintly cheesy macaroni was already

230

cold. It wasn't terrific barely warm; the reduction in temperature hadn't improved upon it much, so I focused my attention on the corn. We didn't eat canned corn at home. I remembered Stephen talking about growing up on canned vegetables, their flavor and nutrients were all but extracted in the canning process, he'd said. I liked it. Actually, another thing Stephen said a lot was that I liked pretty much everything. "If it can be eaten, Caden will give it a shot, *or three*," he said.

"He didn't teach math, did he?" Amy asked. She said it like math was a disgusting thing to choose to voluntarily know anything about. When Meghan answered that he had taught English, I swear, four-eyes breathed a sigh of relief. The thing about having an English teacher as a parent was that he always corrected my grammar. If your parent were a geography teacher, how likely would they have been to correct you several times a day? "Minnesota is west of Wisconsin, not north," or "Texas is the largest state in the US, going by land mass, but California has the largest population, not the other way around." Really, how often did that shit actually come up in normal conversation? The difference between borrow and lend, however, or that time I asked if we could have a friend for dinner? "We're not cannibals, Caden! You may have a friend to dinner." I had started to rethink the "pretty awesome" comment when Kelly put his fork down and looked up, ready to rejoin the conversation.

"What?" he asked his sister. "Grandma says I have a hollow leg."

"And you had no idea what that even meant until Mom explained it to you," Meghan told him. And us.

"So?" he replied.

"So, how is it?" Meghan asked. I was studying my tray, trying to decide what to eat next. No one said anything. When I looked up, I realized she was looking at me.

"Me? How is what?"

"Eleventh grade?"

"It's okay, I guess. I haven't been in it long enough to adequately assess."

231

"Caden skipped a grade," Kelly offered. Keaton nodded. It seemed he already knew that much. Amy was looking down at her tray, moving lettuce around with her fork.

"So what was San Francisco like?" Keaton asked.

"Different than here. That's for sure." I wondered if I sounded like a dick. "It was cool, though. I don't know, it's cool here, too."

Then we all just ate for a couple of minutes. Kelly, having finished all of his food, just sat looking around the cafeteria, as if he was committing every person to memory. Amy continued to play with her food, more than eat it. It turned out the cold macaroni was edible, after all, when that ended up the only thing left on my tray and I was still hungry.

"What class do you have next?" Meghan asked. I looked up right away this time, to see if she meant me. Kelly had turned around and was looking out the window. He wasn't paying any attention to the rest of us at all.

"Computers," I answered.

"The senior class?" Amy mumbled. The spike in the conversation had caught her off guard. Having just taken a bite, she had to half cover her mouth to ensure no food would fly out.

"Yep," I answered.

"How old are you?" She had finally swallowed everything in her mouth.

"I'm fifteen."

"Wow!" Keaton said. "A fifteen-year-old junior taking a twelfth grade class. That's cool, I guess."

"It's completely weird," I answered.

"It's cool though," Amy chimed in. "That classroom is totally cool. They should have computer classes for juniors, too."

"They do," Meghan smiled at Amy. "Caden's in one." Amy took another bite of food, dejected.

232

"But that class is mostly seniors," Keaton added.

"But not all," Meghan concluded. It was almost as if she was defending me to her friends. It didn't seem necessary. The conversation was friendly enough. Still, I kind of liked it. "Kelly, do you know where your next class is?"

He turned back around, looking as if he didn't know what his next class was, let alone where. "It's Math," he finally remembered, after thinking about it.

"Gross," Amy said. The girl quite obviously had something against mathematics.

"You don't like math much?"

"You picked up on that, huh?" Meghan joked. She smiled at me and I swear, it was like my heart might have pounded right out of my chest. I wondered why I hadn't noticed this stuff until today. I'd never felt this nervous around a girl my own age. Well, she wasn't exactly my own age, but close enough. Who could I even talk to about it that wouldn't freak out? She was Stephen's niece, Kev's cousin, Kelly's sister, not that I'd talk about that kind of stuff with Kelly anyway. I looked at the clock on the wall, mostly because I was excited about next period, but also I thought it might be nice to go somewhere the air was lighter. Ten minutes to go.

"I should hit my locker and go look for the computer room, so I'm not late for next period," I said, standing up. It was the one classroom in the whole school that I knew right where it was. None of them knew that, though.

We all said our goodbyes and I made as quick a getaway as I could manage, moving left and right to avoid a head-on collision with other kids making their exits. I should have offered to help Kelly find his next class. I felt a little like his big brother. He was so ill at ease it was embarrassing, but not to me. *Well, too late for that anyway*, I thought as I steered left to the area where other kids were dissembling their trays. I assumed he'd be alright. Me, on the other hand, I seemed to have forgotten how to breathe.

233

Chapter 22
<u>CADEN</u>

The rest of the day was a blur. I was grateful not to run into Meghan or Kelly again. Or Joanna. I was still not sure whether people could tell just by looking at me that I liked Meghan. And I didn't know if it was supposed to matter. I got off the bus on our corner and walked home, wondering how to talk to Stephen about stuff, or if I could just talk to Kev. When I came around the corner, I saw the truck and knew I didn't have to ask either one of them. I nearly ran that last half a block, afraid he'd leave before I got there and my chance would be gone. As I got to our house, Charlie was loading the lawnmower into the back of the truck.

"Hey!"

"Hey there. How was school?" he asked. It seemed like he was happy to see me. Cool.

"It's okay. I'm in the eleventh grade," I offered.

"Stephen said that. That's cool, right? Who knew you were such a smarty-pants?"

"Smarty-pants? Really?" The thing about Charlie was that he was in between Kevin and Stephen. Kevin still said stuff that was cool and he wasn't afraid to just tell me to stop being a dick. Just like that. Charlie swore, but when he swore in front of me his voice got quieter, like he wasn't sure it was okay. Charlie, same as some other grown-ups, seemed like he had to remind himself how to act cool around kids. Stephen was that way a little too, but it was okay because he was a dad.

"Not cool anymore?"

"Was it ever?" I asked, not meaning it to be mean.

"Hey, I was cool." Charlie played along.

"Whatever helps you get through the day. Is Stephen home?"

"Yep," he answered. "In the house."

234

"So — um — can I — um, ask you something?"

"Sounds serious." I was waiting for an answer, so didn't say anything right away. Finally, he got it. "Oh, yeah, of course."

"I think I like this girl at school." He just smiled at me, waiting for me to continue, I guessed. "But it's complicated."

"It always is."

"No, it's *really* complicated."

"Liking someone or not liking them is the most complicated thing in the world." Charlie had stopped what he was doing and gave me all of his attention. I looked to make sure Stephen wasn't coming, but Charlie kept talking. "People think rocket science is hard."

I knew that I was pretty smart. Sometimes kids would pretend they weren't as smart as they were. I didn't know why, to fit in maybe. Sometimes, though, adults say things that, I'd be like, "insert eye roll here." Did you ever wish that you were able to punctuate your conversation with funny faces and stuff? Charlie must have guessed that I hadn't quite followed the rocket science comment, so he tried to explain.

"It's like; you're in a relationship already, with everyone you see every day. All of those relationships are hard in their own way. Some of them are the hardest."

"I guess that makes sense." Right then was another time when props or signs everyone understood would, you know, have come in handy. I sometimes wondered how adults did it. They were always talking, and they seemed to understand what other people meant a lot more than kids did. It was like we only understood half the language.

"Does the girl know you like her?"

"No! I mean — um — how are you supposed to know?"

"Have you talked to her?" he asked.

"Oh, yeah, lots."

235

"You met her at school?" He looked confused.

"Well, sort of."

"It's only the second day. You couldn't have talked to —." Then he just sort of drifted off, like he could have used a cartoony face to illustrate what he was thinking, too.

"What?" I asked.

"It's Meghan, isn't it?" Oh, my God! How did he do that? Maybe it *was* actually obvious. I felt my face start to burn. I looked down at the ground. "Dude, it's not that big a deal."

"But you said it was always a big deal." I studied the sidewalk, like the answers might jump out of the pavement.

"Well, okay, here's the thing. It's a big deal that you like someone and it might even be a big deal that the *someone* is your step-dad's niece. But as things go, I'm guessing it's not half as big a deal as you're thinking it is."

"You're sure?" I looked up at him, my face cooling just a little.

"Well, there's another thing, Cay." He laughed. "Most people have an opinion about who other people like, and they're rarely the same."

"What's not the same?"

"People's opinions. I think you have to decide for yourself and what other people think shouldn't really matter. They're not in the relationship with you."

"Kind of like my dads?" I asked.

"Well, sort of, but a lot more people have an opinion about their relationship, than will have one about yours."

"But you think it's okay?"

"I do, but it's like I said: it doesn't matter what I think. It just matters what you think and what she thinks, and unfortunately, because you're like ten years old, it'll matter what your dad and her mom think."

236

"I'm fifteen," I told him, though I knew he knew that.

"Nooooo," he joked. I smiled even though I didn't think it was as funny as he did, especially since that was like the twentieth time he'd made the joke. "I'm sorry my opinion doesn't really matter all that much."

"Yeah but at least you didn't think I was some kind of freak or something."

"No more than most ten-year-olds," he answered. Okay, sometimes it was funnier than others. We were quiet for a minute, both of us just standing there. I felt better and worse, kind of at the same time. Finally, he continued. "Your dad is one of the coolest people I know. Just talk to him. And you know there's one other person whose opinion is going to matter a lot."

"This kinda sucks." I knew he meant Meghan. I couldn't imagine talking to her about this. How did people do that? Talk to each other? It didn't seem like it was worth all that trouble.

"It's worth it though." It was like he could read my mind or something. "So, are you going to talk to him?"

"I guess." I had no other choice. At least Charlie hadn't freaked out. That was something. "Maybe I'll just try to figure out what Meghan thinks first."

"Good luck with that, man."

"You won't say anything to anyone, right?"

"Of course not," he nodded. "As long as you help me with this mower."

After I'd helped Charlie put the lawn mower in the back of the truck and he drove off, I grabbed my backpack and went inside. I listened for Stephen, trying to figure out how loud I needed to yell.

"I'M HOME!" I screamed, not hearing anything. Maybe he was out back.

"Thanks for the update," Stephen said, from the top of the stairs. "I'm certain the neighbors at the end of the block didn't hear you, though. Maybe you need a little more volume next time."

"Funny. Maybe next time I'll just sneak up on you."

237

"I don't think you have it in you," he told me. "Stealth is not a talent you possess."

"I can be very stealthy. You don't know." He just laughed at me.

"What were you and Charlie talking about?"

"When?" I asked, trying to be cool.

"Just now," Stephen continued.

"Nothing really," I lied.

"Oh, okay." That was easy. "How was school? Those teachers know anything you don't?"

"Not a lot." I played along. "I was thinking of blowing it off. I mean, if I'm not learning anything."

"It's up to you," he joked. "Who needs the hassle?"

"I know, right?!"

"So, really, how was it?"

"It was okay. Ran into Meghan and Kelly at lunch, so I sat with them."

"Oh, awesome! I liked having my sisters in school with me. It felt less, I don't know, overwhelming."

"But they're not my brother and sister. They're not even my cousins."

"No, I guess not. It's nice to know someone when you're in an unfamiliar place, then."

"Totally," I agreed. Then tried to change the subject. "What's for dinner?"

"I don't know. What are you making?"

"Haha. No seriously? What do I smell?"

"Oh, that?" He turned and started towards the kitchen. "I may have made your favorite. To celebrate."

"Celebrate what?" I followed him into the kitchen.

"Your second first day of school."

"You made lasagna, really?" That was a lot. It took Stephen all day to make it. "That's what we have for, like, a special occasion."

"Today is a special occasion," he said.

"I don't know what all the fuss is about." I only half meant that. It was cool for him to make a big deal. "It's just one grade."

"One grade is a really big deal. You have no idea how proud your dad would've been. He'd have bragged to everyone."

"You really think so?" I asked, smiling.

"I know so. I'm proud, too. It's a very big deal. First thing this morning, I called my mom and told her. Oh, Mariana, too."

"In San Francisco?" He hadn't talked about Mariana in a while.

"Yep. I had to do a little bragging of my own and I didn't know who else to tell. Oh, I told Charlie, too. And Kev. And I told Betty. Haha. Charlie is going to come back for dinner. I didn't think you'd mind as many people as I could wrangle on such short notice. I should've invited my mother."

"You just like when we have to sit at the big table," I joked.

"Added bonus!"

"Anyway, it's cool. Thank you."

"It's my pleasure." He stopped messing around with dishes and pans and stuff, and looked up at me. He was smiling. "Now, go get out of kitchen, before I make you cook your own lasagna."

"I'll go upstairs, then, and do my homework," I turned to leave.

"That's what I like to hear. Dinner's at six."

I took the stairs two at a time. It was cool he was making dinner special. Sometimes it really felt as if things were completely normal. I guessed that was okay. I didn't think my dad would've wanted either of us to be sad, not forever, anyway. I didn't see him as much as before. Sometimes I just felt him, and that was enough. It was like I hadn't totally lost him. I had even started to like our new home. Stephen was right. It was cool to have people around that I knew. That was kind of new for us. It felt, I don't know, like comfortable, like we were going to be okay there, no matter what. I thought that was what home is supposed to feel like; the way it did in San Francisco, even though there was just my dad and Stephen. It was safe.

I opened the door to my room and Sonic came running from the other end of the hall. He certainly liked the house, but he basically liked it anywhere. He was okay with the move as soon as he no longer had to be in the kennel. It was that easy for cats. People had it harder. You had to get used to a place and really start to feel like you belonged. When that started to happen, it was like you were finally there. Almost. It's like you were almost home.

Chapter 23
KEVIN

I didn't usually work at the video store on Thursday nights, but Stephen and I had swapped. He and my grandma were going to the casino to play bingo. Stephen agreed to take my Friday night shift so I could have dinner with my mother. I guess we were both going to get to hang out with our moms. I hadn't spoken to mine since April. We hardly ever went a week without talking, but suddenly it'd been seven months. The truth was I hadn't talked to *her* yet. Her new aide had called Stephen's to invite me to schedule dinner. It was like he was scheduling my mom's fucking hair appointment or something, instead of dinner with her only child. I was willing to take what I could get under the circumstances. She'd made the first move, I made the next by agreeing to see her in an effort to make things right. The whole thing was uncomfortable, but it didn't stop me from looking forward to seeing her.

There was a TV mounted on the wall at the video store, like in a hospital. I waited with Colleen when she was getting her cancer treatments a few times; and we'd make fun of the soap operas the other patients were watching on a TV just like it. We were supposed to watch movies on the TV at the video store. I'd seen Stephen watch *Regis and Kathie Lee* before he opened the store in the morning. The movies are cool, though. Who else got to watch movies at work? I'd kind of gotten into *The Real World* on MTV, though, and was asking Stephen about watching it on the TV at the store. He didn't even know what it was.

"I guess it's like *Melrose Place*, kind of. Just with real people, not actors." We were outside smoking.

"And the people know they're being watched? I can't believe something like that would be so popular. I mean how many people are going to whore themselves out like that? And how many people are going to want to watch it?"

"It's pretty popular," I told him.

"Weird. That kind of voyeuristic crap will be just another flash in the pan. You'll see."

241

"You're not going to drag out the 'when I was your age' stuff, are you?" I kidded him.

"Did I sound like a parent, just then? Oh, God!" I was starting to get my uncle's sense of humor.

"Speaking of parents," Caden said, standing in the doorway, holding the cordless. "It's some lady from your mom's office." He pushed the screen door open and passed me the phone. My heart started to race... seven months! I wondered if the first voice I heard would be my mom's.

"Yeah—um, I mean, hi—hello."

"Kevin, it's Adam from the congresswoman's—I mean your mother's office." Caden had said "lady," but this was a guy. I guessed he sounded a little girly. Mostly his voice was just soft.

"Is my mom alright?"

"Yes—yeah, of course. Catelyn—I mean your mother is just fine."

"Then what do you want?" What the hell?

"Your mother was wondering if you were free to have dinner with her tomorrow night," he explained.

"Why didn't she call?" Did she really have this guy, her assistant call me? The better question was if she had really asked me to dinner like we'd just talked a few days ago instead of *seven* months?

"She's very busy this morning, and asked me to find a number where you could be reached and call you to invite you to dinner. I'm not certain what it's about. I can tell her—."

"No that's alright. I am free, I mean I'll have dinner with her," I interrupted. "Where and when?"

"She was hoping you could meet her at the house, say about seven o'clock?"

"I'll be there. Thank you."

242

"No, thank you." He sounded nervous. "And Kevin, I know that your mom is really looking forward to it."

Then he hung up. I wasn't sure how to react. I didn't know what she wanted to talk to me about. And why suddenly did she need to see me the next day? What about her assistant saying she was too busy to call. She'd never had her assistant call me before.

That was in the morning. That evening Stephen and my grandma were at the new casino in Prior Lake. My grandma loved bingo. She asked Stephen to go with because she didn't like to drive, especially at night. That didn't make a lot of sense because my uncle didn't even know how to drive. I guessed it was for moral support and maybe so she didn't have to ask either of my aunts.

She had gone to Las Vegas with my grandpa a few times on vacation. That was grandma's idea of a vacation. Grandpa would have been happy to just stay at home and not work. He hadn't gambled much. Besides Las Vegas, my grandparents went on one other trip each year. It was usually somewhere warm in the winter. They'd been to Arizona, Texas, Florida, even San Diego. Stephen looked hurt when that came up. It'd turned out that they were in San Diego before he'd moved to San Francisco. So he was still living in Southern California and they hadn't made any effort to see him. My grandma told him that San Diego and Los Angeles were pretty far away from each other, but he still brought it up a few times after that. I was the only family member who visited him in California the entire time he lived there. It made me sad for him, and glad that I had gone to see him.

My aunt Colleen was the one who told me my uncle was gay. It must have been about seven years before, right after he'd been back to visit. I loved my uncle, but I didn't know him very well. He was pretty cool when I was a little kid. He babysat me a lot before my parents got weird. I still remembered him holding my hand walking to McDonald's. That was after he had started to babysit me at my grandparents' house instead of ours. McDonald's was a few blocks away and Stephen told me that it would be "our little secret." My mother didn't approve of me eating fast food. I brought it up to her once, and she said she'd never disapproved of McDonald's. I thought she didn't understand how loud her disapproval was.

"Why doesn't Stephen come home more?" I'd asked my aunt when I was about fourteen. I certainly couldn't ask my mother about him.

243

"I don't know. I think he might just be happier in California. Once you've been away and you get used to the way things are somewhere else, it's hard to want to go back to a place where they weren't as happy."

"He wasn't happy here?"

"I don't think he was as happy here as he is in California," Colleen answered.

"Why not?" As soon as I knew what being gay was, I had wondered if my uncle was. I thought about just asking him, but I figured it might hurt his feelings if I asked and he wasn't gay.

"What's going on, Kev?" my aunt asked.

"Nothing," I lied.

"Why all the questions?"

My aunt's hair was long and usually messy. Sometimes she piled it on top of her head and held it there with a huge clip. Strands of hair fell everywhere. Even messy, she had this casualness about her that made it all look like it was on purpose. She was pretty much the chillest person I'd ever known. Stephen wasn't really chill at all. There wasn't very much he kept deep down. Everything my uncle had was right there in front of you. The thing they had in common though was their heart. I heard or read somewhere about a person whose heart was bigger than all the rest of them. That was my aunt and uncle. I missed my aunt, probably way more than I missed my mother, which was pretty fucked up. I got my sense of right and wrong from my aunts and uncles, even Stephen who I barely knew.

When my mom forbade me to go to California and drive Stephen and Caden back, I didn't even have to think about it. Mom had threatened to cut me off completely, but I thought it was the right thing to do. I almost couldn't believe she didn't see that.

That day, talking to Colleen about Stephen, she reached up, tore the clip away from her head and moved her right hand up to gather her hair again. She tried a couple of times and then just tossed the clip on the table in front of us, giving up. Her thick hair fell about halfway down her back; some fell in her face. I'd never forget when she cut it. She tried to look cheerful about it, but I knew my aunt loved her hair. It had to be like losing a really big part of herself.

244

On Election night some people were hanging out at my apartment. I had this picture frame that held two pictures. One was of my aunts. The other picture I had taken of Stephen, Alec, and Caden when I visited them in San Francisco. The pictures were side by side. A couple of my friends were doing coke. It wasn't like I'd never done it, but I wasn't that night. That night I was celebrating and cocaine wasn't my drug of choice. It was the first time I'd ever voted. My mom was a huge supporter of the current President, of course, but I liked the governor from Arkansas. It seemed like most of the people I knew did, too. A lot of the country celebrated when the news broke that he had beaten Bush and Ross Perot. Most of the people I was hanging out with had voted for the first time that day. We'd gotten it right. I had no idea that Alec had died, none of us did until later. I went to the bathroom, and when I got back, I saw the frame with those pictures lying flat on the old footlocker I used as a coffee table. I saw the small pile of white powder in the corner, just above my aunt Joanna's head. I turned down the line they offered me, just before the dumbass friend of a friend set his elbow against the glass and leaned in to put a rolled up dollar bill to his nose. I heard the glass break over the din of the music. When I went to look, I saw that a splinter had shot right through my uncle's family. The frame itself almost broke in half. It wasn't until later that week that I found out Alec had died. I was sad for my uncle and Caden.

The morning after the party I picked the broken frame up and took it over to the garbage can. As I picked away the pieces of broken wood and glass, I realized something. People had frames. Some were other people, their families, and their kids. Some were their light, whatever is inside. Some were just the stuff around them, their belongings. My aunt's frame was her hair. There was other stuff, too. It was just the top part of her frame, I guess. When her hair was gone, though, after two courses of chemo, it was like her light grew more intense. The picture of my aunts was taken after they'd gone to the North Shore, just before my grandpa died. I stared down at it after the pieces of powder-shrouded glass were gone, and realized that Colleen was completely bald in the photo.

"You know you can tell me anything, right?" Colleen asked me. I was sad. I was just beginning to figure out why, but I didn't ever want to talk about that part of it.

"I think I might be gay." The words felt weird to say. You said the same shit over and over again and it was like you hadn't said anything at all. Then you said a combination of words in a certain order, and it felt like you were talking

245

for the very first time. I looked at my aunt, determined not to look down. I hadn't done anything to look down over. Our eyes met and hers had tears in them. She was smiling, though. She didn't say anything for a little while, but when I looked away, she spoke.

"What makes you think so?"

"I don't know." That was a lie.

"You asked about Stephen. Does that mean you were wondering about him?" Colleen asked.

"Is he gay?" I was looking her right in the eye again.

"Did your mom say something?"

"No! She wouldn't though. She would never! She's going to hate me, you know?"

"Oh sweetheart, she will never hate you," Colleen said.

"Yes, she will," I disagreed. I was sure my mother's siblings had stopped — I didn't know how to say it — knowing her.

"She may disapprove, she may not understand, but she will not hate you," she explained.

"What makes you so sure?"

"I know my sisters and neither of them are capable of hatred." She paused for a few seconds. "Stephen is gay, but you already knew that. Why do you think you are, love?"

"I haven't really — I mean — I don't — should I, I...."

"Kev, it's okay. Everything's going to be alright."

"Then why are you crying?" I shot back. I didn't mean it to sound angry.

"I was the first person Stephen told," she sighed. "I was wrong to encourage him not to tell anyone else. We were really young. "

246

"Was it because you thought people would hate him?"

"No, Kevin. NO!" She wasn't mad, just certain. "I hated thinking how hard it was to keep a part of yourself such a secret, but I also knew how difficult it was to be gay. That was almost ten years ago. I didn't want him to have to tell people and then deal with it alone. I was leaving in a couple of days to go back to college."

"Just to St. Cloud, right?" I asked her.

"That's a pretty big distance to be all alone from. It was a different time, Kev. And I was wrong, anyway. You understand that I wouldn't care one bit, if you were, right?" I just nodded and she kept talking. I wasn't sure how much of what she else she said I actually heard over the noise in my head. I'd accomplished two things. I confirmed what I thought about my uncle and gained at least two allies in my family. After that, my mind just wandered. We only discussed it one more time, but by then I was pretty sure I wasn't gay. Maybe bi. I didn't know for sure. I don't know, maybe I still didn't. Did just being open to either experience mean you were immediately saddled with some kind of label?

Back at the video store, a customer was keeping me busy searching for a copy of some movie called *The Philadelphia Story*. I'd never heard of it, so she proceeded to tell me all about it while I looked. I had heard of Katherine Hepburn and Cary Grant, so I had that going for me, the woman told me. I finally found the video in the Drama section. The woman thanked me and even got me to promise that I'd watch the movie after she'd returned it. I waited until she'd left to grab a Jolt cola from the cooler and the remote control. I was only a couple of minutes late to tune in, so I'd probably only missed the "Last Week on *The Real World*" part. I punched a couple of keys on the computer to sell myself a can of pop. They were seventy-five cents, which was kind of expensive. You could buy a can of pop for fifty cents most places.

Aaron on *The Real World* had done something. They were all talking about it. He was kind of a dick. Come on, he was a surfer from Southern California, and he referred to President Clinton as the antichrist. I must have missed a little more than just the recap. When I looked at the computer, it said it was 8:10. The stupid clock on the wall had slowed down again. I wrote a note to Stephen that we needed to get a new one, threw three quarters in the

247

drawer, and looked back up at the TV. I think I liked the cast of Season One better than these guys. Except for Eric.

Just then a couple of guys who looked about eighteen or nineteen came in. They went straight to the back of the store where the New Releases were. There was a big mirror above the counter just opposite the TV. Even though I was facing away from the back of the store, I could see them standing there. One of them turned around to see if I was looking. I knew exactly what was going on. They were there for porn.

The tiny back room was new since my uncle had bought the video store. Charlie had put up the wall for Stephen, who had changed his mind about it at least ten times. The other video store in Uptown had an adult section. Betty said she knew someone who went there instead of our store because of it. That was all Stephen needed to hear. I wasn't sure Betty approved, but she accepted the fact that it was out of her hands. I think my grandma even got it. She went in there once when Stephen and I were both there, and Stephen yelled from the back room.

"Oh, for goodness sake, Stephen! I know what porn is," she called from the other side of the door. "Don't be such a prude. Besides, you shouldn't sell or rent anything you'd be embarrassed for your mother to see." She didn't stay back there long, maybe just a minute, just long enough to make my uncle really uncomfortable.

Sometimes kids came in the store with the intention of stealing a video. You could just tell. That's why the actual tapes were behind the counter. We only had about a hundred of them. The thing that set our store apart from the other one in Uptown was that about half of those were gay. I hadn't realized that gay porn existed. There was nothing wrong with it, obviously. My feeling was if straight people could have theirs, why not gay people? I guessed that the kids who came to steal porn were maybe too embarrassed to rent the gay stuff. Or too young. We didn't get very many kids in the store and the sign on the little half-door to the room clearly said: "18 & Up Only."

Sure enough, as soon as the one kid looked up towards the front of the store, the other kid snuck into the back room. Did the dumbasses think I'd forget there were two of them back there? I walked around the counter, grabbing a couple of videos I had to put back on the New Release wall. I hadn't made it halfway back before there was a noise in the back room.

248

"Gross!" the kid in the back yelled. "Jesus Christ!" Then there was another noise. I could tell it was empty video cases falling on the floor.

"What?" the other kid asked. I don't think he'd noticed me getting closer. Just then, the kid in the back came crashing out of the room, the swinging door slapping back and forth behind him.

"There's fag movies back there. Did you know that?"

"Seriously? That's disgusting!"

"Excuse me," I said, loudly. I felt sick to my stomach all of a sudden.

"Fuck you, man!" I wasn't sure which one said it.

"You need to get out of this store and never come back," I told them.

We were pretty much face-to-face by then and I was taller than both of them. I had never experienced such hate. It was horrible to think, but at least my mother wasn't hateful, all evidence to the contrary. She wasn't. Colleen was right. My mother had a blind spot. I had worked out exactly where it came from. She had not.

"You think we couldn't take your punk ass?" Again, I wasn't paying attention to which asshole said it. I was prepared to fight, even though I had never fought before in my life.

"I think your idiot friend is about ready to piss his pants," I said. I meant the one who'd done most of the talking. Wasn't it the loudest who were really the most afraid? Everything inside me was still except my heart.

"What the fuck is that supposed to mean?" It was a different voice. I was right. It had been the same one talking almost the whole time.

"Come on, man," the other one said. "Let's just get the fuck out of here."

"Maybe we just—fuck man, chill!"

"It's time for you to go," I told them. "I don't want to call the cops."

"I'm out of here. Dude, come on, let's go!"

249

"Burn in hell, faggot!"

They turned and made their way to the front of the store. The angrier one opened the cooler at the front, took out a can of pop, and slammed it against the wall. It exploded and sprayed everywhere. The other one already had the door open. As soon as his buddy exited the store, he turned back around, took a couple of steps forward, gripped the top of the candy rack, and tipped it forward. Then they were both gone, the stupid bell on the glass door rang and rang as I made my way to the front of the store. I pulled the glass door shut and turned the lock. Then I almost tripped over the candy rack. I took a quick right and threw up all over the counter.

I closed the store an hour early that night. I hoped Stephen didn't find out about what happened, any of it. What I was thinking about earlier, why my mom had a blind spot; that was the thing I didn't want my aunt to know, or anyone. I *really* didn't want Stephen to know about it. I hadn't ever told anyone. It would have destroyed my mother. She had gotten it all wrong. My dad was gay; that was clear. Or maybe he just had a thing for little boys. My mom hated my uncle Stephen because, I didn't *know*, but I thought she blamed him for ruining her marriage. She pushed him away, though, to protect him. I didn't think either of us was sure it hadn't been too late. Then she watched me practically every minute. It turned out that wasn't enough.

My dad touched me. That was really the extent of it. I thought he was too much of a coward to do more. I never connected the dots until my mom was so over the top with her supposed hatred of gay people. What she was, though, was jealous. I had put that much together based on what she said about her brother. She was envious of him. It became absolutely clear to me that, at first, she pushed him away in order to protect him. The jealousy came later. I supposed it grew as she felt more and more alone with what she knew. My mom was a smart woman, but she was also one of the dumbest people I knew. That she was able to come away from what had happened believing it was anyone's fault besides my dad's was fucking stupid. For reasons unknown to me, I felt protective of Stephen after I figured out what went on when I was little. I honestly didn't think he had been abused. I think my mom successfully protected him from all of that.

*****

250

I spent an hour after the assholes left cleaning the front part of the store. Very little vomit went past the glass top of the counter. The pop the asshole had thrown was another story; it sprayed everywhere. I had to scrub the wall, even some of the movies on the rack closest to the front. I finally left the store a little before midnight.

I found myself looking over my shoulder as I went around back and got into my car. The kids from before were long gone. I wasn't sure why I was so freaked out. I wondered if that was how my uncle felt all the time. It would've sucked to have to, like, keep an eye out all the time. The whole way home I was on autopilot. I parked in the driveway off the alley and checked to see if there any lights on in the house. It didn't look like it. When I was confident no one would come out of the house and find me; I just sat in my car and cried for a while.

*****

At ten minutes to seven the next night, I pulled into a different driveway. The place never felt like home, even though it had been for several years. I hadn't lived there since I started college at the U of M three years before. I managed to make it through two-and-a-half years of college before I dropped out. My grades weren't that bad. My last semester at the U, I had a 3.40 GPA. My mother expected above 4.0 and had told me my grades weren't good enough to get me into any law school worth attending.

My car was the only thing of value I owned. Stephen offered to pay the insurance for six months. He convinced me that it was because I drove him and Caden around so much. I didn't pay him rent. We'd never discussed that. Sitting there, in the driveway, one thing was clear. I needed very little from my mother at that point. The one thing I wanted, I was unlikely to get.

I'd sought Catelyn Bennett-Amble's approval for years, almost since the moment she'd stopped giving it. She was the woman who held my hand and told me it would be okay the first day of Kindergarten. She was the woman who kissed my forehead when I had the chicken pox. She'd gotten them, too. I looked it up, some years later, and chicken pox are more dangerous for adults. Doctors certainly recommended precautions for parents of children with pox, but my mother was more concerned that I felt safe and loved than she was for her own safety.

251

She sat with me when my aunt Colleen died. I was sure I'd even seen her cry then. She talked about her weird "too bohemian for her own good" sister all the time, but I could tell she was sad. On my twenty-first birthday, the congresswoman had actually gotten drunk with me. Drunk Catelyn inquired about her family as if she hadn't seen them in years. Maybe she hadn't actually looked at them in years. She even asked if her little brother was well, in San Francisco. It was the only time I remember my mother referring to Stephen as her brother. In fact, it was the only time I could ever remember her bringing him up.

I knew that my mother loved. There in the driveway, I finally decided that's all I wanted from her. I'd given up on her financial support, even her acceptance; but she had to love me. She must have all along. I got out of the car and let myself in the house. My key still worked. The alarm immediately started beeping and I had to think hard to remember the code. It was my birthday reversed: 0701. The code still worked. It used to be part of my DNA. We'd never changed it. I had used 0701 to enter this house for months after I'd dropped out of college. I came to the house, usually when Catelyn was not there, to do laundry, to get free groceries from the pantry. My mother stocked things I knew she'd never eat. Someone else did her shopping, and she must have instructed them to buy peanut butter. Catelyn was allergic to peanuts, but there was always a jumbo-size, unopened jar of peanut butter sitting on the shelf. After I turned twenty-one, beer even started to be appear in the pantry, another thing I was certain my mother wouldn't touch with a ten-foot pole.

We had a sort of understanding. The pantry was like a small convenience store for me. Catelyn made sure it was stocked and I made sure to not mention it. Sometimes, there was even cash on the counter. I knew it was for me. I had been to my mom's on Election Day; and although there was no beer in the pantry — that would have been too easy — there was cash on the counter. That day I'd found five twenty-dollar bills. With them I put gas in my car, had a friend buy two cases of beer, and a whole lid of pot. We had some celebrating to do.

I sat at the kitchen counter until seven forty-five. The house was empty and there was no sign of my mom having been there. I hadn't bothered to look in the pantry. The phone rang and I let the answering machine pick it up. The outgoing message was generic. Everyone called my mother somewhere else. After the beep, I heard a voice it took me a moment to recognize. It was soft, though it was clearly trying to get my attention.

252

"Kevin. Kevin, are you there. Pick up the phone, please. Kevin. Kevin." I lunged for the handset on the wall.

"Adam?"

"Oh, good," he said. "I'm glad I got you."

"She's not coming."

"Something came up. I am very sorry. I called your uncle's house an hour ago, but the boy who answered the phone said you'd already left."

"I had something to pick up on my way," I told the voice on the other end of the phone.

"I'm so, so sorry. It's completely my fault." I knew it wasn't.

"What came up?"

"Your mother had an interview in the morning, but the paper cancelled, so she took an earlier flight to Washington. She needed to talk with a lobbyist and felt she could reach him more easily in the morning. It really was my fault. I shouldn't have pushed the interview in the first place."

"The interview was for both of us?" I sighed.

"Why would you ask that?"

"Just a hunch," I said, and put the handset back on the cradle. I threw the flowers I'd bought on my way in the trash and picked up the ten twenty dollar bills sitting on the counter, stuffing them in my pocket. I didn't bother to check the pantry or reset the alarm on my way out.

Chapter 24
STEPHEN

Caden and I had a deal. We were long past the days when he needed a sitter in order to be left at home. He was fifteen years old and a junior in high school. He was going to start driver's training soon. It was definitely a good thing there would be another driver in the house, but the fact that he was old enough to be that driver boggled my mind. I reminded myself to breathe when it came to the passing of time, especially when said passage involved that incredible kid. His father would have been so proud; he would have never shut up about it. However, half of what Caden had become meant that his dad had to leave us. The strength of character, the resilience, the endless empathy this fifteen-year-old boy possessed was a byproduct of what he had faced having been raised by two gay men. It was also, almost certainly a direct outcome of his losing one of them at a young age. Our deal was I wouldn't smother him, and I would try not to obsess over the vast amount of time he was left alone, as long as we shared at least one meal a day.

The meal was usually dinner. Lately, he'd been leaving almost as early as the city bus would carry him to school, so he could spend time in the computer lab before homeroom. Breakfast with me that early was definitely out. I had never been a morning person. That night I was going to the casino with my mother, so Caden and I were having an early dinner.

It was October seventh already. Caden had been in the eleventh grade for over a month. My sister and I had buried the hatchet. I'd been summoned to her office that first day of school to discuss Caden's skipping a grade. Then there was the Saturday, two weeks before, when Kevin invited me to meet him for lunch, then conveniently overslept. We were having lunch with Joey to discuss Moira's sixty-fifth birthday. I wasn't certain why it couldn't be discussed over the phone. Each of us had been told the other had an idea of what to do and was assured by Kevin that he would be there to act as buffer. Surprisingly enough, we both just laughed when we discovered the deceit.

"We need to eat," Joanna said. "And Kev was right, we have to discuss Mom's birthday."

"Are you suggesting what I think you're suggesting?" I joked. Joanna was already seated on the patio.

254

"Stay and have lunch," she almost pleaded. "Please, Stephen."

"I am hungry." I sat down across from her and she smiled, almost warmly.

"I asked for three waters. I hope you're thirsty," she joked. "Do they do that in California; make you order water? I suppose it makes sense. They sell it now at Super America. Plain bottled water, rows, and rows, not carbonated, not flavored. That's probably been a thing in California for a while, designer water?"

"Nervous?" I asked her. My sister always rambled when she was nervous. She had gotten the three of us—Colleen, me, and herself—in trouble more than once because our mother knew to question her first. Though we'd all been guilty of that once in a while.

"I am, a little."

"Because I sat down?"

"I guess so." I moved to get up. "No seriously, just stay. I'm also nervous because I owe you an apology."

"I'm all ears."

"It's not what you think," she started. "I was clearly wrong about your relationship with Caden. I've talked to him, over the summer a little and now in school. He's protective of you. I can't begin to explain how foreign that is to me."

"He's protective of me?" I had begun to wonder if Caden had also played a role in making sure my lunch with Joanna would happen. But protective?

"I know that you two struggled after Alec died. I'm sorry to bring it up; I'm even sorrier I wasn't more understanding months ago."

I couldn't believe what I was hearing. I had to replay it in my mind. Intellectually you knew people must get it, especially people near to you. Near in a way that was supposed to transcend distance and familial crap. There was a weirdness when something so sad occurred hundreds of miles away from the touch of those nearest to you. The understanding was intellectual; felt on a different level when touch wasn't an option. In lieu of that, you'd have to become willing to accept some sort of verbal covenant. I had never hoped for

255

that from my family, but I was getting it now. The server appeared with our waters.

"May I get a very large Miller Light, please?" The server hadn't even spoken yet. She opened her mouth, probably to ask about drinks, and I completed her thought for her. "The largest you have." Joanna started to laugh, then so did I.

"I was just thinking about the day you called," she said, after the waitress had left.

"What day?" I thought I knew.

"The day of Caden's birthday party, what four years ago." Yep, I was right. "How—I mean how are you?"

"What?" I really wasn't sure what she meant.

"Have you been sick?"

"Not yet." I answered, and she sighed. I couldn't get over the leap she had taken. It was like she had covered half of a lifetime in just a couple of questions. Her sigh betrayed how aware of it she was.

"I'm sorry I never met him."

"Uh—I mean—uh thanks. Thank you." Tears were welling in my eyes. Hers, too. I had to do something to stop them. "I assume you mean Alec. No reason to cry over Sean-Fucking-Cassidy again."

"You met him?"

"No. It's not just one big orgy of celebrities everywhere you go. He was just the first person I could think of from when we were growing up. I met Betty White."

"Kelly would be so jealous," my sister said. "He's obsessed, believe it or not, with *The Golden Palace*."

"*The Golden Girls* spin-off," I laughed. "You should have visited, all of you. You'd have liked it."

"You should have invited us."

256

"Would you have come?" I meant it earnestly.

"Probably not," she answered. We had definitely turned a corner. We'd been on the patio for less than twenty minutes. I still didn't have a drink in front of me. The conversation bordered on something mature, certainly nothing as frigid as nearly every conversation we'd had since I'd called from San Francisco four years earlier. I couldn't quite work out what had changed. The server finally returned with our drinks and I lit a cigarette.

"May I have one of yours? Looks like I've left mine in the car again."

For the next few minutes, we made ridiculous small talk. By the time we'd ordered our food, Joanna had made sure I hadn't met Sean or any other Cassidy. Even in small talk, she'd grown animated. There was no hesitancy left. By the time our food arrived, we were working our way back around, past small talk.

"Kev said your house in San Francisco was amazing. It overlooked the whole city."

"San Francisco is a big city. It overlooked the Castro and you could see downtown."

"Do you miss it?" My sister asked.

"Of course. It was like a different world compared to here."

"I can imagine. We should've visited. Colleen brought it up once. Do you remember when we were kids? She wanted to live there."

"California?" I asked.

"San Francisco. I never got it. I've always been happy here. No desire to go anywhere else."

"I don't think you have to be unhappy where you are to want to go someplace else," I asserted.

"I asked Colleen once why she never visited you. It was before she'd gotten sick, and she told me that she'd given you San Francisco."

257

"What did that mean?"

"I didn't get it either," she told me. The waitress returned with our food. I'd ordered a burger and fries and Joanna had ordered a salad with chicken, red peppers, and pea pods. We stopped talking while the waitress refilled our water glasses and asked if we needed anything else. After she'd gone again, my sister stabbed at her salad and moved her fork to her mouth. I stamped out half a cigarette and looked down at my burger.

"I did ask," Joanna finally continued. "Colleen said it was good for you to be there and until you came back to us we could only visit. She thought you needed a place of your own, that it was great you'd found San Francisco."

"I didn't know it was lost," I laughed. "And until I came back to you?"

"You know how she got sometimes. She was convinced, though, that you'd move back eventually."

"We always come home." I shoved a couple of fries in my mouth.

"I guess," Joanna continued. "I told her that I couldn't see you ever moving back and she told me that I was blind. She said you cherished family more than any of us. Remember Sunday dinners?"

"I thought they'd still be happening."

"They did for a while, a few years maybe. After a while, Caty completely stopped coming. Then there was the time Paddy was absolutely trashed. It was right after their son had been stillborn. Mom said something about Jannie being to blame and Patrick got this wild look in his eyes. They went back and forth for a little while and then Mom suggested Jannie had robbed him of more than his manhood."

"Jesus. Didn't Dad say anything?"

"You know Dad. He didn't stay for much of it. He got up from the table as soon as they started going at it. It was just Jim, me, and the kids. And Mom, Jannie and Patrick. He told Mom that Jannie was right about her. Mom asked what that was supposed to mean. Then Paddy tried to get up from the table, knocked the chair out from underneath himself, and fell on his ass.

"They didn't talk for a long time after that. After Paddy got his second DUI, Jannie kicked him out. He slept in a hotel for a couple of weeks before Dad got wind of it. Then he moved back home and Mom pretended nothing had ever happened."

"Wow," was all I could manage.

"That was pretty much it for Sunday dinners. We still did holidays. Caty rarely came, but Kev did. It just never felt the same without Caty and Dad arguing about politics or you and Colleen talking in that language only you two understood."

"What language?"

"It's like you had your own shorthand at times. No one else got it. Can I have a fry?" I had only taken three or four bites of the burger.

"Sure," I said, pushing my plate in her direction. "I'm about finished, anyway. I should have gotten a salad, too. I don't know what's happened to me. We used to eat so much better in California."

"It's so much work being a grown-up isn't it?" my sister asked. "I'm a complete failure at it. I'm certain Kelly thinks pizza is one of the four food groups."

"Caden is drinking coffee now! His father would be mortified. Breakfast, I swear—coffee and Pop-Tarts. For me, too."

"Food is the first thing to go," she said. "I feel like I have to choose my battles. If it's between Meghan not smoking or waiting to have sex until she's at least thirty, or the occasional Twinkie being eaten instead of a Brussels sprout—."

"I'm so happy boys mature more slowly than girls," I interrupted. "Caden's perfect, really. I just wish he'd come with some sort of owner's manual."

"Was Alec a good father?" I was really moved by her sudden interest in my family.

"The best. He had the good cop/bad cop thing down to a science. He let me play good cop far more often than I deserved. I think he felt that anyone willing to co-parent someone else's child was more deserving of the easier role."

259

"After Kevin visited, we all grilled him for information. Colleen more than anyone, but Paddy, too." Maybe the interest wasn't as sudden as it appeared to be.

"How about you?"

"Of course, but I got to play it cooler. The other two were asking all the right questions."

"I wish I'd known." My voice trembled a bit when I spoke.

"I'm so sorry." She looked surprised. Our eyes met and hers were damp. She pushed her plate almost even with mine in the middle of the table.

"We haven't even talked about Mom's birthday," I said, changing the subject. It was obvious she was trying. There were walls that had gone up which would take more than a forty minute conversation to tear down. The water under our bridge, though, seemed to be flowing a little freer than it had in years. "I could have dinner at my house. Do you think Caty would come?"

"I doubt she'd come no matter where we have it."

"I absolutely dread the time that I can't talk to Caden at least once every day. It's coming too soon. How the fuck can our sister just decide not to have anything to do with her own son?"

"Self-preservation?" Joey suggested, and laughed ironically.

That had been a couple of weeks before Mom's 65th birthday, which had come and gone. It was four thirty and Caden would be getting home about the same time as the pizza I'd ordered for dinner. I really needed to hire another part-time person to work at the video store so pizza for dinner became more of a treat than a normality. I asked Mom to join us, but she'd declined. She said she'd pick me up five forty-five. I was standing at the kitchen counter when I heard Caden at the back door. He kicked the door, as we'd begun to do. Sonic had become aware of the world beyond our house and we hadn't decided whether or not it was safe to give him a wider berth. He'd escaped twice before and was proving pretty adept at developing

260

getaway tactics. All of us had taken to kicking the front and back doors before opening them in case the cat was near.

"Sonic sleeping?" Caden asked, closing the door behind him.

"I haven't seen him, so it's a fair assumption. How was school?"

"Fine."

"A little more information, please," I told him.

"What do you want from me?" he joked, tossing his backpack on the floor.

"Name, rank and serial number," I offered.

"You know I really have no idea what you're saying sometimes?"

"That makes many of us."

"As long as you keep your day job," Caden laughed.

"You got that from your dad," I said.

"For the record, he was more funny."

"Funnier actually," I corrected him. "And what makes you say that?"

"I just speak the truth. Are we having pizza again?"

"You like pizza."

"What time is she coming?"

"My mother will be here in about an hour, and yes I ordered pizza. I need to hire another person at the store so I can be home every night for dinner."

"That would be cool, I guess," he started. "I need a mom. I mean seriously, formative years."

"I could wear a dress if that would help."

"Jesus, please don't!" he exclaimed.

"Just wait until you're old enough to appreciate the artistry that goes into drag."

"Oh, I get that. No worries there. I've seen *The Crying Game*." He had started to leave the room.

"Your backpack," I called after him.

"Oh, yeah."

"Pizza should be here soon. What are your plans for the rest of the night?"

"I've got some girls coming over about seven thirty. That's okay, right?" he joked.

"Funny."

"Okay, fine. I have homework. Then tomorrow is garbage day, so I thought I'd partake in a little child labor and drag that shit out. Then cable until I'm sure you and the old lady have made it back to civilization safe and sound."

"Probably best not to refer to my mother as 'the old lady' in her presence, not if you have any hopes of providing me with grandchildren in twenty-five or thirty years."

"In thirty years I'll be like forty-five. Who wants kids when they're that old?" he retorted, grabbing his backpack.

"Wash your hands," I told him. I was thirty-three, yet somehow unable to argue with his logic.

"Whatever, Mother," he said. He was already down the hall, at the foot of the stairs. Just then, the doorbell rang. "Pizza's here!"

"The money's right there," I called to him.

"Seriously, I have to wash my hands," Caden said, taking the steps two at a time.

Chapter 25
STEPHEN

Moira did not actually parallel park as much as she appeared on the street in front of our house and honked the horn repeatedly until I opened the front door and waved at her to stop. Eventually, I took a deep breath and climbed in the passenger seat of the mid-sized Ford something or other.

"Get your seat belt on before I floor this fucker," my just turned sixty-five year old mother exclaimed. She had the radio tuned to a country music station and a cigarette dangling from between her lips. The air conditioning was blasting.

"It's a little cold in here," I said, my nipples hardening.

"Ugh! I don't know how to turn it off."

"You don't know how to operate the air conditioning in your car, but you're up-to-date on the latest slang the kids are using these days?"

"Priorities," she clarified, and hit the gas. When the car lurched forward, I was never more grateful for a seatbelt. Without one, I'd have left my front teeth embedded in the dashboard.

"Mom! Slow down!" I yelled.

"Really, Stephen. There's no need to impersonate your sister-in-law. One Jannie is enough!"

Moira went at least fifteen miles over the speed limit on the highway. I did my best not to distract her too much. We mostly just made small talk. A couple of times she sang along with, but a little off tune to a song on the radio. She didn't seem nervous at all; in fact, she seemed almost giddy.

After we'd made the trip in record time and parked the car in the vast parking lot at the casino, my mother undid her seatbelt and started rummaging through her purse. The women in my family carried purses large enough to comfortably serve as a domicile for a small house pet. The rummaging seemed like it would be necessary to find anything at all. I chuckled, recalling my dad once referring to my mom's purse as "The Mystery Grab Bag." Long after I would've given up the search as fruitless, Moira pulled out a silver flask,

263

undid the top, and took a very healthy swig of whatever it contained. I continued to laugh, by then almost involuntarily. It was like when a child swears. Thinking back on it, it was a little bit like when an old lady swears. I was getting used to that, though.

"A reward for getting us here in one piece," she said, offering me the flask. I shook my head no. "Suit yourself." She stilled for a moment, studying my face, almost as if expecting my disapproval. When she saw none, she took a smaller sip from the flask, replaced the lid, and reached in front of me to put it in the glove compartment. "The casino's dry."

"Well, in that case."

"Help yourself," she offered.

"I think I'll make it through the night just fine on pop."

"I'm sure you will," she answered. "As will I. Now. Let's go."

It took us about five minutes to get to the entrance of the casino, even with my mother rushing. She did move a tiny bit slower than she used to, but I chalked that up to inactivity more than age. She wasn't the least bit feeble. I'd come to see her more as lost. My mother had very little to do anymore and the less she did, the less she wanted to do.

"Out with it," she said, as we neared the front doors of the massive complex. "What are you wondering about?"

"What makes you think I'm wondering about anything?"

"You keep looking over at me and then you go back in your head, so out with it. What are you deciding about me now?"

"I'm paying attention to you, Mom. There is a difference."

"If you say so."

We stepped into the casino and were quickly enveloped by all of the sounds. I heard slot machines and dealers conducting the business of gambling at various tables around the huge room. There was the loud murmur of gamblers everywhere, some clearly ecstatic over winning, some disappointed over what they'd lost, but most of them just enjoying themselves. There was a

264

cloud of smoke that hung thick in the air. The ceilings were high. In the main room, they went up three stories. The smoke didn't travel all the way up. It clung to the atmosphere about four feet above people's heads, just rolling there, like the fog did in San Francisco.

We had stepped into Moira's element. I was a little ill at ease. I enjoyed bingo, but that was the extent of my interest in this world of hers. She could play craps, Black Jack, even Poker; and she loved the slots. Everyone in my family was competitive. We all loved games. That's where I came by my excitement over bingo. There was no rush for me in the risk involved in gambling, though. Moira loved it all. She fit in there. She relaxed upon entering the main room, looking around, and taking it all in. I was happy to be spending time with her and even happier to see her light up.

We made our way to the bingo hall and purchased what they called our packages. My mom knew exactly what she wanted and went about the business of purchasing it, then helped me pick out what she said I could handle. When we were finished, we turned around to survey the room and choose our seats. The hall was huge, perhaps twice as large as any I'd been in. My mother indicated her desire to sit near the restrooms, so we went in that direction. Once we'd chosen our table, I moved to sit across from her, but my mother motioned for me to sit next to her instead.

"If you need help, Stephen, I'll not be able to give you any from that angle." She set her giant purse down. Her silver hair was pulled back and held in place by a series of clips. There were diamonds in the top hole of her twice-pierced ears. Underneath those were small gold hoops. She wore a navy blue tracksuit over a plain white t-shirt, and white tennis shoes. On her right wrist were two different tennis bracelets and on her left, was a gold charm bracelet. There were rings on almost every finger. "Take a seat. I'm going to get myself a pop. Want anything?"

"Something caffeinated and not diet, please. I'll watch your stuff." I watched her walk away, confidently. I knew that she'd never been in that particular hall before. There was a casino in northern Minnesota that I was certain she'd gone to with my dad. The halls must have been similar. There was no tentativeness in her steps. She was gone and back in barely a minute, sitting two plastic cups down between us.

"You're really in your element here," I told her.

265

"I guess," she said, again rummaging in her purse. I wasn't sure I wanted to know what she'd bring out this time. She took out a large Ziploc baggie with several bingo dabbers in it and set those down. She snapped the purse shut and put it on the floor between us, placing one of the straps under one of the legs of her chair. Next, she unzipped her fanny pack and removed her cigarette case. In one fluid motion, she opened the case, removed a lighter and cigarette, put the cigarette between her lips, lit it, and inhaled deeply. She set the cigarette case down next to her, removed three small trolls from the fanny pack, arranging them in front of the ashtray, and finally turning her attention to the packet she had purchased.

"You have a whole routine. I'm completely out of my depth."

"I'll get my act together here and then help you," she said cheerfully.

"You know, I think Jannie and Joey worry about you because they've never seen you like this," I told her.

"That's ridiculous." She looked up from the papers she was arranging in front of her.

"You're so tentative at home, though."

"Slow isn't tentative," she snapped back. "It's not feeble, either."

"I didn't mean to distract you," I told her, feeling bad for disrupting her routine.

"What is so good about rushing everywhere? Did anyone stop to think that I move slower at home because I have nowhere that I need to be; certainly nowhere in a hurry?"

I hadn't considered that and I was certain my siblings or siblings-in-law hadn't either. I guessed there was a lot about our mother's situation that we hadn't taken into account. Both Joanna and I had, in one way or another, lost our significant others, too; but in our situations, the losses came with twice the number of responsibilities than before they occurred. Our mother's loss had left her, for all intents and purposes, with nothing to do. What she seemed to be implying was that it wasn't all bad. I'm certain there were things about being married to my father that Moira didn't miss at all. She had returned to the task of situating her bingo sheets. Some were put to the side, some

266

turned over. Still others were finally placed right side up, on top of the ones she had turned facedown.

I started to ponder if there were things about Alec that I didn't miss. In less than a month, it would be a year since he'd died. I had focused only on not lamenting the process of dying, the sadness, the sickness, the constant reminder of my own mortality. The big things tended to overshadow the petty ones to the point that they barely existed. I chuckled at how easily a few of them came flooding back when I willed them to. After more than eleven years of living together, Alec had never learned the correct way to load the dishwasher or to put the toilet paper on the roll. I was forever following behind him, correcting his "mistakes." The toilet paper went over, not under. I had told him a million times. I assumed it had become a game to him. No one could be that dense accidentally.

"You're not paying attention to me," she was saying. "Stephen!" I looked over and she had arranged my smaller stack of papers for me, just as she had her own. She'd even tested out all four dabbers to insure they worked properly.

"Sorry. Tell me again."

"The numbers on the screens," she motioned to the big monitors on the walls. "Mark those on this sheet." Then she handed me a single bingo sheet.

"How do I know you didn't switch these when I wasn't paying attention?" I joked.

"I guess you should pay attention, then," she snapped back. "You think too fucking much."

The thing that got me about her swearing was that her volume never changed. Some people lowered their voices when they swore. Not my mother. I supposed she didn't raise her voice either, which was a good thing. I found myself looking around, though, to see if anyone had noticed her say fuck. There didn't appear to be anyone offended if they had.

"We have five minutes until the Early Bird session starts. Get going," she ordered.

"Okay, okay, you're much bossier than when we were kids."

267

"I am a lot of things more than I was when you were kids," she clarified. "As is every single one of my children."

"I didn't mean anything by it."

"I know you didn't. It is tedious though, you know, having the ways you've changed lorded over you. Not by you."

"Joanna doesn't mean to," I told her.

"I know that, too," she agreed. "It doesn't make it any less tiresome, but I do know. You're doing well." She motioned to the sheet I'd about half marked-up.

"What is the deal with these?" I asked.

"It's a speed session. It happens right before the break. It's right here on this sheet." She placed a white sheet of paper between us, just south of the ashtray. "This is the schedule for tonight. With the speed session, they'll only call a certain amount of additional numbers, and they'll do so faster than they call regular bingos. If you get to cover up all those numbers, you win whatever the jackpot is. Good, you're almost done!" I *was* almost done. There were five squares unmarked when I finished.

"Pretty good, huh?" I looked over at my mother.

"Really good," she said. "They'll call eleven more numbers. See I have six to go. That's when you stand pat. I think I'll go get some more pop, quick, before they start."

I looked over and even in all that she had accomplished, shuffling papers all around, setting up shop like the table belonged to her, chain smoking, and keeping me in line, she'd also drained her plastic cup. There was nothing left in it but ice. I set my jackpot sheet aside and lit a cigarette. There were a lot of people in the hall, but no one had sat at our table. There were eight seats. The tables on the ends seemed to fill up faster, so I assumed it wouldn't be long before someone else joined us.

"Some people don't play Early Birds," Moira said, back again.

"Jesus, Mom. Did you run?"

We played our way through the first five games. I never came close. By the time the early session was over; two women had sat at the other end of our table. They looked to be about Joanna's age. I was dumbfounded when one of the women lined up an array of troll dolls. The other woman was clearly an amateur, like me, as the two of them repeated the same dance my mother and I had. The troll lady pointing here and there, telling the other one what to do. My mother had gone to the bathroom as soon as they'd called a break.

There must have been a line for the bathroom, because it took her almost ten minutes to get back. I was terrified they'd start calling numbers and I'd have my own, as well as her sheets to watch. She was prepared to play twelve cards and I had another six. There was no way I'd keep up with eighteen. She made it back with seconds to spare.

"Fucking women!" she exclaimed, this time at least sort of under her breath. "I was beginning to think I'd never make it out of that bathroom alive."

"I was scared I'd have to play all these cards."

"So was I," she laughed, lighting a cigarette. "You'll be fine with six."

"Your first number is up," the caller announced over the PA. I looked up and sure enough, there it was.

Before long, we'd made it through another seven games and it was time for the Jackpot. The excitement in the room was palpable. Eleven numbers to go and I only needed five. I wondered what the odds were. We each had just one card to play. The caller began. *B-nine.* I had that one. Four to go. *O-seventy.* I didn't have that on my sheet, but Moira did. We each had the next number: *B-thirteen.* And the next after that: *G-fifty-eight.* We each only needed two more numbers. *O-sixty-nine.* Neither of us had that one. Six numbers left to call and my heart was in my throat. The announcer informed us the prize would be one thousand dollars in forty-six numbers. Jesus Christ. *I-nineteen.* Nope. Neither of us. *I-twenty-two.* I needed twenty-four. I-twenty-four, damn it! My luck seemed to have dried up. The younger lady with the trolls, from a few seats down, whispered to her friend that she was down to two. *Haha lady, glad you finally caught up!* Four numbers left for them to call. *B-twelve.* My mother slapped my arm, motioning to her sheet. All she had left was the one I'd been waiting for. I-twenty-four. I needed that one and N-thirty-four. Three numbers left to call for a thousand bucks! I thought I might pass out.

"Someone else is going to get it," my mom said. "You watch."

269

"Don't say that. Be positive. Unless, you know, the someone else is me. Then you can keep right on talking."

"N—." My heart stopped. "Thirty... Five." *What the fuck ever!* Two left. You could almost have heard a pin drop.

"I... Twenty...." Yeah, I wasn't gonna fall for that one again. "Four!"

"I-twenty-four!" Moira yelled, then. "BINGO! BINGO!" She was waving her hand in the air. No one had called it. She appeared to be the only winner. I looked at her and she mouthed, "*Fucking BINGO.*" I didn't know why she chose the moment all hell broke loose to show some decorum. I did know I hadn't seen my mom that thrilled in, well, since I'd been back. Who wouldn't be thrilled to win a thousand dollars? A woman came over to the table and took my mom's lone sheet to the nearest microphone.

"We have a bingo," she announced. There was a minute or two while Mom's bingo was verified. Then the woman brought the sheet back along with a sheet my mother was instructed to fill out. A voucher which could be redeemed at a cashier stand after the sessions were over would pay the thousand dollars. It was time for another break. Five minutes. I think we were both a little too stunned to move.

"I bet you wish you had that flask back in your purse right about now." I leaned over and whispered to her.

"You got that fucking right!" she exclaimed, and all was well with the world. My breathing finally returned to normal and so had my mother's vocabulary.

The rest of the session was a tad uneventful compared to the Jackpot round. My mother was one number away two more times, but didn't win again. On the second to last round, I was one away for what seemed like twenty numbers called. When the caller finally uttered the number I needed, I could barely get the word out.

"BINGO," I called. Along with five other people. The prize for that game was one hundred dollars, of which I won twenty. After I tipped the bingo server two dollars and deducted what I paid for my package, I ended up almost breaking even. It wasn't a thousand, but it wasn't bad. And I'd had a blast with my mother. It was fun seeing her in control. I vowed to attend bingo with her more often. It would certainly be good for her to get out of the house and I wanted to spend time with her. I'd wasted thirteen years. I didn't intend to waste anymore.

On the drive home, after my mother had emptied the flask, she told me her friend Dawn had asked her to go to Las Vegas for Thanksgiving. "I told her no."

"Why?" I knew why, and I was happy she'd declined.

"It will be your first real holiday back. I didn't even make a turkey last year. Your father had only been dead a couple of months and your Alec had just died. It seemed wrong to give thanks."

"I get it," I said.

"I mean, of course, we were all still grateful, but I didn't think anyone would want to holler it from the rooftops."

"Dawn's husband died two years ago, right?" My mom just laughed, not heartily, more mournfully.

"I guess I'm at that age. The party was lovely, by the way." She meant the almost-surprise birthday party I'd had for her that past weekend. Joanna and I had hatched a plan, then brought Paddy and Jannie, and of course, Kev on board. We'd had it at my house. Catelyn was in DC, but sent flowers.

"Do you miss him?"

"Dawny's husband?" she asked, incredulously.

"No, Dad!"

"Of course I do. Do you miss him?"

"Stupid question. I get your point."

"Not a day goes by, that I don't forget for just a split second. I take two forks out of the drawer when I'm getting ready to eat. Or I start out back to tell him something. It is what it is. I mean: you know."

I did know. It was strange that my mother and I had that knowledge in common. Sad that her piece of it had come from the passing of my dad. I'd

271

barely acknowledged his death. For years, I barely acknowledged his life. I sometimes told myself that I had grieved enough for Alec to cover my father and my sister, but I knew that wasn't true. You couldn't actually grieve for one person through another. It turned out that I'd grieved for Alec about exactly as much as I'd needed to. I guess that meant that I hadn't even begun to grieve the other losses.

"They'll be easier," my mom said, like she'd just read my mind. "They're all different. I mean a spouse is different than a sibling, and a sibling is different than a parent, and a parent is different than a child. Dawn's husband was a friend, and even that is different. You get rather adept at grieving. I imagine you know all about that, as well?"

"Not as well as you'd think."

"I'm glad, Stephen. It's too much."

"You've had a lot," I told her.

"Yes, I have, but then we all have, really. It's a terrible thing to lose a child. I do not recommend it."

It was weird that this entire conversation was happening in the car, both of us with our seat belts on, my mother's weathered hands rigid on the steering wheel. I wished I could reach out to her. A hand on her knee or leg seemed far too intimate, inappropriate actually. At one point, I reached over to squeeze her shoulder. She nodded in my direction as if she'd taken in the awkwardness, as well.

"I think that you should go to Las Vegas, Mom." It came out of nowhere.

"Where on earth did that come from?"

"Let your children repair a little more. We have Christmas, too. That gives us about ten weeks to get our shit together. Dawn doesn't have anyone left." That much was true. My mother's best friend, the woman who'd been her maid of honor, how many decades ago, had one child. Her son had killed himself several years ago, just after Alec and I had moved to San Francisco. Then her husband had a stroke and lingered for four years before dying. It was cold of me, I knew, but I remember thinking *thank God* when someone had told me he'd died. I meant that it was a blessing when someone is no longer in

272

pain. Still I'd have taken it the wrong way had anyone suggested Alec's dying was a blessing.

"You used to adore Dawn," she told me.

"I did?" I didn't remember. I didn't have any memories of very late childhood, just images, through other people's eyes, from stories they had told about me. I knew some people who had vivid memories of when they were four or five or even younger than that. Not me. About my earliest memory was when I was six. There were many after that point, but none before.

"And she loved you. Everyone did. You were such a sweet little boy. Always picking flowers for people. Always wrapping shit from my kitchen or your dad's garage to give away. Even your own toys. You'd have given everything away, if we'd allowed it."

"I really don't remember that."

"And now look at you. You've got Caden and your nephew."

"What do you mean?"

"Just balance it," she explained. "The last thing you want is to have truly given it all away. It is okay to measure it out. That way you have more to give for longer."

"I could tell you the same thing." I understood exactly where she was headed.

"Maybe." She steered the car off of the freeway. My God, we were almost home.

"Go to Las Vegas, Mom. You deserve it. We'll have the biggest Christmas we've ever had. Caden's never really seen snow, a few flurries here and there in San Francisco, but not real snow. I can't wait to show him what Christmas is like here. Last year's holidays were hard for all of us. Not this year."

"Then I'm excited for all of us."

"So you'll go to Las Vegas then?"

"We'll see." It was such a parental answer.

273

"Hey, what do you think the chances are we could get Caty to have Christmas with us?"

"I wouldn't hold your breath, dear."

Chapter 26
JOANNA

The alarm clock started beeping at six o'clock in the morning. At first, I wondered why I hadn't shut it off. It was the Tuesday before Christmas, four days into the break. I could have slept until ten had I chosen to. Then he stirred next to me and I sat straight up, startled. There was a man in my bed. I didn't even have to look to know it was a man. I felt his hairy legs against mine when he moved. I breathed in his scent like something divined by the gods. Or maybe it had just been that long. I laid back down and moved my body next to his. He pushed in closer, and it was like we were one.

The greatest thing about sleeping with him was how we fit. My ex and I never seemed to fit quite right. I slept with Jim through fifteen plus years of marriage. In the beginning, there had at least been spooning, but even then, we didn't fit. After the first couple of years, we stopped even trying to fit together. There was always plenty of space between us for whichever child couldn't sleep on any given night. It had gotten to the point where cuddling felt mechanical. I often sensed he did so only out of duty or to meet my expectations, and honestly, I didn't mind that so much. It was nice to be held for however long it lasted, but it was just as nice when Jim rolled over and shifted his body a few inches from mine. He had his side of the bed and I had mine.

Two mornings prior, there was a man in my bed for the first time in I couldn't remember how long. I was astonished to wake up limb to limb; two bodies pressed together as if they belonged that way. It had become a foreign concept and not just because it had been a year since my divorce. Jim and I had stopped sharing the same bed months before we separated. The kids were both gone overnight on Saturday—Meghan at a friend's, and Kelly with his dad for their family Christmas. It was not often I was completely alone in my own house. When he spent the night, there was no need to set an alarm clock, no need for him to escape quietly before either kid woke up. It was far too early for that discussion. Meghan would probably just laugh at me; she was sixteen and we had been open about sex. I couldn't imagine her giving it a second thought, other than the grossness factor. Who wanted to imagine their parents having sex? I certainly cringed the first time it had occurred to me. Kelly, on the other hand, would've been far more difficult. Somewhere, deep down, I knew that he harbored hopes his father and I would get back

275

together. He had to. It was perfectly normal. All I needed was for my thirteen-year-old to go on a crime spree because his mother had finally gotten some.

Saturday night we had sex twice. The first time we barely made it to the bed. We had sex again Sunday morning before he left, around eleven. He came by Monday night, but did not stay after we fucked. I wasn't ready to call it anything but fucking. I'd thought about it the night before actually, lying in his arms, feeling his breath on my neck. We were having sex, a lot of it, I'd admit that, but sex was all it was. I had to be practical. There were countless reasons I couldn't develop feelings for him, yet I had already begun to smile inside. There were so many warring emotions; I almost couldn't pick a place to start to unravel them. Certainly, I was terrified. There were at least a dozen more feelings I had yet to put names to. But there were also happiness, and satisfaction, a lot of satisfaction. For right then, I just knew enough to not freak out. At some point, we would talk about what was happening between us. I hoped it wouldn't be soon. Talking, if I remembered correctly, was overrated, and just seemed to further complicate things.

"Morning," he whispered, his arms tightening around me.

"Good Morning. How'd you sleep?"

"Like the dead." We were still spooning. I had not turned around to look into his deep blue eyes. He released his hold on me and wriggled out of the embrace, throwing one leg over my body, laying sideways across the bed. I made a quarter turn onto my back and suddenly Charlie was straddling me. He held most of his weight off of me with his thighs, which tightened, one on either side of me. "There you are." He smiled. His long hair twisted all over the place, some of it matted to his face.

"Where else would I be?"

"Nowhere. It was just an expression, I guess." He leaned in to kiss me softly, first on my forehead, then on the lips, before sitting back up. I smiled up at him, tried not to look like a complete fool. The smiling was brand new. All of it was fresh. Fresh was something I guess I'd given up on; didn't really think about. I thought about sex a fair amount, okay, a lot. I thought about passion, I supposed. I just didn't think of affection or anything in its neighborhood.

"How did you sleep?" That was the million-dollar question, wasn't it?

"I slept really well."

276

"God, I love sleeping well." He rolled off me, onto his back.

"You don't usually?" We were lying, side by side, both looking up at the ceiling. It was still very dark. The only light came from the street lamp, outside my bedroom window.

"Sometimes, but your bed is amazing."

"One of the better things I got in the divorce," I agreed, not bitter for a change.

"I sleep on a futon and the space heater buzzes all night long."

"Where is your apartment?" I realized I had no idea where he lived.

"It's in Uptown. Near Loring Park. Not far from the video store."

"Oh, yes." I remembered something. "You're sure you don't mind taking us today?"

"Not at all. Things are slow until it snows."

"Don't forget. Not a word," I said, sternly.

"He'll figure it out, you know."

"Maybe. I'm honestly just not ready to discuss my sex life with my little brother." I swung my legs over the side of the bed, sitting up again. "We've only been talking for about a minute. It's nice, you know, having him back to talk to."

"I just think he'll sense something's changed."

"If he does, then we'll cross that bridge. If not, let's just... well; let's not say anything." I wasn't certain where Stephen and I stood, exactly. It was good. It was really good, like we were brother and sister again. I just wasn't completely sure whether we were friends, as well.

Stephen had gone out and bought a Christmas tree the week before Thanksgiving, he was so anxious. He and Kevin had hung lights outside. Growing up, my little brother had loved Christmas. I knew all kids did, but the

277

magic never went away for Stephen. It was nice that I was getting a chance to see it all through his eyes again. The kids and I had invited Stephen, Kevin, and Caden all over to our house for Thanksgiving. Paddy and Jannie had gone to her parents, out near St, Michael. Catelyn, of course, was nowhere to be found. And our mother had gone to Las Vegas with her best friend, Dawn. The six of us had a fantastic time, stuffing ourselves. We played board games all afternoon.

Last week, I gave Caden a ride home from school. He'd stayed late to work on something in the computer lab and I happened to be leaving just as he was. I went into my brother's house, just to say hello, and he was standing; looking at the Christmas tree in his living room. There were more needles on the floor than were left on the tree.

"It looks like the Charlie Brown Christmas tree," he said, so disappointed.

"It's beautiful," I lied.

"Haha, it certainly is not. Thanks for driving him home." Caden had thrown his coat on the floor. His boots were sideways, half-on, half-off the rug; dripping on the wood floor. "God, that kid! Do you have to get home to the kids or do you have time for a quick glass of wine?"

"I left the car running and Kelly's at home alone. Rain check?"

"Of course." He picked up Caden's coat. "Three feet in either direction. Closet or coat rack."

"Yeah," I agreed. I bent down and moved the boots upright and onto the rug. "Kelly is hopeless, too."

"Do you have a tree, yet?"

"I'm so far behind. You have no idea. So, to answer the question: no."

"Well, if you get one, it'll be fresh," he said.

"Thanks, bright side."

"I think I'm going to have to get a new one. I can't fucking believe it."

"You think so?"

278

"We're still on for Christmas Eve, right?" he asked.

"Definitely," I answered. "And all you want is salad?"

"And wine. Mom is bringing pies and Paddy is bringing bread. I've started stocking the wine rack downstairs, so we always have a backup."

"Oh, wine is no problem. You can never have too much, right?"

"I think I'll ask Charlie if he can manage another ride to Bachman's." He had turned back to the tree, preoccupied. It really did look awful.

"Hey, maybe we could all go?" I didn't relish tying a tree to the top of my piece of shit car. Last year, the tree we'd gotten had almost fallen off twice on the way back home. Charlie had a truck.

"This weekend?"

"Perfect! I'll ask him. I'm sure he won't mind. I'll call you."

"Okay." I nodded. He'd crossed over to me. "I should go."

"Oh, yes. Car running. Kid waiting for dinner. I remember." We embraced quickly, warmly. The hugging was not particularly new, the warmth was. It was nice. Just as I turned to go, I heard Caden on the stairs.

"I'll talk to you soon, then."

"Yes. Thanks again!"

"Yeah, thank you," Caden said, halfway down the stairs. He was telling Stephen that he would've hung up his own coat as I went out the door, closing it behind me. *That's a conversation I have with Kelly almost daily*, I thought as I hurried to my car.

"I'll pick you back up about eleven," Charlie said. He, too, had sat up. He was cross-legged, facing me, or rather my back, in the bed. I looked back at him,

279

naked. God, he was beautiful. There it was again. My smile. I was smiling like a goddamned clown.

"That would be perfect," I told him, trying not to sound giddy.

"I won't say a word." He stood up. His ass was stunning. His cheeks were round, firm, molded to his legs perfectly. I lost my breath every time I looked at it. It was incredible-looking in jeans. I never dreamt how amazing it would look out of them.

"Thank you," I said, taking in the view one last time as he stepped, awkwardly, back into his jeans and pulled them up. I walked around the bed, stood on my tiptoes, and kissed him.

"What's that for?"

"Just because."

"I like it." He smiled that time.

"Good! Now hurry up. It's almost six thirty."

"You're sure there's no time to go once more?" I couldn't tell if he was joking.

"It would have to be quick." I couldn't get over what a whore I had become in three short days.

"Nah, I've got to leave you wanting more. Can't let you use me up so quickly."

"Tease!" I threw his shirt at him.

"Do you see my shoes?"

"They'd be downstairs, still." Both of us were thinking the same thing. Why hadn't he grabbed them and brought them upstairs? One of the kids — .

"I'm sorry," he apologized, finishing the thought out loud.

"It's fine. Neither of them is that observant. We'll be more careful next time."

"For sure." He lowered his head to kiss me again. Our tongues touched that time, and I felt my legs go weak. God, it was fucking insane. We made out for

280

a minute. I pulled away when I was certain if I didn't, there would have to be more sex.

He snuck out of the bedroom and down the hall, so quietly. When I knew he couldn't see me, I was grinning like a fool. I reached for my robe, and realized I'd been naked the entire time. Instead of feeling embarrassed or even surprised, I just giggled. I decided to just throw the robe back down and snuggle into bed. I must have drifted back to sleep, because the next time I opened my eyes, it was light out.

Charlie had called it. It took all of five minutes in the truck together. We had been making small talk and my brother just blurted it out. "What the fuck? Were you two really not going to tell me?"

"Oh, for God's sake," I said, looking at Charlie.

"I didn't say a word, but I did tell you so."

"What is it you think you've figured out?" I asked my brother.

"You two — I mean what you're," he started to laugh, a little uncomfortably. "Don't make me say it."

"I think we should make you say it."

"I mean we don't actually know what goes on in the brain of yours," Charlie agreed whimsically.

"Are you having sex?" Stephen asked neither of us in particular.

"If I say yes, can we not talk about it anymore?"

"No. I mean yes, I guess." All three of us were in the front seat of Charlie's truck. "It's not like I want details."

"Good, because you won't get any from me," I told him.

"It's cool, though," he smirked. "I'm glad somebody's getting some."

281

The three of us laughed like we'd been friends forever. It was comfortable. It had started to snow, just flurries. I could not remember if it had been forecast. Charlie was a good driver. Stephen sat in between us. We were pressed together in the cab. My brother actually put his head on Charlie's shoulder, briefly. The two of them, together, made me smile again. I was glad my brother had a friend. It had sounded like there hadn't been many in San Francisco. It was cool to see the obvious affection between these two men, one gay, one straight. There was not an ounce of pretense. There was no need. They fit, too; I decided, just then. They fit. Then I started to worry again. God, it was all so fucking complicated.

We spent thirty minutes picking out trees. Charlie had as much of an opinion on the two trees as my brother or I. In the end, both trees had been tied and wrestled into the back of the truck, and the three of us were back in the warm cab.

"Where to, first?" Charlie asked.

"Well, I'll need help with mine," I told them both. He had already started the truck, so we were on our way.

"How long?" Stephen asked, a little out of the blue. We all knew what he meant, though.

"Just since last weekend," I said. Charlie was quiet; carefully letting me set the tone. I appreciated it.

"The kids don't know then?"

"Definitely not. It's complicated, obviously. I mean how else is there to put it?"

"I get it," he replied. "Christmas Eve won't be awkward?"

God, I hadn't thought about it. I knew that Stephen had invited Charlie. Charlie had a falling out with his parents over his brother, Liam, and they hadn't talked in a few months. I did not get parents not speaking to their kids. I just couldn't wrap my brain around it. How did that work exactly? From what depths was it necessary for one to muster the selfishness required to abandon one's own child? I could have strangled my sister. Kevin was absolutely wonderful in every way. There was nothing about him that I wouldn't be proud of. Catelyn was a fucking idiot. I had thought about talking to her, but

282

what good would that have done, really? Our mother was certainly against it. Christmas was going to come and go, just like Thanksgiving had, and we'd all just pretend that Kevin hadn't been essentially orphaned.

"Not to change the subject, but do I even need to ask if you've heard from Caty?" I asked Stephen.

"Where did that come from?"

"I mean, yes, Christmas Eve might be awkward, but we're going to be together, all of us. It's Christmas." It was then that my little brother put his head on my shoulder. It was brief, but somehow held more intimacy than we'd managed in years. I knew he had followed my train of thought, even if Charlie hadn't. I actually had no idea how much Charlie knew about our sister. It was a good idea to change the subject, though, before he went where Stephen and I had.

"Who else is coming? Anyone?" I asked Stephen.

"I invited Betty and her granddaughter, but they have other family. Betty seemed genuinely touched by the invitation."

"It was sweet of you."

"This guy is a sweetheart," Charlie piped up.

"So it'll be Mom, you and the kids, Kevin, Caden and me, Paddy and Jannie, and Charlie. Let's talk about Catelyn later. Oh, and Dawn is coming. Wait until you have my lasagna. I've become a pretty good cook."

"So I hear."

"I can attest to that," Charlie added. "And he bakes, too."

"He's like our mother that way. The two of them would bake together, even when he was eight or nine. The kitchen was my mom's, but she let Stephen in. They just bonded there. None of the rest of us could intrude, even if we'd wanted to."

"Oh, that's not true," Stephen said. "I think it's because I was the baby, but none of you ever had any interest. It was that, maybe more than anything."

283

"Colleen and I used to joke that you and Mom had a club, pretty exclusive; membership of two."

"Well, Mom's doing most of the baking Friday. I may have baked some cookies."

"Of course you did," I told him.

"I'm excited," Charlie added.

"I'm glad you'll be there," my brother told him. And I smiled. It was the thought of all of us celebrating Christmas together. We got home, unloaded the tree, and screwed it into the tree stand. Meghan was at work, so after the guys left, Kelly and I spent the rest of the afternoon hauling up decorations and lights from the basement. Meghan got home from work in time for the final tree lighting.

"It's pretty, Mom," Kelly said.

"We do excellent work," I agreed.

"It is pretty," Meghan added, and actually hugged her brother.

I couldn't believe how overcome with happiness I'd been lately. It started even before Charlie. I had held in so much for so long. I truly believed it had been Caden who helped me see how awful it was. It was that first day of school, when he'd told me how sad Stephen had been. How selfish was I to have never noticed? I realized, too, that I had not really allowed myself to be sad. I'd been sad about Colleen and our dad, but there were other losses, and I'd only allowed myself to get angry over those. Anger was safer. It was certainly cleaner. While everything else was falling to shit around me, I had become determined to maintain order where my emotions were concerned. I needed to rearrange the feelings like furniture. Things had changed. There had to be order, or chaos would take over. Grieving people who had died was orderly; it all made sense. The loss of a marriage, the dissolution of my family, immediately and in the broader sense, even; somehow, the loss of self, those were huge and messy, entirely lacking in sense or order. It took a fifteen-year-old boy's concern for his stepfather to show me how cold I had become under the weight of everything I'd buried.

"I love you guys," I said, moving to intrude upon their embrace. They allowed it for a moment, then we all separated. Back to business. "Meghan, you work until what time on Christmas Eve?"

"Just until noon."

"We're expected at Stephen's at three o'clock. Paddy and Jannie are picking up the grandma, but I told Jannie we could get Aunt Dawn, so we'll need to leave here by two. Does that fit into everyone's schedule?"

"You said I could have breakfast with Dad," Kelly said.

"Surely even your father can accomplish breakfast before two o'clock in the afternoon?"

"I suppose," Kelly answered. "Hey, you said we could have pizza for dinner."

"Tonight?" Meghan asked.

"Well, not at Christmas," Kelly answered dramatically.

"Caden said Stephen's lasagna is really good. That's what we're having that night."

"I like that, right?" Kelly asked.

"Yes, it's just like pizza, except with noodles instead of crust," I told him.

"How come we never have that?" he asked.

"Mom would have to cook," Meghan said. I thought she was joking.

"I bet we'd all prefer for your uncle to do that." I decided to play along just in case.

"You're a good cook, Mom," Kelly told me.

"Thanks baby." I touched his head. We were standing together, just looking at the Christmas tree. "I do alright."

"Jim used to cook more than you," Meghan told me.

285

"How come you refuse to call him Dad?" Kelly asked her.

"He's not my dad. Come on. How many times do we have to talk about that? Did you ever think making such a big deal out of it was upsetting to Mom?"

"Leave me out of it," I said. I looked up at my daughter, then at my son. "Jesus, you two are so big. I must be feeding you something."

Meghan moved closer and put her arm around me. "Pizza it is. It's practically your specialty."

Chapter 27
CADEN

"Do you want a pop?" Meghan asked me. She'd been watching me develop pictures for a couple of hours.

"Yeah, that'd be great, except you can't open the door for another thirty minutes."

I was kind of freaking out right then. They were all helping. That's what families did. At least that's what Joanna kept telling me. I hadn't ever experienced anything like it. I was supposed to be working for Patrick, on this house in St. Paul. He was doing that job by himself, but in the morning he would pick me, then drop me off at Joanna's. That was how it went for a couple of days, since Christmas break started. The working in St. Paul was a story we told Stephen so he wouldn't wonder where I disappeared to all day. It seriously sucked since he'd hired the new guy at the video store, and there was another new person starting soon. He was home all the time now.

Joanna was helping the most. I asked her that night she drove me home from school. I just sort of blurted it out in the car. In her basement, in what had been a closet; I'd built a darkroom. A week before that, I didn't know how I was going to pull it off. But almost Stephen's whole family was helping.

A couple of years ago, my dad decided to make a photo album for Stephen for Christmas, but he got sick. Stephen found the album and some of the pictures, but no one did anything about it after that. My dad had ordered this huge leather album with the word FAMILY on the front. Inside were pages and pages for pictures. Before we left San Francisco, I'd snagged it out of some stuff we were donating and snuck it in with my stuff. I wasn't even sure why, back then.

On the first page, Joanna had painted some words on heavy paper. I was going to do it on the computer at school, but when I told her about it, she insisted. I chose the words, but they weren't really mine. I wondered if Stephen would even remember them. Joanna suggested gold lettering, because the leather was sort of brown, but I said black. Stephen hated gold.

Besides the pictures that I had taken and was developing, I'd gotten tons of pictures from Joanna, even some of her and Stephen's sister who had died.

287

There was one of Colleen blowing a bubble with her gum. It was taken at her high school graduation and she had on her cap and gown. It was a really cool shot. Colleen had been very pretty. She reminded me of Meghan. Their hair was the same, only Meghan's wasn't as curly.

I also got a few pictures from Paddy, which Jannie had dug up. In some of them, Stephen looked a little like me. Well, not exactly like me, but the same age. His hair was longer, like it used to be when we moved there, and he wasn't as serious. He smiled in those pictures, like life hadn't happened to him yet.

I wound up with a lot of pictures, so I wanted to make the album like a story. There was so much of Stephen's life that he probably never dreamt of telling me. It always seemed to me that his life began with us. Maybe that was selfish? We never talked about my dad's mom and dad, who were dead, and we almost never talked about Stephen's either. I wondered; looking at these pictures, whether Stephen had mostly stopped talking to is family because my dad didn't have his own. That would've been dumb, though. I didn't know, but I kinda wished my dad had gotten to meet some of Stephen's family.

I could tell Meghan had started to get antsy behind me. I thought it had to be boring just watching me screw around with the paper and stuff. I had all these rolls of film I found when we were packing to move to Minnesota. Some of them, I figured Stephen had totally forgotten about. There were ones I was sure he didn't even know I had taken, like the ones I was developing that day. I shot almost a whole roll of film of him and my dad sleeping. I'd put the paper in the trays a few minutes ago; now I was watching the images begin to appear on the paper. I remembered taking these. I'd only had the camera a couple of months then. I didn't know how good I was now, but then; I mean, I was just fucking around. That was three years ago.

We used to hang out at home on Sundays. My dad called it family day. Sometimes we would go down to the Castro at night and get Chinese food at this little restaurant by Market. After that we would see a movie, or even just walk around and look at people. There were some pretty funny people in San Francisco, and we weren't being mean about it. Stephen called it "people watching." I guess that was a thing. Usually, though, we would just stay home and watch videos. Sometimes one of us had a movie of our own, like I got to rent one that Dad and Stephen didn't want to watch. I mostly got to do that when they had one that was "too adult" for me. On those days, I would watch my movie in the living room on the bigger TV, and they would lie in bed and watch theirs. Lunch, whatever that was, stayed in the kitchen — the middle

288

room. Stephen cooked a lot, mostly healthy stuff, but on Sundays we could have junk food, pizza, or even fast food.

On the day I took the pictures, Stephen whined about the movie my dad picked out. He was complaining about there being subtitles and joked that he was going to watch my movie with me. At least I think he was joking. I can't really remember what my movie was or even if I finished it. I just remember pausing it to go and get more pizza. There was just one slice left. I figured I should ask the dads if I could have it, so I went down the hall to their room. I could hear their movie, voices talking in a different language. I got to their doorway and they were both asleep. My dad was sitting up a little, and Stephen's head was resting on his chest. They were out. They didn't even hear me yelling about the pizza, when I came down the hallway. I thought it would be funny to take a picture, so I got my camera from my room and snapped until I was out of film. They never even woke up. When I was done, I ate the last slice of pizza.

"What are these ones?" Meghan asked. She was looking over my shoulder now. She was a little bit taller than me. When she leaned in closer, I got dizzy. It could have been the chemicals, but I didn't really think so.

"I was just screwing around one day," I told her. "I took a bunch of shots of my dads sleeping." Meghan and I had hung out a few times since November. I was pretty sure she knew I liked her. I was also pretty sure she didn't mind. While it wasn't the exact reaction I had hoped for, it was better than it could have been. She leaned in even closer and I whispered, "Careful."

"They're beautiful. It's like you can tell how much they loved each other. That must've been cool."

"It wasn't weird," I said. I took the first sheet out of the solution and hung it on the line, to my left. "Most people expect it to be weird. I mean, maybe, it was because I never knew that it was wrong. No, I mean, that other people thought it was wrong. I never knew that until way later."

"But you said that you had to keep it a secret?"

"Oh, yeah, but not like... I don't know. They were so open about stuff at home. It was like we didn't need to be in the world. I know it doesn't make sense." I took two more sheets out of the trays of solution and hung them on the line.

289

"No, I get it," she told me. "I think it's so cool."

"Really?"

"That you had each other. I never met my real dad. Kelly's dad was cool, I guess, when we were younger. By the time I grew up a little, he was just a dick. My mom put up with him for a long time. Then she was mad or sad or just over it for so long, she hardly ever seemed happy." She went back to the stool in the corner, but wasn't as much sitting on it as kind of standing next to it. I wondered if she thought she'd been in my way. The room was tiny. Even with her on the other side, there was probably only a couple of feet between us.

"It's weird, right? Does anyone ever know how good things are, until they're not anymore?"

"I'm sorry. I didn't mean to bring up, I mean — ."

"No, really," I interrupted. "You didn't. I mean it's okay. I don't mind." I had three more to develop. I was putting them in the developing solution with a tongs. "About ten minutes."

"That's cool." She moved closer to the clothesline. "I mean it. I really like these. It's fun to watch."

"Haha, you like to watch, huh?" I started to sweat a little as soon as the words popped out. *I mean what the hell? Where did that come from? Jesus!*

"Maybe," she answered. Her brown eyes still twinkled, even in the dark light. Meghan had this look that made you wonder if she was just playing with you, half the time. I guess that was coy. That's what it was called.

"It's cool to be watched," I said. *OH, MY GOD!* I was sure I was blushing. I hoped she couldn't tell in the dark and, you know, with my back to her. Things just kept coming out of my mouth, like I didn't have any control over it at all. Meghan just laughed, not loud, not a giggle either. I didn't know if there was even a name for this laugh, but she did it pretty often. It was sincere, kind of just matter of fact, like she knew something you didn't. One thing I noticed about her is that she almost never seemed nervous. Maybe her brother had gotten all the nervous genes. I wondered where he was then. Every once in a while, we would hear walking above us. The floors creaked like in our house. There hadn't been any noise up there for a while.

290

"They went to the store." It was like she'd read my mind. She did that, too. It was spooky. "They left when I was upstairs before."

We were alone? Was that weird? I supposed it wasn't. It shouldn't have been, right? *Oh God!* Maybe I was just getting dizzy from being so close to her and being in the tiny room working with the developer. I seriously had gotten over that total awkwardness after the first day of school. We were, like, friends by then. I didn't feel dizzy just being next to her, not anymore. And I didn't talk like a dumbass, well not usually.

"So what's next? I want to help," she said, cheerfully.

"I can't believe you don't have anything better to do."

"Nope. I don't even have to work until Christmas Eve."

"You're not coming to our house?" I turned around, and she was, like, two inches from my face.

"Not Christmas Eve Night," she told me. There was the laugh again. "Remember, I can't wait for the lasagna. I think these chemicals have gone to your head."

We were still just inches from each other. I could feel her breath on my face. I lost my balance for a second and sort of fell into her. Meghan just moved into it, and all of a sudden we were touching. I'd looked away when I started to stumble. When I looked back up, our eyes met and the look in hers kind of matched the laugh. There was nothing in them but certainty. Then she leaned in, only like an inch farther, and kissed me. It was quick and on the cheek. Yep, so certain.

I knew I was blushing. No girl had ever kissed me, I didn't think. Maybe Mariana, Stephen's friend. She was always kissing everyone, but she's old, like Stephen and Joanna. Maybe, Meghan sensed I was about to, like, start on fire or something. She took a step back and looked down at the floor.

"I was thinking about doing that for a while," she finally said.

"Cool," was all I could manage in response. Then I turned back around to finish the photos.

291

We were sitting at the kitchen table an hour later. I had cleaned up downstairs. Everything was developed. I still had lots to do, though. Joanna and Kelly were back and it wasn't weird, all of us just sitting there, like we belonged. Somewhere deep down, I was freaking out a little. She'd kissed me. I was like, where did that come from? Then she pretty much said it wasn't even spontaneous. I kind of wanted to go home and think about stuff, but then, I also didn't want to not be in the same room with her. I kind of wanted to go back and have her kiss me again. And then, I decided I never wanted to be kissed, ever again. That one was enough, like so completely perfect. Then, I wondered... if a kiss on the cheek made me feel like that, what would a kiss on the lips do to me? I didn't think it was possible to have so much stuff in my head at one time.

"Do you want some more?" Joanna was asking.

"Um—sure." We were eating lunch. Yeah, that's what was happening. We were just eating lunch, like it was the most normal thing. How did people not just knock into each other, like bumper cars, if they were all kissing other people?

"I'll get it!" Meghan just jumped up from her chair. We were having macaroni and cheese from a box and hotdogs and soda, and I was actually really hungry.

"Thanks sweetie," Joanna told her. Then, to me, she said, "So the developing is done?"

"Yeah, I guess that was the hard part. Now I just have to pick the pictures to use and put them in."

"He's going to absolutely love it," she told me.

"Thank you, again."

"What did I tell you? Stop that," she said.

"Yeah, stop being so polite," Kelly added. "You're gonna make the rest of us look bad."

"That's not hard to do," Meghan announced.

292

"I can be polite," Kelly said, sullenly.

"You're just against it, what, on principle?" Meghan joked.

"Now, I can drop you off at home, right? Because Stephen is at the video store today?" Joanna asked me.

"Yeah. Thank you. I mean — well — uh, yeah. Just, yeah."

"He can't help it," Meghan told her mom, then smiled at me.

"You really could teach these two some manners," Joanna said.

"See?! Mom said you could be more polite, too," Kelly told his sister. She just made a face back at him.

"I cleaned everything up downstairs, but do you want me to take down the clothesline and change the bulb?" I asked.

"No, leave it. I'll talk to you about that in the car. Okay, so I'm going to have a cigarette, and then we can go."

"Thank — um — yeah, okay." I smiled, and kind of laughed.

"Kelly, you've got the dishes," Joanna told him.

"Why me?"

"Because Christmas is two days away and you want your presents to not get donated to the drive at the school," she told him. I couldn't tell if she was kidding.

"Good point," he said.

Then Joanna put her coat on and went out on the deck. I shoved the last third of my hotdog in my mouth all at once, just to see if it would fit.

"Don't even think about it," Meghan told her brother. "Besides Caden just ate the last hotdog."

"I bet I could fit half in my mouth, like, at least," he told us.

293

"Probably," his sister agreed. "I mean you do have a pretty big mouth."

"Shut up," he told her.

"It's not like a period, Kelly. You can't just say shut up at the end of every conversation when you don't have anything smarter to say."

"I don't know, I think it works," I said, and winked at Kelly.

A few minutes later we were in Joanna's car. I hadn't even said goodbye to Meghan. I wasn't sure if I was supposed to do it the normal way or what. I wasn't actually sure of very much right then. I thought about hugging her. Sitting in Joanna's cold car, I was really glad I hadn't done that. That would've totally sucked!

"You know I bought Kelly a camera for Christmas?" Joanna asked me.

"For sure."

"I was wondering if you would teach him how to use it. You know, just the basics. We could leave the room downstairs as it is."

"Sure, that would be cool." It would. I was guessing Meghan would be there a lot on account of it being where she lived and all.

"Oh, thank you! It will be nice for Kelly to look anywhere but in a book or at the television." I really liked Joanna. I hadn't ever had a mom, but she seemed like the way you'd want a mom to be, you know, if you had one.

"Yeah. There's like a whole world out there." Sometimes adults said stuff and you thought about it and then just like tried to work it into a conversation later. It's so you would sound more like them, I guess. Sometimes it worked and sometimes it just sounded stupid.

"Exactly." I guess that time it worked. I wasn't completely sure what it meant. I had an idea. Anyway, she got it and that's all that mattered. "I'm looking forward to Christmas."

"Yeah for sure." People here said "yeah" all the time, only the E-A-H slanted down. It was funny. I still had to do it on purpose. I was from Minnesota now.

"Yes, definitely. I know my little brother can cook. I never picked up that talent. I can do the basics though." She smiled at me, then looked back at the road.

"It's pretty easy, really. I watch him sometimes and it looks like it's just following instructions. I think he memorizes the instructions sometimes. Then I don't know what's happening." I laughed kind of uneasily. Then Joanna laughed, and it didn't sound the same.

"You have an interesting way of observing things, Caden."

"I do?"

"Maybe it's not the way you observe things as much as it is the fact that you pay attention at all."

"I like to know stuff. I like it when it makes sense to me," I told her.

"You're always thinking. That's never a bad thing. You're a lot like Stephen that way." We were finally turning onto our street.

"I never thought of that." We both laughed. I wasn't trying to make a joke, but you just got lucky sometimes.

"Do you need help? Maybe we should have called the house first to make sure he wasn't home," she suggested.

"No it's okay. I know he'll be at the video store until late. We had to have breakfast together this morning. It's sort of a rule."

"Breakfast?"

"No. He wants us to eat together at least once a day, no matter what. We had breakfast because he knew he wouldn't be home until late. I'm supposed to clean my room when I get home," I explained.

"Oh, no! How are you going to get it all done?"

"Oh, my room is clean." I was proud of myself. It probably sounded like it in my voice. "I cleaned it last weekend. I just pretended it was messed up so he would stay out of it." We had pulled up in front of our house a few seconds ago, but were just still talking, like it was normal.

295

"Clever!" Joanna said.

"I can't believe we kept everything secret all week."

"When we put our minds to something — ."

I waited a few seconds because I thought there was more to that. After Joanna didn't say anything else for a while, I undid my seatbelt. "Okay—well, um—thanks for everything."

"Good luck, Caden. He's going to love it. See you Friday."

"Yeah, see you guys on Friday."

I took all the pictures and stuff out of the backseat and went straight in. When I went in the door, Kevin was standing in the kitchen, wearing just pajama pants, and drinking orange juice right out of the carton. That drove Stephen nuts, but we both still did it.

"Hey," I said.

"Hey there. How goes Operation Family Album?"

"It has a name?" I closed the inside door and kicked off my boots. Then I took my coat off and threw it on the floor.

"It needs some work, huh?" Kev wondered.

"For starters, it probably needs to not say exactly what is."

"Like a codename. Cool."

"Like Operation Christmas?" I suggested.

"That might work. Stephen's at the video store?"

"That was the plan, but you'd know better than me," I told him. "I just got here."

296

"I just got up," he countered. It was after one o'clock in the afternoon, but I sometimes slept that late, especially if I was up really late the night before. "Anyway I've got shit to do. Gonna hop in the shower."

"Cool." When he walked by me, I swear, it smelled like he had been drinking all morning.

Chapter 28
STEPHEN

It was finally Christmas Eve. Growing up, Christmas Eve had always been the bigger deal. On Christmas Day, we pretty much went to church; ate again, and people would play around with whatever gifts they'd gotten the night before. Sometimes we were given a family gift, a game, or something, an activity we could all participate in. I liked those gifts. Now it was my turn to set the stage.

I loved to entertain. I thought I particularly excelled at presentation. I had considered the music for the night, chosen candles, and picked out what I was going to wear. That had all happened over a week ago. I had considered suggesting an outfit for Caden, but dismissed it on account of not being a fan of being laughed at. Instead, I focused my energy on baking. I'd told my sister that I hadn't baked that much, but in truth, there were enough cookies to feed the entire street. The decorating was perfect after the awful tree snafu. Caden and Charlie had made so much fun of me over that. The new tree was about eight feet tall and Charlie had strung the lights perfectly. I loved Christmas, but I hated wrapping gifts almost as much as I hated stringing lights. Kev had strung them on the first tree way back before Thanksgiving. That tree had lasted until about two weeks ago. By the time I'd made the decision to replace it, two-thirds of its needles were on the floor. It hadn't escaped my notice that two straight men had proven their mettle as part-time decorators for the gay man obsessed with Christmas. I'd been forced to buy a second tree and had just finished arranging the ornaments perfectly when Caden got home from working for my brother.

"Oooh, it looks awesome," he said. "How long do you think this one will last?"

"Be quiet, please. What do you have there?" He'd set down two bags in front of him, so that he could get his boots and coat off.

"It's Christmas. I refuse to answer any more questions on the grounds that it may ruin the holiday for you."

"Oh, I see." I had started towards him, probably to hang up the coat he'd likely throw in the middle of the floor, but for once in his life, he turned around and sort of haphazardly hung the coat up on the overflowing coat rack just inside the door. He had one boot off. Before I'd made it even halfway, he snatched the bags up. "Relax! I wasn't going to look."

"I don't trust you."

"I beg your pardon." I played along.

"After two Christmases ago, I should think you would."

"What happened two Christmases ago?" I honestly didn't remember.

"Dad hid your gift and you went snooping," he reminded me.

"I did not. That was an accident. I thought your dad was hiding something from me."

"That's the point, dude!"

"I mean I thought he was, he'd just been to the doctor and I thought he was keeping information from me, not a gift." I tried to explain.

"Did you guys do that?"

"Not usually. But sometimes if we felt, I don't know, like it would make the other person sad, we didn't rush to tell them. I honestly was expecting to find a new prescription or some new pamphlet or something. I didn't expect to find the pictures." Alec had decided to put together a family album for me for Christmas. He'd bought a beautiful leather album and had started to gather pictures together. I'd felt so bad. Just after that, he'd had a bad reaction to one of his meds and I'd taken him to the ER in the middle of the night. That was the week before Christmas, two years ago. They ended up admitting him and we were all afraid we'd spend the holiday in the hospital. Alec was released on Christmas Eve and I don't think the album ever came up again. It broke my heart thinking about it now. I was certain it had ended up in the boxes and boxes of stuff we had donated to the AIDS hospice in San Francisco before moving here.

"Hey, I've got stuff to do in my room." Caden brought me out of my memory. I hadn't been there long. He was acting so strangely. "Okay if I just grab a sandwich or something?"

"Sure. I have some errands to run with Kev tonight anyway."

299

"Cool. Thanks. I promise I'll clean my room before Christmas Eve. You haven't been in there, have you?"

"Not in a few days," I told him. I couldn't remember the last time I found his bedroom door open. I tended not to go in if the door was shut. If I had clean laundry or something, I'd set it in the hallway, outside his door. I trusted him. There really no reason for me to snoop through his things. We hadn't ever talked about it. I guess it was just understood. "I don't typically go in your room if the door is shut. See? I told you. I'm so not a snoop."

"Cool." He finally slipped off his second boot. "It's like a Red Cross disaster area in there. I'd avoid it at all costs. I told Paddy I'd help him again tomorrow, but I promise my room will be ready for inspection by Thursday night." He knew I wanted the house clean. Still, the kid was acting all kinds of odd.

"You okay?"

"Why wouldn't I be?"

"Just checking," I told him. "Okay, then. You owe me two meals tomorrow."

"I'll try to be home in time for lunch."

"Oh, wait. I'm at the store all day," I remembered.

"Totally fine. I probably won't be too scarred by then," he joked. At least I think he was joking. God! He turned around to go upstairs, then put the bags down, like he'd forgotten something. He came over and hugged me. "I'll be upstairs in case anything really cool happens."

"I'll send up a flare." I turned back around to take another look at the brand new tree. "I'll let you know when we leave."

"Just yell," he called from halfway up the stairs. "It works. I swear you need to try it."

My entire family was seated around the dining table we'd lugged here from San Francisco. There had never–not once—been any reason for us to have a table that size there, but Alec had humored me. I was at the end of the table. Next to me and across from each other were my mother and Charlie. I tried not to laugh when he and my sister awkwardly tried to sit as far away from

300

each other as possible. No one else noticed. Caden sat next to my mother, looking very handsome in an actual dress shirt. My mother had spent most of the time since we'd sat down flirting with Charlie.

"The lasagna is delicious, Stephen," Dawn said. My mom's oldest friend wore one of those dumb Christmas sweaters. I kind of liked it, though. She had been mostly quiet since she'd arrived with Joanna and the kids.

"It's really good," Meghan said. "Caden was right."

"Thank you. It's his favorite. Can I get anyone more wine?"

"I'll take a topper," my mom answered, picking up her glass and swallowing a fourth of a glass of red wine in one big gulp.

"I'll get another bottle from the kitchen." My brother stood up from the other end of the table.

"But you're not even drinking wine," Dawn exclaimed.

"Paddy doesn't drink, Dawnny. You know that," my mother told her.

"Oh, that's right. Sorry dear."

"No worries. I still play bartender to my wife."

"That's definitely a part time gig," my mother joked.

"Very funny, Mom," Jannie replied.

"Hey, come to think of it, you're not even drinking tonight. No wine?" Joanna asked her sister-in-law.

"I have a little bit of a headache," Jannie answered, and then looked up at my brother.

"Oh, I'm sorry, dear," Dawn told her. Paddy smiled at his wife and even massaged her shoulders a little.

"Oooh, me next," Joanna begged.

301

"He's so good at it." My brother turned towards the kitchen, ignoring our sister.

"There are two more bottles of red on the counter and a white in the fridge," I called after him.

"Does anyone mind if I have a beer?" Kevin asked, getting up from the table and following Patrick into the kitchen, not waiting for an answer.

"You alright?" I heard my brother ask him from around the corner.

"Mom, you were right," Kelly announced, more to his plate, than his mother. "This is kinda like pizza without the crust."

A minute later, Paddy was back with the wine. "Who needs a refill?" Our mother held out a now completely empty glass. "You're not driving, are you?"

"Only if your wife says it's okay."

"Didn't Grandma ride with you guys, anyway?" Kelly asked.

"It's an expression grown-ups say," Caden told him. "Cause you shouldn't drive when you've been drinking alcohol."

"I still don't get it."

"It's not actually that funny, hon," Jannie explained. He just looked back down at his empty plate.

We finished dinner just as Kelly was growing antsy. We'd been sitting at the table for over an hour. He looked like he might fall backwards if he didn't get a book in his hands any minute. Everyone agreed to hold off on desert until dinner had settled. Joanna and Jannie were already in the kitchen cleaning up. Kevin was in the refrigerator grabbing another beer when I walked in with a half a pan of lasagna.

"Leftovers!"

"Awesome," Kevin uttered from behind the refrigerator door. His face was red and he squinted a little when he looked anywhere near the direction of the bright overhead light.

302

"You sure you're okay?"

"Why wouldn't I be?" He set his can down amongst the chaos on the counter and smiled half-heartedly. "I'm chillin'. I swear."

"Yes you are," Jannie told him, smiling reassuringly.

"Merry Christmas, sweetheart." Joanna embraced her nephew. He hugged her back, uneasily at first, but then he relaxed into it.

"I think we should open gifts," Kevin yelled into the other room when Joey released him.

"Sounds like a good idea," Caden called back.

"About twenty minutes," Joanna told them. "We're going to finish up here. Meghan is going to help. Then I'm having a cigarette. Then gifts."

"Go smoke now." Meghan had joined us. "Take Grandma. Kelly, Caden, and I can do these."

"I like the way you think," I told my niece. She was stunning, her long hair for once, was not up in a ponytail. I'd never thought it before, but she looked a little like Colleen.

"Thanks, kids," Jannie added.

"Hey, Caden and Kelly, the sooner you guys get the dishes rinsed and in the dishwasher, the sooner you can open gifts," I said loudly. "Mom, who wants to smoke?"

Twenty minutes later, the smokers were still outside, and Kelly opened the back door. "Dishes are done. You know what that means?"

"Pie?" Joanna asked.

"Very funny, Mom."

"Come on, everybody," I said. "I'm almost as excited for this part as the kids."

I had a couch and a love seat in the living room, but Charlie, the kids, and I still sat on the floor. There were lamps on either end of the long room, but most

303

of the light came from the enormous tree and the fire Paddy had built in the fireplace. Gifts of every size and shape were spread out a couple of feet on three sides of the tree. Towards the back was a gigantic box, one of only a few gifts I'd actually wrapped myself. I needed to make sure that Caden opened that one before a couple of the smaller ones. If he opened the one with that mouse-thing in it, he'd know what the big one was before he'd even gotten to it. For two days, he'd circled the gift, calling out guesses. Of course, that was before everyone arrived tonight, and the pile of presents had grown exponentially.

Caden and Kelly had begun to distribute the presents. They'd each chosen their spots, not far from each other, or the tree. I knew Caden's intention was to tear into the big present as soon as humanly possible. One by one, piles formed in front of everyone, except poor Charlie and Dawn. I had bought Dawn a gift and my mother had brought one for her, as well. Compared to the numerous packages the kids were accumulating, our two guest's piles looked rather paltry. Paddy had brought a gift for Charlie, as had I, on behalf of Caden; so he, too, had two presents in front of him. There was card, I knew, under the tree with his name on it, as well. I had thought and thought about what to give my new friend. I finally decided to present him with something I would have likely given him anyway, except I'd do it as a gift. I thought it would be a nice relief, too. Finally, all of the gifts, even the couple of cards, Charlie's included, had been passed out. Wine glasses had been refilled and Kevin had retrieved another beer from the kitchen.

"I think I need another cigarette after all of that work," my mother joked. At least I thought she was kidding.

"Seriously, Grandma," Kelly groaned. "Not even funny."

"Oh, you're no fun," she answered him, smiling. There was one big, overstuffed chair that usually sat closer to where the tree was now. It had been moved off to the side and from there my mother appeared ready to hold court. She had quite a few gifts surrounding her.

"There're too many gifts to attempt any kind of organized process with this, but let's not make it a free for all, either," Joanna announced.

"How about if we have everyone open at least one before we dive in head first?" I suggested.

"That sounds nice," Dawn chimed in.

304

"Shall we go youngest to oldest?" Jannie suggested.

"Perfect," Kelly agreed.

"Of course *you* like that order," Meghan told her brother. "Poor Grandma won't get to open anything for like an hour."

"I'm not the oldest for a change," my mother exclaimed. "Dawn is."

"We could go oldest to youngest?" Jannie joked.

"Oh, come on," Kelly demanded. "No fair."

"Go!" Meghan told him. "We're just messing with you."

"Yeah, hurry up," Caden said. "I'm after you."

He had begun to slide the big box out from behind him. Kelly searched through his pile, I assumed for a specific gift, like Caden, that he'd had his eye on for a while. He chose a square box about the size of a toaster, then paused, as if willing what he wanted to be inside there. When he finally tore into it, paper landed everywhere. "It's a camera. Just like yours, Caden. Thanks Mom!"

"Sweet. I can totally help you with it." Caden looked up and over at me, or so I thought at first. But then I realized he was smiling at my sister. Was that weird?

"You're up," I told him.

"I don't know which one to pick," he joked, then turned around and attacked the huge box. Five seconds later, he squealed. "No way." He turned back around with the biggest smile on his face, then slid himself over to me.

"Good?"

"Excellent," he said, and hugged me. "Thank you!"

"There's an extra phone jack downstairs," I told him, happily. "The computer can go on the table down there. I suppose, we could get a desk or something."

305

"What in the world is it?" my mother asked.

"It's a computer, Grandma," Meghan told her.

"What's he want with a computer?"

"You'd be surprised, Mom," Joanna added to the chorus. "Meghan, you're next."

Meghan chose a card. She ignored the two pieces of paper inside while she read the inside of the card, chuckling. "Funny, Mom."

"Did you just get paper?" Paddy goaded.

"No, it's —," Joanna started, then realized her daughter was still studying the pages.

"I don't get it," Meghan looked up. "What's the Refinery?"

"It's a spa," Joanna told her. "It's for both of us really. Kind of selfish, I know, but I thought it would be nice to have a mother-daughter day. We each have a massage, manicure, and pedicure scheduled on New Year's Eve."

"You said you were going to go downtown with us?" Kevin said to Joanna.

"I am," she assured him. "This is in the morning."

"Very cool, Mom!" Meghan got up from the floor to go hug her.

"You better not miss my birthday," I turned around to tell Joanna.

"Not for the world," she answered, still hugging her daughter.

"I'm next," Kevin announced. "Unless you all want to plan Valentine's Day, too." Meghan laughed and went over to hug him, too. I think we were all eyeing Kevin. Even Caden and Meghan had picked up on it. I wanted to go murder his mother, then and there. Kevin chose a gift. It was the size of a record album. I looked over at Caden, but he had turned his attention back to the computer. I was so thrilled for him. My eyes traveled up to the tree and I was suddenly overcome with emotion. I didn't cry, but my eyes definitely dampened. It was amazing. I'd never have imagined, even a few months

306

before, a Christmas like it. I looked over at my mother and she winked at me. I wondered if she was feeling the same way.

"It's from Grandma," Kevin called out. "Is it a record?" He ripped paper away from the front of it, revealing a calendar. Rock and Roll Hall of Fame. "This is really cool, Grandma."

"Look inside," she told him. "June is my favorite month."

"I don't get it," he said, at first. He'd immediately flipped to June. "What's the twenty-second?"

"You and I are going to a rock concert."

"What?! No way! Pink Floyd?" It was the first time all night he had lit up.

"You're going to see Pink Floyd, Mom?" Jannie asked.

"Bet your ass," she answered. Kevin was already on top of her, hugging his grandma. "I love you, kid," she told him.

"I love you, too, Grandma! Thank you so much."

"Who's next?" Jannie asked.

"Charlie's next," I answered.

"I guess I am." He had two small packages and the card. I hoped he would choose the card. "How do I even have three to choose from?"

"You're family now," Kevin told him. "Once we adopt you, you can't ever get away."

I watched intently while Charlie fumbled around, finally choosing the card. He seemed a tiny bit uncomfortable, now that all eyes were on him. Immediately, I hoped the contents of the card would not embarrass him. Like Meghan, he took his time reading the card. I couldn't even remember what it said anymore. After a moment, he unfolded the papers that were inside the card. It was a lease. I knew that he struggled to pay rent, especially in the winter months, and I had an empty one-bedroom apartment above the video store. Charlie was reading the first page, carefully. At one point, he looked over at me and smiled. Phew! Then he looked back down at the lease. A minute

307

passed, while others talked amongst themselves. Finally, he seemed to have absorbed the gift and its meaning.

"I'm sorry to hold up the show, everyone," he announced, getting up.

"What is it?" Paddy asked him.

"It looks like a contract. Who does business on Christmas?" my mother asked.

"It's actually a lease." Charlie moved around people and packages to come over to me.

"I was going to do it anyway." I moved to get up, almost tipping over my now empty wine glass. I was definitely feeling the wine.

"But fifty dollars?" he asked, quietly. Joanna looked up and it seemed as if she'd done the math.

"Well, if you're interested, the building needs a super," I offered. "It's probably only a few hours a week, but you'd be helping me out so much."

"I don't know what to say." He leaned over to hug me.

"Somebody should really explain or I'm going to have a cigarette," my mother demanded.

"It's a rental agreement, Mom," Joanna answered, smiling. "Charlie can live in the apartment above the video store in the building that Stephen owns."

"That's a gift?"

"Just never mind, Mom," Paddy said.

"Okay, okay, whatever you say. Can I get a large refill?"

"I'll get you, Grandma," Kevin told my mother.

"I'm sure there's, like, film here somewhere," Kelly broke in, surveying his gifts. "Caden, can you show me what to do first?"

"Sure," he agreed.

308

"Okay, Stephen, you're next." Jannie attempted to regain control of the process.

"So I am! Kev, why don't you bring the bottle?"

"Way ahead of you," he announced appearing around the corner with the bottle of red wine. The big smile on his face made my night. "I'm going to a rock concert at the Dome with my grandma. So fucking cool!"

"Kevin!" Jannie said, shocked. No matter how much she was around us, she just hadn't gotten used to the swearing. Joanna and I looked at each other and smiled.

"Sorry, Jannie," Kev apologized. "Are you sure you don't want some wine?"

"Positive," she said, and glanced over at my brother again. He had moved over by the boys, curious about the computer. I wondered if she was really not drinking in front of us all because Paddy was in recovery. I turned my attention back to the presents in front of me, not knowing which one to choose.

"Open this one," Caden said, pointing out a box, similar in size to Kevin's calendar, only much thicker. It was clearly from him, though I'd not noticed under the tree before. All of a sudden, all eyes were on me.

"From you?"

He nodded, almost unable to speak. He was as excited for this gift, as I'd been for him to open the computer.

I tore off the paper and opened the box. Inside was tissue paper. I was impressed at how beautiful the presentation was and then I saw it. I looked up at the anxious fifteen-year-old boy who was kind of kneeling right next to me.

"Oh, Caden."

"What is it?" my mother asked, loudly from across the room. I realized she seemed to be the only one in the room not in on it. I looked at her friend and was surprised to find Dawn's eyes closed. Was she asleep?

"She always does that! She nodded off at the damn Black Jack table in Vegas."

309

"It's a photo album, Mom." I held it up, letting the box and tissue paper fall onto the floor in front of me. Joanna and Meghan had moved in closer. Then came Kevin. And Jannie. I laid it in my lap and opened the cover, expecting a photo. I read the words and my eyes filled up with tears.

"You remember?" my son asked proudly.

"I wasn't sure you'd even heard," I answered, sniffling. The tears embarrassed me, but what could I do? I just went with it. This was the most thoughtful gift anyone had ever given me, in my entire life.

"I belong where you are." Kevin read the words someone had painted beautifully, in black letters on white paper. "I don't get it."

"It's something I told him once," I explained, my voice quivering.

"It was right after we moved here," Caden elaborated. I turned the page and there was a baby picture of me.

"Where in the world?"

"That one came from Joanna," Caden said. On the next few pages, were pictures of me and my siblings almost from birth until one of me and Colleen at Joanna's wedding. I'd completely forgotten we were in the wedding. Colleen was the maid of honor and I was a groomsman. I looked up at Joanna and mouthed thank you.

"How many people were in on this?"

"Caden had a few elves," Charlie said.

"You knew, too?"

"The gift is from Caden," Joanna said. Of course, I knew that. I turned a page and there was a beautiful black and white rendition of the photo on my dresser of Caden and me asleep with the red dinosaur in our first apartment in Los Angeles. On the opposite page was a photo of Caden and his dad, I could not remember ever seeing. I turned another page and there were pictures of the three of us in Los Angeles, Caden at six, seven, and eight years old. There was a photo of the three of us on the day we moved to San Francisco. Caden was nine years old.

310

"I love it," I said, looking up and over at Caden, my tears abating. He proudly returned my smile, but didn't say a word.

"Caden, I found the film," Kelly said, not paying any attention to what was going on with us. He had started opening enough of each gift to see what it was until he got to what he was looking for.

"You can't blame him." I must have been beaming. "I mean look at this."

"Dawn is really down," Jannie added. Everyone had shifted to one end of the room, even my mother. At some point in the last two minutes, our "Aunt Dawn" had tipped over, thankfully to the side of the couch she was seated on. Kevin started laughing and couldn't stop.

"If she could sleep in a fucking casino," my mom whispered.

"Okay, here. I'll help you." Caden had sat down next to Kelly and was going to show him how to put the film in his camera.

"Joey, God! You should open something," I said, suddenly feeling very selfish. I had halted the assembly line of unwrapping for more than five minutes.

"We'll get there," she replied, smiling. And eventually we did. One by one, Joanna, Jannie, Paddy, and finally my mother opened a gift each. Kevin paid attention, and sometimes Meghan and Caden tried to keep up with what was going on. Even I was a little distracted by the beautiful book in my lap. With each gift opened, I stole another look. Joanna got perfume from our mother.

"At least she's not still buying you socks and underwear." I heard our brother whisper.

I looked over at Caden and Kelly who were woefully behind in the gift-opening count. Caden was explaining something about the camera to Kelly. Then I caught Meghan out of the corner of my eye. She looked from her brother to Caden, smiling; but did her expression change from one to the other? I noticed something, but barely. There were conversations going on all around me and Dawn was snoring softly, having not opened one gift, asleep in the middle of all of the chaos. Eventually, Kelly began to snap pictures. The amateur photographer was particularly interested in snapping them of the old lady asleep in the middle of the room.

311

The order of unwrapping all but abandoned, I somehow missed Joanna open her card from me. Suddenly she leaned down and thanked me. She and Colleen had gone to the North Shore after Colleen had gone into remission. Colleen had decided to be cremated and wanted her ashes scattered there. Not only had she been there with our sister, but she'd been there on a high school class trip, on which she'd lost her virginity to Frankie Zahler. I remembered sitting in their bedroom, hearing all about it, after she had gotten back. I hadn't thought of that for years, until I decided to take a leap of faith and plan a trip for my sister and me. Colleen loved the North Shore. Joanna had taken her ashes there and scattered them, alone. I hadn't realized that until, one night we were drinking with Kev and he mentioned it. I had never been. I lived in Minnesota for nineteen plus years. I wanted to say a proper goodbye to my sister with our sister. I prayed, for days, after booking the hotel that Joey wouldn't find it too forward.

"Not too much?" I asked.

"It's perfect. I can't wait."

The gift opening continued and sometime later, I realized that Charlie and Joanna had disappeared. I decided they had probably gone to smoke and snuck away to join them. I didn't even bother with boots. I wore a size nine shoe. Kev wore a size eleven. Even Caden's shoes were bigger than mine. I was forever slipping into someone else's shoes to go outside to smoke. I slipped on a pair I couldn't immediately identify and grabbed my coat. I was surprised my mom or Kevin hadn't noticed us sneaking off to smoke. At the back door, through the window, I saw Charlie kiss my sister. I hesitated for just a moment, then pulled one door and pushed the other, clearly alerting them to my intrusion.

"Sorry. I needed this." I held up a cigarette. Neither of them was even smoking.

"I can't believe Mom didn't follow you out here."

"I'm stealthy as fuck," I said, then giggled. "I might also be drunk. Oh, God." They both laughed. I couldn't tell. Maybe we were all drunk?

"I stopped drinking an hour ago," Charlie offered.

"What, so you can drive me home?"

312

"The thought had crossed my mind."

"Dawn has to go back to Fridley," Joanna countered.

"Or you guys could take Mom home and we could ask Paddy to take Dawn home. How much sense did it make for them to pick up Mom and you to pick up Dawn, anyway?"

"He has a point. What about the kids?"

"They'll hardly notice who's driving the car," Charlie suggested.

"Meghan has been so distracted the last two days," my sister added.

"Caden, too. It's probably just Christmas. Plus, oh my God, the album! For whatever part either of you played in that, thank you."

"He's such a great kid, Stephen." My sister was all smiles.

"You fuckers!" my mom, well our mom, said. Actually let's go with her mom. Moira was at the back door, Kevin behind her.

"You caught us, Mom."

Kev had pressed past my mother, opened the outside door, and stepped down, reaching back to give his grandmother a hand. I lit a second cigarette. It was dry out and Charlie had dragged over three of the wrought iron chairs from a few feet away. There was no snow on the sidewalk, thanks to Caden's newfound talent at snow removal, so he lined the chairs up along the pavement. Joanna, Mom, and I took seats.

"You're wearing Dawn's shoes?" my mother asked, as soon as I sat.

"Oh my God, you are," Kevin said, practically pointing. He and Charlie started laughing.

"Like I said, stealthy as fuck," I told them.

"Pink Floyd?" Joanna asked our mother.

"Get the fuck off my pudding," Moira shot back.

313

A little more than an hour later, Paddy and Jannie had helped Dawn out to their car and left. Paddy had warmed the car up and carried out gifts and leftovers. None of us were certain whether Dawn would need to be carried out, as well, but in the end; she walked of her own volition, thanking everyone, carrying three unopened gifts and a small Tupperware container of lasagna. I was saying goodbye to the others. Charlie was going to drive Joanna's car to drop Mom off, then I didn't know what. I'd seen the two of them whispering a few minutes ago, so they must have worked something out. I assumed Charlie would sleep over and sneak back in the morning to get his truck. It was twelve-thirty when I watched Joanna's car pull away from the curb.

A couple of minutes later, securely tucked into my own shoes, a fresh glass of wine in hand, I was back outside for one last cigarette. The concrete steps were dry to the touch, so I sat down in my regular spot and looked up at the sky. I couldn't see a single star, or even the moon. There was nothing but black. The only light was cast from the two street lamps I could discern from my vantage point. I sighed, taking it all in. It was a sigh of relief, even happiness. I couldn't have imagined a happier Christmas Eve, not a year ago, and certainly at no time in the interim. Two young men I adored completely and would do anything for were bickering back and forth as they unloaded, then reloaded our dishwasher. I could hear their banter from where I sat.

I was full. Full of food, full of wine, full of love. Full. Maybe it was because I was slightly drunk, because I'd never been much of a lamenter. I finally lit a Kool, then still looking up at the starless sky, I said, "Thank you." Maybe it was to God. Maybe it was the Universe. Maybe it was to the man who had made me whole again, given me a son, then broken me almost completely and finally led me back to my family. Back home.

Chapter 29
JOANNA

"I don't want this to just be about sex."

Seriously? I'd tossed and turned all night long. Even the whole bottle of wine I drank after he left did little to curb my restlessness. Had I become that used to sleeping next to him so soon? I sat up in bed and actually used my fingers to do the math. The first night was a week ago. That was Saturday. He'd stayed over Monday night, then Wednesday and Thursday, and then again on Christmas Eve. Five nights. I sighed and laid back down and covered my face with a tangle of flannel sheet and comforter. I tried to will sleep to come back to me, but sleep wasn't having it. Finally, I peeked out from under the covers and squinted, for about the fifteenth time since I'd crawled into bed six hours ago. Five-thirty. Seriously? I sat back up. Great. Up at five-thirty on a Sunday. I decided to give up on sleep, for the moment at least. I threw my robe on and crept down the stairs to make coffee.

"No Charlie last night?" My daughter had a cup of coffee in her hand already.

"What?" I was barely coherent. "Why are you awake? Wait—what?"

"You couldn't seriously think I wouldn't notice?" She was actually smug.

"How? I mean—no—yeah how?"

"I'm a barista, Mother." What in the hell did that have to do with it?

"But—."

"You're going to have to use your words, Mom." The situation was funny to her. She turned around, grabbed a coffee mug from the cupboard, filled it with coffee, and handed it to me. "I worked early on Christmas Eve and I was already down here, just like now. I watched Charlie come down the stairs. Actually I guess it was more like I heard him come down the stairs. Yeah, then I turned around to see who it was. I saw Charlie go out the front door, barefoot, holding his boots."

315

"You're using enough words for both of us." The conversation, so far, had knocked the wind out of me. I eased myself down into a chair at the kitchen table. "Your brother?"

"God, no. I'm not sure he'd notice if it was his room Charlie was sneaking in and out of," she joked. "I didn't really think that one through, until... yeah, that was gross."

"Why didn't you say anything?"

"I'm saying something now. Besides it was hilarious watching you two sneak around on Christmas."

"It — I mean you — you don't care?"

"You're old. I'm pretty sure you can do whatever you want." My daughter was hilarious at that hour.

"That's not what I asked."

"I do not care," she said, matter-of-factly. "I'd take it easy on dorko upstairs, though. He still thinks his dad will move back in next week."

"I don't want him to know. Not yet. I didn't want either of you to know. I mean there's nothing to know. I don't know."

"Mom, chill! I bet if I hadn't been up already on Christmas Eve, and seen him leave, I wouldn't have figured it out." I'd been staring into my coffee cup. "You're both very convincing."

"Thanks, I think." I looked up at my daughter. I did not know exactly what I expected to see there. I could've said unequivocally that there was barely a sign of the little girl in pink footy pajamas who once stood in this kitchen. I would have sworn it was just last week. "You work at six?"

"Yeah, I should probably take off."

"Okay, then, have a good day." I looked back down at my coffee. Every conversation I'd had lately with the beautiful, interesting, perceptive, amazing human being barely lasted two minutes.

"Mom, seriously! Everybody likes Charlie. And he's super-hot."

316

There was that. By seven o'clock, I had finished the pot of coffee that Meghan made and started a second. I thought about calling him, but it was too early. I thought about getting in the car and driving to his apartment, then laughed. I didn't have any idea where he lived. By eight o'clock, I had showered and had one more cup of coffee and half a piece of toast. Stephen knew where Charlie lived. Was I crazy? I replayed it over and over. "I don't want this to just be about sex," wasn't how the conversation started.

Christmas Eve had been nice. Dinner at Stephen's, gifts, family, it had all been really nice. Charlie drove my car. We dropped Mom off. We left the car running and the two of us went in with her to make sure everything was all right. Mom insisted she was fine. She even said, "I love you, baby girl." She hadn't said that to me since Meghan was born, I didn't think.

Very little was said on the drive from my mother's to our house. It was after one in the morning by the time we got home. I made a show out of thanking Charlie for being so kind to drive us all around and asked if he wanted to come in for a nightcap, certain the kids would go straight to their rooms and that would be the end of it. Kelly had different plans. He wanted to be tucked in. It was odd, seeing as it had been two years or more since the last time he'd requested I do so. He was my baby. He'd always be my baby. If he wanted to be tucked in at thirty-five, I would do it. It was after two o'clock by the time Charlie and I were finally alone in my bedroom. I was surprised when he suggested we just sleep, but I was exhausted and willing to go with it.

We slept like puzzle pieces, his breath on my neck. I didn't even remember drifting off. When I woke up, it was light out. Shit! We hadn't set an alarm. Shit, shit, shit! I listened closely, and I could hear someone in the bathroom across the hall. The door opened and there were footsteps and I heard the creak of the second stair. Charlie was still sound asleep. I wriggled out of his arms and he barely moved. I sat up quietly and turned to look down at him. I had loved my ex. I really did. The last few years, before we separated, were the worst. Before that, there had been disagreements over how to raise our children, fights over money and his drinking. I had almost completely stopped drinking. The smell of him coming to bed at night disgusted me. I could barely stand the taste of it in my mouth. So much had happened; I could not locate that indefinable thing that had drawn me to him in the first place. I am certain though, on at least an intellectual level, he was and remained attractive. Even so, he didn't compare to the man asleep next to me.

317

"What are you thinking about?" Charlie opened his eyes, turned his head slightly, and looked up at me.

"Strangely enough, I was thinking about my ex-husband. Glad you asked?"

"Not particularly." His eyes shot wide open and he sat up, abruptly. "Fuck!"

"Yeah, that ship has sailed," I sighed. "How are you at climbing out of second-story windows?"

"What happened? Didn't you set an alarm?" He was only half-awake and scrambling to get out of the bed and dressed.

"It's alright. Slow down."

"I'm just — I'm — I'm sorry." He sat back down on the bed, wearing only a t-shirt. I looked down at his pants, folded somewhat neatly, on the trunk at the foot of my bed. I was working out things to tell the kids in my head. "We could tell them that I was too tired to drive home."

"So you decided to sleep naked in my bed?" I didn't mean it flippantly, but that's apparently how it sounded.

"I was just trying to help," he said, and reached for his pants. He did not wear underwear, not boxers, not briefs; not those new boxer briefs I'd seen at the store. I'd never encountered a man who didn't wear underwear. Then again, how many men had I encountered in a way that I'd actually have access to that information? I wasn't turned off by it. On the contrary, it struck me as a little sexy. Okay, it was completely fucking hot. I definitely didn't mind looking over at his bare ass as he stretched across my bed reaching for his pants. Finally realizing that he was not going to be able to reach the damn pants from his current location, he got up and walked around the bed. He knew his butt made me insane. The tease turned away from me every single time he put his pants back on. The entire process, in fact, was done as erotically as if he were taking them off.

"I have it! You were too tired, and had too much to drink to drive home last night."

"Didn't I already say that?"

318

"There's more. I woke up pretty early and asked you to look at the heater in my room."

"The baseboard?"

"Whatever it's called." Was that part really important?

"Baseboard." I guess it was that important.

"It's probably fine anyway. Meghan is still asleep and Kelly won't even wonder about it."

He walked around the bed, sat beside me, and kissed me tenderly on my forehead, then put his arm around me. "It might work. I should have reminded you to turn on the alarm, though."

"Jesus Fucking Christ." I stood up angrily. Where was this coming from? "Stop apologizing. Stop being so goddamned fucking perfect."

"What the fuck?" I was just as shocked as he was. Oh God! What had I done?

"I didn't mean that."

"What did you mean exactly?" He was looking up at me. I met his now hurt-filled eyes with my own. I really had no clue what they were registering. I hadn't any idea where that came from. I'd admit he was perfect, but why the hostility? I didn't know what to say.

"I don't know." It was all I could manage. It was true, though hardly original.

"I think you better figure it out." He stood up and I turned away, ashamed. After a minute or more of silence, he sighed. "I should go."

"Don't leave mad. I am sorry. I'm truly sorry."

"I'm not mad," he said. "I'm just disappointed." Oh, God! That was a parental big gun. *"I'm not mad that you took the car. I'm just disappointed that you ran over the cat on your way down the driveway."* How was I supposed to respond to that?

"Look. This is brand new. Don't you think it's too early to have to label it?"

319

"I do, which is precisely why I haven't," he shot back. "You're the one labeling it and freaking out and making it something it's not." He was probably right. No, he was definitely right. I'd freaked out the second I woke up in his arms, that first morning.

"You don't have any expectations at all?" I said, feebly attempting to turn it back on him.

"I just don't want it to be all about sex." Merry Fucking Christmas!

It was December 26th and we hadn't spoken in almost twenty-four hours. By nine o'clock, I had put away clean laundry, washed and dried the flannel sheets on my bed, and was remaking it, when I remembered brunch. Brunch. What time did we say? I had no idea where the cordless was, so I grabbed my coffee cup and hurried downstairs. I dialed Stephen's number and poured out what was left in my coffee cup. It was cold anyway.

"Hello."

"Hey. What time did we say for brunch?"

"I think ten-thirty," Stephen answered.

"I forgot, momentarily, and when in popped back into my brain, I was afraid we were late."

"What's wrong?" he asked.

"Nothing. Everything's good," I lied.

"Well, I'm just out of the shower," he assured me. "I could start the bacon in ten minutes. Why don't you guys head over now?"

"That sounds perfect." My voice rose stupidly on the last word.

"It's just you and Caden, right?"

"Right," I answered.

"Joey, drive safe." He hung up the phone and I sighed, thinking about how long I had stupidly frozen him out. Why did I feel it necessary to do that to men?

By ten o'clock, I was sitting on a stool at Stephen's kitchen counter watching him fry bacon.

"Do you want coffee?"

"No. God, I've had enough coffee."

"Mimosa?" he offered, smiling slyly.

"No. I don't want to drink today."

"That's the entire point of brunch, that and bacon, but alright. How do you feel about arsenic?"

"Very funny," I said, dryly.

"Well, out with it." Almost the entire time we'd been talking, he kept his back to me, his immediate attention reserved for the bacon. I wasn't sure if that made it easier to talk, or more difficult. Stephen didn't even need to turn back around. "They're upstairs in Cay's room and Kev's sleeping like the dead downstairs."

"I yelled at Charlie," I admitted.

"Was there a cause for this scolding?" I sighed; then so did he. "I should've baked this. So much less work."

"Can I just have juice?"

"Can you help yourself? Glasses are there." He pointed at the cupboard to his left with the tongs.

"It's not like I scolded him, exactly. Well, maybe a little." I joined Stephen on the other side of the counter. "We overslept, and it wasn't even his fault."

"Oh, no! Did the kids catch you?"

321

"Not exactly. Do you want juice?" He seemed to have to think about it, as if I had just asked him if he wanted to participate in a marathon or something.

"Why not," he finally answered. "Explain."

"Turns out Meghan already knew," I told him. Stephen just laughed. "What?"

"That one's smart. You know who she reminds me of?"

"Colleen?" It's not like I hadn't seen our sister in my daughter many times before.

"She looks a little like her, too—with all that hair."

"So, we overslept," I continued, changing the subject. "He woke up and was freaking out. So I told him to calm down that we could figure out a lie to tell the kids."

"Did you—come up with something to tell them?"

"Yeah, of course. I'm not an amateur." My brother laughed again. He knew.

"So, then what happened?" He was removing pieces of bacon from the grease in the pan with tongs, placing them in a different pan.

"He kept apologizing or trying to be comforting." I realized how stupid it sounded.

"Damn him," Stephen joked. I just sighed. "What is it? What's going on?"

"I'm sorry to dump all of this on you. I know you're his friend. That's one thing right there. There are so many reasons why it won't work."

"Aren't there reasons it will?" He came over to the counter where I had taken a seat again. "This orange juice tastes funny."

"It doesn't to me," I said, not immediately getting the joke. "Wait you mean without the champagne?"

"It actually doesn't taste that bad. Who knew?"

"You're a funny guy."

322

"That sounds—where'd you get that?" he asked.

"Dad used to say that. You don't remember?" I couldn't believe it.

"It did sound familiar," he admitted.

I knew at some point, we were going to have to discuss our father. It wasn't like Stephen and I had been talking again for very long. Still, I did not think he'd brought up our father once.

"You make everything sound so reasonable." I'd decided to stay on topic. "All I've thought of are the reasons why it's a bad idea to get involved with Charlie."

"That's the thing about cons. They almost don't exist without the pros."

"See?!" I asserted. "There you go again."

"Are there any pros?" He turned his attention back to the bacon.

"He's beautiful," I suggested.

"His ass is a religious experience. Jesus Christ." I was surprised how not weird it was to be having the conversation with Stephen. It actually felt perfectly normal.

"You should see him naked," I told him. He almost dropped the tongs. "He's kind."

"Beautiful and kind. Check. He gets along with both of your kids. He adores your gay brother. That's something you couldn't say about Jim."

"He got along with the kids most of the time."

"I meant the other part. Does Kelly eat eggs? I should've asked before now."

"It depends. We'll figure it out. He loves bacon. He needs to learn to eat what he's served or not eat at all. God, can you imagine one of us dictating the menu when we were growing up?" Stephen just laughed. "Do you remember the battles over Caty eating her vegetables?"

323

"We're going to have to talk about her next week. This stuff with Kev is becoming ridiculous. I've made up my mind to do something. I don't care what Mom says. That kid is hurting."

"I agree." I did. I had pretty much decided the same.

"Anyway, I didn't mean to, you know, change the subject." He had removed a baking dish from the oven and put a pan of bacon in its place. Then he turned the oven off. "He's sweet. I'd date him, you know; if he was into guys."

"He is closer to your age," I offered.

"I am finding I like them younger." I nearly choked on my orange juice. Stephen had opened up somehow. It felt almost as if he had never left. I was certain there were plenty more wounds that needed to heal, but it was nice. "I take it the young thing is a con as far as you're concerned?"

"I'm ten years older than him," I said.

"Almost twelve."

"Thank you for that."

"Why does it make a difference?" Stephen asked.

"I don't know that it does." I really didn't. It wasn't noticeable when we were together, as if that would make a difference. Was I truly not worried about what other people might say or think? I didn't know what my hesitation was.

"So put that in the undecided column. What else? Is the sex good?" My face started to get red. "Oh, get over it!"

"It's amazing," I finally answered, with yet another sigh.

"Okay, so let me get this straight. He's gorgeous; the sex is great. He gets along with your kids and your family. He's sweet. Kind. Employed. But you're worried it won't work out because he's a few years younger than you and maybe too nice?"

"When you put it like that —."

324

"Hey, at some point, I'll probably need to take my own advice," he interrupted. "But does it really matter if it doesn't work out? Whatever happened to living in the moment?"

"It got complicated when the kids entered the picture."

"I suppose, but then I call your attention back to Exhibit A." My kids liked him and he liked them.

"And if it doesn't work out," I argued. "The kids are hurt, and he works for one brother and is friends with the other?"

"Oh, don't worry about me. I can always go back to not talking to you."

All four of us, my brother and I and our two sons ate breakfast at the counter. After we were done eating, Stephen tore a piece of paper off the pad next to the phone and wrote something on it. I was ready for a cigarette, but then my little brother turned back around and handed me the slip of paper.

"What's this?" It was an address.

"What do you think? Leave Kelly here and go talk to Charlie."

"Are you sure?"

"They're upstairs fooling around with their cameras or downstairs on that computer. I doubt they'd notice if both of us left." He had a point. It turned out they were downstairs. Both of their cameras lay on the couch beside them. They were both huddled in front of Caden's brand new computer. My son barely acknowledged my goodbye. At least Caden looked up and smiled in my general direction.

By twelve-thirty, I was sitting in a beanbag chair in a tiny studio apartment in Uptown. The apartment was neater than my house. Add that to the plus column. Charlie had greeted me at the security door to his building, shirtless and barefoot, with a "What's up?" Really? I was nearly out of breath after we climbed the three flights of stairs to his apartment. Each flight seemed to entail twice as many stairs as my house. I was beginning to form a theory about where Charlie Carpenter came by his perfect ass.

He had a little kitchen and a littler bathroom. In the main room was a closet, a dresser, a tiny table with two chairs, and a futon. And the beanbag I was attempting to sit in and still look dignified. The possibility of that had been left back in the early eighties. *Oh, screw it!*

"I don't want this to be just about sex either," I blurted out. He'd just returned from the bathroom where he he'd put on a shirt. He smiled down at me, then climbed into the bag with me.

"The sex is pretty fucking great, though. Right?" He laughed, leaning into me.

"It's alright."

"Better than alright," he demanded, still smiling.

"Look, you have to let me take this slow."

"We can take it at whatever speed you like. This might surprise you, but I don't want to go too fast either."

"Have you ever been in a relationship? There is so much I don't know about you."

"It's weird, right?" he said. "We've known each other for years."

"Not that long."

"You knew my brother when he was, like, Meghan's age," he reminded me.

"That's right." I didn't know why I kept forgetting that Charlie's brother had been a friend of Stephen's. "I didn't know him well. Where is he now?"

"He died about five years ago."

"Oh Charlie, I'm sorry!" How in the hell did I not know that? "What happened?"

"He had AIDS," Charlie said, almost matter of fact.

"Jesus! I really am sorry."

"Stop apologizing," he said, and then started to smile. "And stop being so goddamned fucking perfect."

"Not one of my proudest moments." We were both laughing now. I couldn't believe it. It had not been sixty seconds since Charlie told me his brother had died of AIDS. At that moment, I realized something. "Wait a minute. Liam and Stephen? Really?"

"Yep. I mean seriously, how did you not know that? Your Mom knows. Kevin, Caden. Colleen knew."

"Wait—what? My mom knew?"

"She caught them, I guess," he explained.

"That was your brother?" Charlie nodded. "I wasn't living at home then. It was just Stephen and Colleen. I only heard about it after Stephen came out."

Neither of us said anything for a long time. I leaned back a little and looked up at the ceiling. There were two long cracks. One of them stretched almost the length of the room. Charlie had leaned back too. I was up a little higher than him. His butt was practically on the floor, his head resting on my chest for a change.

"My parents knew about Liam. Well, my mom did for a long time. I didn't know that until I got to know your brother."

"Which one?"

"Stephen. Patrick and I don't talk as much as you'd think. We work separately. Stephen's house was only the second or third time we worked on a project together. After work, he goes home to his wife and I come back here and lay on my crappy futon and think about you." He turned his head up a little so that our eyes met. Then he laughed.

"Be serious," I demanded, trying not to laugh, too. "I gather they didn't like it that he was gay?"

"They disowned him," he said, and turned his face back towards the ceiling.

"They came around before he died?"

"Nope," he said, almost nonchalantly. "I saw him as much as I could. I was seventeen when I found out."

327

"You weren't scared?" His eyes were dry. We were just talking. He wasn't completely emotionless. It was just clear to me that he had worked through it.

"I was fucking terrified, but he was my brother."

"I've been such a bitch to Stephen. I don't know how he even—but it was never about him being sick. I mean—you know what I mean."

"You're his sister," he told me. "I don't know why it's so hard to understand."

"I don't know why it comes so easily to some people, and it's so hard for the rest of us," I offered.

"That's the thing. Shit happens. I'm not judging you or anything. It's pretty clear that you realize you missed out."

"It's that clear, is it?" I asked.

"To me, it is," he said, smiling.

"Well then I guess I better keep you around." I leaned forward to kiss him, but all I could reach was his nose.

"I'm right here." He had the silliest look on his face, just then. He slid down further, rolled over, and climbed back up, until he was almost on top of me. "You can't get rid of me that easily."

"I'm glad," I said, and he kissed me. "So, guess what... Meghan knows."

"About us?"

"She saw you leave on Christmas Eve morning," I explained. "It's okay. She couldn't care less."

"That's good, I guess. And you're alright with that?"

"Yeah, I'm fine. But it brings me to another thing. Kelly goes to his dad's tonight. For the whole week."

"Nice!" he said. "I mean—jeez—um, I like Kelly—I mean—."

328

"I know what you meant," I said, laughing at him. "So what nights do you work?"

"Just tonight and Thursday and Friday. I volunteered to go in at ten and take over for this guy tomorrow night though. That's so he'll work for me on New Year's Eve. It's a fucked switch. I might make twenty dollars in tips on a Monday half-shift."

"And he'll make tons working the last three hours on New Year's Eve?"

"That's the deal. I wanted to celebrate with Stephen."

"He could've celebrated another night. You need the tips."

"Don't tell me you don't know what else it is." He rolled off me and got up. "It's not just his birthday. He met Alec on New Year's Eve. It's their anniversary."

"Oh, God! I did know that, I think. I just forgot."

"Kev said we have to get him out of the house," Charlie said.

"Right! I get it now."

"You see?"

"Yep," I said, moving to get up, as well. "And I'm in, too."

Chapter 30
KEVIN

I did mushrooms by myself a couple of months ago. I didn't want to trip at Stephen's, so without anyplace better to go; I chose my old bedroom at my mom's house. There wasn't any cash on the counter, so I knew she wasn't expecting me. I also knew from the news that she was in Washington D.C. I sat on the floor, leaning against my old bed, and stared up at the Pink Floyd poster on the wall. I did that for what seemed like hours. In reality, it was probably more like thirty minutes. I had started to sweat, so I decided to take a shower. I put my clothes in the washer, downstairs, and ran back through the house naked. I was in the shower when I heard it, something hit the wall, and there was a hiss. That was the first time. I didn't even recognize it yet. I got out of the shower to search the house.

There was a robe in my room; I didn't think I'd ever seen before. It felt new. I put it on and started my search, one room at a time, stopping some places; taking them in. There were pictures of me on the wall, going down the stairs. Or up. Depending on which way you were headed, I either went forward or back in time, like one of those books where you flip the pages, and in the corner, it's like a filmstrip with one changing image. For five minutes, or maybe it was an hour, I ran up and down the stairs, watching myself get younger, then older, then younger again. Finally I remembered I was searching for something. Oh yeah, the sound. Nothing in the living room, or the den. Nothing in the kitchen, or the downstairs guest bathroom. Nothing in the garage. I opened the door to the pantry and was assaulted by all of the letters, so many different sizes and colors. No one in there, so I left.

Back upstairs, I checked my mom's room. I wanted to fuck with stuff, mess it up a little, so she'd know I'd been there. There were papers spread out on the bed, stacks of files on top of the pretty white comforter. The carpet was white, and the drapes, too. There were big, fluffy white pillows on the bed. It was like a fucking snowstorm in there except for the papers. I wondered if a congresswoman kept classified documents at home, all those secrets and lies growing out of the snow. I considered just brushing them all off the bed and sleeping there. She'd know then. Maybe she'd remember she had a son. Then I remembered he used to sleep there. Fuck him. What did I care about either of them? So I closed the door on all that white. It freaked me out a little. Too fucking clean. Too pure.

330

Back in my room, I took the robe off and tossed it on the floor. I laughed out loud at the idea of being naked, no clue why. I was never allowed to play "my music" too loud when she was home, so I turned the stereo all the way up. She'd always said "my music" like it, and I, were from another country; like I was listening to German Folk music or something. There was a CD already in the stereo, so I just pressed play. *Momentary Lapse of Reason.* Pink Floyd. I actually had the empty case for this CD at Stephen's, now I knew where the CD had gone. I didn't like "Signs of Life"; the water at the beginning freaked me out, especially when I was high.

I almost drowned when I was little. It was a stupid swimming class. Looking back, it wasn't actually that bad, but my mom said I never had to go back. I never learned to swim after that. I pressed the button to skip the first track. I loved "Learning to Fly." It was probably my second favorite song on the CD. "Turning Away" was, in my opinion, Pink Floyd's most underrated song. That one was my favorite. I'd listen to that next. At a certain volume, it's almost like you and the music become one. That's what I was going for. I laid on my back on the bed looking up at the ceiling, letting the music just happen to me. I fell asleep soon after that. That night, or early the next morning, I had the dream.

I could hear the voice change back and forth. I only knew one of their names. Adam was my mother's assistant. I'd only ever heard his voice two times. Until the dream. I heard the other voice all the time. It came from far away, maybe behind a door. *Burn in hell, faggot. Burn in hell.* I tried to block both of them out, but now of they were a part of the same dream. Adam's voice would begin, "It's Adam from the congresswoman's office." Then it would morph into the kid's voice, the one with all the hate. Then I'd hear that voice saying "From the congresswoman's office, burn in Hell." Or sometimes it'd be "Faggot, its Adam from the congresswoman's office." I would wake up when the can of pop exploded against the wall.

I just had the fucking dream again. What day was it? What time was it? It was light out. That much was obvious, just opening my eyes. I laid completely still until my breathing slowed down and the day came to me. Oh, yeah, it was New Year's Eve. I'd been looking forward to this day. It was Stephen's birthday and we were all going out. I loved my uncle very much. In a way, Stephen was responsible for keeping me in the family. I didn't really know how or why.

331

I guess I'd felt like I was drifting, separating. Maybe I'd just end up like Stephen, you know, before he moved back. Just before he came back to visit, last March, I started to think about taking off. I could even move to San Francisco. Why not? Truthfully, I was a little disappointed that night we had dinner at my grandma's. I was excited to see my uncle. I hadn't seen him since I went to San Francisco before my grandpa and Aunt Colleen had both died. Before Alec, too. There wasn't anyone in Minnesota to tether him to us. Not anymore. We were exactly alike, except for the gay part.

My grandma had invited me to dinner. I assumed my mother had been invited, too. I also assumed that, since Stephen would be there, we'd not be seeing her. Stephen didn't drive, so he'd taken a cab from his hotel, downtown. He was staying in a hotel. That was weird. It didn't feel like a single member of the family was going out of their way to make him feel welcome. We all started arriving at the same time. Joanna was just sitting in her car with my cousin Meghan when I pulled up. I had no idea where my other cousin, Kelly was. Like a minute later, a cab pulled up and my uncle Stephen got out. The cab was just driving off when Patrick and Jannie parked in front of the house. It was all awkwardly polite hugs, there on the street, before we moved up and onto the front porch. The crowd just sort of pushed Stephen in first. He had an overnight bag, or maybe more like a sort of backpack, even though I knew he was staying at the Hyatt. I would have invited him to stay with me. Fuck what my mom would say. I had a bedroom and I could sleep on the crappy futon in the living room. I did half of the time anyway. My apartment was kind of crap-ass, though, and all the way in Dinkytown.

Everyone was being super polite, like he was a second- or third-cousin, or somebody no one had seen in a really long time. I guessed maybe that was it. Still, I wondered why he hadn't stayed with my grandma. "I could've picked you up, Uncle Stephen."

"Thanks Kev," he said, and it seemed like he meant it.

"I can't believe you got lost from the Hyatt," Jannie said.

"He might have forgotten the way," Joanna suggested.

"I know. I know. I wasn't paying attention," Stephen explained, ignoring the obvious slam from Joanna. "But it kind of worked out for the best."

"Wait, you got lost?" God, my Uncle Patrick wasn't going to belittle him, too?

332

"Yeah, we went way too far; and then we were stuck going around the lake before I actually realized where we were."

"Then how did it work out for the best?" Joanna asked. "I think I missed something."

"I saw this house over on, I don't know, south of Calhoun," Stephen started to explain.

"What house?" Grandma interrupted.

"It's for sale, Mom."

"Wait a minute! Are you thinking of buying a house here?" Paddy actually seemed like he might be happy about it.

"I wasn't until about twenty-five minutes ago."

"You'd move back here?" Joanna asked.

"I don't know—um—I really don't know. It's something to think about." Stephen sounded more nervous all of a sudden.

I actually wanted to tell him not to buy the house. I had a sick feeling in my stomach even then, but I knew I was just being really selfish. I thought it was that I didn't want my mom to freak out. I didn't want her to hurt him. That's what I thought. I was wrong, I guess. Stephen seemed really past the point where she could hurt him. He told me, once, that he had come to think of her more as a politician, than an actual relative; that she only had the power to hurt him as a politician.

"I thought maybe you'd be willing to come and take a look at it with me," Stephen said to Paddy. "I think it'll need a lot of work"

"Glad to," Paddy told him. Okay, maybe it was just the women who were determined to freeze him out.

"Thanks. We don't have to talk about it right now."

"How long are you in town, Stephen?" Jannie asked.

"Just four days. I didn't want to leave Caden too long."

"And Caden is your stepson?" she asked.

"He is. A friend of mine is staying at the house with him while I'm here."

"Caden's awesome," I chimed in.

"That's right! You went out to San Francisco to visit," Jannie acknowledged. "How old is Caden?"

"He's fourteen."

"Joanna, where is Kelly?" my grandma asked.

"He's with his dad. You knew that, Mom."

"I didn't," she disagreed. "But thank you for clarifying."

My grandma and Joanna didn't seem to get along very well since Colleen died. Or maybe it was since my grandpa died. My mom told me once, that Joanna was always grandpa's favorite. And Stephen was grandma's. "None of the rest of us stood a chance," Mom had said, bitterly. "They might as well have skipped their first two kids altogether."

I didn't get it. Uncle Patrick didn't seem bitter at all. "What's for dinner, Grandma?"

"I made Stephen's favorite." My two uncles kind of looked at each other, like neither of them knew what that was. Or neither of them remembered. "Chow Mein!"

My grandma made this kind of Chow Mein. I mean it didn't really taste like any I'd had in a restaurant, but it was good. "Oh, God, I forgot all about your Chow Mein, Mom," Stephen said. "Thank you."

"It's no problem," Grandma told him. "I did have to rack my brain to remember what you liked."

"How long has it been since you've been home?" Joanna asked.

"I think about five years," he answered, almost embarrassed.

334

"That's all?" she replied. I couldn't tell what had happened to her voice. All the warmth there usually was had gone out of it. It was so different, between them then, than it became after he moved.

"Grandma, my mom isn't coming, is she?" I asked. That made Joanna laugh.

"I don't even know if she's in town, kid," she answered. "I'm sure she'd want to see her little brother, if she was." Joanna just laughed harder, so grandma asked her, "What in the hell is so funny, dear?"

"Absolutely nothing, Mother," she answered, then tried not to laugh anymore. Finally, she excused herself to go smoke. When my grandma told her that she smoked inside, my aunt answered, "But I don't."

"Suit yourself," grandma called after her. When Joanna came back in from smoking, Stephen excused himself to go smoke and I went with him.

"There used to be a tree house in that tree," Stephen said, pointing at the big tree at the back of the yard. "I smoked my first joint there."

"Seriously?"

"Oh, yeah! It was with your aunt."

"Which one?" I asked him.

"Colleen." He laughed. "I don't think Joey has ever smoked pot. It doesn't seem like her, does it?"

"I guess not." I was laughing then, too. After we'd gone back in the house, Stephen asked Grandma about the tree house.

"It wasn't in that tree. That was on the other side. We had to take that tree down. Dutch Elm. The city made us."

"I had some fun times in that treehouse," Paddy offered.

"Didn't we all?" Stephen agreed. "Well, except for Joey. She never wanted much part of it."

335

"All any of you ever did out there was stuff we weren't supposed to," Joanna told them.

"That was sort of the point," Paddy said.

"Oh, like what?" Jannie asked.

"Not in front of Mom."

"Mom's not a goddamned idiot," Grandma said.

"Mother!" Joanna said.

"I get to speak however I wish now, dear," Grandma told her. "I knew exactly what was going on out there. Your father, maybe not."

"You didn't tell him then?" Paddy asked.

"He didn't need to know everything. You kids deserved a place that was your own. What you did out there was none of our business."

Before he left to go back to San Francisco, I met Stephen at his hotel. "How come you didn't stay with Grandma?"

"I could have," he assured me. "Of course I could have. I just wanted a place that I could go back to if things got tense."

"I think someone should've insisted," I suggested.

"You know those manners," he started. "You might be surprised to know they come from your mother."

"I don't think so." I laughed.

"No, I'm serious. Caty was always very big on manners."

"I was really sorry to hear about Alec," I told him, not wanting to talk about my mom.

"Thank you for saying so." He seemed touched that I had.

336

"He was funny," I offered.

"He liked you," Stephen told me. "A lot. He wondered if you were an indication of how the rest of my family was."

"What did you tell him?"

"I told him no," he laughed. There was no bitterness in his voice.

"I'm really glad you bought the house," I lied.

"Good, because I'm scared shitless."

"I think Grandma's glad, too."

"I know she is," he told me. We talked for a little while. It was mostly small talk. Right at the end, though, was when he asked me. "So, I was wondering if you'd do me a really big favor?"

"Really, what?"

"Do you think you could drive a small truck?"

"Definitely," I answered.

"I'll hire movers for most of our stuff, but I was wondering, if you'd want to fly out to San Francisco and drive Caden and me back in a couple of months?"

"Um, yeah — I mean, um — I guess."

"Are you sure? You don't think it will cause problems with anyone?"

"By *anyone*, do you mean my mom?"

"She did come to mind," he answered.

"Maybe, but it's really up to me," I asserted.

"Well, the other night didn't go exactly as expected," he said.

337

"I was sort of hoping you didn't notice," I told him. "Why did you even decide to move back?"

"It's important to have family around," he told me, not ironically.

"Yeah, but—."

"They'll come around," he interrupted. "This is as much my doing as any of theirs."

"How do you figure?"

"I left, Kev." He sounded a little pissed at himself. "People think I'd been disowned or told to go. I wasn't, though. Not by anyone who mattered."

"I don't understand," I said.

"It was my decision to go and my decision to come back as infrequently as I did. It was more comfortable for me not to rock the boat, but I blamed them for a lot of that. In the end; it was on me."

"What makes you think that they'll all come around?"

"Well, I'm irresistible," he said, with a big smile on his face.

I couldn't believe how much had happened since then. I was living with him and Caden. He was more of a parent to me than my mother had been in years. That's when I remembered the card. I had a birthday card for him somewhere. What had I done with it? I bought it, like, three months ago. I was buying flowers for my mother and there was a rack of cards. Right there, at eye level, "You're Not Just an Uncle, You're a Friend." That, too. I sat up in bed and decided to go find Stephen and wish him a happy birthday.

Caden was right there when I opened my bedroom door, screwing around on the computer, which Stephen had given him for Christmas. Stephen had given me a bunch of clothes, a really cool leather jacket, and a pair of tennis shoes I had looked at a couple of months ago and said were cool. They were the kinds of things, at one time; my mom would have bought for me, the kinds of things that Stephen bought Caden.

338

"Hey. What time is it?"

"Don't you have an alarm clock in your room?"

"It kinda broke," I answered. "I should get a new one."

"Ya think?" Caden said.

"Where's the music coming from?"

"From the computer." He looked at me like it was a dumb question.

"Really? How was I supposed to know?"

"It's a drive just like a CD player," he told me.

"I just put the shit in the CD player and punch a button. I don't need to know it works."

"You will," he said, like it was a warning.

"Then I have your ass to show me."

"Maybe."

"Your dad home?" I asked.

"Yeah, upstairs."

"Did you wish him a happy birthday?"

"What do you think?" he asked, sarcastically.

"Just checking."

"Let me warn you, he's in an extremely good mood."

"Nothing wrong with that. Is that Radiohead you're listening to?" Caden just nodded. "Where'd you get it?"

"The store," he said, again with the sarcasm.

339

"They sell that stuff to little kids?" I was actually kind of serious.

"It's British. They don't have Parental Advisory stickers and almost no one knows who Radiohead even are, yet."

"Has Stephen heard 'Creep'?"

"Don't know, but I was thinking it might be a little too much for him. So maybe, you know, we can keep the CD between us?"

"I don't know," I offered, laughing. "He's pretty open-minded."

"Well, that's the thing, the CD isn't actually mine. Stephen might be okay, but my principal probably wouldn't approve."

"It's Meghan's?" I laughed. Again, he just nodded. He was being super-weird.

"Yeah, Aunt Joanna probably isn't a huge fan of British Indie Rock. Your secret's safe with me. It's cool you and Meghan are friends."

"It's alright," he said drolly.

"Why do you have to be such a sarcastic little fucker?" I went around behind him and got him a headlock with my right arm, bringing my fist up to the top of his head to give him a noogie.

"Dad!" he yelled, not loudly. "Hey, hey too hard. Too hard." After I let go, he said, "So you for sure won't say anything about the CD?"

"I can't promise anything, douche," I told him, smiling.

"You're the douche! Go wish him a happy birthday. He's getting older by the minute."

I found Stephen in the living room, sitting in the big chair, reading. "What are you reading?"

"Lasher, finally." He looked up from the book.

"Anne Rice?"

340

"I've had it for two months. I can't believe it's taken me that long to start. Two years ago, when I finished The Witching Hour, oh my God, I couldn't wait!" he exclaimed.

"Yeah, I think you mentioned it."

"I was obsessed for a little while."

"I think you had just finished the first one when I was out there," I offered.

"In San Francisco?" he asked. "How do you remember that?"

"Like you said, you mentioned it one or two *hundred* times. Hey, happy birthday!"

"Thank you, sweetheart! Excited for tonight?"

"You know it," I told him. "I bought you a card. I just can't find it."

"Give it to me next year," he joked.

"I might have to. Sorry."

"Don't worry about it. I'm just really happy we're going out. It's going to be fun."

"Should be," I told him. "I'm gonna go jump in the shower. Oh hey, what time is it?"

"Like two o'clock. You slept in." He smiled up at me.

"I didn't mean to. My alarm clock broke."

"How did that happen?" he asked.

"It kept going off, so I sorta threw it," I admitted. "I'm sorry."

"You threw it? Where?"

"Against the wall," I said, embarrassed.

"You didn't hurt the wall?" He had closed the book. I wondered if I was going to get a lecture.

"Nope. Just the alarm clock."

"You okay, Kev?"

"I'm fine, really." I knew that he had been paying attention to, and worrying about, how much I'd been drinking. I saw it on his face.

"You can talk to me about it, you know."

"I know." I did know. I just wasn't ready. I wasn't sure if I'd ever be. I wasn't sure even what it all was. I mean there was Mom. That's what everyone thought it was. If that was all it was, I'd have it made. "Do you ever regret coming back?"

"Why would you ask that?"

"I don't know; it's just different here."

"Different how?"

"People are meaner," I said. I wasn't going to tell him about the shit at the video store. I didn't think I needed to give an example.

"There are stupid people everywhere, Kev. They even have them in California."

"I guess. Well, I'm glad you came back."

"For the record, so am I." The phone started ringing. Saved by the bell. Stephen jumped up, but he didn't go immediately to answer it. He came over and hugged me instead. "Everything is going to be okay," he said, quietly. "I promise."

342

Chapter 31
STEPHEN

It was December 31, 1993, my thirty-fourth birthday. Kevin, Joanna, and I were taking the bus downtown. We'd meet up with Charlie at the Brass Rail and go where the night took us, if in fact; it took us anywhere, but the Rail. By the time the four of us shared a cab home, it would be 1994. I could not begin to recount what had taken place the past year, not in a way that would make any sense at all. The most important thing was that we were finally happy, so much so that I had been living in a state of euphoria for a week.

Our last New Year's Eve had been spent at home, just Caden and me. Dinner was meatloaf, mashed potatoes with cheese and bacon, and salad. Every year, before that, I had made lasagna, but neither of us could stomach any more lasagna for a while. I suggested meatloaf, and Caden offered his stock approval: "Whatever." We sat on stools at the counter, not at the dining room table, ten feet away, and hardly said a word to each other.

After dinner, Caden started to help with the dishes, but I told him I would do them. I knew he was anxious to get back to his book. For Christmas, I had given him Tolkien's <u>Lord of the Rings</u> and the past few days, I'd noticed the bookmark travel the pages until it rested more than three quarters of the way back. The book sat next him on the counter through dinner. It was nearly 1,200 pages! Was his having read probably a thousand of those in four days a sign of how little we connected anymore? He'd spent his entire Christmas break in his bedroom with the door closed. I had allowed it. In fact, I was grateful for it.

He certainly didn't argue when I told him I'd do the dishes. He thanked me for dinner, and then hesitated for a few seconds before retreating to his room. The hesitation when we separated was new. To hug or not to hug. It seemed a question best not answered. I listened for the sound of the door shutting before pouring my second glass of wine. As I set the stopper back in the bottle, I decided to use the stereo.

Music had all but left our lives. Alec and I used to be the cool parents, well mostly me. The stereo was cranked most nights after dinner. Doing the dishes had become a family affair, the three of us singing along to James Taylor, Billy Joel, or Fleetwood Mac. Alec played along, though he preferred the gayer

343

stuff—Streisand, Midler, and show tunes. I liked just about all music. To me it was more than just background noise.

There was a thin film of dust on the edges of the four components to the state of the art sound system Alec had assembled. The dust seemed to suggest it had been weeks since I had even looked at the stereo. The silence had grown deafening. I adjusted the volume, then turned a dial until the little red light above CD lit up. I scanned the shelves above the stereo for a specific CD. God, what had happened here?! There was no organization whatsoever. The sadness, the silence, the complete lack of proper alphabetizing was about to send me careening over the edge when I spotted it. Dan Fogelberg's *The Innocent Age*. I pushed another button and a tray shot out from deep within the elaborate system before me. I removed CDs that had likely been in there for months, not paying any attention to what they were. Then I replaced those CDs with just one. I pressed the skip button seven times to get to track eight and took a sip of wine. When the music started, I couldn't help but smile.

Met my old lover in the grocery store
The snow was falling, Christmas Eve
I stole behind her in the frozen foods
And I touched her on the sleeve

I loved Christmas music. Though most people didn't consider Fogelberg's "Same Old Lang Syne" a Christmas song, it was perfect for right now.

She didn't recognize the face at first
But then her eyes flew open wide
She went to hug me and she spilled her purse
And we laughed until we cried

I was feeling a little giddy, all of a sudden; maybe I was just drunk. I'd only had the one full glass of wine. And a shot of tequila. The bottle was practically empty when I was straightening the liquor cabinet earlier. When did we ever drink tequila anyway? I was no longer a "we," certainly not one made up of a minimum of two adults anyway. I wondered for a second if I, *not we*, had a lime. Not likely. I was going to have to do it without training wheels, all for the sake of organizing the liquor cabinet and not wasting alcohol. I looked around before just tipping the bottle to my lips. That was a couple of hours earlier. Now I was drinking wine. It took me the rest of my second glass to get the CDs properly organized. Then I finished the dishes.

344

After they were done, I grabbed a specific champagne flute from the cupboard and a bottle of champagne from the refrigerator. I was afraid to open champagne. Alec had always done it. I considered going down the hall to my fourteen-year-old son's room to have him open the bottle, but not wanting to be interrogated by Child Protective Services, I tossed that option aside. I could do it. I ended up peeking out through a single eye in the general direction of my outstretched arms with each twist of the cork. When it finally gave, my heart was where my throat usually went.

I'd been dusting the wine rack a couple of days earlier when I discovered the bottle of champagne. It had been a gift to me, from Alec, and I had meant to save it for a special occasion. I was sickened when I saw it there. I should have drunk it with Alec. There were so many things that we'd never share. It had been that way for a few weeks or more. The crippling despondency would subside and I'd only feel a sort of dull grief. The grief and I had become intimately acquainted, even before Alec died. The other stuff, the stuff I felt like I was suffocating beneath, was newer. It had crept in around Thanksgiving. For the life of me, I hadn't known what to do. The holidays? The least Alec could have done was die in June. Who gave a fuck about the Fourth of July?

Caden and I had to get through the five weeks during which Thanksgiving, Christmas, my birthday, and Alec's and my anniversary all occurred. Alec and I had met on New Year's Eve, 1980. He died fifty-eight days before what would have been our twelfth anniversary and my thirty-third birthday. New Year's Eve had become quintessentially poignant to me, being that it marked the anniversary of my birth and the anniversary of the night I met the love of my life. All clocks reset for me on December 31st. Silk or linen was to be gifted on the twelfth anniversary. That hadn't happened.

The tenth anniversary is tin. Along with the champagne, Alec had given me two of the most beautiful champagne flutes I'd ever seen. The bases of them were adorned in tin. Back to 1992, I had changed into flannel pajama pants and an oversized t-shirt, and was settled into my bed, remote control in one hand and champagne flute in the other. *Dick Clark's New Year's Rockin' Eve* began at 10 p.m., so I was just a few minutes late to the party.

I tried to remember why we hadn't just drunk the goddamned champagne when he'd given it to me. Or last year, even. Oh, yes. Last year he had just gotten home from the hospital. There'd been a pretty serious reaction to one of his HIV meds and I'd had to rush him there in a cab a few days before Christmas. It seemed more like five years—not one—had gone by since then.

Alec was well over six feet tall. When we slow danced, it felt as if he held my entire body. I never felt as safe as when his arms folded around me. On our last New Year's Eve together, we'd slow danced to Boyz II Men. They performed "It's So Hard to Say Goodbye to Yesterday" on *Dick Clark's New Year's Rockin' Eve.*

I thought we'd get to see forever
But forever's gone away

Alec had to have known I was crying. My head was turned away from his, resting against his chest, and my tears just fell upon the worn t-shirt he wore. His once strong arms had begun to weaken. He'd lost thirty pounds by that point. His chest wasn't as full as it had always been. I did not feel nearly as safe.

Those anniversaries had begun to feel almost as if they had happened to another couple. Charlie, Joanna, and Kevin were determined to take my mind off of the anniversary thing anyway. We were going to focus on my birthday, instead. I was being forced into a too-crowded bar, surrounded by crazy drunk people, and I was actually thrilled about it. It might have been any other Friday night, were it not for all the hoopla.

We got to the Rail about nine-thirty. Charlie still had an hour and a half to sneak us free drinks. He had worked out some shift change with another bartender and was probably going to take a big hit, giving up the tips he would have made from eleven to one on New Year's Eve. I had a fifty-dollar bill ready to tip him for the sacrifice. Even at nine-thirty, we could find only one seat at the bar. Joanna took that and Kev and I stood one on either side of her. Charlie came over as soon as he saw us. I thought Kev was going to faint as soon as Charlie leaned over the bar and planted a kiss on his aunt.

"What the fuck?"

"Yeah, that's happening," I told Kev, smiling from ear to ear.

"To be fair that was about the same reaction I had when she kissed me two weeks ago," Charlie announced. "Drinks?"

"Oh, yes!" Joanna looked from Kevin to me and back again. "I had no idea he'd do that. Is my face red?"

346

"You couldn't tell in this light anyway," I told her.

"Congratulations, I guess," Kevin offered.

"It's important Kelly not find out, Kev. Not yet. So please, let's keep this between us," Joanna said to our nephew.

"My lips are sealed," he told her. "I will have a beer, Charlie. Please."

"Same for me," I added.

"I guess beer it is," Joanna agreed.

"You're full of surprises tonight." I hadn't seen my sister drink beer in months.

"This is my first," she countered. "If you want to point fingers, though, the bartender started it."

Forty-five minutes later Kevin and I were nearly halfway through our second beers. Joanna hadn't finished her first. We had agreed no shots until Charlie was just about out from behind the bar. "Why don't you order something you'd rather drink?"

"I felt like a beer," she told me. "It happens. It's just clearly not going down as easily for me as it is for the two of you."

"I'm pacing myself," Kevin told us. "I'm actually thinking of cutting back. New Year's resolution."

"I think that's a fabulous idea," Joanna said.

"I thought you might. Hey, look it's snowing." Joanna and I turned to look out the big tinted window at the end of the bar, and sure enough, it was snowing.

"That wasn't supposed to start until much later," Joanna commented, finally finishing her first beer. As if on cue, Charlie appeared. "Can I get a water? I'm getting a headache." She'd started rummaging through her mystery grab bag. "I'm going to take something. Don't worry. I'm not nearly done drinking."

"Hey, did you notice Jannie not drinking on Christmas Eve?" I asked her.

347

"Now that you say something," she started. Just then a car backfired on the street. Traffic was literally twenty feet from where we were seated. The backfire sounded like a gunshot.

"Jesus Christ."

"Kev, are you okay?" Joanna asked. I looked over and our nephew had turned almost white as a ghost. "You look worse than I feel."

"It just freaked me out," he told us. People on either side of us had gotten up to leave. I motioned for Kev to sit and he took the bar stool to the left of Joanna. "Okay, fuck it. Let's do a shot. Please!"

"Give me two minutes and I'm in," Joanna agreed. Charlie had set a bottle of water in front of her. She moved the palm of right hand to her mouth, swallowed the pills she had dug out of her purse and proceeded to drink half of the bottle. "I'm going to go splash some water in my face. I'll be right back."

"Should we order shots?" Kev asked, the color already returning to his face.

"Surprise me, but don't get too wild and crazy."

"I can't believe she and Charlie are together," Kev commented, once Joanna had left.

"It's kind of cool, right?"

"Completely!"

"You sure you're alright?" I asked him.

"I'll be way better when people stop asking me that every five minutes."

"You're right. I'm sorry."

"I don't know why. That car scared the crap out of me. That's all." Charlie came back and I ordered four windshield washer fluids

"Can I get one of those, too?" a voice said from behind us. I turned around to see Matthias, the guy Charlie had been pushing on me, the guy with the green eyes and awesome tattoo.

348

"Sure! Charlie, make that five," I said, grinning like a fucking idiot.

"You got it!"

"I thought you didn't like 'em young and that's why you never called?" Matthias motioned to Kevin.

"Matthias, this is my nephew Kevin," I explained. "Kev, this is Matthias."

"He's pretty," Matthias whispered.

"What?" Kevin asked, loudly.

"He says you're pretty," I answered, just as loudly.

"Oh, so he's gay?" Matthias asked, looking at Kev.

"I don't believe in labels," Kevin answered. I thought he might actually be flirting.

"That's cool, man."

"Hey bartender," I called out. "We're gonna need more beers, too."

"Yeah, yeah!" He had the shaker in his hand already, mixing the shots. "Kev?"

"Yeah, sure," Kevin nodded. Charlie had set a beer each in front of Kevin and me, and filled a drink order for Matthias before Joanna got back from the bathroom. "We thought you were lost."

"It's busy back there," she explained. Introductions were completed before Charlie came back to pour our shots. After that, Matthias excused himself and my sister reclaimed her bar stool. "He was pretty."

"Funny, that's exactly what Matthias said about Kev here."

"You are a hit," Charlie announced. "The gentleman at the end of the bar would like to buy you a shot."

"Me—what—um—No, thank you."

"Kev, you have to take the shot," I advised, laughing.

349

"It's not a marriage proposal," Charlie agreed.

"Really?" Joanna seemed genuinely surprised. "People just do that?"

"No one has ever bought a drink for you before?" I asked her.

"No one I didn't already know."

"Um—okay—I guess," Kevin stammered. "What do I do now?"

"Well, you tell me what you'd like to drink and I get it for you."

"Okay. I'll have—um—a Jack and Coke."

"Seriously?" Joanna looked at Kev. There was no judgment, just still surprise.

"I dabble from time to time," he joked. "Hey, are you feeling any better?"

"Not really. Not yet." She still had not ordered a second drink. "It's only been twenty minutes since I took the aspirin and it's loud in here. I'll be fine."

"There are so many people here," I offered.

"God, when did we get so old?" Joanna asked, disgusted.

"Speak for yourself."

"It's just that I'm sitting here thinking how much nicer it would be to be at home in my pajamas with a glass of wine and a video," she sighed.

"Not nicer, just different, but I get your point. Hey, where's Kev going?"

Kevin had gotten up; it appeared, to thank the guy who bought him the drink. We watched, and sure enough, Charlie delivered the drink to our nephew at the other end of the bar. Hands were shaken; there was conversation, probably small talk. And there was laughter. Our nephew didn't look out of place or the slightest bit uncomfortable.

"God, I love that kid," Joanna exclaimed.

"I know! Who the fuck raised him? It can't have been Caty."

350

"I think it was a combination. I mean Mom, you when he was younger; Colleen was there a lot, but mostly Catelyn."

"It doesn't make any sense," I wondered. "He's one of the most loving and open-minded people I know. How did our sister make that?"

"He's got a mind of his own," Joanna offered. "Maybe that's all it takes. And he worshipped you when he was younger. No matter what she said or did, he could never hate you."

"He worshipped me?"

"He followed you around like a puppy dog. Not unlike Kelly with Caden."

"Well, they're a lot closer in age." I looked up and Kev was on his way back already. He was grinning from ear to ear. I was so happy he was having a good time.

"Miss me?" he asked, to a chorus of nods.

"My relief just got here. I'm gonna finish these glasses and close out my till and then I'll join you guys," Charlie told us.

"Can we get another round, quick, before you're done, please?" I had forgotten all about the fifty-dollar bill in my pocket.

"Actually, I'm good for now," Kev said.

"I'm alright for now, too," Joanna added.

Charlie set a beer in front of me, then he winked at my sister. "Buck-twenty-five," he demanded.
I handed him the bill in my hand. "Really a fifty?" He went to make change and I looked at Joanna and Kevin and smiled.

"Thank you for coming out."

"Wouldn't miss it." My sister smiled back at me.

"Yeah, I'm having a blast," Kev added.

"Of course you are." Joanna looked back at him. "Mister Popular. So what's the story with the kid from before?"

"Matthias?" I asked. "Charlie says he likes me."

"He's so young," she exclaimed. I just looked back at her about to roll my eyes. "Okay, I can't believe I just said that."

"How old is Charlie anyway?" Kev asked.

"He's only twelve years younger than me."

"For the record, Matthias is way closer to Stephen's age than you and I are to each other." Charlie had returned with change. He handed me two twenty-dollar bills and eight ones.

"Oh, that's for you."

"Shut up," he said.

"No, I'm serious. You're the best fucking bartender I know, and I know a lot. Most of 'em are back in San Francisco, but there ya go."

Charlie went to close his till, and I went to the bathroom. By the time I got back, he was standing beside my empty bar stool with a beer in his hand. He hugged me and whispered happy birthday in my ear. I whispered that I loved him. Maybe I was getting drunk again. All I knew was that I had everything to celebrate and I was doing so with people I loved.

"I love you, too," Charlie said, and hugged me tighter.

"Awwwwww," Joanna started, then grimaced.

"Headache still?"

"Aspirin hasn't done a thing."

"Should we go?" I offered.

"No! We're not gonna go," she insisted.

"Are you sure?" Charlie asked her.

352

"I was thinking maybe I would," she told him. Then to me, she said, "I'm really sorry."

"I'll go with you," Charlie told her.

"No. God! I am a big girl. I can hail a cab and be home in no time. I'll be fine. I just feel bad."

"Let's all go," I announced.

"If you don't stay out and have a good birthday, I'm gonna be fucking pissed," she directed. Kevin and I laughed.

"Hey, she said fuck," Kev said.

"Oh, for God's sake," Joanna exclaimed.

"I'm at least going out with you to hail a cab," Charlie said. "God, it's really coming down."

"Yeah, it's snowing pretty hard," I noticed. "I'm glad we took the bus down. You left your car at home, too, right?" I asked him.

"No, I drove. I'm parked around the corner. Okay, let's get you a cab."

Joanna put her coat on and hugged both Kevin and me goodbye. She whispered sorry to me and I told her not to worry about it. She had turned to go, but then turned back around. "Happy Birthday, little brother."

"Be right back. Save me that bar stool," Charlie said, pointing.

I watched the two of them go out to the street. Charlie had his arm around my sister and they both slid a little in the new fallen snow. He hadn't even put a coat on. He was wearing a tight white t-shirt and jeans. They stood there, together, for another minute. That was all it took for a cab to pull up. Charlie kissed her and opened the door to the cab. Joanna got in and the cab pulled away from the curb.

"I should have grabbed my coat," he said, when he came back in.

"You're all wet!" I brushed a few flakes of snow off his shoulder.

353

"My nipples are hard. Wanna feel?"

"I think I'll pass." I was thinking that I wouldn't mind it, but my big sister might. "Kev, you wanna touch Charlie's nipples?"

"Sure," he answered, and moved in closer.

"Don't even think about it," Charlie told him.

"You shouldn't have invited me," Kev snapped back, playfully.

"The invitation was for your uncle!"

"Don't you have another shirt?" I asked him.

"Yeah, I'm not that wet, though. Besides, wait for it." He had barely finished speaking when the new bartender came over, placing a beer down in front of him.

"From Joe," he said.

"Hey Josh, these are my friends, Stephen and Kev. Stephen's the birthday boy."

"Happy Birthday," Josh told me. Then to Charlie he half-whispered, "You were right."

"You were right about what?" I asked Charlie, after Josh had left.

"You're cute," Charlie told me.

"You told him I was cute?" I asked. Kevin just laughed.

"Well, he agreed," Charlie shot back.

"You're hopeless!

"No, I believe that would be you."

"Charlie's determined to get me laid," I told Kevin. As soon as I said it, I wondered if I was drunker than I had originally thought.

"Sounds like a good plan to me," Kevin announced.

"Oh God, you're on his side?"

"Yeah, but beyond that, let's not discuss it too much or I might need therapy."

"Okay, we need shots," Charlie said, changing the subject, for which I was grateful.

The three of us sat at the bar for another two hours. People would come up and talk to the gorgeous bartender sitting between Kevin and me and, I swear, he'd must've been given at least four beers and a couple of shots. Josh did a birthday shot with me, which he paid for. And even Kev's benefactor from the beginning of the night came down and bought us all a round. Charlie stopped drinking about twelve-thirty, turning down two drink offers. He told me the three of us could stay behind, once Josh closed the bar, so he could sober up a bit more. I was having a great time. I flirted a little with Matthias, when he came back to the bar to announce he was heading to the Saloon. It was harmless. After Josh had turned up the lights and all the other patrons had exited the bar, he turned the lock on the door, and came back behind the bar to finish up.

"Let me help you, man," Charlie told him.

"No, that's cool. You're off the clock. One last drink for the birthday boy?"

"God!" I exclaimed.

"Oh, go for it," Charlie said, patting me on the back.

"Kevin, you, too?" Josh asked.

"Sure!"

"He's cute," I told Charlie, I think, for the tenth time since he'd become our bartender.

"He has a boyfriend."

"Why didn't you say that before?"

355

"I don't know that he'd be opposed to a quickie in the back, though," Charlie joked. At least I hoped he was joking.

It was almost two-thirty in the morning when we left the bar. Josh let us out. We heard him turn the lock once we were on the other side of the door. It was barely snowing anymore, but the sidewalk was slippery.

"Let's cut through the alley," Charlie suggested.

"I had such a good time, you guys," I told them, shivering a little.

"I did, too," Charlie agreed.

"You're pretty quiet, Kev."

"Just thinking," he told me.

"About what?"

"Nothing really. I just think it's going to be a good new year, you know, as soon as Charlie and I get you laid." He started laughing, then so did Charlie. They hurried in front of me. I bent to gather snow for a snowball, but it was too powdery and fine.

"Hey, hold up," I called after them.

There were two guys over by the alley, smoking. I suddenly shuddered. Kevin turned back around and was waiting for me to catch up. Charlie kept going. He was twenty feet ahead of Kevin. It must have been just seconds before everything changed.

I wasn't sure what was happening at first. I didn't hear what one of the smoking guys had said to Charlie, but something was said. Then the two of them were on top of him. I made out one word. It was a pretty hard one to miss. I'd certainly heard it before, and every time it filled me with terror. *Faggot.* I hated the word so much. Kevin turned back around when I'd nearly caught up; we just kept going. By that time, punches had been thrown; things seemed to be moving in slow motion. I don't think any of us had figured out what we were walking into until we were actually in it. Charlie slipped in the snow and went down. It looked as if he had turned his ankle. He tried to get back up and then doubled over again.

356

"It's you," one of the guys said. I thought he was talking to Charlie, but then I realized it had been meant for Kevin.

"It's the fucking queer from the video store," the other guy yelled.

"Fuck you, man." I heard Kevin tell them. His voice was completely different. There was fear in it.

"No, faggot; fuck you!" I thought it was the first guy who had spoken. I didn't know what to do. I turned to Kevin. Our eyes met for a split second and I saw his shine in the street light. Charlie had made it to his feet, and then I saw his face change.

"What the fuck, man," he screamed. That was when I noticed it. It shone brighter than Kevin's eyes in the light. One of the guys had produced a knife. He was closer to me than to Kevin or Charlie. I couldn't move. I could not form a coherent thought. Everything had gone silent. I felt someone, Kevin I thought, push me down, but then one of the guys was on top of us. He punched me in the face and then he and Kevin were rolling around on the ground a couple of feet away. I didn't know where Charlie had gone. Maybe he was right behind me; I just couldn't see him. For a few seconds, I could not see the second guy either. I moved to get up and fell back down. I finally made it to standing and turned to look for Charlie. He was on the ground, not moving. I wondered if he had been stabbed. I finally made out the second guy, the one with the knife and as soon as I did, he was on me. I heard Charlie call out to me, but even from a few feet away, I couldn't make out what he had said. I saw the knife again and followed it as it moved in slow motion up into my chest. I felt a sharp pain and fell backwards. I think I hit my head. The guy had raised the knife again and then went out of sight, as Kevin stepped between us. Then Kevin fell hard.

It was as if I were underwater, drowning. Our voices were muffled. I thought I could make out crying. Or was it screaming? The snow was falling; a flake settled on my face and melted into the tears there. I realized I was lying in the snow, but I wasn't cold. Something warm, like a blanket, was spreading across my chest. When I looked down, though, I saw that it was blood. My blood. There was so much blood. I watched the snow go red with it. And then everything... everything went black.

357

Epilogue
JOANNA

My head was pounding by the time I made it home. I couldn't even be sure how big a tip I'd given the cab driver. The streetlight reflecting off the thin layer of new fallen snow was blinding. The cab had pulled up in front. I stood there for a split second, and wondered when the last time I'd gone in the front door was. It was snowing hard. This was going to be one of those nuisance snowfalls, a couple of inches, almost not enough to shovel, but definitely enough to make driving, and yes walking, difficult. I slipped at my first attempt to take a step, and almost went down. "I hate winter," I said to absolutely no one.

As I approached the front door to my house, I could see the light from the television dancing across the walls. Other than that, the living room was completely dark. I considered walking around back, so that I could have a cigarette on the deck, but a shooting pain in my left temple told me that might not be such a great idea. I climbed the three cement steps that lead to my front door carefully and fumbled around for the keys in my purse. I thought about knocking, then, but decided to try the door and see if it was unlocked first.

The handle turned and I pushed the door open and saw them. It took me, honest to God, a few seconds to realize what it was that I was seeing. My daughter was on top of a boy and they were making out. That much was obvious immediately. It was seconds, though, before I realized the boy was Caden. I dropped my purse, right there on the threshold, and it turned over, fell off the door jam, onto the cement, and slid across the step.

"Jesus Christ, Mom," Meghan shouted.

"Oh, shit." I heard Caden say. I had turned to grab my purse, bent over, and felt my right leg go out from under me, and down I went. Before I knew it, there was Caden, my brother's stepson, standing in the doorway, reaching out to me.

"Fuck. Mom, are you okay?" I looked up, and she was standing beside Caden. Both of them were fully dressed. Thank God! But at that level, it was impossible to miss. I assumed he was unaware of how visible it was. I looked down, quickly, unwilling to scar either one of us any further. I wondered how

358

long it would take me to erase the image of Caden's hard-on, through his sweat pants, from my aching brain.

"Let me help you," he begged. I took his outstretched hand, trying not to look up, and he helped me to my feet.

"Thank you, sweetheart." A million thoughts were racing through my mind. As he pulled me up, I almost slipped again. Caden held tight, and pulled me closer, and we were almost hugging.

"Before you freak out," Meghan started.

"Just give me a minute. I'm not certain freaking out is going to be my next step."

"Did you hurt anything?" Caden asked.

"My pride, mostly." He pushed me into the house. It was slippery on the tile and I was desperate, all of a sudden, to be on dry ground.

"Here." Caden handed me my wet purse.

"Is Kelly asleep?" I asked anyone who cared to answer.

"Yeah, for like, an hour. Are you going to be okay?" Meghan asked.

"Yes. I'll live. It's been a really long day. I have a terrible headache. And I'm really disappointed — ."

"We're sorry," Caden interrupted.

"No, sweetheart! I'm disappointed I had to leave the boys downtown. I'm so not disappointed in either of you. Shocked. Not disappointed." I shook my head to emphasize the point, and it felt like it might fall off and roll across the carpet. "Meghan, go get Mommy about a hundred aspirin."

Caden just stood there. Almost since I'd opened the door, however many minutes ago it had been; he had been standing over me. That needed to change, so that I was able to actually look straight ahead. "Caden, sit down."

"But—um — I'm uh," he stammered.

359

"Just sit," I said, as if I was commanding a dog. Thankfully, at last, he did. I looked over at him, across the room, lit by the light of the television, and smiled. He tried really hard to smile back, but couldn't quite manage it. This poor kid was mortified. From out of nowhere, I started to laugh. I just laughed and laughed. I couldn't make myself stop.

"What's going on in here?" Meghan was back with the aspirin. I couldn't form words. Another few seconds and poor Caden started laughing uncomfortably along with me, like he couldn't quite figure out anything else to do. The look on my daughter's face, concern mixed with embarrassment mixed with complete dread set me off again. Before long, we were all laughing and not long after that, the pained expressions on those two teenagers faces seemed to vanish. Caden seemed to relax almost entirely. My daughter seemed to be reserving judgment, at least until the laughter had died down. When I was finally able to stop laughing entirely, and swallow the aspirin, I drank the entire glass of water. It had never tasted so good. Maybe I had just been dehydrated? I held out the empty glass.

"More water?" Caden stood up and took the glass from me. He turned and went into the kitchen, probably relieved to be excused. He was gone less than a minute. After he handed me the glass, I looked over at my daughter. She was looking at Caden, and I'd be damned if I didn't see something in the neighborhood of love. I sighed, then looked back up at Caden. I took the glass of water and said, "Okay, both of you sit down."

An hour later, we had decided that Caden would spend the night on the couch downstairs. I called my brother's house and left a message on his answering machine, so he wouldn't worry. Neither of us had even known the kids were hanging out together tonight. Without the loud music and din of a hundred simultaneous conversations at the bar, the second dose of pain reliever worked almost right away. By the time I had given Caden bedding and Meghan and I started up the stairs, the headache was gone. "I'm keeping my bedroom door open, you two. Unless Caden needs to use the bathroom, you're to remain on different floors. No more making out tonight."

"Mom!"

"Thank you," Caden called, from the living room.

"Goodnight, sweetheart," I called back.

360

I could feel a bruise forming across my entire left butt cheek; my ankle, while not swollen, definitely hurt, so I decided to take a long hot shower. I must have been in there for thirty minutes before I felt the water start to go cold. I got out, dried myself off, and put my robe on. I checked on the kids one more time before finally retreating to my room. Stephen and I would have to discuss where to go from here. I honestly couldn't see him having any different a reaction than I had. Our kids were fifteen and sixteen years old. I had no reason not to trust my daughter's judgment. They were in no way related by blood. They didn't live under the same roof. My only concern was what would happen when one of them broke the other's heart. What then? They were kids. It was bound to happen. I didn't have the strength to bring that up downstairs earlier, not after I saw the look on my daughter's face.

It was certainly a unique situation. I had come to care about, perhaps even love Caden. How often does a parent feel actual love for her teenage daughter's boyfriend? I also happened to be his high school principal and closely related to his father. I turned and crept back down the hall to my own bedroom. I didn't even bother with the light. After I had shut my bedroom door, I removed my robe and slipped into a pair of flannel pants and oversized t-shirt and slid beneath the flannel sheets and comforter on my bed. I drifted off to sleep wondering if Charlie would show up here drunk in a couple of hours. I hoped he did, if only so that I could feel his body fit against mine. I must have fallen asleep almost right away.

I hadn't any idea how long I'd been asleep before the phone woke me. Not at first. I reached for the cordless, fumbling in the dark. I was barely awake. "Hello," I croaked.

"Mrs. Bennett? Is this Mrs. Bennett?"

"This is Joanna—uh—Bennett is my maiden name. This is Joanna Bennett-McCullough." I couldn't take me eyes off the digital display on the alarm clock. No phone call coming in at 4:45 a.m. was ever good. My first thought was of my mother. Something must have happened to her. I felt completely panicked. "Please tell me what's wrong."

"This is Sharon King at Hennepin County Medical Center. I was given your name by Charles Carpenter."
I didn't recognize the name right away. Who the hell was this? As soon as I worked out who Charles Carpenter was, my panic grew. Oh, my God, what had happened?

361

"Charlie Carpenter, yes; he's my boyfriend." Strangely enough, at that moment I wondered: does Charlie really not know my last name isn't Bennett?

"Mrs. McCullough, Charles Carpenter, Stephen Bennett, and Kevin Amble were brought in to the emergency room here an hour ago. It's extremely urgent that you come down here as soon as possible."

"What happened?" I begged, desperate now.

"There was a fight. I don't know a lot more than that. Can you please notify Mr. Bennett and Mr. Amble's next of kin? You should all come to the Emergency Room entrance of the hospital as soon as possible. Do you know where Hennepin County Medical Center is? Are you nearby?"

Next-of-kin. Jesus Christ! "Can't you please tell me anymore?"

"We have taken Mr. Bennett into surgery. If you — ."

I hung up the phone. I'd sat up in bed at some point. I did not remember when. I just knew that I had to pull myself together. There was not time to cry. I took a deep breath and tried to stand up. My legs felt wobbly beneath me. I struggled out of the flannel pajama pants I had on, replacing them with the first thing I saw, sweat pants. It felt like I had changed into the same thing. Shoes. I needed shoes. I turned an almost tripped over a pair of white tennis shoes. That was helpful. I took another deep breath and tried to think. Meghan could stay with Kelly. I needed to wake her and explain where I was going. Oh, God, Caden was right downstairs. Should I wake him? Of course. I had to reach my sister. How the hell was I going to do that? I wasn't even sure where or who to call. My mother would know. I went back to the bed and looked for the cordless phone. I had just been on it. Where the hell was the phone? Then I saw the antenna sticking out from under my comforter. I grabbed the handset and punched in my mother's number. It must have rung seven or eight times before she picked up.

"Mom, its Joey."

"What's wrong, dear?" Stay calm.

"There's been some kind of accident. I need for you to stay calm. I don't know a lot more than that, except that HCMC called just now and said that it's

362

urgent for us to get down there. Stephen and Kevin have been hurt. Stephen has been taken into surgery. I don't know how to reach Catelyn."

"Oh, my God! Oh, no."

"Come on, Mom. We need to be strong. Can you find a way to reach Caty and call Patrick to have him come and get you and bring you to the hospital? Can you do that?"

"I'll see you there, dear," she said, and hung up.

Okay, that was done. Without hesitation, I hurried across the hallway to Meghan's door. I didn't knock. I opened the door and went to her bed. She was so peaceful, sound asleep. I bent down, so that my face was just a couple of feet away from hers. As soon as I called her name, she opened her eyes. I explained the situation to her, proud of how calm she remained. I was hurrying out of her bedroom, onto the next early morning wakeup call, when my daughter said she loved me. I knew if I turned back around, I might start to cry, so I said I loved her too and kept moving. I stepped on the creaky second step, and took the rest two at a time. I turned the corner and Caden was sitting up on the couch, awake.

"What's wrong?"

"Why are you up?" I was not prepared to face him yet.

"I heard the phone ring in the kitchen, then I heard you moving around upstairs. Something's wrong, isn't it?" This boy had the sweetest, softest face. It registered emotion like a TV screen. It broke my heart what happened next.

"There's been an accident, sweetheart. Your dad's been hurt. He's having surgery right now. Would you...."

"I'm going with you," he cried. "You can't make me stay here. Please!" There was so much fear in his voice, I went to hug him, reassure him somehow. He put out his hand and got to his feet in one motion.
"No. We have to go. We have to go now."

My coat and purse were still on the arm of the loveseat. I barely had to move to grab them. Caden was already at the back door, calling to me to hurry. I threw on my coat and turned around to see Meghan sitting about halfway down the stairs.

363

"Drive safe, Mom," she said, her voice shaking.

"I'm going to have a cigarette. Okay, sweetheart?" I asked Caden, once I'd turned the car onto Minnetonka Boulevard.

"I don't care."

"It's going to be okay," I told him, fumbling around for my pack of cigarettes in my purse.

"Here, let me do it." He grabbed my bag and looked at me. I could barely make out his face at first, but then we drove right under a streetlight and I could see clearly that he was crying. "Can I go in here?"

"My purse? Of course." He opened it up, took out a pack of cigarettes, removed a cigarette from the pack, and handed it to me. Then he resumed the search until he found a lighter and handed that to me.

"You can't possibly know it's going to be okay," he told me. There was no tremble in his voice, just determination. "How far is it?"

"We'll be there fifteen minutes."

"Can we just be quiet until we get there?" He laid his head back against the seat and looked out the window, turning his face as far away from me as it would go.

Fifteen minutes later the two of us rushed into the Emergency Room entrance. I explained to the person behind the counter who we were. She said something to another nurse and we were escorted back. The nurse talked the whole way back, but I didn't hear a word she was saying. We turned a corner and I saw two policemen talking to man who appeared to have been beaten up. The nurse almost walked right by them, but stopped. There was a partially drawn curtain and I was not paying attention, not until Charlie called my name. I turned around, to follow the voice, but he was right there.

"Jesus Christ," I nearly shouted. His face was partially covered in blood and his left eye was swollen and black and blue, but that wasn't the worst of it. His white t-shirt was almost completely covered in blood, his hand had been bandaged, and his jeans were wet. He was only wearing one shoe.

"It's not my blood," he assured me. Something about his voice was just wrong.

"Where's my dad?" Caden pleaded. "Please tell me where Stephen is!"

"He's in surgery, buddy. He was stabbed."

"What happened?" One of the police officers said they would have more questions for him later, but that they would let him be examined and talk to us, and they both left. I asked him again what had happened and he started to explain. Every once in a while, it was clear he was editing the story in his head for Caden's sake. Even the edited version was horrifying. I watched every awful emotion possible register across the faces of Charlie and Caden as the story was told.

"I couldn't move." It seemed to me as if he were asking forgiveness, all the while fighting back tears. "They think it's broken. I couldn't stand up to go for help." He motioned to the foot without a shoe.

"If the blood isn't yours?" I asked, but he wouldn't answer. He couldn't answer. Tears were now silently streaming down his face. This was so much worse than even he had let on.

"What about Kevin?" Oh, my God. I had almost forgotten he was there. Charlie reached up to swipe the tears from his eyes and cringed when he grazed where his eye had gone black. "Charlie, what about Kevin?"

"They only told me about five minutes before you got here."

"Told you what?" I demanded.

"Kev was stabbed twice. The guy with the knife had already stabbed both of them, I think. Stephen was on the ground and the guy had raised the knife and Kev moved in between them. He was stabbed in the stomach."

"Charlie!" I already knew what he was going to say next. I put my hand up to my mouth. I thought I might vomit.

"Kevin died before we even got here."

As he said the words, I reached over and pulled Caden to me, and he started to shake. All three of us were crying. With one arm around Caden, I reached

365

out and touched the part of Charlie's shirt that had not been stained with blood. I thought that I had mentally prepared myself for any possible outcome on the drive to the hospital. Not that. Not fucking that.

For some reason, I happened to glance up. At the other end of the hallway, the police officers were talking to a woman. I would not have recognized her, at first, except for the numerous times I had seen her on the news. I looked away quickly like she had been a mirage. When I looked back, she was still there. How had she gotten here so fast? And where was my mother? The next time I looked, the woman wasn't there.

"Joanna?" I turned in the direction of the voice, and there was my sister. There was Catelyn.

Trademark & Copyright Acknowledgments
The author acknowledges the copyrighted/trademarked status and copyright/trademark owners of the following trademarks mentioned in this work of fiction:

A Charlie Brown Christmas: CBS Corporation and CBS Broadcasting Inc.
A League of their Own: Columbia Pictures Corporation, Parkway Productions
A Nightmare on Elm Street: The Elm Street Venture
Almond Joy: The Hershey Company
Boyz II Men, *It's So Hard to Say Goodbye to Yesterday*: Freddie Perren and Christine Yarian
Campbell's: CSC Brands LP.
Coke: The Coca-Cola Company
Dan Fogelberg, *Same Old Lang Syne*: Dan Fogelberg
Dan Fogelberg, *The Innocent Age*: Dan Fogelberg
Dead Poets Society: Touchstone Pictures, Silver Screen Partners IV, Buena Vista Pictures
Dick Clark's New Year's Rockin' Eve: Dick Clark Productions, ABC Network
Disney World: Disney
Doc Martens: Airwair Intl. Ltd
Duran Duran, *Hungry Like the Wolf*: Simon Le Bon, Andy Taylor, Duran Duran
Ford: Ford Motor Company
Formica: The Diller Corporation
Garth Brooks, *Ropin' the Wind*: Troyal Garth Brooks
Geo Metro: General Motors, Suzuki
Girl Scouts: Girl Scouts of the United States of America
Good Morning Vietnam: Touchstone Pictures, Silver Screen Partners III, Buena Vista Pictures
Hawaiian Punch: Dr Pepper/Seven Up, Inc.
Hazelden: Hazelden Betty Ford Foundation
Hyatt: Hyatt Hotels & Resorts
Jack Daniel's: Jack Daniel's
Jolt Cola: Wet Planet Beverages
Kansas, *Carry On, Wayward Son*: Kerry Livgren, Kansas
K-Mart: Sears Holdings Corporation
Knots Landing: Columbia Broadcasting System (CBS), Lorimar Television, Roundelay
Kools: R. J. Reynolds Tobacco Company
Lasher: Anne Rice
Live with Regis and Kathie Lee: WABC, Buena Vista Television
Lord of the Rings: J. R. R. Tolkien
Louis Armstrong, *What a Wonderful World*: Bob Thiele and George Weiss
McDonald's: McDonald's
Melrose Place: Darren Star Productions, Fox Television Network, Spelling Television, Torand Productions
Menards: Menard, Inc.
Midol: Bayer
Miller Light: Miller Brewing Co.
Minnesota Twins MLB Team: MLB Advanced Media, LP.
Ms Pacman: General Computer Corporation
MTV: Viacom International Inc.
My Girl: Columbia Pictures Corporation, Imagine Entertainment
Nike: Nike, Inc.
Perkins Restaurant & Bakery: Perkins & Marie Callender's, LLC
Pink Floyd, *Learning to Fly*: David Gilmour, Pink Floyd
Pink Floyd, *Momentary Lapse of Reason*: Pink Floyd
Pink Floyd, *On The Turning Away*: David Gilmour, Pink Floyd
Pink Floyd, *Signs of Life*: Pink Floyd
Pizza Hut: Pizza Hut, Inc
Polo: Ralph Lauren Coproration

367

Pop-Tarts: Kellogg NA Co.
Pretty in Pink: Paramount Pictures
Radiohead, *Creep*: Thom Yorke
Saab: National Electric Vehicle Sweden AB
Scooby Doo: Hanna-Barbera Productions
Scope: Procter & Gamble
Sharpie: SANFORD
Shel Silverstein, <u>The Giving Tree</u>: Evil Eye, LLC
Six Flags: Six Flags
Slumberland: Slumberland, Inc.
Sonic: SEGA Corporation
Southern Comfort: Brown-Forman Beverages, Europe, Ltd.,
Star Trek TNG: Paramount Television
Sunkist: Sunkist Growers, Inc. and Dr Pepper/Seven Up, Inc.
SuperAmerica: SuperAmerica
Target: Target Brands, Inc.
The Big Chill: Columbia Pictures, Carson Productions Group Ltd.
The Crying Game: Palace Pictures, Channel Four Films, Eurotrustees, Nippon Film Development and Finance, British Screen Productions
The Fisher King: Columbia Pictures Corporation
The Golden Girls: Touchstone Television, Witt/Thomas/Harris Productions, NBC
The Golden Palace: Witt/Thomas/Harris Productions, Touchstone Television
The Philadelphia Story: Metro-Goldwyn-Mayer (MGM), Loew's Incorporated
The Real World: Bunim-Murray Productions, MTV Networks
The Silence of the Lambs: Strong Heart/Demme Productions, Orion Pictures
<u>The Witching Hour</u>: Anne Rice
Twinkies: Hostess Brands, LLC
Tylenol: McNEIL-PPC, Inc.
U-Haul: U-Haul International, Inc.
Variety: Variety Media, LLC, a subsidiary of Penske Business Media, LLC.
Visine: McNEIL - PPC, Inc.
Walkman: Sony Electronics Inc.
White Fang: Walt Disney Pictures, Silver Screen Partners IV, Hybrid Productions Inc.
Ziploc: S. C. JOHNSON & SON, INC.

ACKNOWLEDGEMENTS

Tina, editor extraordinaire – I could not have hoped for a gentler "first time," and feel as if I've made a wonderful new friend in the process. Thank you so much!

Paul – thank you for your formatting expertise!

Colleen, Lindsay, Alyssa – thanks for your efforts on the cover. Let's try again next time.

Jess – I am blown away by all you've done. The website is brilliant! THANK YOU!

Jennifer D – I truly appreciate your contribution to get the editing started! Thank you!

Jess, Carey, Wen, Jenny, Shelly and Kade – thanks for BETA'ing for me my first time out!

Nik – You read almost every word as it was written. Your support and encouragement was invaluable. Thank you, thank you, thank you from the bottom of my heart!

Kami – I loved reading this to you! Your encouragement, too, was truly a blessing! Love you!

Colleen and Kathy – there are parts of you in Joanna and Colleen and none of you in Catelyn. Thank you for that and for being the most amazing sisters! I love you!

To my "Twitter family" – it's been an absolute trip and I wouldn't change a thing! The hugs, whether virtual or in person, the support and encouragement, and the friendship: I could never have done this without you!

To my friends and family – I am so grateful to have all of you to share this journey with. You have lightened my load and filled my heart in ways you couldn't possibly imagine. I am an extraordinarily blessed man. Love and gratitude!